Finn couldn't stand seeing her in distress.

"I'm sorry," Eva murmured. "I don't know what's wrong with me."

"Nothing is wrong with you, Eva." Finn's own voice was low and husky with emotion. "You have every right to be upset. There's been nothing but threats and danger at every turn."

She didn't answer. Finn had promised himself to offer comfort, nothing more.

Even if it killed him, which was a distinct possibility.

If he had one single functioning brain cell in his head, he'd assign someone else to protect her and the boy.

But even as the fleeting thought went through his mind, he rejected it.

He didn't want anyone else here, watching over them.

He trusted only himself and his K-9 partner to keep them safe from harm.

D0054912

USA TODAY Bestselling Author

Laura Scott

and

New York Times Bestselling Author

Lenora Worth

Deadly Secrets

Previously published as *Blind Trust* and *Deep Undercover*

LOVE INSPIRED
INSPIRATIONAL ROMANCE

If you purchased this book without a cover you should be aware that this book is stolen property. It was reported as "unsold and destroyed" to the publisher, and neither the author nor the publisher has received any payment for this "stripped book."

LOVE INSPIRED®
INSPIRATIONAL ROMANCE

ISBN-13: 978-1-335-20963-4

Deadly Secrets

Copyright © 2020 by Harlequin Books S.A.

Blind Trust
First published in 2019. This edition published in 2020.
Copyright © 2019 by Harlequin Books S.A.

Deep Undercover
First published in 2019. This edition published in 2020.
Copyright © 2019 by Harlequin Books S.A.

Special thanks and acknowledgment are given to Laura Scott and Lenora Worth for their contributions to the True Blue K-9 Unit miniseries.

Recycling programs for this product may not exist in your area.

All rights reserved. No part of this book may be used or reproduced in any manner whatsoever without written permission except in the case of brief quotations embodied in critical articles and reviews.

This is a work of fiction. Names, characters, places and incidents are either the product of the author's imagination or are used fictitiously. Any resemblance to actual persons, living or dead, businesses, companies, events or locales is entirely coincidental.

This edition published by arrangement with Harlequin Books S.A.

For questions and comments about the quality of this book, please contact us at CustomerService@Harlequin.com.

Love Inspired
22 Adelaide St. West, 40th Floor
Toronto, Ontario M5H 4E3, Canada
www.Harlequin.com

Printed in U.S.A.

CONTENTS

Laura Scott is a nurse by day and an author by night. She has always loved romance and read faith-based books by Grace Livingston Hill in her teenage years. She's thrilled to have published over twenty-five books for Love Inspired Suspense. She has two adult children and lives in Milwaukee, Wisconsin, with her husband of over thirty years. Please visit Laura at laurascottbooks.com, as she loves to hear from her readers.

Books by Laura Scott

Love Inspired Suspense

Justice Seekers

Soldier's Christmas Secrets
Guarded by the Soldier

Callahan Confidential

Shielding His Christmas Witness
The Only Witness
Christmas Amnesia
Shattered Lullaby
Primary Suspect
Protecting His Secret Son

True Blue K-9 Unit

Blind Trust
True Blue K-9 Unit Christmas
"Holiday Emergency"

Visit the Author Profile page
at Harlequin.com for more titles.

BLIND TRUST

Laura Scott

Hear, O Lord, when I cry with my voice:
have mercy also upon me, and answer me.
—*Psalms* 27:7

This book is dedicated to Gregory
and Marianne Iding, and their chocolate Lab, Moose.
It's fun to dog-sit for you when you're on vacation.

ONE

Eva Kendall slowed her pace as she approached the single-story building housing the modest training facility where she worked training guide dogs. Lifting her face to the sky, she basked in the sun warming her skin. June in the Forest Hills area of Queens, New York, could be incredibly hot and humid, but today was the perfect summer day.

Using her key, she entered the training center, thinking about the male chocolate Lab named Cocoa that she would work with this morning. Cocoa was a ten-week-old puppy born to Stella, who was a gift from the Czech Republic to the NYC K-9 Command Unit located in Queens. Most of Stella's pups were being trained as police dogs, but not Cocoa. In less than a month after basic puppy training, Cocoa would be able to go home with Eva to be fostered during his first year of training to become a full-fledged guide dog. Once that year passed, guide dogs like Cocoa would return to the center to train with their new owners.

A few steps into the building, Eva frowned at the loud thumps interspersed with a cacophony of barking.

The raucous noise from the various canines contained a level of panic and fear rather than excitement.

Concerned, she moved quickly through the dimly lit training center to the back hallway, where the kennels were located. Normally she was the first one in every morning, but maybe one of the other trainers had got an early start.

"Hello? Kim, is that you?" Rounding the corner, she paused in the doorway when she saw a tall, heavyset stranger scooping Cocoa out of his kennel, a tire iron lying on the floor beside it. Panic squeezed her chest. "Hey! What are you doing?"

The ferocious barking increased in volume, echoing off the walls and ceiling. The stranger must have heard her. He turned to look at her, then roughly tucked Cocoa under his arm like a football.

"No! Stop!" Panicked, Eva charged toward the man, desperately wishing she had a weapon of some sort.

"Get out of my way," he said in a guttural voice.

"No. Put that puppy down right now!" Eva stopped and stood her ground, attempting to block his ability to get through the doorway.

"Last chance," he taunted, coming closer.

Fear was bitter on her tongue. She twisted the key ring in her hand, forcing the jagged edges of the keys between her trembling fingers. As he approached, she braced herself, hoping to find a way to stop him. He punched her with his right arm, roughly hitting her shoulder. Pain reverberated down her arm and into her hand, but that didn't stop her from lashing out with the keys, scratching him down the length of his forearm as she tumbled to the ground.

He called her a vile name as he went by, but she

didn't care. Ignoring the pain, she surged to her feet and took off after the assailant. Roughly five feet from the doorway leading outside, she lunged, grabbing ahold of the waistband of his black cargo pants and pulling back on it with all her might.

"Stop! Help! Please help! He's stealing a puppy!" She raised her voice, hoping someone outside might overhear.

"Let go!"

No! She couldn't let him get away with Cocoa!

The big and strong assailant dragged her along for a couple of feet before he abruptly turned on her. His meaty forearm, lined with three long, bleeding scratches from her keys, lashed out again, and this time he struck her across the face.

Her head snapped back, sharp pain blooming in her cheek, bringing tears to her eyes and blurring her already diminished vision. The sheer force of the blow knocked her off her feet, and she fell against the wall with a hard thud. Unable to hang on, she released him and slid down along the wall, collapsing on the floor in a crumpled heap. The sound of the puppy's panicked yipping tore at her heart.

"Cocoa," she managed in a choked voice. It was too late. The heavy door leading outside opened and slammed shut with a loud bang.

The assailant was gone, taking her precious puppy— the one she'd hoped to use one day as her own Seeing Eye dog—with him.

Eva forced herself upright. She rushed back to the main reception desk and picked up the phone.

If only she'd got a better look at the guy, she thought, as she dialed the number for the NYC K-9 Command

Unit. Her retinitis pigmentosa was already impacting her ability to see clearly. Especially in areas that weren't well lit. The dim interior of the kennels along with his baseball cap had shadowed his face.

With trembling fingers, she clutched the phone to her ear, hoping it wasn't too late to find Cocoa.

"Hey, Gallagher!"

Finn stood and looked over the edge of his cubicle. "What?"

"Pick up line three. Something about a missing dog."

K-9 Officer Finn Gallagher abandoned the notes he was reviewing on Chief Jordan Jameson's murder to pick up the phone. "What's going on?" The NYC K-9 Command Unit headquarters was located in the Jackson Heights area of Queens but served all five boroughs in New York City.

"One of Stella's puppies has just been stolen," Officer Patricia Knowles informed him. Patricia manned the front desk of headquarters, ruling the place with her no-nonsense attitude. "The pup that's missing is Cocoa, the one donated to the guide dog program."

"Stolen?" Finn scowled and glanced down at his yellow Labrador retriever, Abernathy. His K-9 partner's specialty was search and rescue, fitting for finding a stolen puppy. Finn clipped a leash onto Abernathy. All the K-9s were named after fallen K-9 officers, and his was no exception. Abernathy was named in honor of Michael Abernathy, who was killed in the line of duty while trying to rescue a child from his suicidal father. The child had survived, but Officer Abernathy had been hit in the cross fire and ultimately died. "I'm on it. Thanks." He hung up the phone. "Come, Abernathy."

Wearing his K-9 vest identifying him as a law enforcement officer, Abernathy was all business, keeping
pace beside Finn as he left the K-9 Unit headquarters.
The guide dog training center was located in Forest Hills, a ten-to-fifteen-minute drive from Jackson
Heights. Finn opened the back of his white K-9 SUV
for Abernathy and then slid in behind the wheel.

Rush hour made the ride to the training center take
longer than he'd hoped. A beautiful blonde hovered just
inside the doorway, anxiously waiting for him.

With Abernathy at his side, he assessed the woman.
She appeared to be in her late twenties, her heart-shaped
face and stunningly beautiful features framed by long
straight blond hair. He scowled as he noticed she was
holding an ice pack against a dark bruise marring her
cheek. She stepped back and gestured for him to come
inside.

"I'm Officer Finn Gallagher. What happened?" he
asked with concern. "You were assaulted? I was told
that Stella's puppy has been stolen."

The blonde offered a lopsided smile. "I'm Eva Kendall, and I'm the one who reported the puppy-napping."

"You're hurt. I'll call an ambulance." Finn reached
for his radio.

"No need," Eva said quickly. "It's more important
to find Cocoa."

Finn knew Cocoa was a chocolate Lab. A valuable
animal, sure, but worth stealing? He had to believe the
other guide dogs at the facility might be worth just as
much, maybe more. He looked at Eva. "Tell me what
happened."

She moved the ice pack so she could speak, and he
was struck anew by her clear porcelain skin and bril-

liant blue eyes. He did his best to avoid being distracted by her beauty, focusing on her story. "I came in early to work with Cocoa. The minute I entered the building, I heard thumps and loud barking from the dogs. I feared something was wrong, so I headed back toward the kennels."

"Alone?"

She lifted a shoulder, then winced as if the motion hurt. "I convinced myself that it was nothing, until I found a stranger grabbing Cocoa from his kennel."

Finn clenched his jaw, imagining the scenario. Was it possible the chocolate Lab had been targeted on purpose?

"I shouted at him to stop, but he didn't listen." Distress darkened Eva's blue eyes. "He punched me in the shoulder, knocking me to the floor, but I managed to scratch him with my keys." She gestured to the key ring sitting on the counter. "I thought you might be able to get a DNA sample from them."

He lifted a brow, secretly impressed she'd thought of that. "We can try. Go on, what happened next?"

"I ran after him and grabbed him from behind, but he hit me again and got away."

Hearing that the perp had hit her twice had him grinding his teeth in a flash of anger. It deeply bothered him when men used their strength against women. "Are you sure about not calling an ambulance? I think it's best if you get checked out at the ER."

"I'm fine." Eva waved a hand dismissively. "I've been hurt worse tussling with my older sister. We used to wrestle a lot when we were younger."

"Your older sister?" Finn felt a bit confused by the change in topic.

"Yes." Eva's gaze reflected a deep sorrow. "Unfortunately, Malina died three weeks ago when she was struck by a car."

"I'm sorry to hear that." He wanted to offer comfort but told himself to focus on the issue at hand. "I have to ask about the attack. Did the guy look at all familiar?"

"No. But I still don't understand. Why steal a puppy? Especially since we have older dogs here, too. Although it's possible the older dogs might try to bite more than a puppy would."

"Good question." He flipped his notebook shut and cast his gaze around the interior of the building. "Take me along the assailant's path. I'll also need to review the security video."

"The video won't be available until my boss gets in, I don't know how to use the equipment. But aren't you going to head out to try to find him?" Eva asked, exasperation ringing in her voice. "I specifically asked for a search-and-rescue team."

Finn flashed a wry grin. "Abernathy is the best search-and-rescue K-9 on the force, and, yes, I plan to head out to search for Cocoa. But I need to see the path the guy took, and I need something belonging to either the perp or Cocoa to use, as well."

Mollified, Eva wheeled around and led the way back through the training center. "There's a tire iron on the floor near the kennel. I think he used it to break inside the building then dropped it here by the kennel."

Finn took note of the tire iron on the floor. Metal wasn't the best substance to use for obtaining a scent, but Abernathy was exceptionally smart. "Don't touch anything," he warned. "We may be able to use the tire iron or the keys to pick up the perp's scent."

"I won't."

He went back to put the keys in an evidence bag, then led his K-9 partner to the tire iron. He pointed at the object and offered the evidence bag of keys as two ways for the animal to pick up the scent. "Find, Abernathy," he commanded.

The yellow Lab sniffed along the entire length of the tire iron, going back and forth as if to distinguish the smell of the metal compared to the person who'd held it, and then buried his nose in the evidence bag.

"Find," Finn repeated. Abernathy put his nose to the ground and began following the scent. Finn let his K-9 take the lead, following his partner as the dog made his way from the kennel out to the main corridor toward the main entrance, alerting at several spots along the way.

"He's on the trail," Eva said excitedly.

"He is," Finn agreed, energized by his K-9's ability to track the perp. "Stay here. We'll be back shortly."

"Wait! I want to come with you." She tossed the ice pack on the counter and hurried to catch up with him. She didn't like leaving the place unlocked and hoped they wouldn't go too far.

"We work better alone," he protested.

"I'm coming. If we find Cocoa, he'll be scared to death, but he knows me. Cocoa might even respond to the sound of my voice." She sent him a frustrated glance. "Come on, Officer Gallagher. Stop wasting time. Let's go!"

"Call me Finn," he told her. Giving up, he reluctantly allowed Eva to tag along as he and Abernathy went to work. The K-9 alerted at the doorway leading out the main entrance, then turned to the left as he followed the perp's scent.

Eva didn't say anything but seemed to watch in awe as Abernathy alerted again a short while later. They went one block, then a second, the K-9 picking up the scent at regular intervals.

"Good boy," Finn encouraged his partner, giving him a nice rub as a reward for his good work. Then he straightened. "Find, Abernathy."

The yellow Lab put his nose back to the ground, sniffing and moving in a circular and seemingly random pattern. Abernathy made a circle and then came back, alerting on the same spot he had before.

"I guess this is it." Finn battled a wave of disappointment that their attempt to find Cocoa had come to such a quick end. He glanced back the way they had come. Three blocks. The perp had clearly gone in this direction for at least three blocks. "Abernathy has lost the scent, here at the intersection in front of the Grocer's Best convenience store."

"Maybe we could go up a block or two, just to be sure?" Eva suggested.

Finn nodded. "I'll take him a few blocks each way."

Twenty minutes later, Finn knew it was no use. The attempt to pick up the perp's scent had failed. Abernathy didn't alert once.

"It's likely the guy had a car waiting here for him," he told her as they walked back to the training center. "Otherwise, Abernathy would have picked up his scent."

"I guess I hadn't thought of that," Eva acknowledged, her slim shoulders slumping in defeat. Then she brightened. "Maybe we'll be able to catch the vehicle make, model and license plate number from the video."

Again he was impressed with her cop-like instincts. Most of the women he'd dated—of which there had been many, although no one serious—didn't have a clue about what law enforcement really entailed. He looked up at the security cameras posted on the outside corners of the training center building. "Maybe, but it will depend on the camera range and the quality of the lens. It would be a huge break if we could get something from the tapes. How soon can I check it out?"

Eva shrugged, then winced, putting a hand on her injured shoulder. "As soon as Wade gets in."

"Your boss?"

She nodded, her straight long blond hair shimmering in the sunlight. "Wade Yost is the director in charge of the guide dog training center. He reports to the owner."

"Have you seen anyone lurking around over the past few days?" Finn asked. "The fact that this guy broke in through the back door, makes me think he cased the center before deciding to grab Cocoa."

"No, I haven't noticed anyone. Although maybe the security video will give us that information, too."

"How far back do they go?"

She pursed her lips. "I'm not sure. Maybe a week or two? I know they run on loops."

Two weeks wasn't very long, but he'd take what he could get. "Do you think you'd recognize the guy if you saw him again?"

"I'm not sure." Eva looked away, gazing off into the distance. "Maybe."

Her tone lacked conviction, but he wasn't deterred. "Tell you what. How about you work with a sketch artist to give us an idea of what this guy might look like? Witnesses are always surprised at how much they remember."

"I don't know," she hedged. "I don't think it will help.

I honestly didn't get a good look at his face." Her lack of enthusiasm toward working with the sketch artist bothered him. Where was the woman who had insisted on coming with him to find Cocoa?

"Give it a try," he persisted. "It can't hurt."

There was a long pause before she gave a curt nod. "Okay. But please don't pin all your hopes on the sketch. The keys I used to scratch him with will likely help more than the brief glimpse I got of him."

"DNA takes time, and if this guy isn't already in the system, having it won't help until we get a suspect to use as a potential match. The sketch is a better place to start."

"Okay."

He held the door of the training center open for her, wondering once again why Cocoa had been targeted. The pup was only ten weeks old—what was the point of stealing him? Especially since there were other, more valuable dogs in the kennel?

Did someone have a grudge against the training center? Had the pup been taken as a way to ruin their reputation? He made a mental note to ask Wade Yost for a list of employees who had been fired in the past year.

Finn waited fifteen minutes before Wade showed up. The director was roughly five feet eight inches tall with a husky build. He had dirty-blond hair and non-descript features.

"Eva? What happened? How did you let Cocoa get away?" Yost demanded.

"I tried my best to prevent it," Eva said. "I'm sorry."

"The man attacked her," Finn said, speaking up on her behalf. He shot the director of the training facility a narrow glare. "She's fortunate she wasn't seriously injured or killed."

"Yes, of course," Yost said, backpedaling. "Eva, I'm so sorry you were hurt. Do you want to take the rest of the day off?"

Finn glanced at her and she rubbed a hand over her shoulder.

"Maybe. But first Officer Gallagher wants to see the security video."

"Yes, I do," Finn said. "And you don't seem to have a security system, correct?"

"With all the dogs in here, didn't think I'd need one." Wade Yost led the way to his office and the computer screens he had sitting on a table in the corner. The director went over and pulled up the video feed, going back a few hours. There was no sound from the video, and a heavy silence fell among them as they watched.

Finn rested his hand on Abernathy's silky head. He saw Eva entering the guide dog training facility through the front door. The cameras were only on the outside of the building, not on the inside. They waited, watching various cars driving by on the street, as the timer clicked through. Nine minutes later, the door abruptly swung open and a man dressed in black rushed out. The guy instantly turned left, the same way Abernathy had tracked him, then disappeared from view. The man's face was averted, a ball cap pulled low on his forehead as if he'd known exactly where the camera was located.

"Do you have another camera?" Finn asked. "Something pointing down the street?"

"Afraid not," Yost said. "The other camera points to the parking lot in the back of the building."

"That might show him breaking in," Eva pointed out.

Yost went to work pulling up that security feed. As Finn watched, he could see a tall man wearing black from head to toe, along with the baseball hat pulled over his brow, coming out from behind a dumpster. He again kept his head down as he made his way to the back door. Using the tire iron, he opened it up and disappeared inside. Once again, the angle of the camera made it impossible to see his face beneath the rim of the cap.

Finn blew out a frustrated breath. "I want copies of the video going as far back as you have it."

"Should be about a week's worth," Yost said. "Maybe eight days at the max."

Great, that was just great. The video they had wasn't helpful, and Eva hadn't got a good look at the guy. He'd still have Eva work with a sketch artist, but at this point they had very few clues.

Finn turned toward Eva's boss. "Tell me, do you have a list of employees who were let go in the past twelve months?"

"Uh, yeah, sure." Yost looked uncomfortable as he glanced at Eva, then back at Finn. "I'll, um, get that for you."

Yost rummaged around in his desk drawer, then pulled out a sheet of paper. He glanced again at Eva before handing it over. "You'll, uh, keep that confidential, won't you?" he asked.

"Of course." Finn didn't understand why the guy was so uncomfortable until he scanned the list, his gaze stumbling across a familiar name.

Malina Kendall-Stallings.

Eva's older sister.

TWO

Eva could feel Finn's intense gaze boring into her and desperately wished she could see him more clearly. Unfortunately, he was standing with his back to the large window overlooking the street, and the light coming in behind him cast a shadow over his face.

"Is something wrong?" she asked, finally breaking the strained silence.

"No, of course not." Carefully, Finn folded the paper her boss had given him and tucked it into his pocket. "Wade, do you mind if I take Eva down to the station with me? I'd like her to work with a sketch artist. We need all the help we can get identifying this assailant in order to get Cocoa back."

"That's fine," Wade agreed. "Eva, why don't you take the rest of the day off? You were planning to leave early anyway, right?"

"Yes, I was." Normally working with the animals relaxed her, but since her brother-in-law, Pete Stallings, had just left town to attend a conference, she needed to pick up her three-year-old nephew, Mikey, from his preschool program. Spending extra time with him would be nice. The poor little boy was struggling after his mother's death just three weeks ago.

She picked up her purse from the counter, wishing there was a way to get out of going with Finn. She really didn't want to work with the police sketch artist, knowing that what little she'd been able to see of the man wasn't enough to recreate a good likeness. Yet she wasn't about to reveal her degenerative eyesight issues to Finn Gallagher, either. She knew only too well that men treated her differently once they discovered the truth. Sure, her ex-fiancé, Rafe Del Rosa, had denied breaking off their relationship because of her diagnosis, but she knew the truth.

Rafe was an artist and the ability to see was very important to him. The fact that one day she wouldn't be able to see or appreciate his work had bothered him. Considering they'd met at one of his art exhibits, she could somewhat understand.

Despite what she'd heard on the rare times her parents had taken them to church, love did not conquer all.

Losing Rafe, her sister, Malina, and all too soon her vision had been three life-changing events too many. She'd turned away from the church, unable to believe that all of this adversity was part of God's plan.

There was no plan. Wasn't she living proof of that?

"Eva? Are you ready to go? Joey, our sketch artist, will meet us there."

She realized Finn and his yellow Lab, Abernathy, were hovering near the main entrance, waiting for her. She shook off her depressing thoughts and moved toward him.

She wasn't blind yet. She cleared her throat. "How far away is the K-9 headquarters?"

"In Jackson Heights. Don't worry, I can drive you home afterward." Finn held the door open, and in the bright sunlight she was able to see him more clearly. Earlier, she'd been too worried about Cocoa to notice, but now she could see just how broad Finn's shoulders were and how handsome he was. His dark brown hair was longer than most cops she knew generally wore it, a lock falling over his forehead and his green eyes were incredible. There was a tiny part of her that wanted to take the time to memorize his features so she could picture him in her mind's eye forever, but she gave herself a mental shake.

A relationship was out of the question. In a few years she'd be deemed legally blind. Her diagnosis was such that her field of vision would narrow over the next few years, until she could only see through a small circle. She'd already accepted the fact that she'd spend the rest of her life alone. At least she had her nephew, Mikey, to help care for. And the dogs she trained were also important to her.

She didn't need anyone else.

"Where do you live?" Finn asked.

"Not far. I don't need a ride home, but maybe you could bring me back here to the training center. I live a short subway ride away."

"We'll see," Finn said, his tone noncommittal. She sensed he wasn't the type to take no for an answer, but she didn't need his help.

Remaining independent was very important to her. No way was she going to start leaning on a man now. The more she took the same route to and from work, the better she'd be able to navigate once her eyesight vanished for good. Granted, she'd have a guide dog of her own by then, but still it was important to establish a routine so she could continue to work. Who better to train guide dogs than a blind woman?

Finn opened the back of the police SUV so Abernathy could get into the back. Then he came around and opened the passenger-side door for her.

"Thanks," she said, sliding inside.

"Not a problem." Finn closed the door behind her, and instantly she became aware of the musky scent of his aftershave, which seemed to permeate the interior of the vehicle.

"You mentioned your sister passed away three weeks ago. What happened?"

The change of subject was odd, but she sensed he was making small talk. "Malina was hit by a car and killed on impact. It's been a difficult time for all of us—her husband, Pete, and their little boy, Mikey."

"I'm sorry to hear that." Finn paused, then asked, "Did your sister have a job?"

"She worked with me at the training center for a while as the receptionist slash part-time bookkeeper, but then decided it was too hard to juggle her responsibilities there while caring for her son." Eva didn't add that Malina suffered from the same disorder she did, retinitis pigmentosa. Her sister was three years her senior and in the months before her death, Malina's eyesight had begun to rapidly deteriorate.

"I see. And how old is Mikey?"

"Three and a half." She glanced over at Finn, sensing there was more to these questions than mere curiosity. "Why do you ask?"

"No reason." Finn grinned and, ironically, the softening of his features made him all the more appealing.

"Sorry I was playing twenty questions. As a cop, it's my nature to be nosy."

"Occupational hazard, huh?"

"Yep." Finn expertly navigated the busy Queens traffic as he drove to the K-9 headquarters. Eva paid attention to the streets they passed to familiarize herself with the area.

"I really appreciate you taking the time to do this, Eva."

She did her best to smile, hoping it didn't look too forced. "I want to find the man who took Cocoa as much as anyone."

"How's the cheek?"

"I'll live." Truth was, her face was tender and sore to the touch, but not bad enough that she needed medical care.

Finn drove until he found a parking spot in the tiny lot adjacent to the building. She climbed out of the white SUV while he released Abernathy from the back. With Abernathy between them, she followed him through the double glass doors that led into the main lobby area. Finn punched in the code that allowed them access so they could go inside.

A woman in uniform sat behind a large U-shaped desk wearing a headset. She appeared calm despite the never-ending ringing of the phone.

Finn waved at the officer, who handed a visitor badge to him while still talking on the phone. He clipped it to Eva's collar, then led the way inside. The interior of the police station smelled like old coffee, animal hair and the faint odor of gun oil. There were cubicles separating the desks, but she could still hear cops talking at the same time, some on the phone, some to each other. The din made it difficult to hear specific conversations, and the entire place seemed to be one of perpetual chaos.

"Is Joey Calderone around?" Finn asked the officer closest to him. "He's supposed to meet us here."

"I'm here." A man about her age came over. He also had a visitor badge clipped to his collar. "What's going on?"

"Joey, this is Eva Kendall, and she saw the man who dognapped one of Stella's puppies."

Joey, a man who was as short as he was wide, looked horrified. "That's awful. Why would anyone steal a puppy?"

"No clue, but I intend to ask when I find him." Finn's jovial tone held an underlying note of steel. "Have a seat, Eva. Joey is a master at getting sketches done from witnesses just like you. This shouldn't take too long."

Eva sat down in the uncomfortable plastic chair, thinking that Joey hadn't ever had to work with someone with such limited vision as hers. Still, she was determined to give this her best shot.

The questions started out easy, the shape of his face, his build. Eva relaxed as the drawing materialized in front of her. But when it came down to identifying details like the shape of his eyes, his nose and his mouth, helplessness washed over her.

"I'm sorry, but I don't remember." She sensed Joey's frustration, but he kept his tone light and easy.

"It's okay. Just close your eyes for a moment, see if anything comes back to you."

She closed her eyes, forcing herself to remember the brief flashes she'd got of the attacker's face. After several long moments, she opened her eyes. "I'm sorry," she repeated. "But other than a unibrow over his eyes and the five-o'clock shadow, I can't tell you anything more specific."

"That's okay. It's better to have something than nothing," Joey assured her. He put a few finishing touches on the drawing, but even she could tell the face lacked depth.

It could have been anyone. Even Joey.

"How does it look?" Finn and Abernathy crossed over to see the portrait. She imagined Finn was disappointed, but he didn't say anything. "Thanks, Joey." He took the drawing and handed it to another officer. "Calvin, I need you to spread this sketch around to the rest of the precincts, so all cops can keep an eye out for him. He's the one who stole one of Stella's puppies."

Calvin looked surprised at the directive, but then nodded. "Yeah, sure. I can do that."

Eva knew when she was being patronized and couldn't prevent a flash of anger. She jumped up from the plastic chair, grabbed her purse off the back and threw it over her shoulder. "I told you this wouldn't work. I told you I didn't get a good look at him. It wasn't well lit inside the building and everything happened so fast."

"It's okay," Finn began, but she'd had enough.

She turned quickly and made her way through the various desks of the precinct toward the door.

It wasn't until she was outside and walking away from the police station that she realized she was more upset with herself than with Finn Gallagher. She should have tried harder to get a good look at the guy. She knew the limitations of her vision but hadn't attempted to compensate for it.

Instead of trying to stop the big hulk of a man with

nothing more than her keys, she should have studied his features, memorizing them for future reference.

Her shoulders slumped with defeat. It would be her fault if Cocoa was lost forever.

Finn was flabbergasted by Eva's abrupt departure. What had he said to set her off like that? He couldn't imagine. He knew civilians didn't have the same observation skills that were drilled into new recruits during their training at the academy. Having her come work with the sketch artist had been a long shot, but he'd felt it was worth it.

He hadn't expected her to become so angry and upset.

"Wow, you must be losing your touch," Joey said dryly. "What happened to the infamous Gallagher charm?"

"No clue," he admitted. He wasn't necessarily proud of his reputation with women but hadn't actively done anything to change it, either. He dated often, but never more than a few times with one woman before moving on. Despite that, he hadn't left a trail of broken hearts behind. He'd worked hard to make sure the women he went out with knew he was all about fun and nothing more serious. He had Christian values after all, so he'd never crossed the line. And they'd always parted as friends.

But Eva was different from the women he usually went out with. Not just because she was stunningly beautiful, but because of the many complex facets to her personality. Layers he was dying to peel away in order to catch a glimpse of the real woman hiding beneath.

Not that he would be getting that chance anytime

soon, he thought wryly. Which was too bad, since she intrigued him in a way the others hadn't. Unfortunately, he wasn't relationship material. His dad had been a cop and his mother had left them both when he was just a kid. He remembered being huddled in his bed, listening to his parents fight. His mother had railed at his father that sitting around waiting for him to get home wasn't fair, especially when she wasn't even sure he'd come home safely. She'd screamed at him that the reality of being a cop's wife wasn't what she'd signed up for and that she was leaving.

Finn's mother had never come back.

"She's a looker. You gonna just let her leave like that?" Joey asked, breaking into his thoughts.

"No. Come, Abernathy." He followed Eva outside, figuring that once she'd got outside she'd change her mind and wait by the police-marked SUV for him to take her home.

But he was wrong. Emerging from the building, he headed toward the spot where he'd left his vehicle, then stopped when he noticed Eva wasn't waiting by the SUV. In fact, she wasn't anywhere in sight. He frowned, sweeping his gaze over the area, trying to imagine which way she'd gone. Had she called a car service?

A glimpse of golden-blond hair caught his gaze, and he was shocked to see that Eva was already several blocks away. Did she really intend to walk all the way home? Or was she heading toward the subway station?

Was she familiar with the Jackson Heights area? He wasn't sure.

Muttering under his breath, he and Abernathy picked up the pace in order to catch up with her. Not because he believed the neighborhood was dangerous, but he had promised to take her home. She'd been assaulted just a few hours earlier, and it didn't sit right to have her leaving on her own like this.

"Eva!" He called her name, hoping she'd stop and wait up for him. But the streets of New York were always packed with people and, from what he could tell, she didn't act as if she heard him.

She seemed to be heading toward one of the subway stations, so he tried to move faster, bumping into people as he attempted to navigate around them.

"Excuse me. Pardon me. Sorry," he said as he jostled the pedestrians around him. Abernathy kept up with him, as if sensing they were on the hunt. "Eva! Wait up!"

She hesitated, turning to look behind her. He waved, hoping she'd recognize him.

But she simply turned back in the direction she'd been going. He scowled, wondering if she was purposefully leading him on. He'd never chased a woman in his life and wasn't sure why on earth he was doing it now.

For some illogical reason, he didn't want her to go off alone. The dognapper was probably long gone—the perp had no reason to stick around—but Finn still didn't like it. Abernathy brushed against his legs as they attempted to close the gap between them. Eva paused at the next intersection, her gaze focused on the subway station up ahead.

"Stubborn as an ox," he said to Abernathy as they reached the same intersection. He'd only taken two steps when he heard her shriek.

"No! Let go of me! Help! Help!"

"Eva!" Finn managed to shove past an older guy standing in front of him as he attempted to catch up to her. His gaze narrowed when he realized there was a big man tugging on her arm. Realizing the man was trying to get her into a waiting car, he yelled again. "Police! Let her go!"

Finn barreled through the crowd just as Eva was pushed backward directly toward him. He took his eyes off the assailant in time to catch her.

"It's Finn. I've got you!" He clutched Eva close to his chest, breathing hard. His heart—or maybe it was hers—thundered against his ribs. The man jumped into the car and it took off, disappearing into traffic. Finn squinted in an effort to see the license plate, but the cars were too close together. Hopefully he'd get something off one of the cameras nearby. Frustrated and worried, he turned his attention to Eva. "Are you all right?"

"I think so." Her voice was breathless, and he was grateful she made no move to push him away. He wanted—needed—to keep holding her, making sure she was truly not harmed. Abernathy sniffed at her, his tail wagging as if he was also glad she was okay.

As other subway goers brushed past them, Finn could hardly wrap his brain around what had just happened. If he hadn't been there, the big man would have succeeded in getting her into the car, abducting her.

Finally, she straightened, putting a little distance between them. "I'm okay," she said.

"That was too close," he said, more than a little upset at the attempt so close to their K-9 headquarters. He pulled out his phone. "Patricia? Tell Danielle Abbott I need to get the video feed from the cameras located near the subway station to the south of headquarters."

"Will do," the officer promised.

He turned back to Eva. "Sure you're not hurt?"

"I'm sure." She allowed him to gently tug her out of the stream of pedestrian traffic. Abernathy sat beside him, waiting for his next command. He bent to give the K-9 a quick rub, then focused on Eva.

"What happened?"

Eva lifted a trembling hand and tucked a strand of long blond hair behind her ear. "A guy came up beside me and grabbed my arm, telling me I had to go with him in the black car, a four-door sedan. I screamed for help, then I heard you call out. That's when he pushed me backward and jumped into the car to escape."

Finn nodded. Her story was exactly what he'd seen. He wanted to pull her close again but managed to refrain. He thought back, trying to put an image in his head of the man who'd been beside her. He'd seen the guy only from the back, and he was dressed from head to toe in black. There had been a tattoo of sorts peeking out from beneath the sleeve of his T-shirt. Eva hadn't mentioned a tattoo but said she'd got only a glimpse of the guy. "Did you recognize him? Was it the same man who stole Cocoa?"

There was a long pause before she finally shook her head. "You're going to think I'm nuts, but no. It wasn't the same man."

He wasn't sure he agreed but let it go for the moment. This latest attempt on Eva had to be related to the Cocoa dognapping. It was the only thing that made sense.

But how? And why?

THREE

Shaken by her second attack in less than a couple of hours, Eva longed to step into Finn's broad arms, soaking up his strength. What in the world was going on? She had no idea, other than she knew the man had almost got away with dragging her into the car. If not for her cry for help, and the way Finn had announced he was a cop and called her by name, she was certain she'd already be a hostage in the car being taken to who knows where.

She shivered, realizing how stupid she had been to leave the police station alone. Especially since her motivation was nothing more than wounded pride.

"This has to be related to the incident from this morning." Finn's voice broke into her thoughts. "And from what I could tell, the guy was dressed in black and wearing a ball cap, the same as how you described the man from this morning. If we can get the camera footage, we may catch a glimpse of his face or the license plate of the car."

"That's fine, but it wasn't the same man," she insisted, battling a wave of frustration. She tried to think of a way to make him understand. "This guy was slighter in build and sounded—different. His voice was raspy and he smelled kind of dusty."

"Raspy and dusty?" His voice held a note of skepticism. "Okay, then, did you notice anything different about the voice or scent from the guy who took Cocoa from the training center?"

"He smelled stinky, like he needed a shower, not dusty." She thought back for a moment. "And there was a twang in his voice, as if he may have been from somewhere else. A hint of the South, maybe." When Finn's eyebrows levered upward she felt defensive all over again. "Never mind. I know this may seem crazy to you as a cop, but that's the only way I can describe the difference between the two men. Thanks again for coming to my rescue."

"Hold on, Eva." Finn reached out and caught her hand. Ridiculous that she liked the feel of his warm fingers cradling hers. "I'm sorry. Sounds and smells are important, so I appreciate the extra clues. We'll get this guy, and the one who took Cocoa, too. But right now, I'm going to take you home."

The word *home* brought an image of Mikey. *Mikey!* What if her presence put the child in danger? For the first time in years, she was tempted to pray, to ask God to watch over her young nephew. "Okay, but can we please hurry? I'd like to pick up my nephew from preschool. My brother-in-law is out of town for the week at a training conference in Atlanta, so I'm taking care of his son. It's a bit early to pick him up, but I'll feel better once he's with me."

"Not a problem. Let's head back to the station, where I left my SUV." Finn put his arm around her waist and, despite her determination to remain independent, she was grateful for his support. Abernathy walked along Finn's other side, and she couldn't help thinking about Cocoa.

Why had the pup been taken by the stinky Southern-twang guy? And why had the raspy-voiced man tried to drag her into the car? None of it made any sense.

Worst of all, she feared for her nephew.

"Do you think Mikey will be in danger?" she asked as they made their way toward his SUV. "Maybe I should move to a hotel temporarily."

"Where do you live?" Finn asked.

"I'm staying at my brother-in-law's for now, while I take care of Mikey. He has a small house in Forest Hills, not far from the training center."

"What about when you're not staying at Pete's place?" Finn asked. His tone was casual, but she sensed he really wanted to know.

"I rent a room in a three-bedroom house owned by one of my college roommates. Her parents are doctors at the hospital and bought it for her. The house is only about five miles from Pete's. I can walk to the training facility or take a short subway ride if the weather is bad."

"Okay, let's pick up Mikey and head back to the house. We'll figure out the next steps later." Finn steered her toward the SUV and opened the passenger door for her, then the back hatch for Abernathy.

Traffic was always a challenge, especially getting from Jackson Heights over to Forest Hills. Eva could feel her nerves fraying with every stoplight and every bumper-to-bumper slowdown. Logically she knew the two men in black had been after her and Cocoa, not

Mikey, but she wouldn't rest easy until she had the little boy safe at home.

The preschool wasn't far, and when Finn pulled up beside it, she told him she'd be right back, shoved open her door and jumped out. Quickly, she went inside, then paused, waiting for her eyes to adjust from the bright sunlight to the dim interior of the building.

"Auntie Eva!" She heard Mikey before she saw him running toward her.

"Mikey!" She swept the little boy into her arms, cuddling him close. His blond hair was so much like hers that people often assumed she was the boy's mother. "I'm here to take you home."

"You're early." Peggy Harris, Mikey's preschool teacher, came over to stand beside her. "We were in the middle of a Father's Day art project."

"I know. I'm sorry." Eva didn't want to go into the events of her morning, so she simply offered a wan smile. "Tomorrow he'll be here for the full day."

"That's fine." Peggy reached out to smooth Mikey's hair. "You can finish your art project tomorrow, Mikey. Be a good boy today for your aunt Eva, okay?"

"'Kay," Mikey said agreeably.

Eva held her nephew in her arms as she turned to head back to the doorway, assuming Finn was waiting outside in the SUV. It occurred to her that she didn't have Mikey's car seat, and the thought of walking back to Pete's house, the way she normally did, wasn't very appealing. Being outside made her feel vulnerable, and she refused to risk anything happening to Mikey.

She turned around and went back to find Peggy. "Do you have a car seat I can use temporarily?"

"Sure, you can borrow this one." She pulled a bulky

car seat from the supply closet. "We have a few extras, but try to remember to bring it back as soon as you can."

"I will. Thanks, Peggy." Eva carried the car seat with one hand while holding Mikey's hand with the other.

Finn and Abernathy were coming into the building as she and Mikey came out. "Next time, wait for me," Finn chided without heat. "Parking is a nightmare around here."

"Doggy!" Mikey tugged on her hand, reaching out toward Abernathy. "I wanna pet the doggy!"

Finn laughed, a hearty sound that sent shivers of awareness down her spine. She had no idea why on earth she had this strong reaction to the sound of his laugher, but she found herself smiling as she released her nephew.

Finn crouched next to Mikey, placing his hand on Mikey's shoulder. "Friend, Abernathy," Finn said.

"Good doggy," Mikey said, stroking Abernathy's silky fur. "Nice doggy."

"His name is Abernathy," Finn explained, then cocked his head to the side. "That seems like a mouthful for such a little guy like you. Maybe you can call him Abe."

"Abe," Mikey repeated.

"And I'm Officer Finn," he added.

Abernathy attempted to lick Mikey's face, which sent the little boy into gales of laughter. Finn chuckled, and for a moment she could easily imagine the K-9 cop with a child of his own.

It was enough to snap her out of her reverie. Having a child—a family of her own—wasn't part of her future.

Losing her eyesight would make it difficult enough to take care for herself, much less a child.

The sooner she accepted that reality, the better.

* * *

Finn loved watching Mikey and Abernathy together. Boys and dogs went together like peanut butter and jelly. But it was time to get going, so he called Abernathy over.

"Come," he commanded.

Abernathy instantly wheeled around and came to sit beside Finn, looking up at him expectantly. "Time to go." He led the way down the street to the parking spot he'd managed to find. When they reached the vehicle, he opened the back. Abernathy jumped inside with lithe grace.

Finn came around to help Eva with the car seat. Once she had it secure, she set Mikey inside, buckling him in. He opened the front passenger-side door for her, and she hesitated for a moment before climbing in.

After sliding in behind the wheel, Finn glanced over at her. "I was thinking once you're safe at home, I could go out and grab something for lunch."

She hesitated, then nodded, seemingly relived. "That would be great. I'm still too shaken up to cook."

"Any particular food Mikey likes best?" NYC was well-known for its variety of restaurants, but he had no clue what three-year-old kids preferred to eat.

"Pizza!" Mikey said excitedly. "I love pizza!"

"I know you do," Eva said, glancing back at her nephew. "It's your favorite, right? We'll eat as soon as we're home."

"Speaking of which, I'll need directions."

"Keep heading north, then turn left at the next intersection."

Eva continued to give him directions until he pulled into a narrow driveway in front of an older-model brown brick home wedged in between two others. It was a nice place to raise a child, he thought as he slid the gearshift into Park. He thought there might even be a little sliver of a fenced-in backyard for Mikey to play in.

"We're home," Eva said, as she carried Mikey out of the SUV. Finn went around to the back to let Abernathy out, grabbing the dog's water dish and tucking it under his arm as he followed Eva and Mikey inside.

Eva hesitated for a moment in the doorway, and he wondered if she'd noticed something out of place. "What's wrong?"

"Oh, nothing." She flushed as if she were embarrassed, then moved farther inside. The small kitchen was crowded with two adults, a little boy and a dog, but Eva acted as if she didn't notice.

"Okay, what's for lunch?" he asked, filling Abernathy's water dish and setting it in the corner of the kitchen.

"Ordering pepperoni pizza would be easiest, then you don't have to leave." There was an underlying note of fear in Eva's voice and he understood she was loath to be alone.

"Not a problem." He caught a glimpse of a local pizza flyer on the fridge. Using his cell, he dialed the number and ordered a cheese-and-pepperoni pizza. When that was done, he took Abernathy's vest off, giving him a bit of freedom to explore. Abernathy lapped at the water, then began sniffing around the edges of the room.

Finn's phone rang and he quickly answered it. "Gallagher."

"We got the video feed you requested," Danielle Abbott, their technical guru said. "But it's not a lot of help. The camera angle isn't great. The cars are too close together to get a view of the license plate, and the crowds of people on the sidewalk obscure the view of the perp's face. I'll keep trying to clear up the video, but I can't make any promises."

Finn battled a wave of frustration. "Okay. Thanks, Danielle."

"What?" Eva asked.

"We haven't got anything off the subway camera. At least, not yet."

Eva shook her head. "It figures."

The pizza arrived twenty minutes later. Eva opened her purse, but he shooed her away to take care of the bill himself. Eva set the table, and he opened the pizza box, then picked up Mikey to place him in his booster seat. Eva took out a small slice of pizza and placed it on Mikey's plate, giving it a chance to cool off. He took the seat across from Eva's and, when she finished, he clasped his hands together and bowed his head to say grace.

"Dear Lord, we thank You for this food we are about to eat. We also thank You for keeping Eva safe in Your care. Please provide us the wisdom and guidance to find Cocoa, too. Amen."

There was a brief pause before Eva murmured, "Amen."

Mikey had already taken a bite of pizza, completely oblivious to the prayer. Finn smiled and made a mental note to include the boy next time.

Whoa, wait a minute. Next time? There wasn't going to be a next time! He was only here because Eva had been attacked twice in one day.

This might look like a nice cozy scene, but Eva wasn't his woman and Mikey wasn't his son.

"Finn?"

He looked up from his food, belatedly realizing he was staring at it without making the slightest effort to eat. "What is it?"

"Do you think we'll be okay here?"

"I think so, yes." He picked up a slice of pizza and took a bite, chewing thoughtfully. He didn't want to say too much in front of the boy. "It's probably better for you to be here than at your own place."

She nodded thoughtfully. "I hope so."

"How many people know that your brother-in-law is out of town?"

"My roommates know, of course. So does my boss." She nibbled at her pizza.

"How long will he be gone?"

"About six more days, he left yesterday. He's a paramedic and firefighter, stationed not far from Mercy Medical Center here in Queens. He's their trainer, and there's some new strategies about caring for patients in the field he has to learn, so they sent him to Atlanta." She was silent for a moment before adding, "It wasn't easy for him to leave so soon after…" Her voice trailed off.

Finn nodded his understanding. He couldn't imagine losing your wife and then leaving your son behind as you went off on a business trip. "It's great that you're able to be here for Mikey."

"Yes." Her smile held a hint of sadness. "Between the two of us, we'll help him through this."

It was on the tip of his tongue to ask about God and faith, but then remembered how she hadn't immediately joined him in saying grace. Maybe that was part of his

role here. Not just to protect her, but to help Eva understand God's grace and the power of prayer.

Mikey played with his food, pretending his slice of
pizza was a plane and dive-bombing his silverware.
Crumbs from the pizza crust were falling everywhere,
and he noticed that Abernathy had taken up residence
next to Mikey's chair, gobbling up every morsel the
kid dropped.

Finn tried not to wince. Normally Abernathy
wouldn't eat from anyone other than him, but with his
vest off, he obviously thought Mikey's crumbs were
fair game.

"Don't play with your food," Eva said, putting her
hand on Mikey's arm. "Are you full? Or do you want
to eat some more?"

"Eat," Mikey said, popping what was left of his pizza
into his mouth. "Can I visit Cocoa?"

Eva froze, her gaze locking onto his. She drew in
a shaky breath, then told the little boy the truth, "I'm
sorry to say Cocoa is lost, Mikey, so you can't visit
now. But Officer Finn is going to work really hard to
find him."

"Yes, I will." Finn wasn't exactly sure how he would
accomplish that feat since he didn't have a clue where
to start. Earlier, he'd taken Eva's keys with him back
to the station and had asked Ilona, the lab tech, to run
the DNA. Once those results came back, they'd know
if the perp who'd hit Eva was in the system or not. But
how long would that take? Despite what was portrayed
on TV, fast turnaround times for DNA happened only
in rare circumstances. A puppy-napping wouldn't be
high on the list.

"I'm sorry about what happened this morning," he

said. He couldn't imagine what he'd do if someone took Abernathy from him. The dog was more than just his partner.

Abernathy was the only family Finn had since his father had passed away last year. The other K-9 officers were like his brothers, but Abernathy was more than that. The K-9 was his best friend.

"I know." She offered a lopsided smile. He knew she was worried about more than just Cocoa's fate.

"I'll take a look around the place when we're finished," Finn offered. "See if there are any extra security measures I can add."

"I'd appreciate that," Eva said gratefully. "I know we're probably fine here, but I don't want to take any chances."

He wanted to offer to stay there with her but knew he shouldn't get too emotionally involved. Bad enough that he was tempted to ask her out for dinner and maybe a movie. What was it about her that made him want to toss his two-date, nothing-serious dating rules out the window?

Five minutes later it was clear Mikey was finished eating. Eva washed tomato sauce off his face and his hands, then lifted him down to the floor. Finn finished his meal so he could help clean up.

"I'll take care of it," she said, shooing him away with a wave of her hand. "Do me a favor and check things out, would you? I know I'm being paranoid, but I want to be sure we're safe."

"No problem." Finn moved through the house, taking note of the layout. A living room was located through the doorway from the kitchen, along with a small bathroom and a bedroom. From what he could tell, the bedroom was used as a playroom, toys strewed everywhere.

There were steps leading up to the second floor, where he surmised the other bedrooms were located.

Sure enough, he found two bedrooms separated by a full bathroom. The master suite didn't look frilly, and he wondered if Pete had already got rid of things that reminded him of his dead wife. Crossing the room, he looked out the window. Just as he'd suspected, there was a narrow fenced-in area containing a patio in which a turtle-shaped sandbox was located. There was a grill out there, too, perfect for spending summer evenings outside.

He did the same routine in Mikey's room. A look out the window revealed a wooden trellis from beneath his window to the ground. The window had a sturdy lock, but he wondered if there was something more he could do to prevent anyone from using the trellis to gain access inside. It might not hold a man's weight, but he didn't want to take any chances.

Finn made his way back downstairs to the main level. He found Mikey in the playroom. Abernathy was stretched out on the floor, his tail thumping against the linoleum.

Eva joined him a few minutes later. "Any thoughts?"

Finn glanced at her. "Just the trellis against the wall outside Mikey's window." He kept his voice low so the little boy wouldn't overhear.

Her blue eyes clouded with fear. "Maybe I'll have him sleep in the master suite for the rest of the week."

"Not a bad idea," he agreed. "I'll call the 110th Precinct and ask for cops to drive by on a regular basis."

"That would be nice." Once again her smile was

sad, and Finn found himself wishing there was a way he could lighten the burden she seemed to be carrying around with her.

"Auntie Eva, look!" Mikey picked up the small furry stuffed replica of Cocoa she'd given to him the day she started working with the puppy. "Here's my Cocoa. I wanna play with your Cocoa."

Finn knew that a missing puppy was a difficult concept for a three-year-old boy to understand, and Eva glanced at him as if she wasn't sure how much to tell her nephew.

Since he was hardly an expert on little kids, he had no clue, either.

"I already told you, sweetie, Cocoa is missing," Eva said gently. "He's lost, but Officer Finn and Abernathy here are going to find him."

Mikey's expression clouded, and Finn was afraid the little boy was about to burst into tears. "Maybe the bad man has him."

What? Finn glanced at Eva, wondering if he'd heard the child correctly.

Eva had gone pale. She dropped to her knees beside Mikey so she could look him in the eye. "What bad man, sweetie? Did you see a bad man?"

Mikey dropped his stuffed Cocoa and picked up two plastic dinosaurs, slamming them together with glee.

"What do you think?" Finn asked in a soft voice. "Do you think he saw something?"

"I don't know." Eva's expression was full of concern. "He's only three years old. Maybe he just heard something on TV."

"He watches cop shows?" Finn asked wryly.

"No, but have you seen some of the cartoons? Several have bad guys in them."

"Bad guy," Mikey repeated. "Mommy said the bad guy is real, not make-believe."

"Mommy said that?" Eva asked in horror. She swayed as if she might go down, so Finn put his arm around her waist.

"Easy," he murmured near her ear. "If Mikey sees that you're upset, he'll cry."

"I don't understand," she whispered. "What does he mean? Why would Malina tell him the bad man is real?"

Finn had no clue, but he remembered seeing her sister's name on the list of people who had been fired from the training center. Something Eva didn't seem to know.

He wondered if there had been more going on in Malina's life than Eva was aware of.

FOUR

Eva pulled herself together with an effort. She sat down on the floor next to Mikey and picked up one of his dinosaurs before casually asking, "Do you remember when Mommy talked about the bad man?"

Mikey shook his head and picked up the T. rex, his favorite dinosaur, and began making growling noises. "Grr! I'm gonna eat you for breakfast."

"No, don't eat me!" Eva cried as she pranced her dinosaur away as if trying to escape. "My dinosaur is scared of the T. rex. Mikey, was your mommy scared of the bad man?"

This time, Mikey nodded. "Bad mans are scary. But my T. rex is scarier." He went back to making growling noises.

Eva glanced up at Finn, who was watching their interaction with a thoughtful expression on his face. While playing with the dinosaurs, she tried several times to probe about her sister's bad man, but Mikey was too focused on the dinosaurs and didn't provide any additional information.

Giving up, she set down her stegosaurus and began to stand. Finn was there, offering his hand. She took it and allowed him to help her up, keenly aware of the warmth of his fingers cradling hers. "Thanks," she said, releasing his hand while hoping her cheeks weren't as pink from embarrassment as they felt.

Finn lifted his chin toward the kitchen. "I need to talk to you for a moment about Malina." He glanced down at his K-9 partner. "Abernathy, stay and guard."

The yellow Lab instantly sat and lowered his nose toward Mikey. The little boy laughed and abandoned his dinosaurs to give the Lab a hug. "I love Abe," he said, his voice muffled against the dog's fur.

"Me, too," Finn agreed with a smile.

Eva moved into the kitchen area. When they were out of earshot of the little boy, she glanced at Finn quizzically. "What about Malina?"

He hesitated, then asked, "Why did she leave the guide dog training center?"

"Because she was finding it difficult to keep working as the receptionist there while taking care of Mikey."

"Isn't Mikey in preschool?"

"Yes, but Pete's schedule requires him to work twenty-four hours on and then he gets forty-eight hours off. The calls come in all night long when he's on duty, so he rarely gets any sleep. Once he gets home, he heads straight to bed. By the time he's on a normal sleep schedule, he ends up going back in for another shift." She shrugged. "I think Pete's long hours were getting to her, so she decided to quit."

"Is that what Wade Yost told you?"

"No, that's what Malina told me." She frowned, not appreciating Finn's skeptical tone. "Why? What difference does it make why Malina left the training center?"

"It doesn't," Finn said, averting his gaze. "I just think

it's an odd coincidence. Less than a month after she quits her job, she's hit by a car and Mikey is talking about some sort of bad man. I'm just trying to understand how the puzzle pieces fit together."

Eva folded her arms over her chest. "You're making a bigger deal out of this than there is. Mikey has been through a lot, losing his mother and adjusting to life without her. How do we know he isn't just a bit confused? Maybe heard something on television? I'm not sure we should jump into action based on a three-year-old's statement."

"You're probably right." Again his tone lacked conviction. "Still, do you know if she had any enemies? Or if Pete has any? Any issues at all?"

Eva let out a heavy sigh. "None that I know of. Why would they? They were happily married and both doted on Mikey. I just don't see how they could be involved with some sort of bad man."

"Was her death investigated?"

"Yes, but it was deemed a hit-and-run, and there wasn't reason to think she was purposely hit. No one nearby got the license plate or paid any attention to the driver." She thought back to those turbulent and sorrowful days after Malina's accident. "The police didn't have any leads and told us that unless someone stepped forward with more information, they likely wouldn't find the person responsible."

"That must have been difficult for you to hear," Finn said. His green eyes were so intense she found it impossible to look away.

"It was," she admitted. "I'm sure the driver was texting behind the wheel, since a few witnesses mentioned noticing erratic driving. To think that a text message cost my sister her life makes me so mad."

Finn nodded but didn't ask anything further. Eva's initial annoyance faded as she looked at Finn. Dressed in his uniform, he was handsome enough to make her wish for a cure for her retinitis pigmentosa.

But that was akin to longing for the end to world hunger, so she did her best to pull her gaze away. Finn was good-looking enough to have any woman he wanted. He wouldn't be interested in a woman who would be declared legally blind in a few years.

"Listen, I need to get back to headquarters. I still have paperwork to write up about Cocoa's kidnapping and the attempt on you. Is there anything else you need before I go?"

The thought of him leaving brought a flash of panic, but she did her best not to show it. Remembering the hard grasp of the raspy guy's fingers against her arm made her shiver despite the warmth. She forced a casual smile. "Um, no, I don't think so. Thanks for lunch and, well, for everything you've done for us."

"You're welcome." Finn stared at her for a moment, then reached for his phone. "Do you mind taking down my personal cell number? I'd like yours, too. You know, in case we find someone who matches the sketch."

Eva wasn't holding out much hope for the sketch but readily agreed to take Finn's number. "Of course."

They exchanged cell numbers quickly, then Finn called Abernathy over. "Eva, don't hesitate to call if you need something, okay?"

"I won't. Oh, I need to get Mikey's car seat out of your SUV."

"Leave it," Finn said. "What time do you work in

the morning? I'll stop by and pick you and Mikey up, so you don't have to walk or use the subway."

His offer was sweet. "Are you sure? I hate to take you out of your way."

"I'm sure."

"Okay, then. I usually try to get to work by seven thirty in the morning. The preschool opens at seven."

"I'll meet you here at seven, then. That way you'll still get to work on time."

She nodded and watched as Finn took Abernathy outside and put him in the back of the SUV. After sliding behind the wheel, he backed out of the driveway and was gone before she could think of an excuse that would allow him to stay.

Reminding herself of her goal to remain independent, Eva locked the door and returned to the playroom to spend time with Mikey.

But as the hours dragged by, she found it impossible to concentrate. She made spaghetti for dinner and then gave Mikey his bath before tucking him into Pete's bed, using the master suite because she was leery of the trellis.

Too wired to sleep, Eva moved through the rest of the house, going from window to window, peering into the darkness to make sure no one was out there. A mostly futile effort, since her eyesight was especially limited in the darkness.

People walked briskly along the sidewalks, and she did her best to catch a glimpse of them as they moved beneath the streetlight. From what she could tell, there was no sign of the stinky guy or raspy guy anywhere.

But the two men followed her into her dreams, turning them into nightmares, and her throat was raw from her silent screams.

* * *

At headquarters, Finn finished up his paperwork, then quickly performed a background check on Malina Kendall-Stallings to see if there could be any possible link between the attempts on Eva and the dead woman. He came up empty. Eva's older sister had a clean record.

He squelched a flash of guilt for thinking the worst about her. As a cop, he wouldn't be doing his job if he didn't follow up on every possible lead. Yet he could understand why Eva had got upset with him. Her sister had been the innocent victim of a tragic hit-and-run accident. From the 110th Precinct officers, he'd easily validated that there had been no indication of foul play.

So what if she'd been fired from the guide dog training center? That didn't mean she was involved in anything criminal. He needed to stay focused on finding Cocoa and the men responsible for the assaults against Eva.

Less than an hour later, he and Abernathy were called out for a missing ten-year-old child. Lilliana Chow was late getting home from school, and her mother was desperately worried. Finn didn't hesitate to take Abernathy with him to head over to the Lindenwood area of Queens.

By the time he fought the never-ending traffic to get there, the little girl had returned home. According to her mother, Lilliana had missed her subway stop and, rather than taking the subway back, had decided to walk.

Finn was glad his and Abernathy's services weren't needed and, since he was in the area, decided to take a drive, see if he could find any clues related to the two men who'd attacked Eva.

It was crazy to think he'd be able to pick up the

raspy guy from the rather generic sketch that Eva had produced, but it was better than dwelling on the loss of his chief, Jordan Jameson, who'd been found dead with a needle mark in his arm. At first the rumor was suicide, but Finn and the rest of the NYC K-9 Command Unit knew their chief had been murdered. They continued to work together in an effort to crack the case, but the longer it took, the more likely it was that the perp would get away with the crime. A confusing part of the crime was that Jordan's K-9 partner, a German shepherd named Snapper, had been missing since Jordan's death.

The K-9 should have stayed with the fallen officer as he was trained to do. Finn had thought Snapper must have been stolen, but there was a recent report of a male German shepherd on the loose in a Queens park, and everyone was looking for him. Had Snapper been stolen and escaped? Finn had no idea, but he couldn't help wondering if the stolen puppy was related to Jordan's missing K-9.

Finn returned to headquarters and viewed the subway video for himself, frustrated by the lack of information to be gleaned from the limited view of the street where Eva had been accosted. With few clues to go on, Finn finished his shift and decided to head back toward Forest Hills, telling himself that driving past Pete's house was on the way home. He lived in Briarwood, in the same house where he'd grown up with his father. His dad had passed away last year from a sudden heart attack. At the time, Finn had half expected his mother to show up to claim her portion of the property, but she never did.

The house was too big for a single guy, but there was a small yard that was good for Abernathy so Finn had decided to stay. He was slowly renovating the place, putting money into updating the bathrooms and, ultimately, the kitchen, with thoughts of one day putting it on the market.

Although he wasn't sure he was ready to leave his childhood memories behind. Looking back, the good memories outweighed the bad.

Driving slowly past Pete Stalling's house, he searched for any indication that someone was watching the place. He went around the block twice before he was convinced no one was lurking around.

It was tempting to pull into the driveway, to check in on Eva and Mikey, but he told himself to keep going. It wasn't like him to get hung up on a woman, and he was irritated with himself that he hadn't been able to get Eva out of his mind.

She wasn't like the other women he dated for fun and laughs. She was serious and intense. Stubborn and smart. Courageous and gentle. And so beautiful she took his breath away.

All very good reasons to keep their relationship professional and friendly.

No matter how much he secretly wished for something more.

The next morning, Eva took Mikey through the routine of getting dressed and his teeth brushed before heading down to the kitchen to make breakfast. Yawning, she made a half pot of coffee. She'd been awake more than she'd slept, thanks to the troubling nightmares, which didn't bode well for the rest of her day.

When she spilled coffee down her yellow knit top, she headed back upstairs to change. It wasn't as if she needed fancy clothes working with dogs all day, but she still wanted to look nice. For Finn? Maybe. As she rifled through the items in her small suitcase, she realized she'd underestimated how many times she'd have to change clothes because of being around a three-year-old. Mikey had got jelly smears over one top already the previous day, then there had been the tomato sauce handprint from the spaghetti dinner last night and now the coffee spill. She could do laundry but didn't have enough yet for a load, so she made a mental note to stop by her place to grab more clothing before picking up Mikey from preschool.

Returning to the kitchen, this time wearing a burnt-orange short-sleeved blouse with her jeans, she made Mikey breakfast. Her nephew loved pancakes, so she whipped up a batch, making half a dozen for them to share. As she set his plate before him and dropped into the seat beside him, she was reminded of how Finn had said grace the day before. It had felt a little awkward watching him pray, yet, at the same time, she was touched by his faith.

She and Malina had been raised to believe in God, but their parents hadn't attended church on a regular basis and had never prayed before every meal. The little childhood customs had gone away after her mother lost her eyesight, the same way Eva was destined to do. Her parents now lived in Arizona, and she only saw them a few times a year.

After learning about her diagnosis and Malina's untimely death, she'd begun to doubt that God existed.

"More syrup," Mikey said, breaking into her thoughts.

"How do you ask nicely?" She reached for the bottle

of maple syrup but didn't pour any onto his pancakes until Mikey responded.

"Please," Mikey said, stretching for the bottle.

"I'll help you." She poured a generous dollop of syrup on his pancakes.

It was at times like this when she struggled the most with her diagnosis. As much as she tried to fight against the bouts of self-pity, the feelings remained buried just below the surface, ready to pop out at the least provocation.

A knock at the door made her heart jump crazily in her chest. Shaking her head at her foolishness, Eva peered through the window to see Finn and Abernathy standing there, and she unlocked the door.

"Hey." Finn greeted her with a broad smile. "I'm a little early. For some reason traffic wasn't as bad as usual."

"That's fine, come on in." She opened the door wider, giving them room to enter. "We're eating breakfast. There might be an extra pancake or two if you're hungry."

"I already ate, but I wouldn't say no to a cup of coffee."

She laughed at the hopeful expression on his face. "Of course, there's plenty."

"Hi, Officer Finn," Mikey said, waving his fork. The little boy peered down from his perch at the table. "Did you bring Abe?"

"Sure did." Finn gestured to the boy and Abernathy eagerly gave him sloppy kisses. Or maybe, Eva thought, he was simply licking the sticky syrup off him.

"Thanks," Finn said when she handed him a mug filled with coffee, then returned to finish her pancakes.

"No news on yesterday's events?" She studiously avoided using Cocoa's name, so Mikey wouldn't ask once again what happened to the puppy.

"I'm afraid not." Finn's smile faded. "But don't worry. We're keeping an eye on things."

Fifteen minutes later, using Mikey's car seat so they could return the borrowed one, they arrived at the preschool. Peggy was grateful to have the car seat back, and Mikey waved happily before running over to play with the others.

After ten minutes, they were on their way to the training center.

"I'll come inside with you," Finn said. "I need to pick up the video your boss promised me anyway."

She nodded and led the way inside the center. Finn and Abernathy followed close behind.

"Wade? Officer Gallagher is here."

Her boss came out of his office with a harried expression on his face. "Did you find Cocoa?"

"Not yet, but I'd like to view the video you have from over the past week or so, if you don't mind."

"Oh, yeah, almost forgot." Wade disappeared into his office, returning a few minutes later with a disk. "Here you go."

"Thanks." Finn took the disk and glanced at her. "I'll see you later. Stay safe, Eva, okay? And call if you need anything."

"I will." She quickly turned and went to the kennel to begin training another puppy, a black Lab named George. George was a week younger than Cocoa, and needed more work than Cocoa had. Young puppies were left at the training center until they were twelve weeks old, then were fostered out with a trainer for a full year.

After the first year, the dog would be paired with an owner, and the training continued at the center until both trainer and owner were adjusted to each other.

She couldn't help wondering why Cocoa had been targeted instead of George or any of the other dogs. They had several that were about to be paired with their future owners, which made them more valuable than a young pup.

The rest of her day went by without any issues. She even went across the street to a little bodega for lunch. At two thirty in the afternoon, she went to find her boss.

"I need to leave a little early today."

"Uh?" He looked distracted, and it occurred to her that he'd made it in earlier than she had, which was highly unusual. "Oh, sure, that's fine."

"Thanks." She turned to leave, then glanced back at him. "Is something bothering you?"

He looked startled but then waved a hand. "No. I mean, other than Cocoa being gone. I've been fielding phone calls about it all day."

"Sorry to hear that." She sensed there was more going on than he was telling her but let it go. She was a trainer and preferred working with the dogs rather than the business side of things. Malina hadn't been as much of a dog lover but had enjoyed doing the books. Malina had talked about going back to school to take bookkeeping classes, but after learning about her diagnosis, she'd abandoned that dream.

Now her sister was gone.

Eva shook off the painful memories. "Bye, Wade. See you tomorrow."

"Uh-huh." Wade was already back at work, shuffling papers.

Heading into the sunshine, Eva decided to walk home. She'd been thrilled when Alecia had invited her to move into her new place, as the location was close to her work. It also wasn't far from Mercy Medical Center, where Alecia and Julie worked as nurses. Her thoughts returned to Finn, and she wondered what he was doing today, then chastised herself for caring. If he had news about Cocoa or the two men who'd assaulted her, he'd tell her. No sense making up excuses to call him.

The home she shared with her roommates was a narrow two-story building. Feeling safe in the bright daylight, she went up to the front door and used her key to unlock it. Eva had dropped out of nursing school when her sister had been diagnosed, fearing she had the same genetic disorder. And she was right. She'd switched to training guide dogs and loved it. Thankfully, she had a knack with puppies and it was something she might be able to do years from now, even after losing her eyesight.

Currently, Eva had trouble seeing at night and in dim lighting and had already noticed some limitations in her peripheral vision. As the months went on, she knew the loss of peripheral vision would continue to grow more and more noticeable until she could only see straight ahead through a round circle. Eventually the circle would narrow to a pinpoint where she might only be able to see light and dark.

Her eye doctor told her there was a potential treatment that could slow the vision loss but couldn't cure it completely. She had to go back to see him in another month to find out if she'd qualify.

"Hey, Eva, what are you doing here?" Alecia looked surprised when Eva entered the kitchen. "I thought you were staying at your brother-in-law's for the week, taking care of your nephew?"

"I am, but I need more clothes." She eyed Alecia's scrubs and then glanced at her watch. "I was expecting you to be at work."

"I'm on my way, running late as usual." Alecia rolled her eyes and sighed. "I think my boss is getting tired of me, but we're so short staffed she always ends up letting me off the hook."

Eva smiled, knowing Alecia's tardiness all too well. She and Julie had waited many times for Alecia to show when they'd made plans. "Don't let me keep you," she said, heading over to the stairs leading up to her second-floor bedroom. "I'll only be here a few minutes anyway."

"Okay, see you!" Alecia picked up her stethoscope and dashed out the door.

Eva went to her closet, pulled out a small bag and began packing a few more items, especially tops. Hopefully by the weekend, she'd get some laundry done.

A sudden crash echoed through the room, followed by a distinct thud. Her heart thumped wildly as she instinctively ducked down beside the bed. What was that? A gunshot? She pulled out her phone, intending to dial 911 when she noticed the large object sitting in the center of her hardwood floor, between the window and the bed.

What in the world? Crawling on her hands and knees, she peered closer at what she could now see was a large rock with paper wrapped around it.

Her mouth went dry as she recognized the picture of Cocoa on the paper with a crude threat written beneath.

"If you want to see the dog alive, find the package your sister stole from us."

Her sister? A package? Eva's thoughts whirled as she called Finn's cell number to report what had happened, unable to deny Cocoa's disappearance was linked in some way to Malina.

FIVE

Finn pulled up in front of Eva's place ten minutes after her call. It had helped that he'd already been on his way back to the training center to talk to her about the video. There was a brief image of a man lurking near the edge of camera range, and he hoped she might be able to identify the guy as one of the attackers.

He let Abernathy out of the SUV and took the K-9 with him as he quickly headed inside the house. He'd barely knocked at the door when it swung open. Eva stood there, trembling, so he stepped forward and wrapped his arms around her.

"Oh, Finn, it's awful." Her voice was muffled against his chest and her tear-streaked cheeks tugged at his heart. "Thankfully, my two roommates were gone when this happened, but Alecia had left barely five minutes before the incident. What if one of them had been hurt?"

"It's okay, you're safe now." She felt good in his arms, and he wanted to continue holding her and offering comfort but needed to focus on this most recent threat. "Ready to show me the crime scene?" Eva had been so upset when she'd called that he'd had trouble understanding what she meant about a rock and a threat against Cocoa.

She pulled away from him, subtly swiping at the dampness on her face. "Yes. It happened in my room."

Finn followed her up the stairs to her second-floor bedroom, decorated with cheerful yellow paint on the walls and frilly white curtains. His gaze zeroed in on the broken window, and then at the rock on the floor surrounded by bits of broken glass.

"Stay back," he warned. "Abernathy, sit."

The yellow Lab sat beside Eva as if guarding her. Finn didn't want his K-9 to walk over the shards of glass glittering on the hardwood floor.

He pulled a large evidence bag from his pocket and picked up the rock carefully, noticing it was big and heavy enough to leave a dent in the hardwood floor. He wrapped the edges of the bag around it to preserve it. There was a chance he'd be able to lift fingerprints, either from the rock or the paper itself.

Examining it further through the clear plastic evidence bag, he could see what Eva had meant by a threat against Cocoa. The note beneath the dog's picture said clearly that if she wanted to see the dog alive, she needed to find the package her sister had stolen.

Stepping carefully around the broken glass, he approached the shattered window. It faced the tiny backyard, which wasn't fenced in. It was empty now except for two garbage cans, one tipped over on its side. He could easily imagine someone throwing the rock from there. Eva's room was on the second floor, so not too high. The bigger question was how the perp had identified Eva's window. Being followed to the house was one thing, but knowing the specific window that belonged to her bedroom rather than her roommates? That was something different.

Or had it simply been a coincidence?

Most cops didn't believe in coincidences, and Finn was no exception. Sure, they happened on occasion but not often.

His instincts had been right all along. Whatever Malina had got involved with before her death had caused Cocoa's dognapping and three assaults—if you counted the rock incident—against Eva.

He backed away from the window and turned to look at her. "Do you have any idea what package they're talking about?"

She shook her head vehemently. "No! Absolutely not."

Her response was exactly what he'd expected, but this time he wasn't going to let it go. "I need you to think back to the time before Malina's death. Did you ever see her with a package? Did she carry a large purse? Or did you sense something was amiss?"

"No!" She lifted a shaky hand and pushed her hair behind her ear. Again he had the crazy urge to pull her into his arms to comfort her. "She had a medium-sized purse, not a large bag. I promise, Finn, I'm not lying about this. I want Cocoa back just as much as you do. If I knew anything I'd tell you."

"What about money?" Finn asked, stepping closer. "Did she seem to have enough? Or was she always broke?"

"I never had the impression she was broke or had more money than she should." He could sense the frustration in her tone but ignored it.

"Eva, I have to ask. Is there any way your sister could have been involved in something illegal?"

"No. Absolutely not." Her instant denial seemed to come from loyalty rather than certainty.

"I need you to think carefully about this," he pressed. "Cocoa's life depends on it."

She met his gaze head-on. "I know what you're thinking. Drugs, right? What else could be in a missing package?"

"Drugs, stolen goods such as precious gems or cash itself," Finn pointed out. "But yeah, those are the three main possibilities floating through my mind at the moment."

Eva shook her head. "I just can't imagine Malina being involved in anything like that. It's surreal. She had a loving husband and a beautiful son. I can't believe she'd risk her family for something like that."

"Yet the two men who assaulted you obviously believe that you know something about their stolen package."

She fell silent for a long moment. "I know. But she may have got the package by accident. Like they think she stole it, but someone set her up."

He levered one eyebrow skeptically. "Doubtful."

"But possible. I'll search my brother-in-law's house, see if I can find anything."

"Good plan. I'll help." Finn glanced back at the window. "It's interesting that the vandal knew which window to target. Are you sure you haven't noticed anyone lurking around outside? Not just today but over the past few weeks?"

"I'm positive." Again there was no hesitation in her tone. "You know as well as I do that there are always people coming and going. I had no reason to believe I was being watched, no reason to notice anyone in particular behind me." Her expression turned grim. "But you're right about the window. It freaks me out that they know so much about me. I guess I've been a bit clueless, huh?"

"Hey, it's okay." Finn reached over and took her hand in his, giving it a reassuring squeeze. "We'll figure it out."

"I hope so." Her crystal-blue eyes were troubled. "I can't bear the thought of anything happening to Cocoa. And what about my roommates, Alecia and Julie? I hate to think they may be in danger."

Finn didn't much like it, either. "You'll have to warn them, encourage them to stay someplace else for a few days."

"I will."

It was clear to him that the perps had decided to use the dog as leverage against Eva as a way to get their precious package back. What if they weren't able to find it? If the package contained drugs, and if Malina was a user, it was highly likely the package no longer existed.

Except…he kept coming back to the hit-and-run that had taken Malina's life. What if the accident that had turned deadly had been intended as more of a scare tactic? A way to get her to turn over the stolen goods? He imagined the driver could have been a bit overzealous in an attempt to appear to be a distracted driver, hitting Malina with more force than was necessary.

The end result had been that she'd died, making it impossible for the perps to get the location of the missing package.

Warming to his theory, he decided to go back to

recanvass the area around Malina's accident to see if he could resurrect any witnesses the original officers might have missed.

First, though, he needed to get this rock logged into evidence. Fingerprints would go a long way in helping them identify the perps and what they might be involved in. And he wanted to stop by the training center again to talk to Yost. He'd fired Malina for a reason and Finn wanted to know the details.

"I have a few stops to make, and then we can pick up Mikey from preschool and I'll take you home." Finn turned, hesitated and glanced back at her. "Do you have anything in the basement that I can use to board up the window?"

She nodded. "I think there are some odds and ends down there. The previous owners had done some renovation work."

"Good." He hurried to the basement and found a board large enough to nail over the broken window. When he finished the task, he made a call to Wade Yost.

"I need a few minutes of your time," he told the manager of the guide dog training center. "I need to ask you about Malina."

"Okay, but not in front of Eva."

Finn glanced at Eva, who was scratching Abernathy behind the ears. "She already knows something is up with her sister," he told Yost. "I don't think you need to worry."

"I can't afford to lose her as a trainer," Yost argued. "She's the best I have."

"I understand, but you need to trust me on this. We'll be there in a few minutes."

"Fine," Yost agreed in a resigned tone.

"Don't forget I have to pick up Mikey by five thirty," she reminded him.

He nodded. "Okay."

Eva was quiet as he drove to the training center and Finn knew she was likely thinking about her sister and the missing package. He hoped he wasn't making a mistake including her in the conversation with her boss, but he needed Eva to think hard about what her sister might have been up to.

Wade looked distinctly uncomfortable when they walked into his office, as if he was dreading what was to come. "Hey."

Finn greeted him with a nod. "We have reason to believe that Cocoa was taken by someone Malina was acquainted with." He was being vague on purpose, not wanting to give too much away. "I need to understand what happened before she left your employment."

"Uh, sure." Yost cast a furtive glance at Eva. "Uh, Malina worked as a receptionist and also did some of the bookkeeping for me. But I, uh, noticed she'd made several mistakes and that her behavior had grown erratic. She was late or left early or didn't show up at all."

"For how long?" Finn asked.

The manager shrugged. "A couple of months." Yost glanced at Eva, his gaze pleading. "Please don't be upset with me, Eva. I'm really sorry—I had no choice but to let her go."

Eva sucked in a harsh breath. "You fired her?"

"I had to!" Yost looked distressed. "I didn't want to because I respect you so much. But Malina changed. She messed up my bills, caused me to be overdrawn at the bank. I was getting pressure from the owner to take control of the finances or I'd be fired. I needed to do something, so I let her go and took over doing the books and being the receptionist myself. Please, don't quit. I need you."

Eva didn't say anything, but he knew she wasn't happy about what she'd learned.

Finn put a reassuring hand on Eva's arm. "Don't take this out on him. It's not Wade's fault." He kept his tone soft and soothing. "He cares about you. And Malina, too. But your sister must have got herself in trouble, doing something she shouldn't have been."

Eva bit her lip, her eyes filling with tears. As if sensing her distress, Abernathy nudged her with his nose. "I don't blame you, Wade, but I wish you'd confided in me! Maybe I could have done something to help her."

Understanding she had a right to be upset yet doubting that there was much Eva could have done to rescue her sister, Finn kept his hand on her arm. "And Malina could have come to you, too."

Eva didn't have a response to that.

Finn glanced back at Yost. "Anything else? Did she have her own office?"

"No. She sat up front or used mine." Yost's face was pale, and he sent worried glances at Eva. "I'm really sorry, Eva."

"Yeah. Me, too." Despite the slight edge to her tone indicating she was still angry, at least she hadn't quit.

Erratic behavior, bookkeeping errors and not showing up for work all pointed to one thing in particular.

Drugs. He was fairly certain Eva's sister had got herself hooked on drugs. Worse, she'd likely stolen some from her supplier.

The impact of her poor choices had not only caused Malina to be killed but had reached Eva, as well.

He needed to figure out who Malina had taken the package from, and soon.

Before anyone else ended up hurt or, worse, dead.

Reeling from hearing the truth about her sister, Eva struggled to hold herself together. She didn't want to believe the things Wade claimed Malina had done. Didn't want to consider the fact that her sister might have got involved in something nefarious.

Still, it was impossible to ignore the truth staring her in the face. Wade had fired Malina. Her sister had lied to her. And now Cocoa was missing. All because of a stupid package.

Looking back, she had to admit that Malina had seemed distant a couple of months before her death. Preoccupied. Sometimes excited and other times depressed. At the time, Eva had assumed that Malina's diminishing eyesight was the reason for her behavior. Even when it came to the accident, she'd thought that Malina must not have seen the car swerving toward her until it was too late.

What if she was wrong? What if the accident had been deliberate? Eva shivered.

"Do we have time to drop off the evidence before picking up Mikey?" Finn's voice broke into her thoughts.

"I don't think so," she said, glancing at her watch. She wore one with a large face with the numbers in bold. "The traffic seems to be picking up and we're closer to the preschool than we are to your headquarters."

"Okay, we'll pick up Mikey first." Finn took the next

right, toward the preschool. "How are you doing? I'm sure this hasn't been easy for you."

She let out a heavy sigh. "I'll be fine, although it's hard to believe Malina would have got mixed up with drugs."

"It can happen to anyone," Finn said. "Try not to hold it against her."

Eva hadn't told Finn about her retinitis pigmentosa or about the fact that Malina had suffered the same progressive disorder. Was her impending blindness the reason her sister had turned to drugs? It didn't jibe with what she knew about Malina. How her sister had worried about her ability to take care of Mikey and whether or not Pete would continue being supportive.

Pete. Surely, if Malina was using drugs her husband would have known? Granted, the same thing could be said about Eva, but Malina and Pete were living in the same household day in and day out. It would have been much harder to hide something like drug abuse from a spouse.

At least Mikey's reference to a bad man-made sense now. She'd tried to pooh-pooh Finn's concern, but clearly the little boy had been exposed to something.

Why, Malina? Why would you risk your husband, your son, your life for something like drugs? Why?

Her desperate questions remained unanswered.

"Hi, Officer Finn!" At least Mikey seemed to be oblivious to her somber mood. "Hi, Abe!"

Abernathy licked Mikey's face, making him laugh. Upon returning to the car, Eva quickly buckled Mikey into his car seat and then slid in beside him.

Finn headed back toward the K-9 headquarters. Eva knew he was anxious to find fingerprints from the paper or the rock itself. She wanted the same thing, hating to think about what the raspy guy or the stinky guy might be doing to Cocoa.

Finn left them in the SUV with the engine running. He returned less than five minutes later. "They'll call me as soon as they get anything off the rock."

She nodded, exhaustion weighing heavy on her shoulders. Not just from the lack of sleep the night before, but from the most recent developments.

What else hadn't she known about her sister?

"Officer Finn, I'm hungry." Mikey's voice broke into her thoughts.

"We'll order dinner once we're home," Finn promised. He glanced at Eva as if half expecting an argument.

"If you're tired of ordering out, I can make grilled ham-and-cheese sandwiches," she offered.

"I love grilled ham and cheese, but ordering something might be easier. Not only do we need to do some searching, but I'd like you to look at the video tape. There's only one brief moment where a man in black comes into view, and I need you to tell me if he might be the raspy guy or stinky guy."

"Sure." She nodded and then glanced out her window, knowing that it was highly unlikely she'd be able to see the man's features clearly enough to identify him.

Mikey's chatter filled the silence as they fought the traffic back to Pete's house. Finn ordered food while Eva kept busy providing Mikey with a snack to hold him over until dinner arrived.

Finn opened his laptop computer and showed her the screen. "Here's the video," he said, hitting the play icon.

The clip was so brief she almost missed it. A man

dressed in black stepped out from behind the dumpster, stared at the building for a moment and then disappeared from view.

"I'm sorry, but I don't recognize him."

"I was afraid of that," he said wryly. "But I had to ask." He put the video in reverse and paused it when the man's face was on the screen. It was a profile view, and grainy due to the distance. "How about now?"

The guy had a unibrow thing going on, but she hadn't got a clear view of his facial features. "Maybe," she hedged. "The unibrow is similar, but I wouldn't be willing to testify in a court of law."

"Okay, I understand." Finn shut down the video. "Thanks for trying."

It was on the tip of her tongue to confess about her limited vision, to tell him everything, but she just couldn't do it. Besides, her issues didn't matter one way or the other. She wasn't dating Finn. Being together like this was temporary.

Her impending blindness wasn't.

"Do you think Malina's purse might be here somewhere?" Finn asked, changing the subject.

Grateful for something to do, she jumped to her feet. "I'll check."

Leaving Finn and Abernathy to keep an eye on Mikey, she went up to the master suite. The closet was split in half, and one side held Malina's things. She rifled through them, searching for the black purse her sister favored. Finding it near the back, she pulled it out, her heart pounding. It was bulky, and heavier than she'd expected.

Was it this simple? With trembling fingers she unzipped the main pocket and drew the edges apart to see what was inside.

No package. Her shoulders slumped in defeat. There was a thick black wallet inside, which accounted for some of the weight, along with a variety of other things, including a hairbrush and makeup kit. Opening the wallet, she found the usual credit cards and several receipts. Her eyes widened when she saw there were five crisp one-hundred-dollar bills tucked inside.

Cash and a missing package didn't bode well. She wondered if the cash alone would be enough to satisfy Cocoa's captors but doubted it. She suspected the value of the package was much, much more.

Where was the puppy? And what would the men do if she couldn't find the missing package?

SIX

Finn kept an eye on Mikey playing with Abernathy while he subtly searched the playroom. Although he didn't believe Malina would hide drugs in the place where her son spent time playing, he wasn't about to make any assumptions. If she had been using, she might not have been thinking clearly. So he'd do what was needed to check this room off the list.

Maybe he should get one of the drug-sniffing K-9s here to see if they could find the drugs. That, of course, would only work if the package was actually drugs and not cash or other stolen goods.

By the time he finished with the playroom, Eva had returned from the master suite carrying a large black handbag in one hand and a wallet in the other.

"This was all I found," she said, holding up the wallet. "Five hundred dollars in cash. If the package contained drugs, it's likely gone."

He raised a brow and came over to see the crisp hundred-dollar bills. "I don't know, to be honest, five hundred doesn't seem like enough to risk a dognapping. In the world of drug dealing, it's chump change."

"She may have spent most of it," Eva said, her eyes

full of sorrow and resignation. "Maybe this five hundred was all she had left. I don't want to admit that she was involved in anything criminal, but even I can see this doesn't look good."

Finn glanced at Mikey, making sure the little boy wasn't listening. He was still playing with Abernathy, who was good-naturedly taking the hugs and tail tugging without protest.

"I was thinking of arranging for one of the drug-sniffing K-9s to come sweep the house, just in case."

Her brow furrowed. "It doesn't feel right to do that while Pete's not here. It's his house, not mine. Can't we just look ourselves?"

There was a bit of logic in what Eva proposed. Bringing in a K-9 meant he should go through official channels and have a judge sign off on a search warrant. Since Eva was living here, taking care of her nephew with Pete's permission, she could search her sister's things without going through the legal system.

"Yeah, okay. For now."

Eva's face relaxed with relief, and he found himself wondering if she didn't really want to find the package her sister had taken. As soon as the thought formed, he brushed it off. From the very beginning, Eva was an innocent bystander in this mess. She'd brought Malina's purse down to show him the cash, something she could have hidden easily. He also knew she wanted very much to find Cocoa.

And the more he thought about the cash, the more he believed Eva might be onto something about the package being gone. Where else would Malina have got that much cash? Five hundred wasn't much for a drug dealer, but it was to your average citizen. Malina hadn't been working. If she was a drug user, the money wouldn't have lasted long.

"I'll take a look through the kitchen," Eva offered, interrupting his thoughts.

"Sure." He forced himself to concentrate on the issue at hand. "I'll check the living room."

They went their separate ways. Fifteen minutes later, when the deliveryman from Gino's Italian Ristorante arrived with their lasagna, he discovered they'd both come up empty-handed.

"I'm sure it's gone," Eva said morosely. "How will we get Cocoa back if we can't find it?"

"Cocoa?" Mikey echoed.

Eva winced, and he realized she hadn't meant to say that in front of the boy. "Officer Finn and Abernathy are still looking for him," she promised. "They'll find Cocoa."

Finn helped unpack the food, then took the seat to Eva's right, placing her between him and Mikey. "I have a good idea about what we need to do," he said, holding out his hand. "We'll pray."

Eva stared at his open palm for a long moment, before placing her hand in his. With her other hand, she reached for Mikey's. "I'm willing to try."

The little boy didn't seem to understand the concept of prayer, but at least this time he was paying attention. Finn wrapped his fingers gently around hers and bowed his head. "Dear Lord, we ask that You bless this food we are about to eat. We also ask for Your strength and guidance as we continue to search for truth and justice. We ask You to guide us on the right path to find Cocoa and to bring him home safely. Amen."

"Amen," Eva said.

"Amen," Mikey mimicked. "Cocoa safe."

That made Finn smile. "Yes. God will keep us all safe. Now we can eat."

"Noodles!" Mikey gestured with his chubby hand. "I want noodles."

"I know you do," Eva agreed wryly. "They're one of your favorites."

"Nothing wrong with his appetite," Finn said, grinning at the boy. "He's holding up really well."

Eva's expression softened. "Yes, he is. He still has the occasional nightmare, but overall is adjusting well."

"Don't like nightmares," Mikey said, tomato sauce and cheese smeared along his cheek. "Good dreams, right, Mommy?"

Eva froze at the little boy's slip, but then she leaned forward to press a kiss on his forehead. "Yes, Mikey. Good dreams."

Finn watched the interplay between Eva and Mikey, thinking about how his own mother had abandoned him all those years ago. He only vaguely remembered being hugged and kissed by her, accompanied by a hint of perfume. She'd seemed to love him the way Eva obviously loved Mikey, and to this day he couldn't understand how his mother could have just walked away. Oh, sure, he'd found her eventually, happily married to a businessman with two pretty little daughters, who were eleven and twelve years younger than him. He'd watched them for a long time, his mother smiling with her second family after abandoning the first.

He'd considered confronting her, forcing her to acknowledge him and what she'd done, but in the end he'd simply walked away without letting her know he'd been there.

"You look sad, Finn," Eva said. "What's wrong?"

"Nothing." He forced a smile and took a bite of his lasagna. "Yum. Mikey is right—this is amazing."

She tipped her head to the side, studying him thoughtfully. He fidgeted in his seat, feeling as if her blue eyes could see through his outward jovial facade to the depths buried beneath. To the secrets he'd never told anyone.

To the family he'd always wanted and at the same time refused to allow himself to have.

He was a cop. It was all he'd ever wanted. To be like his father. To protect and serve.

But watching Eva, so stunningly beautiful he could barely stand it, hug and kiss Mikey made him want to reconsider his priorities. Was it possible for him to have both his career and a family? As if sensing his inner turmoil, Abernathy came over and nudged him, placing his head in Finn's lap.

He stroked his K-9 partner's silky fur and reaffirmed this was what he was meant to be. A K-9 cop focused on bringing the bad guys to justice.

Not a family man.

Eva sensed there was something bothering Finn, but he clearly wasn't interested in sharing whatever thoughts were weighing on his mind.

For some odd reason, Finn's prayer had touched her deeply, unexpectedly providing a sense of calmness in a chaotic world. The distress she'd felt at finding the cash in Malina's purse was replaced with a sense of peace after Finn's prayer.

It occurred to her that Mikey deserved a chance to learn about God and faith. She knew Pete hadn't grown up with religion, and that he and Malina hadn't attended church on a regular basis after their wedding five years ago.

Her cell phone rang, startling her. After warily picking up the device, she relaxed when she saw Pete's name on the screen. "Hello?"

"Hi, Eva. How is Mikey doing?" Her brother-in-law's voice was difficult to hear amid the background noise.

"He's great. Do you want to talk to him?"

"Sure. I'll try to find a quiet corner." The background noise muted a bit and she held the phone out toward Mikey, putting the call on speakerphone.

"Mikey, say hi to your daddy," she instructed.

"Hi, Daddy," the child said.

"Hi, Mikey. I love you, buddy. Are you being good for Auntie Eva?"

Mikey nodded his head, apparently not understanding his father couldn't see him.

"Say yes," she encouraged.

"Yes, Daddy. When are you coming home?"

"In a few days, buddy." Pete's voice thickened with emotion. "I miss you, Mikey. Be a good boy and I'll see you soon."

"Okay, bye, Daddy."

Eva took the speaker function off and put the phone to her ear. "Listen, Pete, I need to ask you a quick question about Malina."

"What about her?" Was it her imagination or was there a hint of defensiveness in his tone?

She hesitated, glancing at Finn. He gave her a nod of encouragement, so she moved away from the table, out of Mikey's earshot and continued. "Malina may have mentioned the newest puppy I'm caring for, a chocolate

Lab named Cocoa. Well, he's missing. He was taken by a thug who threw a rock through the bedroom window in the house I share with my roommates. The rock had a threatening note attached, telling me if I wanted to see the dog alive I needed to find the package my sister stole from them."

"Package? What package?" Pete asked, confusion lacing his tone.

"I don't know. I have a K-9 cop, Finn Gallagher, and his yellow Lab, Abernathy, helping to find Cocoa, but we need to know what Malina was involved in before she died."

Pete was silent for a long moment. "I don't know anything about a package. Malina and I…were going through a rough patch for a few months before she was struck by that car."

Hearing him admit that much sent a chill down her spine. "What were you two fighting about?"

"Just the usual." Pete's voice was evasive. "Nothing major, but we had a big argument about a week before the accident. Now I wish I hadn't yelled at her like that. It's all I can think of now that she's gone."

Eva sensed Pete didn't know about the five hundred dollars she'd found in Malina's wallet. "I'm sorry to pry into your personal life, Pete. The reference to the stolen package is confusing to me. You're sure you don't know anything about a package?"

"I'm sure. I never saw Malina with a package." Pete's tone was firm. "Is Mikey really doing okay? I'm worried about how he's adjusting."

She glanced over her shoulder at the little boy liberally smeared with pasta sauce. "He's holding up very well. Try not to worry about us."

"This package business is worrisome," Pete admitted. "Maybe I should just leave the conference and come home."

"I don't think that's necessary and I wouldn't want you to get in trouble with your boss. As the paramedic training coordinator, you have to learn what's new. I have the police looking for Cocoa, and Mikey is doing great. I promise to call if that changes."

"Yeah, okay. But please be careful, Eva. Mikey needs you now more than ever. You're the only mother figure he has at the moment."

Tears pricked her eyes at the concern in Pete's tone. "I'll be very careful. See you in a few days, okay?"

"Yeah. Bye."

Pete disconnected from the line and she stared at the blank screen of her phone for a long moment, her emotions churning. She couldn't imagine what her brother-in-law was going through, losing his wife and becoming a single parent overnight. She was glad she could be there for him and for Mikey.

What was the usual stuff married couples fought about? Money? Spending time together? Or had Pete suspected drugs? She knew from her nursing roommates how the opioid crisis was infiltrating every corner of the city. How people got addicted to painkillers and, when they couldn't get the pills any longer, turned to either heroin or cocaine because they were cheaper and easier to get.

Malina had got her appendix out about five months ago. Was it possible her sister had somehow become addicted to painkillers? An addiction that had sent her searching for something cheaper and more readily available?

"Eva? Everything okay?"

"Huh?" She lifted her head and focused her gaze on Finn. "Yes, fine. Pete doesn't know anything about a package. And while he admitted to fighting with her over the usual stuff, whatever that means, he didn't say a word about Malina using drugs."

"Are you sure he'd tell you something like that?" Finn's question cut through her like a knife.

"Yes, I'm sure." She brushed past Finn to return to the kitchen although her appetite had vanished.

After Mikey was finished eating, she looked at the mess he'd made and sighed. "Bath time," she said with a smile.

"I'll clean up in here," Finn offered. They hadn't said much during the remainder of the meal.

"Thanks." She picked up her nephew and carried him upstairs to the bathroom, wondering if Finn planned on re-searching the areas of the house she'd done. As a cop, she knew he had to be suspicious of everything, but it still hurt that he'd think the worst of her—and of Pete.

Mikey enjoyed splashing in the bathtub, and Eva had to smile at how he played with the bubbles. When the water went cool, she lifted him out, dried him off and dressed him in his jammies.

When she returned downstairs, she found Finn and Abernathy waiting in the now-spotless kitchen. "I didn't want to leave without telling you."

"Thanks for cleaning up."

"I'll come by to pick you and Mikey up again in the morning," he offered. "Unless I'm called away for something."

"Okay." It seemed foolish to turn down a ride that

was intended to keep her and Mikey safe. "Let me know."

"I will." Finn stared at her intently for a moment, then turned toward the door. "Come, Abernathy."

"Bye, Abe," Mikey called out.

"Bye, Mikey," Finn said with a smile.

It was tempting to ask Finn and Abernathy to stay overnight, but she told herself that it wasn't smart to get any more emotionally involved with Finn than she already was.

Still, after he left, the silence in the house seemed suffocating.

Just like the night before, she didn't sleep well. Thankfully, Mikey slept through the night. She'd heard from Pete that he sometimes woke up with nightmares. Still, she couldn't stop thinking about the moment the rock had crashed through her window and how she'd initially thought it might be the sound of gunfire.

As a result, Eva overslept, having fallen into a deep sleep at some time after three in the morning. She quickly showered and changed, and then fed Mikey cereal for breakfast. Finn arrived and drove them to Mikey's preschool, and then he dropped her off at the training center.

"I'll call to let you know if I'm able to drive you home, okay?" Finn's expression reflected his regret. "Unfortunately, there are a few things going on that I have to take care of."

"That's fine," she assured him. "I know you have a job to do."

Though he looked like he wanted to argue, he simply nodded. She headed inside and spent the day working with George, the black Lab puppy who was a week younger than Cocoa. When Finn called to let her know he couldn't pick her up, she understood.

Taking the subway for the first time since the incident at the training center was unnerving. The dark clouds hanging overhead, an indication of an impending rainstorm, only added to her depressed mood. She found herself acutely aware of the people around her. She didn't smell the dusty, the raspy guy or the stinky, twangy guy, but for all she knew they'd sent someone else to watch over her.

Being surrounded by strangers was suffocating, and she couldn't help wondering how she'd manage to ride the train once she'd lost her eyesight. Her determination to remain independent wavered in the face of what that really meant.

Moving around Queens, among the people and traffic, seemed a daunting task. Even with a guide dog. That was what she trained them to do, but experiencing it firsthand wouldn't be easy.

Time ticked by slowly before she arrived at the subway stop near Mikey's preschool. She exited the station and waited for the stoplight to turn green. After crossing the street, she headed down the sidewalk toward the preschool.

She smelled a hint of dust seconds before a man wearing black stepped out from between two buildings and grabbed her arm roughly, yanking her into the alley and up against the wall. He was behind her, so she couldn't see his face.

"Did you find the package yet?" he whispered harshly in her ear.

"No, but I'm looking for it," she admitted, realizing this was the raspy-voiced guy, the one who had tried to drag her into the black sedan. "I promise to keep searching."

"You better look harder or you'll never see that puppy again. And you never know who'll be next."

"I'm trying," she insisted. Was the threat against her? Or Mikey?

The raspy guy yanked her from the wall and shoved her sideways. The momentum sent her falling hard against the concrete.

Her hands and knees stung from the force of the blow, but she ignored the pain, jumped up quickly and headed out to see which way he went.

The raspy guy was long gone. She struggled to breathe against a wave of panic. Fearing the stinky guy might be nearby, she turned and ran to the safety of Mikey's preschool before using her phone to call Finn.

"Gallagher."

She tried to control her racing heart. "It's Eva. The raspy guy just threatened me, or maybe Mikey. I'm at the preschool now, but I need you to come and get us. *Hurry!*"

"I'll be right there," he promised.

"Thank you." She disconnected from the call and leaned heavily against the wall near the doorway. Knowing Finn was on the way wasn't as comforting as it should be.

You never know who'll be next.

The subtle threat against her or, worse, a three-year-old boy was nearly her undoing. If anyone was the true innocent in all this, it was Mikey. These men wouldn't stop until they got what they wanted.

No matter the cost.

SEVEN

"I have to go." Finn glanced at a fellow K-9 cop, a rookie named Faith Johnson and her partner, Ricci, a German shepherd named after fallen Officer Anthony Ricci. They'd been searching the Rego Park area because someone had reported seeing a German shepherd running loose. The K-9 team had hoped the dog might be Jordan Jameson's missing K-9 partner, Snapper. So far, they'd come up empty-handed. "You'll be okay?"

"Yeah, Ricci and I will be fine." Faith waved him off. "We'll do one more sweep, then head back to headquarters before the storm." She sighed. "I was really hoping to find Snapper."

Finn nodded, but his mind wasn't on the mystery surrounding the missing K-9. He needed to get over to Mikey's preschool as soon as possible. Knowing that the raspy guy had accosted Eva and threatened her and Mikey so close to the preschool made his blood boil.

Bad enough that they'd dognapped Cocoa, but to threaten an innocent woman and a three-year-old child? The two men must be desperate to get their package back, and he knew only too well that desperate men did equally desperate things.

Traffic was horrible, and it hadn't even started raining yet, but thankfully Rego Park wasn't far from Forest Hills, so he made it to the preschool quickly. When he and Abernathy walked up, Eva came out from the doorway, where he surmised she'd watched and waited for him. Her eyes were wide with fear and horror.

He instinctively pulled her into his arms, cradling her close. "Are you sure you're okay?"

She nodded her head, her voice muffled against his chest. "Bruised and sore, that's all."

He closed his eyes, thanking God for keeping Eva safe. He never should have let her head home alone. He should have told her to wait for him until he'd finished searching for Snapper. "I'm so sorry," he whispered.

"It's not your fault." She lifted her head to gaze up at him, her eyes bright with unshed tears. "I'm worried about Mikey. We have to find that stupid package, Finn. We have to!"

"Shh, it's okay. We'll keep looking, I promise." He pressed a gentle kiss to her temple. "Mikey is inside?"

She sniffled, swiped at her eyes and nodded. "They were working on a finger-painting project for Father's Day. Mikey wanted to finish it for his dad and told me it was to be a surprise. I assured him I'd wait for you and Abernathy. I also called Pete, but he didn't answer so I left a message. I didn't go into detail, because I didn't want to panic him, but I told him to call me back as soon as possible."

Finn nodded and glanced around the sidewalk. "Show me where this went down."

Eva looked a little nervous, so he took her hand in his, noting the rough abrasions on her palm. She led him two blocks away from the preschool and gestured to the narrow alleyway between two buildings. "Here. He grabbed me as I was walking past and shoved me up against the brick building."

Thinking about how frightened she must have been had him clenching his jaw to keep his temper in check. As if the bruise darkening her cheek wasn't bad enough, these guys just kept coming after her. He swept his gaze around the area, but there was nothing resembling a clue as to who raspy guy might be. Finn wished he had the tire iron that was used at the guide dog training center with raspy guy's scent on it, but he'd left it at the crime lab.

With a resigned sigh, he turned back toward Eva. "Okay, we have to assume he's been following you and knows the location of Mikey's preschool. I'll take you and Mikey home, and you'll need to stay there. It's too risky to continue bringing him here and going to work. I'll make sure the cops drive past the place on a regular basis."

She never hesitated. "I know. I'd never forgive myself if something happened to Mikey. His safety has to be my primary concern."

He wouldn't be able to forgive himself either if anything happened to Mikey or Eva. He took her hand again. "I'll keep you both safe. Let's get Mikey."

The little boy greeted them enthusiastically, proudly displaying his finger painting for them to see. Amid the blue-and-green swirls, the child had drawn a family portrait. There were stick figures of a man and a woman with long hair each holding the hand of a little boy who looked just like Mikey. "Auntie Eva, will you help me hide it from my dad? I want it to be a surprise."

"Of course," Eva assured him as they walked to the

vehicle. Finn could tell she was getting choked up all over again. "How about if we frame it and wrap it up for him? I'm sure he'd love to have your painting hanging on the wall."

"I'd like that." Mikey grinned as she placed him in the car seat. "Can we do that today?"

"Um, maybe not today, but soon." Eva glanced at Finn and he nodded in agreement.

"I have a day off coming up, I'll be happy to take you and your aunt to get the picture framed."

"Can Abe come, too?"

"Sure."

"Goody!" Mikey clapped his hands. "I love Abe."

Finn almost told Mikey he and Abe loved him, too, but held back, reminding himself that he wasn't part of Mikey's family. A family he'd decided was not meant for him because of his career, but now couldn't stop thinking about.

He concentrated on navigating the traffic to reach Pete's home. Earlier that morning, he'd looked into Pete Stallings's background but hadn't found anything unusual. The guy appeared on paper to be just as Eva claimed, a dedicated firefighter and paramedic who loved his son. There were some money problems, but nothing too terrible. And if Malina was using drugs, the money problems made sense.

He'd pulled the autopsy results on Malina's death, too, but surprisingly, the medical examiner had not found any track marks indicating IV drug use. There was some indication that she might have been snorting cocaine, but there hadn't been any hard evidence of recent use. Damaged nasal passages could be from severe allergies as well as cocaine, especially if the user was early in the level of abuse.

All of which brought Finn back to the immediate threat. Did the two men who'd assaulted Eva know that she was staying at Pete's place? He had to assume they did. After all, they knew Malina had stolen their mysterious package. What was to prevent them from breaking into Pete's to look for the package themselves?

Unless they already had? Was it possible they'd managed to get inside the house to do their own search? And when they hadn't found what they were looking for, had gone after Cocoa and Eva? And maybe, now, Mikey?

His gut told him it was a distinct possibility.

Once he and Abernathy had Eva and Mikey safe inside the house, he decided to go through the entire place one more time. Leaving Eva and Mikey in the kitchen, eating a snack of animal crackers and milk, he took Abernathy and started up in the master suite.

He and Abernathy made their way through the upper level without finding a thing. Downstairs, he went through the living room, the playroom, bathroom, finally ending up in the kitchen.

"I already went through all the cupboards," Eva said wearily.

"I know." He glanced over his shoulder at her. "I just feel like I need to do something."

"Me, too." Her sad smile squeezed his heart. "All finished, Mikey? You want to play?"

"Yep."

She washed Mikey's face and hands, then lifted him from his booster seat. For a moment she snuggled him close, kissing his cheek, before setting him on the floor.

He gave Abernathy a pat on the head, then ran toward the playroom, laughing when the K-9 followed.

Eva dropped her chin to her chest for a moment, as if struggling to remain composed. Finn couldn't stand seeing her distress. He pulled her into his arms once again, marveling at how right it felt to hold her.

"I'm sorry," she murmured. "I don't know what's wrong with me."

"Nothing is wrong with you, Eva." His own voice was low and husky with emotion. "You have every right to be upset. There've been nothing but threats and danger at every turn."

She didn't answer. He stroked his hand over her long silky blond hair, reveling in the softness against his fingertips and her clean citrusy scent. He ached to kiss her, but had promised himself to offer comfort, nothing more.

Even if it killed him, which was a distinct possibility.

After several long moments, Eva pulled out of his arms, offering a watery smile. "Thanks, Finn. You've been incredible through all of this." She surprised him by going up on tiptoe to press a soft kiss against his cheek before stepping away. "I feel safe with you and Abernathy, here."

"I'll stay for as long as you'd like," he offered rashly, willing to do anything if she kissed him like that again. Yeah, it wasn't smart to stick around where he'd only get more emotionally attached. If he had one single functioning brain cell in his head, he'd assign someone else to protect her and the boy.

But even as the fleeting thought went through his mind, he rejected it. He didn't want anyone else here watching over them.

He trusted only himself and his K-9 partner, Abernathy, to keep them safe from harm.

Once again, he lifted his heart in prayer that God would help watch over them, too.

Leaving Finn's embrace was the hardest thing she'd ever had to do. As she went into the playroom to check on Mikey, she put her hands over her warm cheeks, willing the crazy attraction away.

How was it possible to feel so attached to the man in such a short period of time? She hadn't felt this emotionally connected to a man before, not even Rafe Del Rosa. It was easy to look back and acknowledge that they'd had some fun, shared a love of art—and that was about it. No wonder he'd broken things off when learning about her retinitis pigmentosa.

She needed to tell Finn about her condition, sooner rather than later. But after the emotional turmoil of the day, she didn't want to open up that subject. Especially since once he knew the truth, those hugs and chaste kisses would likely end.

Be honest, she told herself sternly. *The main reason you kissed Finn on the cheek was because you were hoping he'd kiss you in return.*

Yeah, okay, so what? Kissing wasn't a crime. And it had been so long since she'd met a man she truly liked. Respected. Admired.

"Can I play outside in my sandbox?" Mikey asked.

"Not today. Looks like rain." She went over to the small television in the corner of the room. "How about if I put on some cartoons for you?"

"Okay."

Once Mikey was settled on the floor, lying next

to Abernathy to watch television, she returned to the kitchen to think about dinner. Malina had been the cook; Eva was more of a carryout kind of woman. But for Mikey's sake, she should at least try to provide a homemade meal. Especially since they were going to be housebound for the foreseeable future.

She opened the fridge and peered inside, hoping for inspiration.

"Hey, what if we head over to Griffin's for dinner?" Finn offered.

She closed the fridge and turned to face him, wrinkling her nose. "I don't know—it looks like rain. Besides, I can't bear the idea of being followed by the raspy guy or stinky guy or anyone else who might be looking for that stupid package."

Finn nodded. "I hear you, but Griffin's diner is a cop hangout, I don't think anyone would be dumb enough to try anything there. And you and Mikey won't be alone—Abernathy and I will be with you the whole time. Along with plenty of other cops."

She'd never been to Griffin's but had heard it was a cop hangout. Cooking wasn't her forte, and going someplace to eat rather than going for takeout once again held a certain appeal. Yet she didn't want to do anything that might put Mikey in harm's way, either.

"It's located just a couple of blocks from the K-9 headquarters," Finn added. "I'll park there, and we can walk over."

"Okay, let's do it," she agreed. "I can't lie, my cooking is atrocious."

Finn laughed, and despite her earlier assault, she found herself smiling in return. "I'm actually not a bad cook," he said modestly, "But it would take too long to get groceries and to start a meal from scratch. I know Mikey's safety is most important and a cop hangout near our K-9 headquarters is the only place that fits the bill."

"All right. I'll get Mikey's raincoat."

Ten minutes later, they were tucked in Finn's K-9 SUV and heading back toward the K-9 headquarters. Eva remembered seeing Griffin's, when she'd been at the K-9 Command Center.

A light rain was falling, the air thick with humidity. Welcome to summer in Queens. After parking at headquarters, Finn and Abernathy escorted them down the few blocks until they reached the diner, an old red-brick building that had aged to a deep rusty brown over the years.

The interior of the café was a typical diner decor, royal blue vinyl seats in the booths, and wooden tables and chairs in the open area. Beyond that, it wasn't typical at all. There were two sides to the place. One side appeared to be a dog-friendly patio, shielded from the weather by an aluminum rooftop and walls that were little more than screens that were open in the nice weather. It was homey, and she could understand why the K-9 cops liked it here. A pretty woman greeted them at the hostess stand, a large diamond ring flashing on the fourth finger of her left hand. Eva told herself that it was petty to be jealous of this woman's happiness.

"Hey, Violet, how are you?" Finn turned and pulled Eva close. "I'd like you to meet Eva Kendall and Mikey Stallings. Eva, this is Violet Griffin. She's Lou Griffin's daughter."

"Nice to meet you." Eva shook Violet's hand. "Let me guess, your father owns the restaurant?"

"Yes, he does." Violet's smile didn't reach her eyes

and she glanced at Finn, who frowned as if he'd noticed too. "Dad is here, Finn, if you'd like to talk to him. You know how he likes to keep up on the cop gossip. Follow me. We're busy, but there's a table available in the doghouse."

"The doghouse?" It took a moment for the pun to register in Eva's brain. The sign above the French doors helped. It read The Dog House—Reserved for New York City's Finest.

"Sounds good. Thanks, Violet." Finn held out Eva's chair for her and then glanced around. "We'll need a booster seat, too."

"Got it." Violet returned a few minutes later with a booster seat, a paper place mat and three crayons. "For Mikey, to keep him busy."

"Thanks." Eva was grateful for her thoughtfulness.

"Finn, where have you been?" An older man with grizzled ruddy features and a shock of white hair came over to shake Finn's hand. "Haven't seen you all week."

"Been busy," Finn agreed. "This is Eva Kendall and her nephew, Mikey Stallings." After the quick round of introductions, Finn added, "Hey, Lou, are the rumors true?"

"Rumors?" The older man's attempt to sound surprised was abysmal.

"Yeah. Zach Jameson mentioned something about how you were offered a lot of money by a real estate developer for this place. Did you really turn it down?"

"Zach should learn to keep his mouth shut," Lou muttered, avoiding the question. The older man glanced back over his shoulder at his daughter. "Although I have to admit, he makes my Violet very happy. The Jamesons are a fine family, such a shame about Chief Jordan. Honestly, I couldn't ask for a better soon-to-be son-in-law."

"So you're not selling," Finn pressed.

"Not yet," Lou admitted. He waved a hand. "Go on now, enjoy your meal."

A waitress came by to take their order. Eva ordered a burger and Finn ordered the same. Mikey wanted chicken strips and a glass of chocolate milk.

"It's nice they allow dogs here in the patio area," she said once their server left to place their order.

"Yeah, well, being so close to our headquarters helped. Lou quickly figured out that half his business came from K-9 cops, so he added this outdoor patio for customers with dogs. And he constructed it in a way that it can be sheltered from the elements." Finn glanced down at Abernathy lying on the floor between his seat and Mikey's. "The dogs are all very well trained, so it hasn't been a problem."

"It's a nice place," she agreed.

"Yeah, Lou treats us all like we're his kids, checking up on us and making sure we're doing okay." He leaned forward and lowered his voice. "That's why everyone is upset to hear some rich real estate mogul wants to buy the building. We're hoping Lou doesn't cave to the temptation to sell."

She nodded, understanding his point. Mikey continued coloring his picture while they waited for their food. Despite how busy the place was, their meals arrived quickly. She cut up Mikey's chicken so it would cool off.

"Let's say grace," Finn said, picking up her hand and Mikey's. "Dear Lord, bless this food we are about to eat. And provide guidance to Lou as he decides his future. Amen."

"Amen," she echoed, feeling self-conscious about praying in public. Then she realized she needn't have worried. No one seemed to pay them any attention, and, to her surprise, she noticed another couple at a table several rows back also praying before their meal.

"Yummy," Mikey said, taking a bite of his crispy chicken.

"My burger is good, too," she confided.

A few minutes into their meal the sound of raised voices from the other side of the restaurant caught Finn's attention. With a frown, he rose to his feet. "Stay here, we'll be right back."

He and Abernathy made their way over to where two men were arguing loudly. Eva craned her neck, trying to see what was going on. She stood to get a better view, gasping in horror when she noticed one of the men punch the other one in the face mere inches from Finn.

"Who starts a fight in a café known to be a cop hangout?"

She was talking to herself, as everyone's attention was centered on the ruckus. She took a step forward, not liking the thought of Finn getting in the middle of a fight. But she needn't have worried. Between Finn and a man she assumed was another cop, they managed to separate the two men, each slapping cuffs on their respective perpetrator.

Relieved the crisis was over, Eva turned back to the table, looking for Mikey. His chair was empty.

"Mikey? Mikey!" She shouted to be heard over the din, raking her gaze around the restaurant. But there was no sign of the boy.

Mikey was gone!

EIGHT

"Finn!" The panic in Eva's voice caught his attention. He released the guy he'd just handcuffed, pushing him toward Ian, one of his fellow officers, to look over toward Eva. "Mikey's gone!"

"Gone?" He and Abernathy charged past the diner onlookers to reach her side. "What happened?"

"I don't know!" Eva's blue eyes were wild with fear. She gripped his arms tightly. "I turned my back on him for only a minute when I thought that man was going to punch you in the face. When I looked back, he was gone. It's my fault, Finn. This is all my fault!"

"No, it's not." Fighting a sense of panic himself, Finn surveyed the patio, then the interior of the diner, thinking it was possible the child had decided to head to the bathroom. He hurried over to check, but the restrooms were empty. There was no sign of the little boy's blond head anywhere in sight. Returning to the table, Finn's gaze landed on the child's blue raincoat draped over the seat. He grabbed it.

"Find, Abernathy," he commanded, opening the coat so that his K-9 partner could sniff the interior closest to where Mikey's skin had been. "Find Mikey."

Abernathy buried his nose in Mikey's raincoat for several long moments. Finn knew that Mikey's scent was well-known to Abernathy, considering how much time they'd spent at Pete's house, but this was part of the K-9 training process, signifying they were on the job.

Abernathy put his nose to the ground around the chair Mikey had used. He alerted there, but Finn encouraged him to keep going. The K-9 followed the invisible trail of Mikey's scent through the open patio space to the sidewalk outside the diner. Finn's stomach clenched as he realized that despite his assurances to Eva that she and Mikey would be safe here, he'd been wrong.

So very, very wrong.

"Find, Abernathy," he encouraged, following the K-9 outside. Similar to the day of Cocoa's dognapping, the dog turned and headed down the sidewalk to the next intersection. There, Abernathy sniffed along the ground, turning in a circle before sitting down. When the Lab looked up, Finn thought he perceived a concerned and pleading expression in the dog's dark eyes, as if he was waiting for the next command.

"I know. I'm worried about him, too." Finn bent over to give Abernathy a quick rub and a treat before leading him back to the doorway of Griffin's diner.

"He lost the trail?" Eva's hopeful expression collapsed, and her eyes filled with tears. "I can't believe this is happening. What if they hurt him, Finn? He's just a little boy! We need to find him!"

"I'll call the team. We'll have all officers drop whatever they're doing to search for Mikey." He used his radio to call for backup, putting out the word that a three-year-old child had been taken from Griffin's. He requested an Amber Alert, too, informing the dispatcher of what Mikey had been wearing. A red-and-white-striped shirt with navy shorts and slip-on athletic shoes.

"Eva, do you have a recent picture of him on your phone?"

She nodded and quickly texted it to him. He in turn sent it to the dispatcher to use for the Amber Alert.

Within five minutes, additional cops and their respective K-9 partners arrived. He held out Mikey's raincoat to the newcomers—Carter Jameson and his white German shepherd, Frosty, Reed Branson and his bloodhound, Jessie, and Tony Knight and his chocolate Lab, Rusty. They were the first three responders, and he was grateful that each of their K-9s were trained to follow a very specific scent. Even those who weren't would join in the search, but he appreciated the extra expertise.

"Use Mikey's raincoat for his scent," he directed. He wasn't the highest-ranking officer there but took charge anyway. "Abernathy followed the trail outside to the intersection. The scent ended there, and I'm afraid that likely means the kidnapper had a ride waiting for him. We need to divide up the city, searching quadrant by quadrant."

"Done," Carter Jameson agreed, concern darkening his eyes. "You're taking charge of this operation, so let us know where you want everyone to go."

A feeling of helplessness washed over him. The two men who'd taken Cocoa and now Mikey could be anywhere in the massive city of New York. He hoped and prayed that concentrating on the Queens borough was the right thing to do. It made sense to him that these guys must be staying somewhere close by. Especially considering how frequently they'd been striking out at Eva and those around her.

Carter pulled out a map of Queens and spread it on the table. Finn bent over it, concentrating on the best strategy. "I'd like to take Forest Hills, since that's where a lot of the incidents took place." He glanced up at the three officers surrounding him. "Carter, I'd like you to take Rego Park. Reed, maybe you and Jessie could take Corona."

"You want me and Rusty to take Elmhurst?" Tony Knight asked. "Those are the three closest areas to where we are now. Assuming that the bad guys are smart enough to stay away from Jackson Heights, since that's where our headquarters is located."

"Sure, although I'd like officers to stay around here, too. Griffin's is the location of the crime, so we can't ignore it." There was so much ground to cover, and the bad guys had a vehicle to go wherever they wanted. Yet by his estimation and, apparently, the others as well, these were the most logical places to start. When more officers arrived, he doled out more assignments until they had pretty much an entire circle around Pete's place and Griffin's covered. Between searching and putting out the Amber Alert, he thought they had a good chance of getting Mikey back soon.

The alternative was unthinkable.

"Eva, stay here at Griffin's for a while, I'll check in with you if I find anything," he said as he prepared to leave.

"No. I'm coming with you." The stubborn thrust of her chin and steely determination in her eyes made him groan. There wasn't time to argue. He wanted to hit the streets now, before too much time had passed.

Each minute would feel like a lifetime to a three-year-old child.

"Fine," he capitulated, unwilling to waste another second. "Let's go."

Eva nodded. She accompanied him outside as they hurried back to his SUV. The drive to Forest Hills took longer than he wanted, but his gut told him that these two men would be staying someplace close. They'd accosted Eva near the preschool and at the training center, both located in Forest Hills. This was the place he knew instinctively they'd be found.

"This is all my fault," Eva said in a low, tortured tone. "I never should have taken my eyes off Mikey, not for a second."

"It's my fault for suggesting we go to Griffin's in the first place," he countered in a grim tone. "I thought we'd be safe surrounded by so many cops. Stupid to assume any such thing."

Eva shook her head. "I'm the one responsible for watching over Mikey in Pete's absence." She pulled out her cell phone. "I need to call him again, before he hears about it on the news."

Knowing the Amber Alert would go out on the local news and possibly be picked up by the national networks, he nodded. This time she reached Pete, who'd tried to call her earlier, but she must have missed his call while in the noisy diner. Listening to her side of the conversation, it was easy to hear the alarm in Pete's voice after Eva explained what had happened.

"I can't believe they kidnapped my son!"

"I'm so sorry, Pete. I failed you and Mikey." Eva's voice grew thick with tears.

"Ask for permission for a drug-sniffing K-9 to search

his house," he whispered. Finding the missing package would be the best way to negotiate with Mikey's kidnappers.

She did, and Pete must have calmed down some, because Eva nodded to him. "We'll let you know if we find anything," she promised.

Finn missed the next part of the conversation.

"If you can get a flight home, that would be great," Eva finally said. "Just let me know when to expect you."

Finn wasn't surprised that Pete's plan was to fly home immediately. That was exactly what he would do if it was his son who had been taken. The way Eva sat looking so forlorn made him long to offer comfort. He tightened his grip on the steering wheel, willing the traffic to part like the Red Sea, allowing him through.

"Pete's never going to trust me with Mikey again."

"Eva, please stop berating yourself. The real fault lies with the men who would stoop so low as to use a child as hostage to get a package back."

Eva wiped the tears from her face. He pulled into Pete's driveway and got out from behind the wheel. After freeing Abernathy from the back, he approached Eva. Fresh tears streaked her cheeks, ripping at his heart.

"You don't understand," she said as he approached. "Remember how you asked me if I'd noticed anyone following me?"

He frowned, trying to understand where she was going with this. "Yes, but you can't beat yourself up for not noticing someone tailing you. You're not a trained police officer and, even then, clearly we were followed tonight without my knowledge. No one is invincible. And these guys could have two vehicles for all we know.

Switching them out would make it even harder to find a tail."

She shook her head, looking impatient. "No, it's not that. I wasn't entirely truthful with you." She took a deep breath, as if bracing herself, before she met his gaze head-on. "I didn't tell you about the problem with my vision. About how my peripheral vision is limited. Not only that, but it's hard for me to see clearly in dim lighting. Facial features are often blurry."

He was surprised by her admission. "Is that something new you've been dealing with? Maybe you need to see an eye specialist."

"I have seen a specialist, and no, it's not anything new. I have a degenerative vision disorder called retinitis pigmentosa. It's a progressive blindness disorder that is hereditary in nature. I'll likely be deemed legally blind in three years."

Finn was shocked at the news, although it helped drop a piece of the puzzle into place. He understood now why she hadn't been able to give a detailed description to the sketch artist and why she was so in tune to the way the two men sounded and smelled rather than how they looked. "I don't understand. Why didn't you say anything before now?"

"I had my reasons, and really, none of that matters right now. I wanted you to know the truth." She glanced down at Abernathy standing patiently at his side. "Let's keep searching for Mikey."

Finn wasn't keen on the idea of dropping the subject as if it were a rotten tomato, but she was right about time being of the essence in finding the boy. Yet, as he put Abernathy to work, his thoughts whirled. Was her limited eyesight the real reason she'd pulled out of his arms earlier in the day? He didn't like thinking she was ashamed of her diagnosis.

He made a mental promise to approach the issue of her eyesight later, once they'd found Mikey safe and sound.

Eva should have felt better after telling Finn the truth, but she didn't. Plagued by guilt, she couldn't help thinking that if her eyesight had been better—or if she'd told Finn the truth before now—Mikey wouldn't have been kidnapped right under her nose.

They walked up one street and down the other, a painstaking process wherein Finn worked hard to encourage Abernathy to pick up Mikey's scent. They stopped at each apartment building, each intersection, anywhere that one of the two men who'd kidnapped the boy might be holding him hostage.

She replayed the conversation with Pete in her mind, wondering if he'd got a flight home yet. As Finn and Abernathy took another detour up to a rather run-down apartment building, she used her phone to call him.

"Did you find him?" Pete asked, his tone betraying his hope.

"Not yet," she said, feeling even more miserable. "We're doing our best, and everyone is helping in the search."

"Eva, I can't lose Mikey—I just can't." Pete's voice was full of harsh desperation. "I never should have come to this stupid conference. I don't care if I'm the training coordinator. I should have told my boss to forget about it."

"I'm sorry, Pete. I feel terrible. Did you get a flight home?"

"Not yet. There's a huge thunderstorm moving in, so there is a delay on all outgoing and incoming flights." He sounded upset, not that she blamed him. "I'm trying to find another option, see if I can rent a car to get to another city that is outside the range of the storm."

"Pete, don't do something rash," she cautioned. "The storm might blow past before you reach your next destination. Stay put for now. I'll update you on a regular basis, okay?"

There was a long silence from the other end of the line. When Finn and Abernathy turned away from the apartment building, her hopes plummeted. But she did her best to sound upbeat for Pete's sake.

"Pete? Really, we're going to find him. We have cops and search-and-rescue K-9s combing the entire Queens borough."

"This is all because of some stupid package Malina took from them?" Pete finally asked.

"Yes. I'm afraid so." She fell into step beside Finn and Abernathy. "I've searched the entire house twice but haven't found anything. Are you sure you don't know of any other hiding place Malina might use?"

"I've been racking my brain about it since you called. I don't know of anywhere she would use other than her work or our place. You have my permission to search every nook and cranny."

She wasn't sure if Pete knew Malina had been fired from the guide dog training center but decided this wasn't the time to tell him. There was something else nagging at her. "Did Malina have a gym membership?"

"She used to," Pete acknowledged. "But we stopped paying for it a few months before she died."

"Yeah, okay." She vaguely remembered Malina talking about some new gym she was going to that was located near her home. The Fitness Club. "Stay in Atlanta until it's safe to fly," she repeated. "And I'll call you as soon as I know anything."

"Thanks, Eva."

She closed her eyes momentarily, thinking that she was the last person Pete should be thanking. "We're in this together," she finally said. "And we won't rest until we find him."

"I know." Pete didn't say anything more as he disconnected from the call.

"What was that about a gym?" Finn asked.

"Malina used to go to a place called The Fitness Club to work out, but Pete says that they let their membership lapse a few months ago. I keep thinking of the stinky guy and how he reminded me of how a gym smelled." As they started down another block, Eva noticed the sun was slowly beginning to set. In another hour or two the city would be shrouded in darkness.

Her heart squeezed painfully. Surely the two men wouldn't hurt the boy, but would they understand he was afraid of the dark? Would they care enough to put a night-light on for him? Would they give him a bath and a snack before bed?

Of course they wouldn't, and the overwhelming feeling of despair almost sent her to her knees. She stumbled, instinctively reaching out for Finn.

"Eva? What's wrong?"

"I just…can't stand it. The thought of Mikey being scared and alone, it's killing me."

Finn put his arm around her shoulders, giving her a reassuring squeeze. "Let's pray for Mikey," he suggested. "Let's pray that God will watch over him, keeping him safe. That he'll be strong and brave, secure in the knowledge that we're coming for him."

"Okay," she whispered.

"Dear Lord, we ask that You please keep Mikey safe in Your loving arms. Give him the strength he needs to hang on until we can get there. Guide us on Your chosen path and provide the light we need to find him. Amen."

"Amen," she echoed. "Thank you, Finn."

"Let's keep going," he encouraged. "There's another place up ahead that has potential as a hiding spot."

She nodded and kept pace with Finn and Abernathy. As she walked, she repeated Finn's heartfelt prayer over and over in her mind.

It was strange to open her heart and her mind to God. Yet, despite her fears, she felt a slight measure of peace at knowing that Mikey wouldn't be all alone with those evil men.

God would be there with him.

The next building was a dead end, as was the next one. Abernathy worked tirelessly, and she appreciated having the K-9's keen scent offering them assistance.

She'd kept the Amber Alert on her phone, looking down at Mikey's smiling face periodically as a way to reassure herself that everything possible was being done to find him.

Fighting fatigue, she kept pace as they started down another street. Finn had identified that houses with for-sale signs were sometimes used as short-term rentals, so they went to each of those, as well.

Her phone rang again and, assuming it was Pete, she answered it quickly. "Did you get a flight?"

There was a moment's hesitation before a mechanically distorted voice said, "If you want to see the kid again, find the package."

"You have Mikey?" Her gaze clashed with Finn's, and he rotated his index finger in a way she knew meant *do everything possible to keep the caller on the line*. "How do I know he's alive? I'm not turning over anything to you without some proof that you haven't harmed the child."

"He's fine, or he will be if you bring the package," the mechanical voice repeated. "If you don't…" The caller let his voice trail off.

Eva gripped her phone harder, aware of Finn talking to headquarters, asking for a trace on her phone. There was some kind of noise in the background, but she continued to press her point. "Please, he's only three years old. Just let me talk to him for a moment. He won't be afraid if he knows I'm coming to find him."

"Find the package."

The call ended abruptly, and it took all her willpower not to throw her phone against the closest brick wall.

If she knew where the package was, she'd gladly trade it for Mikey's life. But she didn't.

And was very afraid these men wouldn't blink at hurting a little boy to make their point.

NINE

"We didn't get the trace."

Finn let out a harsh breath and drew his hand down his face at their technical specialist Danielle Abbott's response. "Thanks for trying."

"We'll keep her phone queued up so we can trace the next call."

"Thanks." He'd known tracing the call that had come in on Eva's phone was a long shot, especially since it had taken precious seconds to get the phone pinged, but he'd hoped for something—anything—they could use to find Mikey.

He hated to admit that he and Abernathy were coming up empty-handed.

"They want the package," Eva's voice was dull with resignation. "I don't understand why they haven't figured out that I would have already turned it over if I'd had it."

Finn didn't know what to say to that. If the package was drugs or money, they'd have to get permission to use it as a way to draw out the kidnappers. No way would they be allowed to simply hand it over to secure Mikey's freedom. There would be a whole task force involved, something he sensed Eva wouldn't appreciate. Since it was a moot point, he decided not to go down that path.

"What exactly did he say?"

"If I want to see Mikey again, I'll find the package." She looked as if she might cry. "He refused to let me talk to Mikey, and at the end of the call repeated the demand to find the package. I tried to see if I could hear Mikey in the background, but I can't be sure."

Adrenaline spiked as he moved a step closer. "Think, Eva. You have astute hearing. Go over the call again in your mind. Can you remember if you heard any background noises during the conversation? Anything that would give us a clue as to where Mikey is being held?"

She shook her head automatically, then frowned. "Wait, maybe."

"What was it?" He practically held his breath as he waited for her to respond.

Eva was quiet for several long moments, then she started to hum a few bars of a tune.

"It sounds familiar," he said. "Do you recognize what it's from?"

"It's a cartoon that Mikey's watched before." The hint of tears vanished from her eyes. She reached out to grasp his arm. "They wouldn't put cartoons on the television if Mikey was hurt, would they? He must be okay."

He nodded thoughtfully. "I agree. Having Mikey watch cartoons is a good way for them to keep him quiet and less likely to cause trouble."

"I'll call Pete to let him know," she said, glancing down at her phone.

"Hold off for a moment," he advised. "If you call

Pete, he's going to think we found Mikey. Let's not raise his hopes up over nothing."

Her shoulders slumped, and she nodded. "You're right. It's just that even knowing this much helps."

Was he making a mistake by holding her back from contacting Pete? He wasn't sure. The cynical cop inside him couldn't help wondering if Pete had arranged for these guys to kidnap Mikey and to hold him for ransom in order to get the package back. Pete being out of town at a conference provided a rock-solid alibi.

He just kept coming back to the fact that it was difficult to believe that Pete hadn't known what Malina was doing. That she was using drugs and possibly selling them, too.

The ringing of his phone interrupted his dark thoughts, and he lifted the device to his ear, recognizing the number as coming in from the K-9 headquarters. "Gallagher."

"We got a tip about the missing kid," the dispatcher told him.

His pulse spiked and he locked gazes with Eva. "What kind of tip?"

"Some woman saw the Amber Alert. She claims she was driving by Griffin's when she saw a man dressed in black running from the patio with a child matching Mikey's description. She saw him run down the block and then jump into a midsize black sedan."

"Did she get a license plate?" He held his breath, hoping and praying that she had.

"A partial. First three letters are Bravo, Delta, Tango. She wasn't sure, but she thought the first number was five, but it also could be an eight. We checked Griffin's video and saw the car but couldn't get the plate number.

We're running a trace on the partial plate now, looking for matches with a black four-door sedan."

He remembered how, a few days ago, one of the men had tried to get Eva into a vehicle. That one, too, had been a four-door sedan. Not a coincidence and the first tangible lead they'd got since Mikey's disappearance.

"That's great, thanks. Let me know when you get a list of potential matches."

"Will do." The dispatcher disconnected from the call.

"We have a license plate number?" Eva's wide eyes were full of hope. "That's good news, right? We'll be able to use that information to find Mikey?"

"It's good news, but it's not a complete license plate number. We'll be able to narrow it down to a manageable list of possibilities." He glanced up, noticing the sun was beginning to set, dipping low on the horizon. There was less than an hour of daylight left. "Let's get back to the house. They'll call when they have some information for us."

"I don't like giving up the search," Eva said in a low tone. "We need to keep looking."

He understood where she was coming from. Hadn't he felt the same way? But waiting for the partial plate information was far better than wandering aimlessly around Forest Hills. "I need to check in with the rest of the team anyway. See if anyone came up with something." When she opened her mouth to argue, he gestured toward Abernathy. "My K-9 partner needs food and water. Resting for a while until we have something more concrete to go on is the best thing for him, and for us."

Eva bent down to give Abernathy's golden-yellow fur a rub. "All right. Let's go."

The walk back to Pete's place wasn't very long because Finn had taken a circular route, with the house remaining in the center.

After providing food and water for Abernathy, he and Eva sat at the kitchen table. He noticed her gaze traveling over the kitchen, and he wondered if she was trying to find something they'd missed during the first two searches.

"Since Pete gave us permission to search, I'll ask Zach Jameson to bring Eddie, his drug-sniffing beagle, to come out." Scrolling through his contact list, he found Zach's number. "That way we'll know for sure the package isn't here. Getting our hands on that package can only help get Mikey back."

"Unless the package is money and not drugs," Eva pointed out wearily. "You're assuming they're drugs."

"One problem at a time," he said. Zach picked up on the other end of the line. "Hey, do you have time to bring Eddie out here to Forest Hills to sweep the Stallings' house for drugs? We have reason to believe that Mikey has been kidnapped in an effort to get a package of drugs back."

"Not a problem, we can be there in thirty," Zach agreed.

"Thanks." Finn gave Zach the address, then set his phone down. "Zach and Eddie are on their way."

Eva nodded, her expression troubled. Whether the package contained drugs or money didn't matter much. The money could have easily been related to buying or selling drugs. In fact, considering the money troubles he'd found in Pete Stalling's bank account, he was leaning toward a stash of cash. It made the most sense.

Especially since he didn't believe Malina would have risked her son finding drugs.

Zach and Eddie made good time, arriving twenty minutes later. The K-9 partners started in the kitchen and searched the entire house, room by room. Finn followed from a distance, watching the team work. Eddie, the beagle, alerted in the master bathroom.

"We've looked here, but let's do it again," Finn said.

There were no packages but, upon further inspection, Zach found a tiny bit of white powder in the corner of the cabinet beneath the sink. "I think this must be what Eddie picked up." Zack glanced up at Finn. "We can take a sample and have it tested, but I believe it's cocaine."

"I agree." Finn watched as Zack managed to get a tiny bit of the white powder into an evidence bag, and Finn hoped it was enough to run a decent test. That Eddie had picked up on the scent was impressive. "Let's finish the upper level."

Zach nodded and instructed Eddie to find. The dog went back to work gamely, but the rest of the house was clean.

No package of drugs—or anything else.

"Thanks," Finn said. "Sorry to drag you out here for this."

"Hey, we likely found evidence of cocaine, so it was worth it." Zach's expression turned grim. "I thought we'd done a good job busting up the drug ring at the airport last month, but it's clear we only made a slight dent in the problem. I wonder if the guy who escaped is involved in this, too. We haven't found the ringleader yet, either. He's likely involved."

"We'll get him." Finn led the way down to the first

floor. Eva was still in the kitchen, lightly petting Abernathy as he lay on the floor near her feet.

"Find anything?" Eva asked.

"Just a trace of white powder that needs to be tested." Finn glanced at Zach, who remained silent. "Nothing else. I think if the package is drugs, we can safely say it's not here at the house."

Eva grimaced. "I should have asked him what was in the package," she berated herself. "Next time, I'll push for an answer."

Though Finn wasn't sure there would be a next time, he nodded in agreement. "Couldn't hurt."

"I'll let you know what we find," Zach said. He and Eddie moved toward the door. "If you need anything else, holler."

"Will do." Finn walked them to the door, watching as they climbed into the K-9 SUV. It occurred to him that they should search the training center and The Fitness Club gym. He doubted either would be fruitful, but at this point he needed to cover every possibility.

No matter how remote.

Upon returning to the kitchen, his phone rang. His heart thumped wildly as he recognized the number. "Tell me you have a plate number and address."

"We have a plate number and that led to an address— an apartment located in Forest Hills. It's registered to an R. Talmadge. Got a pen?"

Finn glanced around the kitchen, found a pen and pad of paper and began scribbling as the dispatcher gave him the address. The apartment wasn't far from Pete's house, and it galled him to know that if he'd widened his search by another block, he might have found it.

"Thanks, I'm heading over there now with Abernathy. We're the closest. Send backup."

"Will do."

"I'm coming with you," Eva said as he buckled Abernathy's vest in place and clipped on the leash. The yellow Lab stretched and then sat at his side, waiting for his command.

"Not happening. It's too dangerous." He was bound and determined not to drag Eva along. Especially since darkness had fallen and he knew her vision was compromised.

"Mikey needs me. He doesn't have a mother or a father here. *He needs me.*"

What was it about her that he couldn't deny her anything? Finn swallowed an exasperated sigh. "Fine, but you better do exactly as I say. No argument. I can't allow you to be anywhere close to danger, understand?" They hurried outside to get into his SUV. "If a civilian gets hurt on my watch, my career is over."

"I won't get hurt," Eva insisted. She slid into the passenger seat as he put Abernathy in the back and then climbed behind the wheel.

He didn't want to acknowledge that keeping her safe was more important than his career, but it was. And he couldn't stand the thought of Mikey suffering at the hands of his captors. If having Eva along helped the boy adjust, then fine. He'd break the rules for a three-year-old any day of the week.

Navigating the streets to the address he'd programmed into his cell phone, Finn prayed silently that they'd find Mikey safe and unharmed.

* * *

Eva barely glanced at the apartment building Finn had double-parked in front of, intent on unbuckling her seat belt to follow him inside.

"You need to stay here," he said, releasing Abernathy from the back of the SUV. "My backup will be here any minute, but I'm going in."

"I might be able to recognize the sound of the cartoon through the door." She'd come this far and didn't see what the problem was in going the rest of the way. She'd prayed that God would show them the way to find Mikey and knew they were close. "Do you even have a clue as to what apartment number they're in?"

He scanned the mailboxes. "I don't see the name Talmadge listed anywhere, and wasn't given one, but that's where Abernathy will help." He took out Mikey's raincoat for his K-9 partner. "Find Mikey."

Abernathy put his nose to the ground and alerted on Mikey's scent near the front doorway. Eva's heart was beating so fast she thought it might burst from her chest. The security lock was intact, so Finn pressed the buzzer for the building's superintendent, informing him he was with the police and asking him to open the door.

Abernathy seemed eager to work, sniffing along the hallways as they made their way around the ground floor. When the K-9 didn't alert on that level, they went to the second floor.

"How many floors does this place have?" she asked in a whisper.

"Ten."

Eva's hope began to wane as Abernathy didn't alert on the third floor, either. Ten floors could take forever to search.

On the fourth floor, Abernathy alerted at an apartment door halfway down the hall. Eva sucked in a quick breath as they cautiously approached. Sounds were coming through the thin doorway, and as she came closer, she heard the television.

Straining to listen, she slowly nodded at Finn when she realized the same cartoon show was still on. Maybe the men had recorded it to play over and over again to keep Mikey occupied.

"Go back outside," Finn whispered. Gently he tried the door handle, but of course it was locked. He pulled his weapon and then hammered on the door with his fist. "Police! Open up!"

Eva had begun to retreat down the hallway when she heard a series of loud thumps from inside the apartment.

No! They were going to get away!

Finn lifted his foot and kicked at the door near the handle. Once, twice. The wood frame splintered and gave way, the door swinging open beneath the pressure. Finn entered the apartment, weapon held ready with Abernathy at his side.

"Stop! Police!"

The thumping grew louder, drowning out the sound of the television. When Mikey started crying, Eva decided she wasn't leaving. Not now. Not when they were so close to finding Mikey. Ignoring Finn's directive, she followed him inside the apartment. Where was his backup? Shouldn't they be here by now?

Creeping farther into the room, the shouting from the man and Mikey's shrill screams grew louder. As she rounded the corner, she saw a man dressed in black holding Mikey in his arms as he tried to throw one leg over the windowsill.

"Get him, Abernathy!" Finn commanded.

The yellow Lab ran across the room and latched onto the guy's ankle. Labs weren't trained as attack dogs, but she believed Abernathy sensed Mikey was in danger. The man howled in pain, which only made Mikey scream louder.

"I want my mommy!"

"Stop! Get him," Finn repeated.

Abernathy continued to tug on the man's leg, growling low in his throat. Eva kept her gaze trained on Mikey, trying to send reassuring vibes. The man wasn't very far away, half in and half out of the window. His gaze was locked on Abernathy, and he was so busy trying to shake the dog off that the gun in his right hand was pointed away from her and Finn.

It was now or never. Ignoring Finn's harsh cry to stay back, she rushed forward, grabbed Mikey and yanked him from the man's arms. The hand holding the gun came over to hit her on the shoulder at the same moment the sound of gunfire echoed through the room. It was so loud it caused a ringing in her ears.

She dropped to the floor, instinctively curling her body over Mikey's in an attempt to protect him.

"I'm here. You're safe, Mikey. It's okay, you're safe." She repeated the words over and over even as the room suddenly filled with cops. Finn came over to take her arm, helping her stand.

"I told you to stay outside!" His voice was hoarse with fear and anger. "You almost got yourself killed!"

Mikey's crying increased in volume and she raked him with her gaze. "Not now. Yell at me later. Mikey is frightened enough. Did you get him?" She looked around the room, relieved to note that the guy was sitting in a chair, his hands cuffed behind his back. The odd dusty smell that clung to his clothing helped her identify him as the thug who'd grabbed her arm and tried to get her into the waiting car not far from Finn's headquarters.

Was he here alone? Or was the stinky guy here, too? If so, where was the puppy?

Cops swarmed the apartment quickly, searching for anyone else who might be inside. She heard one of them shout, "Clear!" and knew that meant no one else was there.

Eva sat down on the edge of the sofa, cradling Mikey close, stroking his back and whispering to him, "It's all over, sweetie. You were so brave. Abernathy was smart enough to help us find you."

Mikey's arms were wrapped so tightly around her neck it was difficult to breathe. Her shoulder from where the man had punched her, but she ignored it, refusing to release her hold on the little boy.

Too close. The gunshot had whizzed past her and Mikey before wedging into the wall. The replay of the night's events would haunt her for a long time. So many things could have gone wrong but hadn't. They'd caught one of the bad guys and rescued the little boy from harm.

As she held the precious child in her arms, Eva knew she had God to thank for keeping Mikey safe.

TEN

Upset at how Eva had rushed in to grab Mikey, Finn was also angry at himself for losing his cool. He shouldn't have yelled at her. Thankfully, everything had turned out okay. They'd found Mikey and had the perp handcuffed. He wished Eva hadn't put herself in danger but knew that, given the same set of circumstances, she'd likely do the same thing again.

Watching Eva holding Mikey on the edge of the sofa, rocking back and forth as she attempted to calm him down, he let the last vestiges of his anger go. The way Mikey was clinging to Eva only proved her point. The boy didn't have his mother or his father here, and he deserved to be comforted by Eva, the closest thing to a mother figure he had.

"We got nothing," Zach Jameson announced. "No sign of Cocoa or anyone else staying here."

Finn blew out a frustrated breath. Clearly the two men were smart enough to remain separated. As much as he wanted to find Cocoa, he couldn't help being glad they'd found Mikey so quickly. The Amber Alert had worked in their favor. Too bad there wasn't a dog version of an Amber Alert. They could put one out for Snapper and for Cocoa.

He approached the handcuffed perp on the floor. Just because the apartment was registered to Talmadge, didn't mean this was the same man. "What's your name?"

The guy stared straight ahead, refusing to make eye contact with any of the cops swarming the apartment.

"You're facing serious charges here," Finn pointed out. "Felony kidnapping, not to mention the attempted kidnapping of Eva that I witnessed a few days ago. I'm sure once we run your fingerprints through the system, we'll find other outstanding warrants. Enough to put you away for a very long time."

He noticed the perp flinch, but he still didn't look at him. Finn waited for a long moment, hoping the impact of what the man was facing would sink into his tiny brain.

"I want a lawyer." Although the perp still hadn't met his gaze, Finn had to admit his voice was indeed raspy, the way Eva had described. "Not talking till I get my lawyer."

While expected, the request didn't make him feel any better. He gestured for a couple of the beat cops who'd arrived on the scene to escort the perp out to their car. "Read him his rights and get him his lawyer. I'll meet you at the jail soon."

The two beat cops nodded and escorted the cuffed kidnapper out of the apartment. Zach and his K-9, Eddie, were still searching the place for drugs. "Gallagher! In here," Zach called, a hint of excitement in his tone.

Finn headed into the back bedroom. "Find something?"

"Eddie alerted here." Zach gestured to the bedroom closet. "I want you as a witness before going inside."

Finn nodded. "Let's do it."

Zach opened the closet door and Eddie alerted again. Finn leaned close and saw a sprinkle of white dust similar to what they'd found in the master bathroom at Pete's house. Finn glanced at Zach. "We can bag it as evidence, but I was hoping for something more substantial."

"Me, too." Zach bagged the evidence, then they went on to search the rest of the closet. Finding nothing, Zach let out a sigh. "Guess that's it, then."

"I'd like the lab to compare the two samples you collected today, the one from the house and this one, to see if they share the exact same chemical makeup," Finn said.

"Good idea." Zach raised a brow. "And if they do?"

Finn shrugged. "It's a connection. I'm not sure what it means yet, but I don't believe in coincidences."

"True." Zach placed the evidence bag in his pocket. "Every bit of evidence counts. I'll let you know what the lab says."

"Thanks." Finn returned to the main living area of the apartment. Eva and Mikey were exactly where he'd left them. Abernathy was hovering near Mikey, trying to lick his face. The obvious affection between Mikey and his K-9 was endearing.

"Eva? Are you and Mikey ready to get out of here?"

She looked up at him with a wan smile. "Yes, please."

"I'll drive you both back to Pete's and have a cop stationed outside for protection, then I need to head back to headquarters to grill this guy. By then we should at least know who he is and maybe will get a lead on known associates."

"He's not the stinky guy," Eva said. "He doesn't smell right, have a Southern twang or scratches on his forearm. But I think he's the raspy guy."

She was right, and again he was impressed with how well she used her senses besides her eyesight. "Don't worry," Finn said reassuringly. "We'll find him."

Rising to her feet, she carried Mikey toward the broken apartment door. He and Abernathy followed close behind. There were dozens of nosy neighbors peeking out of their doorways as he escorted Eva and Mikey outside to his double-parked police-issued SUV. He put Abernathy in the back first, then came around to help Eva.

"I'm sorry," he said, opening the back passenger door open for her. "I shouldn't have yelled."

"Yelling is bad," Mikey said, having calmed down from his scare. "Mommy and Daddy aren't supposed to yell, either. But sometimes they do."

Eva's gaze clashed with his and he gave a brief nod. "Do you know what they were fighting about, Mikey?"

"Mommy spends too much money." Mikey yawned widely, his eyelids drooping as the events of the evening caught up with him. "Daddy said so."

"It's okay, Mikey," Eva said. She buckled the boy into his car seat and then kissed him. "Grown-ups sometimes yell, but you should know that both your mommy and your daddy love you very much."

"I love them, too." Mikey yawned again, his eyelids fluttering closed. His head slid to one side as he appeared to fall asleep.

Eva closed the back passenger door and moved as if

to brush past Finn. He stopped her by gently cupping her shoulders in his hands. "Eva, please don't ever jump into danger like that again. My heart nearly stopped when you rushed in to grab Mikey. When I heard the gunshot, I feared the worst."

She lifted her head to look up at him. "Don't ask me to apologize for saving Mikey's life."

"I know, I get it. But your life is precious, too." He knew those moments when she'd run into harm's way would reverberate in his mind forever. "I can't bear to lose you."

She looked surprised by his admission and that made him grin. Unable to help himself, he pulled her close, his mouth hovering above hers. "I want to kiss you," he whispered.

"I'd like that." The words were barely out of her mouth when he covered her lips with his. Their kiss was soft, chaste at first, then grew intense as he allowed the passion he felt to come through.

"Finn? Oh, uh, sorry. I didn't realize the Gallagher charm was striking again."

The interruption was unwelcome, and he lifted his head regretfully. Reed Branson, one of the K-9 officers who'd gone out to look for Mikey was standing nearby. Finn narrowed his gaze, not happy that Reed had mentioned his so-called charm in front of Eva, and didn't bother to hide the edge to his tone. "What?"

"I wanted to know if you still need me to watch over the Stallings' house." The cheeky grin on Reed's face made Finn inwardly groan. This kiss was going to be talked about throughout the K-9 community, no doubt about it. The guys were merciless with their teasing, especially on the basketball court during their informal pickup games. At one time, he'd earned his reputation for dating women with a friendly, no-strings-attached approach. He didn't want Eva to know that.

The feelings he had toward her were different. More intense. More—*everything*.

"Yes. I'm driving them home now, so if you'd follow us that would be great." He opened the passenger door for Eva, who quickly slid inside.

"Just driving them home or sneaking another kiss?" Reed teased. Thankfully, Finn had already closed the door, so he hoped Eva hadn't overheard his remark.

"Just follow us," he said in an annoyed tone.

The ride back to Pete's house didn't take long, and Eva called Pete on the way to reassure him that they'd found Mikey safe and sound. Apparently, Pete hadn't been able to get a flight out because of the storm but was still planning to come home early the following morning. Finn offered to carry Mikey inside, but Eva insisted. He escorted them both into the house, waiting until Eva carried Mikey up to bed.

"Everything okay?" Finn asked.

"Pete claims he doesn't blame me, but I'm not sure I believe him," she said with a sigh.

"Knowing Mikey is safe will be all that matters in the end." Although he ached to hold her, he stayed where he was. "I need to go. If you need anything, Reed Branson will be outside. I want you to feel safe here, okay?"

"Will Reed stay all night?"

"Just till I get back. Since Pete's flight was delayed, I, uh, plan to sleep on the sofa down here in the living room, if that's okay with you."

Eva nodded. "I would feel better having someone here all night, thanks."

Finn wanted desperately to kiss her again but forced himself to leave. Interrogating their perp had to be his top priority.

Down at the local police station, the man they'd arrested for kidnapping Mikey sat in an interrogation room with his wrists handcuffed to the table, his expression defiant. When Finn walked toward the room, he was stopped by the officer who'd transported the man and handed him a folder of information.

"His name is Roger 'Roach' Talmadge," the officer informed him. "Nice nickname, huh? He has a rap sheet mostly related to selling drugs, although there is an aggravated assault on file. More recently, he was a suspect in the airport drug-running operation that Zach investigated. Unfortunately, Roach slipped under the radar and disappeared. Until now. Zach said to go ahead and start the questioning without waiting for him."

"Sounds good to me." Finn took the folder into the interrogation room. "So, Roach, why don't you tell me what's in the package you're so desperate to find?"

Roach stared at him with flat eyes.

Finn tapped the file folder with one finger. "You might want to consider cooperating with us because, with your history, you're looking at hard time. One kidnapping and one attempted kidnaping, both felony convictions. Not to mention aggravated assault and dognapping. You can wait for your lawyer, or you can do yourself a favor and tell us what's going on."

"Not till I speak to my lawyer," Roach said in his raspy voice.

Finn knew what the guy wanted, and that was to cut

some sort of deal. The very thought of this jerk getting less prison time because of snitching on his pals made him sick to his stomach, but that was the way the criminal justice system worked. As much as he wanted to shake the truth out of the guy, he knew that there was nothing more they could do until he met with his lawyer.

Frustrated and exhausted, Finn called Zach to let him know Roach wasn't talking, then left the police station to return to Pete's house. Mikey was safe, which was the most important thing. Still, it galled him that they were still no closer to finding out the truth about what was really going on. Or finding Cocoa.

Although patience wasn't one of his strengths, he had no choice but to practice it now. Leaning on God's strength helped, but he wouldn't be satisfied until they had some answers.

The stinky guy with the Southern twang in his voice was still out there somewhere. Finn needed to find him before he could believe Eva and Mikey were safe once and for all.

Eva collapsed on the sofa, her mind reeling with everything that had taken place over the past six hours. Losing Mikey, finding Mikey, calling Pete, kissing Finn.

She'd been caught off guard by Finn's kiss, especially the sweet way he'd asked her permission. No man had ever done that before. What was even more shocking was that Finn had initiated their kiss despite knowing about her retinitis pigmentosa. She'd been honest with him when she'd informed him of what her diagnosis meant—that she'd be declared legally blind in a few years.

Didn't he realize the impact it would have on her life?

Or was it possible the kiss didn't mean as much to him as it had to her? Maybe this was how he treated all the women in his life. What had that other cop said? Something about the Gallagher charm striking again? It wasn't a stretch to believe that Finn was a "date 'em and dump 'em" kind of guy.

Her cheeks burned with embarrassment, and she covered them with the palms of her hands. Finn might have initiated the kiss because he was accustomed to kissing women, but she'd been a willing participant, agreeing to the kiss and then losing herself in his embrace.

That it meant more to her than it likely had to him shouldn't be a surprise. What man would willingly sign up for dating a woman who'd end up blind? Rafe, the man who'd claimed to love her, had quickly moved on after learning the truth.

Exhaustion weighed her down, but Eva knew she wouldn't be able to rest until Finn was back. How was that for being messed up? The man she shouldn't have kissed was the only man who made her feel safe. Reed Branson, who was keeping watch, was probably a fine cop, but she didn't know him.

Not the way she knew Finn, and believed that the K-9 cop and his partner, Abernathy, would put their lives on the line for her and the little boy sleeping upstairs.

As if on cue, Mikey began to cry. "Mommy. *Mommy!*"

His shriek had her rushing upstairs. She'd left a night-light on for him and could see he was sitting upright in bed, tears streaking down his face. She knelt on the mattress and pulled him close. "Shh, Mikey, it's okay. You're safe. I'm here. We're all safe."

"The bad man is here." He sobbed, a wild look in his eyes. "We have to hide. The bad man is here."

The words were eerily similar to the day Mikey had been playing with the dinosaurs, claiming the bad man was real because his mommy said so.

Was this a nightmare from the recent events? Or something that had happened in the past?

"Mikey, I'm here, and I love you. You're safe. Officer Finn will be here soon with Abernathy. You love Abe, don't you?"

Mikey nodded, and he repeated, "We have to hide from the bad man. Hurry!"

Eva cuddled him close and chose her words carefully. "Why, Mikey? Because Mommy said so?"

The little boy nodded. "The bad man came to the door. She told me to hide, so I went into the closet. I'm scared. I don't want the bad man to get me again."

A chill snaked down her spine as the implication of his words sank deep. Mikey's recent bad man might have been the same one her sister had told him to hide from in the past. Was that why the two events had been linked in the little boy's mind?

It made sense that if Malina had stolen something from the men, they'd come to confront her. She wished she knew when this hiding incident had happened.

If it had happened at all.

"Mikey, Officer Finn has arrested the bad man who took you," she said, rubbing her hand on his back. "We're safe. The bad man is in jail and can't hurt us anymore."

Mikey buried close, his little body still trembling with fear. "I miss my mommy," he whispered.

Tears filled her eyes. "I know, sweetie. I miss her, too."

She held Mikey close until the little boy went lax against her, falling back asleep. She didn't want to leave him, worried he'd be plagued by nightmares again.

When she heard noises coming from downstairs, she realized Finn was back. Moving carefully, she gently placed the child back onto the mattress and pulled the sheet up to cover his shoulders. She kissed the top of his head, then eased off the mattress, hoping to not wake him.

Finn waited for her at the bottom of the stairs, his gaze full of concern. "Everything all right?"

She shook her head slowly. "Mikey had a nightmare, and I think events from the past are mushed together in his mind with everything that happened tonight."

"What do you mean?"

She repeated what Mikey had told her about hiding in the closet from the bad man because his mother told him to. "I'm thinking he meant the closet in the playroom," she added. "It's actually meant to be a third bedroom." She hated the idea that her sister had exposed the little boy to danger. "I wish we could find that stupid package."

"We searched that closet already," Finn reminded her. "Eddie, Zach's drug-sniffing K-9, didn't alert in there."

"I know." She let out a heavy sigh. "Did you learn anything more?"

"Unfortunately, no. Perp's name is Roger Talmadge, but he won't deal until he's talked to his lawyer."

"Deal?" She stared at him in horror. "Surely he'll pay for what he's done."

"Yes, he will." Finn took her arm and drew her into the living room. "Trust me, he'll go to jail. But we still need to find Cocoa. Not to mention Roach's accomplice."

"You're right." Her knees felt wobbly so she sank onto the sofa. "I understand, truly, but it's just horrible the way Mikey is the one suffering in all of this."

"And you, too," Finn added, his gaze dark with concern. "Don't forget, you were assaulted three times and almost kidnapped. You're in danger, probably more than Mikey. Their next attempt will likely be on you."

She wasn't nearly as worried about herself as she was the innocent little boy sleeping upstairs. "Maybe, but that doesn't matter."

"Yes," Finn said forcefully. "It does."

Touched by his concern, she met his fierce gaze. The kiss they'd shared a short time ago shimmered in the air between them. When it looked as though he might kiss her again, she forced herself to stand, putting distance between them.

"What's wrong?" Finn asked.

"You. Me. This." She waved an exasperated hand between them. "Us. Surely you understand there can't be anything between us."

"If this is about Reed Branson's big mouth," Finn began, but she cut him off.

"It's not." Well, maybe it was a little, but that wasn't the point. "You don't realize what my future holds, Finn, but I do. My eyesight is okay now, not great with my limited peripheral vision, yet I can still see. As the next few years go by, that will change dramatically. My vision will narrow further until I'll only be able to see through a small pinhole, darkness and light, shadows and shapes, and nothing else." She squared her shoulders, facing him. "I won't be treated as an invalid. I train guide dogs for a living and plan to continue doing so even after I lose my eyesight. Don't underestimate my determination to remain independent."

"Okay, I won't." Finn took a step closer, drilling her with his intense gaze. "If you promise to do the same."

She frowned. "What do you mean?"

He came closer and stole a quick kiss before stepping back. "I won't underestimate you if you don't underestimate me."

She gasped in surprise, not sure what to make of that. Finn didn't move, so she finally turned away. "I need to get some sleep. Good night, Finn."

"Good night."

As she headed upstairs, Eva replayed their conversation in her mind. Was he serious? Was it possible that she could have the future she'd always dreamed of?

A husband and family of her own.

ELEVEN

Finn was able to catch a few hours of sleep, but woke early, anxious to continue working the case. After taking Abernathy outside and giving his K-9 partner fresh water and food, he sat down at the kitchen table to make notes. He'd already sent two samples of cocaine to the lab, and needed to check if Ilana Hawkins, their forensic lab tech, had any updates on the cocaine matching, the fingerprints from the paper-wrapped rock or the DNA from Eva's keys, and finally, there was the interview with Roach. The last issue was the one where he had the greatest hope of getting something to crack this case. Guys like Roach were always willing to make a deal in exchange for a lighter sentence.

When he heard movement from upstairs, he headed into the kitchen to make coffee and start breakfast. He knew, deep in his bones, that Eva was the primary person in danger now. Mikey was safe, and he didn't think there'd be another attempt on the child, not when they'd been able to find him so quickly. Yet Finn understood that until the missing package was recovered and the stinky guy with a twang had been captured, they had to be extremely careful.

"Good morning." Eva's husky voice had him turning toward the doorway. His breath caught in his chest at how beautiful she was, even after just waking up and without a bit of makeup. Her natural beauty needed no enhancements. The kiss they'd shared flashed into his mind, and he wished he had the right to greet her with a kiss.

She'd drawn a line in the sand last night, one he couldn't bring himself to cross.

"Morning." Had that croaky voice come from him? He cleared his throat, noticing Mikey scampering over to pet Abernathy, and tried again. "I'm making pancakes for breakfast if you're hungry."

"I'm very hungry," Mikey said. The little boy gave Abernathy one last pat, then turned toward Finn, raising his arms in a way that silently indicated he wanted to be lifted up.

Finn obliged him by hauling the boy into his arms. The child wrapped his arms around his neck, resting his head on Finn's shoulder.

"I miss my daddy."

Finn's gaze clashed with Eva's, catching the hint of tears shimmering in her eyes. "I know, buddy. He'll be home soon." He rubbed the boy's back reassuringly before setting Mikey into his booster seat.

"Thanks for making breakfast." Eva brushed past him, and her citrusy scent made him forget what he was about to say.

"Uh…" He glanced around the kitchen, then remembered. "Oh, I have fresh coffee here if you're interested."

"I'd love some." She looked tired, and he wondered if Mikey had suffered more nightmares during the night.

He hadn't heard crying but knew that didn't mean the child hadn't woken her up.

He poured a mug of coffee and pulled milk out of the fridge for her, too, knowing she preferred it that way. Turning back to the stove, he flipped the pancakes and then glanced at her.

"You're staying here with Mikey today."

She nodded. "With police guarding the house, right?"

"Yes. Any idea when Pete is getting in?"

"Not sure. He was hoping to get the first flight out of Atlanta."

After watching the pancakes for another minute, he flipped them off the griddle and onto a plate. He set them on the table, then chose a seat between Mikey and Eva. "Let's pray."

"Pray?" Mikey echoed with confusion.

Finn took the boy's hand and then held out his other hand toward Eva. She placed her small palm in his. "Yes, we need to pray before we eat."

"But I'm hungry," Mikey insisted.

"This will only take a minute." Finn bent his head. "Dear Lord, we thank You for this food we are about to eat. We also thank You for keeping Mikey safe in Your care and for providing us the strength to find him. We ask that You continue to guide us on Your chosen path. Amen."

"Amen," Eva said, her voice clear and firm.

Finn glanced at Mikey. "You need to say 'Amen,' too," he encouraged.

"Amen," Mikey repeated. "Now can I eat?"

Finn chuckled and released the boy's hand. "Yes, now you can eat." He glanced at Eva and winked before releasing her hand.

She blushed. He found himself hoping that meant she was remembering their kiss and that soon the line she'd drawn would be wiped away. She avoided his gaze, taking a deep sip of her coffee.

Pulling himself together, he helped cut up Mikey's pancakes and added a nice dollop of maple syrup. "I have to report in to work," he told her. "There will be two officers in a squad car parked out front, keeping an eye on the place while I'm gone. I'll head back here as soon as possible."

"I appreciate that." She helped herself to a pancake. "Hmm. This is delicious."

"See? Told you I could cook," he teased.

She blushed again, and his heart squeezed in his chest. This wasn't good. He was getting far too emotionally attached to Eva. He forced himself to remember how his own mother couldn't handle being a cop's wife. How he'd been determined not to make the same mistake his father had.

He finished his breakfast quickly, then rose to carry his empty plate to the sink. "I'm sorry to leave you with the dishes, but I have to go."

"It's not a problem," Eva insisted. "I need to clean the place up before Pete gets home anyway."

Finn hesitated, then nodded. "Come, Abernathy."

The yellow Lab came instantly to his side. Finn leaned over to rub his silky fur, then clipped on Abernathy's vest and leash. He tucked the food and water dishes under his arm. "Call if you need something."

"Okay. Let me know if you find anything."

"I will." Finn went over to press a kiss on the top of Mikey's head. "See you later, buddy. Be good for your aunt Eva."

"I will." Mikey grinned, his face sticky with syrup.

The domestic scene was becoming a bit much, so Finn quickly left with Abernathy. It pained him to realize how much he suddenly wanted what he'd told himself he could never have.

A family.

Eva called Wade to let him know she wouldn't be at work that day. Her boss was uncharacteristically upset with her decision.

"Eva, with Cocoa missing, it's even more important that you work with George. He needs to have the basics in place so he's ready to be fostered."

"Finn is going to find Cocoa." She truly believed in Finn and Abernathy. "And it's only for one more day. Pete should be home later this afternoon."

"Listen, Eva, I need your full attention on training these pups. I have owners who have paid a lot of money for guide dogs and they're expecting results."

"I know, I know." She didn't understand why Wade was getting upset over one additional day off. "I'll be in tomorrow," she repeated. Without giving Wade time to argue, she disconnected from the line. She understood this was all getting to her boss, but she was under even more stress than he was. Normally he didn't mind when she adjusted her schedule as needed.

She hoped the guide dog training center wasn't having financial difficulties. She decided to ask Wade about it tomorrow when she reported in for work.

By late morning, Mikey was getting bored. "I wanna go to preschool," he whined. "I miss my friends."

"Not today," she said, glancing at her watch. How she'd keep Mikey occupied indoors for the rest of the day was beyond her. The rain from yesterday had moved on, leaving bright sunlight behind. "Tell you what? I'll see if Officer Finn will take us to get your Father's Day finger painting framed when he's finished with work. How does that sound?"

The boy nodded eagerly. "Okay."

Before she could call Finn, her phone rang. She answered immediately when she noticed Pete's name on the screen. "Hi. Are you on your way home?"

"Just getting on a flight in the next thirty minutes," her brother-in-law responded. "The earlier flight was overbooked, so I had to wait until this one that's scheduled to go out at noon. The storm messed up a lot of flights, so I'm stuck with a layover in Chicago. I probably won't get in until well after dinnertime." There was a pause, then Pete asked, "How is Mikey?"

"He's fine. Truly. I kept him home from preschool and we have a cop stationed outside. We're safe, don't worry. Do you want to talk to him?"

"Yeah." Pete sounded choked up, and she could only imagine how difficult it must have been for him to be in stuck in Atlanta while knowing his son had been kidnapped.

"Mikey, say hi to your daddy." She turned the phone so that the little boy could see his father's face.

"Hi, Daddy!" Mikey waved at his father. "Are you coming home soon?"

"Yes, Mikey. Very soon. I'll be there before you go to bed tonight."

"I have a surprise for you," Mikey said eagerly.

"Don't tell him," Eva cautioned. "Remember? It's a secret for Father's Day."

"I can't wait to see your surprise, Mikey." Pete's

voice grew husky. "I love you and will see you soon, okay?"

"Okay. Bye, Daddy!" Mikey waved again, and this time Eva could see Pete's eyes were moist.

"Bye, son. I'll call you when I land, Eva," Pete added.

"I'll talk to you then." She disconnected from the call, knowing that once Pete returned she'd have to go back to her place. After the rock incident, she'd convinced her friends to stay at a hotel for a couple of nights.

She could stay at a hotel, too, but didn't like being in a strange place overnight. Her night vision wasn't great, and she always ended up walking into furniture in the dark. She preferred being at home, among her own things and where she was familiar with the layout of each and every room.

Something to worry about later. She called Finn, but he didn't answer. She left a quick message related to Mikey's request to get his painting framed, then chastised herself for bothering Finn while he was at work.

This attachment she'd formed with Finn couldn't go anywhere. She knew it. He knew it. They might be attracted to each other, but that didn't mean they needed to do anything about it.

Once they'd arrested the stinky guy with the Southern twang and got Cocoa back, she wouldn't be seeing Finn any longer.

And that was exactly the way it should be.

Finn spent the morning getting caught up. He focused on writing up his report of Mikey's kidnapping and subsequent rescue, a task that took longer than he'd anticipated. When he finished with that, he followed up on the other outstanding issues. The news related to the paper-covered rock that had sailed through Eva's window wasn't good. No fingerprints, nothing unusual about the paper or the color printer the photo had been printed from.

In other words, a dead end.

The lab didn't have any DNA results back yet but was still checking the two cocaine samples to see if they were similar. Cocaine was often cut by other substances to dilute the drug, enabling the dealer to make more money. If the chemical composition of the two samples was exactly the same, it was likely they'd both come from the same batch. What that meant wasn't clear, but he intended to cover every possible angle.

"Noah, I'm heading over to interview Roger Talmadge, aka Roach." He glanced at Noah Jameson, who had recently been named the interim chief, filling his brother Jordan's role in the wake of his murder, which had been staged to look like a suicide. Finn and the rest of the close-knit K-9 team did not for one minute believe their former chief killed himself. It bothered Finn that he hadn't been able to get much done on Jordan's case, and he made a silent promise to work on it later that afternoon. Once he'd got whatever information he could squeeze out of Roach.

"Don't bother," Zach Jameson said, walking toward him. "His lawyer has been delayed in court, so he's still not talking."

Finn let out an exasperated breath. "Great. Now what?"

"Now we wait." Zach shrugged.

"Not happening." Finn dragged his hands through his hair. "I'm going over the list of known associates again. One of them has to be the stinky guy with the Southern twang."

"The stinky guy with the Southern twang?" Zach raised a brow.

"That's how Eva describes him." He abruptly remembered what Eva had mentioned last night. "Stinky with sweat, right? Maybe they originally met at the gym Malina used to go to. The Fitness Club." He could barely contain his excitement. He'd planned on checking out the gym for the package anyway, but the idea that the stinky guy might have used the place as well only cemented the connection. "Come, Abernathy."

"You need backup?" Zach asked.

He was about to refuse, then realized that Eddie's drug-sniffing nose might come in handy. "Yeah, in fact, I think we need to check the place out, see if we can find any hint of drugs there."

"We should get a search warrant," Zach pointed out.

Finn hesitated, then nodded. "You're right. I'll write up the paper on that while you find a judge who will grant it."

Writing up the request and finding a judge to sign off took another hour, and then they had exactly what they needed to access Malina's locker—if she had one—at The Fitness Club.

They took separate cars because the K-9s needed to be safely transported in their own spaces. When they arrived at The Fitness Club, Finn and Zach led their respective dogs inside. Their agreement was that Finn would take the lead on asking questions and providing the warrant while Eddie searched the main area for the scent of drugs.

"I'm K-9 Officer Finn Gallagher and this is my

search-and-rescue partner, Abernathy. I'd like to know if Malina Stallings had a membership here?"

"Uh, do you have a warrant?" The woman behind the desk had a name tag that identified her as Yasmine.

"Yes." He handed her the paperwork.

"I need to call my boss," Yasmine said. "This is above my pay grade."

"No need to call your boss. Just tell us if Malina had a locker here. She died in a car crash that was deemed accidental, but I'm formally requesting to reopen the case. I believe she was murdered. If there's no locker, then there's nothing for us to search, right?"

"Oh, she's the victim of a crime?" Yasmin's expression softened. "That's horrible. Let's see what I have on file." She tapped a few keys and then glanced up. "Yes, Malina Stallings has a membership here."

"A current one?" Finn tried to keep the surprise out of his tone.

"Yes. Her membership is paid through June. She prepaid for six months."

That was interesting and made him doubt Pete's claims of innocence once again. "And what about a locker?"

"Yes, she paid for that, as well. Locker number twenty-six." Yasmine glanced between Finn and Zach. "But it's in the ladies' locker room, and I think it would be best if I called my boss before I let you search the locker."

"This warrant gives us permission, regardless of your boss says," Finn pointed out. "You can either help us out, or we'll just go back there on our own. Your choice."

Yasmine looked indecisive for a moment, then

shrugged. "Okay. I'll get the master key and make sure the locker room is empty so you can go in."

"Thanks for your cooperation, Yasmine." Finn waited until she went to clear the locker room before glancing at Zach. "Eddie pick up anything?"

"Negative."

"The contents of the locker might be exactly what we're looking for," Finn said in a low voice.

"I hope so," Zach agreed.

"It's all clear," Yasmine announced. She held the locker-room door open and handed Finn a key. "I'll keep everyone out until you're finished."

"Thanks." He and Zach took their respective K-9s inside the women's locker room. They found locker twenty-six without trouble, and Finn could feel his heart pounding in his chest as he opened the locker door.

But all he found were sweaty clothes, a bag of makeup and other toiletries. No package.

"Hey, what's this?" Zach put his pinky finger against some white powder clinging to the corner of the locker.

Eddie alerted on the scent and Finn nodded grimly. "We'll bag that as evidence, too, and compare it to the other samples."

"Will do."

The trace of cocaine wasn't what he'd been hoping for; yet, knowing Malina had kept her gym membership was an interesting tidbit of information.

Unfortunately, they didn't have any way to link Eva's stinky guy to the gym. Finn began to despair they'd ever find Cocoa.

Or the man searching so desperately for the missing package.

TWELVE

Eva told herself to stop staring at her phone, waiting for Finn to return her call. He was busy working the case, which was the most important thing right now. Not getting Mikey's finger painting framed.

When her phone rang, she pounced on it. Disappointment washed over her when she saw Pete's name on the screen. "Hi, how was your flight?"

"I'm in Chicago, but there's an engine problem with the plane so we have to wait for a replacement." Sharp frustration laced his tone. "It's as if everything is working against me this trip."

"I'm sorry, Pete, but please know that things here are fine." She found herself wishing Pete might find some solace in prayer, but she didn't say anything. She was too new to the idea of praying. "I haven't let Mikey out of my sight and we still have a squad car sitting in the driveway."

"Yeah, I know." Pete sighed heavily. "It's just that I need to be there, to hold Mikey close. I never should have left him—" He broke off what he was about to say, but Eva could easily fill in the blank.

"With me," she said.

"That's not what I meant," Pete interjected, back-pedaling.

"No, it's okay. I'd probably feel the same way if our situation was reversed. And Mikey was taken right under my nose. I never should have turned my back on him, even for a second."

"Don't, Eva, please?" The pent-up frustration left Pete's tone. "If you blame yourself, then I have to take my share, too. This is all related to Malina stealing some package, which makes me culpable. I should have known something was seriously wrong between us. Should have figured out she might be involved in something criminal. The way she was going through money..." He didn't finish his thought.

"We were both close to Malina," Eva pointed out. "How about we stop playing the blame game and do our best to move forward from here?"

"I'll try." There was a pause before he added, "I'll text you when we finally have a plane so you can figure out when my flight might get in."

"Okay, see you later, then."

Eva set her phone aside and went to the playroom to check on Mikey. He was curled up in a beanbag chair, his eyes drooping as a Disney movie played on the television. She knew the little boy hadn't got much sleep last night between bouts of nightmares, so she left him alone, returning to the kitchen.

She'd taken a package of chicken breasts out of the freezer, determined to make at least one home-cooked meal for her nephew. She found one of Malina's recipes for a cheesy chicken and veggies dish that looked easy enough.

Finn returned her call a few minutes later. "Hey, I'm

getting ready to leave headquarters. I should be there within twenty minutes or so, and we can leave for the custom-framing craft shop whenever it's convenient for you."

She was glad Finn wasn't there to see the silly smile that had bloomed on her face. "Mikey's taking a nap now, but I don't expect him to sleep for long. Oh, and I'm cooking dinner—nothing fancy, but hopefully edible. You're welcome to join us."

"I'd love to." Her silly smile widened at his words. "See you soon."

"Bye." Once again, she set her phone aside, then turned toward the food items she had sitting on the counter. Determined to prove she wasn't a complete imbecile in the kitchen, she painstakingly followed the recipe and then set the covered dish in the fridge so she could bake it in the oven later.

"Auntie Eva, I'm hungry." Mikey's plaintive tone had her moving quickly to the playroom. She scooped the boy into her arms and kissed his cheek.

"How about a snack while we wait for Officer Finn?"

Mikey perked up. "We're going to get my picture framed for Daddy?"

"Yes, we are." After all the excitement from the night before, having normal plans for the evening seemed strange. There was a small part of her that feared leaving the house, but she shrugged it off. Finn wouldn't let either of them out of his sight, and they'd have Abernathy with them, too. "We'll do that first, then when we get back home we'll have dinner."

Mikey nodded. "Pizza?"

"No, I'm making dinner tonight, one of your mommy's recipes."

Mikey's lower lip trembled, and she instantly wished she hadn't mentioned his mother.

"It's okay, Mikey. Your mommy is here, in your heart." She tapped his chest lightly. "She'll always love you."

Mikey patted his chest, too, following her lead. "Is my daddy coming home? Or is he in my heart, too?"

"Oh, sweetie." Her heart ached for the little boy. "Your daddy is in your heart, but he'll also be home tonight, hopefully before you go to bed. But even if he can't get home until later, he'll give you a hug and a kiss when he arrives, okay?"

"Okay." Mikey seemed mollified by that, and she let out a soundless sigh, feeling good that the impending crisis had been adverted. For now.

She gave Mikey animal crackers and milk for his snack and put the finger painting off to the side of the table, in case of a spill. Finn arrived ahead of schedule, Eva greeted him with a warm smile.

"You made good time."

"I did." Finn took a moment to fill Abernathy's water dish, then came over to ruffle Mikey's hair. "Hey, buddy. Ready to head out to get your picture framed?"

"Yes!" Mikey's tone was full of excitement.

"All right, then. If you're finished with your snack, we can leave."

"Goody!" Mikey squirmed out of his booster seat and the three of them, along with Abernathy, went outside.

The drive to the craft store took longer than picking out a frame. While they waited in the checkout line with the finished product, an older woman smiled at them. "Oh, look at that, your son made a family portrait! How sweet."

Eva smiled and nodded, not bothering to correct the woman's assumption that Mikey's drawing was of the three of them. But when Finn glanced at her and winked, she blushed.

Finn's carefree attitude confused her. His playfulness was helpful during times of stress, and at other times, like now, it seemed to be his way of telling her not to take this—whatever it was between them—too seriously.

Just another reminder of how she needed to protect herself from becoming emotionally attached.

Finn loved the way Eva blushed and had to stop himself from stealing a kiss right there in the middle of the store. The framed finger painting turned out better than he'd expected, and he hoped Pete Stallings knew how fortunate he was to have a son like Mikey.

Despite digging deep into Pete's background, he hadn't found anything suspicious. That fact didn't preclude Stallings from being guilty, but proving the guy was involved in his wife's death or with drug dealing in general would be impossible without some hard evidence.

When Eva had told him about Pete being delayed in Chicago, his doubt around the guy's innocence in this mess had grown exponentially. One man couldn't have that much trouble flying home from a trip, could he? Sure, anything was possible, but Finn wasn't buying it. Not yet. Not until they knew for certain who was behind the attempts against Eva and Mikey.

Maybe once Pete was back in Queens, he'd slip up somehow, giving Finn and his K-9 team the proof they needed.

Stallings wasn't the only lead he was following up on. The Fitness Club was another angle. He couldn't dismiss the possibility that Eva's stinky guy was also a member and maybe even had met Malina there. Finding the cocaine in her locker wasn't a total surprise, but he'd really hoped to have found the missing package, even though he knew the stinky guy might have already tried to search there for it. If he could find a way into the women's locker room without being seen.

The longer it took to find the package, the more convinced he was that there was no package to find. Malina had already used the drugs or the money for herself.

"Finn? We're ready."

Eva's voice broke into his thoughts. He glanced over in surprise to see her holding Mikey on her hip and the framed picture under her arm. He'd followed them through the checkout line, but he'd been so lost in thought he hadn't realized Eva had finished up at checkout.

"Sorry, here, let me carry that for you." He took the picture from her and led the way outside. They had to walk a few blocks to his SUV, and he made sure to keep an eye out for any sign of danger as they did so. His gaze landed on a black four-door sedan, but it disappeared from view before he could catch a glimpse of the driver. Was the stinky guy following them? The possibility was like a fist squeezing his heart.

No way was he going to allow anything to happen to Mikey. Or to Eva.

He opened the back of his white SUV for Abernathy and then tucked the framed painting on the floor. Eva buckled Mikey into his car seat.

The ride back to Pete's house was filled with Mikey's

chatter. Eva carried Mikey inside, leaving Finn to follow with Abernathy and the framed picture.

"It will just take me a minute to pop this into the oven," she said in the kitchen, pulling a shallow baking pan from the fridge. "Dinner will be ready soon. Oh, and would you mind helping me wrap this for Mikey and Pete?"

"I don't mind at all. Give me a minute to take care of my partner." He noticed Abernathy standing at the door, looking over at him as if to say, *What's taking so long?*

"Coming," he said, talking to Abernathy as he always did. Some might think he was weird for talking to his dog. For a long time it had just been him and Abernathy. Until he'd met Eva.

Now all he could think about was her. Seeing her. Kissing her. Spending time with her.

If he didn't watch out, he'd fall in love with her.

The notion of being in love was something he'd never really believed in. His parents hadn't been shining examples of everlasting love. And while he'd watched a few his colleagues claim to be in love, he wasn't sure how they knew their feelings were real or whether those feelings would survive the bad times, despite the wedding vows that claimed otherwise.

All women weren't like his mother. But he also knew that cops had the highest divorce rate of any profession. Not just because of the unpredictable nature of the job, but also because cops witnessed firsthand the horrific things people could do to each other.

Often, a case took a piece of a cop's heart, until there was nothing left for himself, much less his family.

When Abernathy finished with his nature call, Finn cleaned up the mess and went back inside. He left Abernathy with Mikey and went into the bathroom to wash up.

"Dinner will be ready in thirty minutes," Eva said when he walked into the kitchen. The way she twisted her hands together betrayed her nervousness. "I used Malina's recipe, so there's no reason it shouldn't turn out."

"I'm sure it will be delicious," he assured her. "Now, where's that wrapping paper?"

It was a good thing nobody was there to critique their wrapping job, because it left a lot to be desired. His fingers tangled with Eva's more than once, and they both ended up with tape and bits of paper stuck to their skin.

Listening to Eva laughing at the final product made Finn realize how little she'd had to laugh about in the past few days. Since the day he'd met her, she'd faced one struggle after another.

He made a silent promise to work harder at bringing her joy.

The atmosphere in the kitchen was homey as he cleaned up the mess on the table and Eva took the cheesy chicken out of the oven.

"Mikey, time for dinner," Finn called. "Abernathy, come."

His K-9 partner came into the kitchen with Mikey, grabbing at the dog's tail, hot on his heels. "Don't hurt Abe," Finn warned.

"I won't. I love Abe." As if to prove it, Mikey put his arms around the animal's neck and gave him a kiss. Abernathy licked him in response.

"Up you go." Finn lifted Mikey into his booster seat. "Don't forget we have to pray," he told the child.

"I won't forget." Mikey leaned over to see the dog,

who'd taken up his usual position as sentry on duty beside Mikey's chair. Abernathy was too well trained to beg, but he wasn't going to allow any food to hit the floor for long, either.

In a matter of minutes the table was set and the steamy cheesy chicken bake was in the center of the table.

"This time, I'd like to say grace," Eva said as she took her seat beside Finn.

"Of course," he agreed, pleased she'd taken the lead. He took her hand in his and then grasped Mikey's hand. To his surprise, Mikey reached down to put his other hand on Abernathy's head, as if including his partner in their prayer.

"Dear Lord, thanks for keeping Mikey safe. Please help Finn and the other officers working the case find the men responsible for their crimes. Please continue to keep us safe. Amen."

"Amen," Finn echoed.

"And Abe, too," Mikey added. "Amen."

That made Finn laugh, and he was grateful that Eva smiled, as well. Mission accomplished, he thought.

He helped cut up Mikey's food and then took a bite. "Yum, this is fantastic."

Eva blushed again and shook her head. "It's Malina's recipe, not mine."

"Better than takeout any day." He didn't like the way she put herself down and made a mental note to talk about that later. Her phone chirped and he glanced at her expectantly.

"Pete texted me that he's on the plane heading home," she said and set the phone aside. "He probably won't land here until nine o'clock, though."

"I can pick him up at the airport," he offered, thinking it might be a good time to question the guy about his relationship with Malina and the missing package.

"Oh, no, that's too much of a bother. Pete told me he'll call a car service."

"Okay." Finn figured he'd wait here for Pete to get home and talk to him then. "I may stick around for a while if you don't mind. I have some computer work to take care of."

"Fine with me."

After finishing their dinner, Finn helped clear the table while Eva took care of Mikey. It was beyond Finn how the kid always managed to get food in his hair, but Eva didn't seem to mind taking him upstairs to give him a bath.

Abernathy licked his chops and sniffed along the floor as if looking for any spare crumb he might have missed. Once Finn had the dishes taken care of, he took Abernathy outside again, looking around to make sure the house wasn't being watched by anyone nearby. Thankfully, there was no sign of the black sedan. Finn grabbed his laptop from the SUV and carried it inside.

He set up a makeshift office along one side of the kitchen table. Listening to Eva and Mikey with one ear, he booted up the laptop and began organizing his notes.

If the three separate cocaine samples from the upstairs bathroom, Malina's locker and the apartment Roach was using all matched, that would mean the cocaine had come from the same batch. How could he use that to their advantage? He listed off the questions as they popped into his head.

Had Malina worked for Roach? What was her job? To sell the drugs or to simply transport them from one place to another? Was she involved in handling the cash inflows? Why had she taken the package from Roach and his accomplice? For personal use? Or to sell on her own? Had she really thought she could get away with doing something like that without repercussions?

He stared at the list of questions, thinking about how Malina had got fired from the guide dog training center yet had maintained her Fitness Club gym membership. What other secrets had she kept hidden from those closest to her? Remembering the five hundred dollars Eva had found in Malina's bag, he couldn't help but believe there had been many.

But the real question revolved around motive. Why would Malina get involved with these guys in the first place? She had a husband, a beautiful son, a job at the guide dog training center. Why risk it all?

He turned his attention to the list of patrons that had been provided by the woman behind the desk at The Fitness Club. He'd had to fax in a court order for the list and she'd immediately sent it to him.

Scanning the names of gym members was depressing. There were so many of them, and even if he split the list in half, he had over 250 men's names to sift through.

Frustrated, he closed the document as Eva entered the kitchen. "Something wrong?"

"Other than that I'm sitting here spinning my wheels on this case? Not at all."

"No new evidence today?"

He hesitated, not sure he should be confiding in her. Sure, Eva was a victim in this crime, but it was an ongoing and active investigation. She deserved to know the truth, but he wasn't so certain his boss would agree. "Not really."

"I thought Roach wanted to make a deal?"

"He will, but his lawyer was tied up today and the DA's office wants to be involved, so we aren't set up to meet until tomorrow."

"Bummer." Eva sighed and then yawned. "Oops. Sorry. I guess my lack of sleep is catching up to me."

He longed to take her into his arms but forced himself to stay where he was. This attraction he felt toward her was getting out of control. Maybe it was time to pack up and head home. Pete would be here in an hour or so and he had a cop stationed outside the house. There was really no reason to stay here with Eva like this.

Mikey and Abernathy came running into the room. "Can Abe sleep with me tonight? Please?" Mikey looked squeaky-clean in his Superman pajamas.

"Oh, I'm not sure that's allowed," Eva said, responding before he had a chance. "Abe is a police dog, not a pet."

"But I wanna sleep with Abe so I won't be scared." The little boy's clear blue eyes were wide and pleading.

"You can sleep with Abe for a little while," Finn offered. "Until I need to head home."

"Yay! Thanks, Officer Finn." Mikey ran over and gave Finn a hug. Finn kissed the top of the boy's head, breathing in the comforting scent of baby shampoo.

"You're welcome." He cleared his throat and glanced at Eva. "I won't be in your hair for much longer."

She gave him an odd look and simply nodded. "Come on, Mikey. I'll read you a bedtime story."

The kitchen felt empty after they left, and it occurred to Finn how much he'd grown accustomed to having Eva and Mikey around. Annoyed with himself, he turned his attention back to his work.

As he reviewed the information he'd dug up on The Fitness Club, he stumbled across the name of Grant Ulrich. *Ulrich, Ulrich.*

Why was that name so familiar?

He pulled a thick file from his computer case and began searching through the paperwork he had in there from other drug-related cases. In particular, from the recent drug bust Zach Jameson had uncovered at La-Guardia.

There! He pulled a sheet of paper from the pack and stabbed the name with his index finger. Grant Ulrich. Not only did he own The Fitness Club but also the furniture store, located near the airport and found to be central to the drug-smuggling operation.

Was The Fitness Club another undercover operation for dealing and smuggling drugs?

THIRTEEN

Eva read Mikey one of his favorite bedtime stories, touched by how the little boy snuggled up against Abernathy. When Mikey finally drifted off to sleep, she set the book aside and watched him for a moment.

Pete would be home soon, putting an end to her babysitting duties. Oh, she'd still help out, especially on the nights he had to work twenty-four hours, but it wouldn't be the same. These past few days had only shown her what her diagnosis was taking from her.

Not just her sight, which was bad enough, but no one would want to risk starting a family with her given the chances of passing retinitis pigmentosa on to her children. Besides, remaining independent even after she'd lost her vision was important. She refused to be a burden to anyone.

Especially not to Finn Gallagher.

So this was it. She'd move on with her life alone. The best she could do was to continue helping Pete with Mikey as needed.

It would have to be enough.

Easing off the mattress, Eva left Mikey sleeping. Abernathy lifted his head, his tail thumping against the bed. She reached over to pet the dog's silky head, silently encouraging him to stay with the little boy for a while longer.

Abernathy set his head back down on the mattress and closed his eyes. She smiled and took a quick picture with her phone of Mikey and the K-9.

She returned downstairs to find Finn still working on his computer. She dropped into a chair next to him. "Mikey's asleep."

Finn nodded, his gaze searching hers. "I'm sticking around until Pete returns home. I don't want you to be upset, but it's important I ask him a few questions."

"About what?" She frowned, not liking where this was going. "You can't seriously believe that Pete hired Roach and the stinky guy. Why would he?"

"I don't believe anything, but as part of the investigation, I need to rule everyone in or out." His gaze bored into hers. "To rule Pete out once and for all, I need to talk to him. Get more detailed information from him."

She sighed heavily and glanced away. Finn wasn't going to let it go, so there was no point in arguing. "Fine, but the poor guy is going to be exhausted by the time he gets home," Eva said. "You might want to give him a chance to rest up before you begin interrogating him."

"It won't be an interrogation," Finn said in a mild tone. "And the sooner he answers my questions, the sooner he can get back to his normal routine."

A wave of panic hit hard. "You're going to keep a cop stationed here until the stinky guy is caught, right?"

"Yes. Don't worry, Mikey will be safe."

"Good." She put her hand over her heart, willing it to slow down. Those moments when she'd realized

Mikey had been kidnapped would be forever etched in her memory.

"What about you?" Finn asked. "Are you staying here tonight?"

"Oh, I don't think that's necessary." The thought of going back to the house she shared with her college roommates wasn't appealing, especially since she'd encouraged them both to stay in a hotel for a few days. Which hadn't gone over well, since Alecia owned the place and hadn't liked being moved out of her home. On the other hand, she couldn't help thinking that Mikey would be safer once she was gone.

"I think it is," Finn countered. "At least for tonight. Tomorrow we'll have a chance to work something out with Roach, and we should have your stinky guy in custody by the end of the day."

She nodded slowly, considering his point. What was one more night? No reason not to sleep on the sofa. "Okay, as long as Pete doesn't mind."

"Why would he?"

She shrugged. "You said yourself that I'm a potential target. By now, the stinky guy must know we've searched the house up and down without finding the stupid package. And he still has Cocoa."

"Yeah, but if the guy was smart, he'd return the puppy and get out of town. He must know we have Roach in custody. Why not save himself?"

His theory made sense. "I hope you're right. I've been praying to get Cocoa back safe and sound."

"I'm glad to hear you're leaning on your faith," Finn said in a low, husky tone.

She ducked her head, hoping he wouldn't notice her blush. "Thanks to you, Finn."

Their gazes caught and held, awareness simmering between them. The kitchen shrank in size, creating a cozy atmosphere as if they were alone in the world.

"Eva?" The way Finn said her name in that deep, husky tone made her shiver. She couldn't tear her gaze from his, and when he slowly stood, her heart thudded wildly with anticipation.

"We shouldn't," she whispered as he drew her to her feet.

"Why not? What's wrong with one kiss?"

The only thing wrong with one kiss was that it made her long for two kisses. Three. And more. Yet she couldn't find the strength to push him away. Finn pulled her close gently, and she willingly wrapped her arms around his neck, drawing him toward her.

"Yes," she whispered as he stared at her for a long moment. "One kiss."

His mouth caressed her lips, and she knew in that moment that one kiss would never be enough. Clinging to Finn's broad shoulders, she reveled in the kiss, memorizing his touch, his taste, his musky aftershave.

The sound of a car door slamming outside startled them both. Instantly Finn lifted his head, reaching for the weapon on his hip with his right hand while pushing her behind him with the other.

She heard the jangle of keys and put her hand on Finn's arm. "It's Pete."

Finn didn't lower his weapon as he cautiously approached the door to peek through the window. Eva ran her fingers through her hair, hoping Pete wouldn't notice what he'd interrupted even as she tried to understand Finn's motive behind the kiss.

* * *

Pete's timing was awful, but Finn told himself to get over it. Still, it wasn't easy to focus with his head full of Eva's citrusy scent.

Abernathy appeared next to Finn. The K-9 must have heard the sound of Pete's arrival and had come down from the master bedroom in response.

"Heel," Finn commanded as he holstered his weapon. Abernathy sat on his haunches and looked up at Finn, waiting for the next command. "Stay."

The door swung open, revealing a tall, dark-haired twenty-eight-year-old man standing there. Pete looked surprised to see them as he crossed the threshold.

"What's going on?" Pete demanded. "Did something happen with Mikey since we last spoke?"

"No, everything is fine." Eva's smile didn't quite reach her eyes, and Finn wondered if she thought that Pete held her responsible for Mikey's kidnapping.

"Thanks. It's good to be home." Pete dropped his carry-on duffel bag on the floor and eyed Finn curiously. "And you are?"

"Officer Finn Gallagher. This is my partner, Abernathy." Finn didn't offer his hand as he gestured toward the kitchen table. "Take a seat. I have a few questions, if you don't mind."

Pete frowned and rubbed his hand over his lower jaw. "Now?"

"It won't take long and then I'll be on my way." Finn's tone was firm.

There was a long pause as the two men stared at each other. Finn could tell Pete wanted to tell him to shove off, but managed to maintain his cool.

"Fine. Give me a minute to check on my son." Pete

brushed past Finn on his way toward the staircase leading to the second floor.

"He's in your bedroom," Eva called after him.

Pete raised a hand, indicating he'd heard.

She rounded on Finn, her blue eyes flashing with anger as if the amazing kiss they'd shared hadn't happened. "I told you to give him some time."

"And I need to do my job." He tried not to take her verbal attack personally. As a cop he knew what needed to be done, and if Eva didn't understand that, then maybe their kiss had been a mistake.

An uncomfortable silence hung between them, and he tried to think of a way to ease the tension. He was about to apologize, for what he wasn't sure, when he heard the sound of Pete's footsteps.

"Mikey seems fine," Pete said, his voice husky with emotion. "I owe you both a debt of gratitude for finding him so quickly."

"Oh, Pete." Eva rushed over to give her brother-in-law a quick hug. "Finn and Abernathy get the credit for finding Mikey. I just hope you'll forgive me."

"I told you, it's not your fault." Pete returned her hug awkwardly, patting her back before breaking away to face Finn. He crossed his arms over his chest and asked, "What do you want to know?"

"Please, take a seat." Finn didn't want to conduct his interview under hostile circumstances. When Pete reluctantly sat, Finn took a chair beside him. Eva was on Pete's other side, and again he had to ignore the flash of hurt. "I need to understand what you know about your wife's activities before she died."

"I don't know anything about what she was doing." Pete stared blindly off in the distance. "I guess I should have noticed the signs—her emotions were all over the place. One minute she'd be furious, then a few hours later she'd act happy and full of enthusiasm." Pete shrugged. "It was so bad that I was constantly on guard, never sure which Malina would walk through the door."

"And you don't know anything about a package?" Finn pressed.

"Nothing." Pete spread his hands in a helpless gesture. "Ever since Eva mentioned it, I've been racking my brains trying to figure out if I saw anything that could have been a hidden package."

"Do you have a safe-deposit box?"

Finn's question caught Pete off guard and he frowned. "Not that I know of."

"Do you know where Malina's keys are?" Finn wasn't going to let it drop. A safe-deposit box was the only other place he could imagine where Malina might have put a package.

"Uh, I don't know, maybe in her purse?"

"I'll get it," Eva offered, getting up from the table.

Finn was glad to have a few minutes alone with Pete. "You're telling me that you didn't once suspect your wife was using drugs?"

"Yes. That's exactly what I'm telling you. Why would I suspect Malina of doing something like that?" Anger flashed in Pete's dark eyes. "Sure, it's easy to look back now and see the signs, but at the time, I thought she was struggling with losing her eyesight. Her vision had got dramatically worse in those last few months before…" His voice trailed off.

"Before she was killed," Finn finished. "I've officially requested to reopen the investigation on her death. I'm not convinced it was an accident."

The blood drained from Pete's face and Finn knew he was truly shocked. "You—you think she was murdered?"

Finn wasn't sure how much to tell him. "I think it was meant to be a warning—return the package or else. Only they didn't realize how bad her vision was. She didn't react in time to jump out of the way and was killed rather than getting a little banged up."

Pete dropped his head into his hands, his body slumped as if he didn't possess an ounce of energy. Finn actually found himself feeling bad for the man.

"It's all so surreal. Finding out that Malina was using drugs and was killed over some stupid package that she stole." Pete lifted his head, his expression full of angst. "She had abdominal surgery five months ago, her appendix burst so they had to open her up. It's possible that's when she got hooked on painkillers, but to steal from her suppliers? Why on earth would she do that? Why?"

Finn remained silent, unable to provide an answer to Pete's questions. The guy appeared sincerely distraught and, as much as he'd hoped to get key information, Finn sensed he was wasting his time.

Pete hadn't known anything about what he suspected was Malina's apparent drug use or her activities. As sad as it was, the spouse was sometimes the last to know.

Eva returned to the kitchen carrying the purse she'd discovered during their earlier search. "Found the keys." She tossed the key ring on the table.

Finn picked it up before Pete could to examine each of the three keys. "Which one is the house key?"

"This one." Eva pointed at the dark brass key. "And this one is to the back door."

"And the third?" Finn held that one up.

Eva frowned. "That looks like it might be for the guide dog training center. I'll get my keys so we can compare."

The training center? Finn found it curious that Malina would have a key after being fired. Wouldn't Wade have asked for it back?

Eva returned and offered her key in comparison. They were a match. Finn nodded and took the keys. "I'll need to borrow these for a little while, then I'll get them back to you."

"Whatever."

Eva snapped her fingers. "Oh, by the way, you should know I found this cash, too." She set the five crisp one-hundred-dollar bills on the table in front of her brother-in-law.

"Five hundred dollars?" Pete stared at the cash as if it were a snake that would lash out and bite him. "Drug money?"

Finn exchanged a knowing glance with Eva. That was exactly what they'd thought, but there was no reason to add to Pete's distress. "We don't know that it's drug money. It could be from something else."

"Yeah? Like what?" Pete roughly pushed the bills toward Finn. "Take it away. I don't want it." He stood abruptly and moved to the other side of the room. "I'm finished answering your questions. I need some time alone."

"Pete, please…" Eva reached out to touch his arm, but he moved away.

"Not now, Eva. I need some peace and quiet. Time alone with Mikey. I have the next few days off work, and I'd like to spend that time with my son."

"I understand." Finn rose to his feet. "But you need to remember to stay inside for the next few days. I'll keep a squad posted outside your home, but until we get the guy who dognapped Cocoa, you and Mikey are still in danger. And so is Eva. I'd like her to stay here tonight."

Pete looked through the window at the police car that was parked in his driveway. "Yeah, that's fine."

"I can head home," Eva interjected. "I think Pete and Mikey have been through enough. They deserve time alone."

"I don't like that idea," Finn protested. "If you insist on leaving, then you need to stay in a hotel."

"I'll figure something out."

Finn wasn't sure he trusted that she'd actually go to the hotel, although he did see that she had her own suitcase packed and ready to go. "I'll drive you."

She looked as if she wanted to argue, but he held up the keys. "We'll make a stop at the training center first, if you don't mind."

She looked relieved and nodded. "Sure."

Pete turned from the window. "There's no reason to leave, Eva. I didn't intend to make you feel unwelcome. The sofa is yours for as long as you want it."

"Thanks, Pete, but I think you and Mikey deserve some quality father-son time. He's missed you." She gave Pete's arm a gentle squeeze, then retrieved her purse and looked at Finn expectantly. "Ready?"

Finn nodded and picked up Abernathy's food and water dishes, along with her duffel bag.

As they headed outside to his SUV, he hoped taking Eva with him to search the guide dog training center wasn't a mistake.

FOURTEEN

The training center looked different at night with only one light shining through the front window. It was well after eleven o'clock, so Eva knew none of the caretakers for the puppies would be around. As Finn parked his SUV and got out, she followed suit, feeling nervous for some reason, as if they were doing something wrong. They weren't, since Finn had taken a good hour to jump through the hoops to obtain a warrant, but still it felt deceitful for some reason.

Finn let Abernathy out of the back, and together the three of them approached the front entrance.

Malina's key, which looked shiny and new compared to hers, unlocked the front door. Since finding Malina's key, she'd tried to understand why her sister would have made a copy for herself. Why would Malina have needed access to the training center after being let go? Eva had no clue. Using this place as a hiding spot for the package was risky. There were plenty of people who went in and out of the training center. Too many to make sure you could get in and out without being noticed.

Unless of course Malina had done exactly what they were doing. Going inside at night.

As they entered, the puppies in the back kennel began to bark. She wanted to go there to reassure them but followed Finn and Abernathy into the office area.

"We're searching for the missing package," he told her. "Nothing more."

She nodded. "I can look through the drawers in the reception area."

"Thanks."

Leaving Finn to look through Wade's office, something she'd rather not do anyway, Eva went through the small reception area. There weren't many hiding places in general, and she found nothing in any of the drawers located along the right-hand side of the desk.

The dogs' barking was getting on her nerves, so after verifying there was no sign of the mysterious package, she went back to the kennel area.

"It's okay," she crooned. "It's just me."

The dogs continued to bark, wanting out of their kennels. She didn't blame them. Seeing them like this was always difficult for her. The puppies stayed alone in the kennels during their basic training, starting when they are eight weeks old, until they were twelve weeks old. Once that was finished, they went with trainers to be fostered for almost a year before returning to the center for formal training. Still, it wasn't easy to turn her back on them.

"Find anything?" she asked, returning to the office area.

"Just another bit of white powder." Finn held up an evidence bag. Eva squinted at it and saw a few grains of what might be cocaine.

"No package?"

"Nope." Finn tucked the evidence bag into his

pocket, his expression reflected his frustration. "There must be somewhere else to search. Why else would Malina have a key?"

"There's a storeroom in the back near the kennels," she offered. "It's mostly filled with dog food and treats, along with some spare supplies."

Finn's green eyes brightened with excitement. "Show me."

She led the way back toward the kennels and opened the supply closet. They never kept it locked since it didn't house anything of real value, unless you counted the dog food.

Thinking of that made her worry about Cocoa. Did the stinky guy still have the puppy? Was he taking care of the animal? Feeding him regularly? Was stinky guy aware that puppies needed to be fed twice a day? It was horrible to think that Cocoa might be suffering at the hands of the man who would clearly do anything to get his stolen package back.

She prayed that Cocoa wasn't being mistreated and would be returned safe and sound.

Soon.

There wasn't a lot of space in the closet for two people and a K-9 partner, so she stayed back and let Finn perform the search. Abernathy was excited about the supply closet, no doubt smelling the food and treats within. Starting at the top, Finn moved everything around on the shelves, looked into a large box of doggy treats and made his way to the bottom shelves. There was a giant bag of dog food in the corner and she saw him eyeing it speculatively.

"You're not planning to dump all the food out, are you?"

"Yeah, I am." He hauled the bag toward him, shooing Abernathy out of the way. "The bottom of a bag of dog food would be a great hiding place."

"Until the bag is empty," she argued. Glancing around, she looked for something to use. "You can't just toss the food on the floor."

"Give me a minute to feel around in there." He shoved his hand into the bag, wiggling it all the way down until his entire arm was encased in brown pellets. A few were knocked onto the floor and quickly gobbled up by Abernathy.

Despite the seriousness of the situation, her lips curved into a smile. Finn looked ridiculous, and she didn't for one minute believe that Malina had buried the stolen package in the bottom of a bag of dog food.

"Can you find something I can use to empty part of the bag?" He glanced over his shoulder, frowning when he noticed her grin. "What's so funny?"

"You. This." She waved a hand. "Give it up, Finn. We don't have anything to put all this food in. If we did, we wouldn't keep it in the bag. Besides, you're not thinking logically. How would Malina get the package to the bottom of the bag in the first place? Look at how you're struggling, and you're much stronger than my sister would have been."

He didn't give up for several long minutes. When he finally pulled his arm out from the bag, it was covered in brown crumbs. He tried to brush them off, but without much success, especially since Abernathy eagerly licked them up before he could stop him.

"Sit," Finn commanded.

Abernathy sat, which didn't prevent him from taking another few licks.

Eva giggled. "You look ridiculous. There's a bathroom over there." She gestured to the staff restroom.

"Stay," Finn ordered.

The yellow Lab's large brown eyes looked mournful as Finn crossed over to the bathroom. Eva knew she shouldn't, but she wanted to give Abernathy a treat to reward him for being a good boy.

Instead, she reached down to scratch the silky spot between his ears.

When Finn returned he pulled a small doggy treat out of his pocket. Abernathy went still, his gaze locked on Finn. Finn gave him several commands, all of which Abernathy executed perfectly, before rewarding the K-9 with the treat.

"I like to use toys when training, but figured he was pretty well behaved surrounded by food like that." Finn shrugged. "He's a good partner."

"You make a good team." She pushed the bag of dog food back into the corner and closed the door. "I guess that's it, then."

"Yeah." Finn looked disappointed.

"It bothers me that you found cocaine in the office," she said as they made their way back through the center to the front door. "Malina hasn't been here for at least four months, and we have a cleaning crew that comes in once a week."

"Maybe they're not a very good cleaning crew." Finn relocked the front door and headed toward the SUV. "Clearly, your boss is overpaying for their services."

"Maybe." She'd never noticed the lack of cleaning before now. And since the white powder was in the office, where Malina had often sat to do the books, she thought it was odd that Wade Yost hadn't noticed the mess. Normally her boss didn't tolerate mediocrity.

It was likely he'd been distracted with the center being broken into and Cocoa being dognapped. A thorough cleaning job wasn't high on his list of priorities.

"Which hotel?" Finn asked once they were seated in the SUV.

She wrinkled her nose. "I'd rather just go back to my place. I'm sure it's safe enough. No one would expect to find me there tonight. And by tomorrow, you'll have the stinky guy in custody."

"Eva." Finn let out an exasperated sigh. "We already discussed this. I'd feel better if you stayed in a hotel."

She pursed her lips, then turned in her seat to face him. "Finn, with my vision issues it's hard for me to be in a strange place, especially at night. I'd really rather be surrounded by my own things in a room where I know exactly where the furniture is located."

He drew his hand over his face in a resigned gesture. "Okay, fine. I'll drive you to your place."

She narrowed her gaze, distrustful of how easily he'd capitulated. But he didn't say anything more, simply turning right and taking the familiar route to the small house she shared with her two college roommates.

Finn carried in her duffel bag, then insisted on searching through the house with Abernathy to make sure no one was hiding inside. She unpacked her things, noticing that one of her roommates had swept up the broken glass on the floor of her bedroom.

"I could sleep on your sofa," Finn offered when she joined him in the living room.

"I don't think that's a good idea. I'm not entirely sure whether or not Alecia or Julie are working tonight. I think they're still staying at the hotel, but if for some reason they come home unexpectedly, they'll be shocked to see you."

Finn didn't look happy as he shrugged. "Okay, that's fine. Sleep well, Eva. Come, Abernathy."

The yellow Lab trotted over to Finn's side. Eva walked them to the door and stood in the doorway, watching as they headed toward Finn's car.

"Bye," she said before shutting the door and locking it. She walked back into the living room, feeling vulnerable and alone.

She pulled out her phone to call Finn, ready to ask him to come back and sleep on the sofa. She stopped herself and slipped the device back into her pocket.

Leaning on Finn the way she had over the past few days had to stop. She needed to be independent. Finn had watched the rearview mirror like a hawk, so there was no way they could have been followed. No one knew she was home.

Staying here was perfectly safe.

And maybe if she told herself that over and over again, she'd be able to shake off the sense of unease long enough to believe it.

Finn drove his SUV around the block, looking for a sign of someone who might be watching Eva's place. He didn't see anything out of the ordinary, and no one resembling the sketch she'd made of the stinky guy.

No matter how safe Eva likely was there, he couldn't bring himself to leave. If anything happened to her, he'd never forgive himself.

He made a second loop around the block before pulling into the driveway and parking his vehicle in front of the two-story house. The light was still on in Eva's room, but the rest of the place was dark. He waited, wondering if she'd look out to find him sitting there, half expecting her to come out to confront him, but she didn't.

After cracking the windows open on either side to let the fresh air circulate through the interior of the SUV, he put his seat as far back as it could go and tried to relax.

Sitting in the car wasn't remotely comfortable because he couldn't stretch his long legs all the way out, but he'd been in worse situations, so he made the best of it. He yawned and shifted in his seat. With the windows open, he should hear the sounds of traffic going by and, hopefully, would also hear if anyone tried to approach the place. Thankfully, Abernathy's keen hearing would alert Finn to anything he might miss.

He stared at the house wondering how he'd ended up here. Somehow, he'd instinctively known she'd pull something like this. Eva was stubborn, especially when it came to maintaining her independence, and while he admired that about her, at times like this he found it frustrating.

"Women," he said to Abernathy. "Sure, I like to have fun. Normally it takes only two dates for me to know it's time to move on. Yet here we are. I'm telling you, I have no clue why I'm letting this woman get under my skin."

Abernathy yawned and then, as if in agreement, shook his head, making his ears flap.

Finn thought about their fruitless search of the guide dog training center. He'd thought for sure that he'd find the package hidden in there somewhere. Why else would Malina have kept a key to the place?

The shiny brand-new key nagged at him. Obviously, Malina had got it made just prior to being let go. Had she known Wade Yost was onto her drug use? She must have suspected the hammer was coming down or she wouldn't have had time to get the key made. He had to believe Yost would have taken the key from her after firing her. And again, why had she bothered? Was it possible she'd had the package hidden in the training center for a short time? Maybe as a temporary hiding place? It clearly wasn't there now.

Unless Wade Yost had found it. As soon as the thought popped into his head, Finn disregarded it. Yost would have notified the authorities about something like that.

Eva might be right in concluding that Malina had used the drugs or spent the money that they were relentlessly searching for. Their best chance of cracking this case open was to convince Roach to talk in exchange for a lighter sentence.

Coming across the small dusting of white powder had been interesting. He'd have it matched to the other samples they'd found, but he wasn't sure that information would add much to the investigation. Malina was the common denominator between three of the four locations where they'd recovered the drugs. The house she shared with Pete, the locker at The Fitness Club and now the training center. Matching them to the drugs they'd found in the apartment Roach was using would connect the drug dealer to Malina, which wasn't necessarily a surprise, either. Not if Malina had stolen the package from them.

Roach was small-time. No way was he in charge of

the entire operation. Zach mentioned something about the kingpin being known as Uno, whatever that stood for.

Finn turned his thoughts back to Grant Ulrich, the owner of The Fitness Club and the furniture store across from the LaGuardia airport. That was a key connection and he made a mental note to talk to the DA tomorrow about his requirements related to Roach's deal. Finding Cocoa was a top priority, but so was obtaining the name and identity of the leader in charge of the drug ring.

So far, the bit of background he'd dug up on Ulrich hadn't provided any clues that might be used against him. No sudden influx of cash or outgoing cash or any other red flags in his bank account. But he hadn't been able to get into the books related to the two businesses. Finn planned to dig deeper into The Fitness Club and the furniture store first thing in the morning. After he dropped off the latest bit of evidence he'd found at the training center.

The window of Eva's bedroom went dark. Finn glanced at his watch and realized it was nearing midnight. He decided to take Abernathy out one last time. The K-9 sniffed around Eva's house for what seemed like an eternity before doing his business. Back inside the SUV, Finn relaxed against his reclined seat, ready to settle in for the night.

Sleep didn't come easy. He could blame it on the fact that sleeping in a car was never restful, but the real reason was that his mind was overwhelmed with thoughts of Eva.

Pete had interrupted their kiss and Finn wished he'd kissed her earlier. Okay, sure, logically he shouldn't have kissed her at all, but his common sense had apparently taken a long hike up a steep mountain.

Tomorrow. He'd get back on track tomorrow. Breaking Roach was key. Once they had the stinky guy in custody and Cocoa back with Eva where he belonged, life would get back to normal.

It occurred to him that after spending these past four days with Eva, he wasn't so sure what normal would feel like. Letting her go wasn't going to be as easy as it had been to move on from the other women he'd dated.

In fact, he and Eva hadn't even gone out on a date. Unless you counted dinner at Griffin's, which had ended abruptly with Mikey's kidnapping.

He'd told her not to underestimate him with regard to her diagnosis, but that wasn't what would ultimately keep them apart. Despite the fact that Luke Hathaway and Zach Jameson had both recently got engaged, he was convinced that marrying a cop was a proven path to unhappiness. A relationship like that wasn't for him.

Imagining a future without Eva caused his heart to ache for what he'd never have, so he did his best to push those thoughts aside. Instead, he concentrated on watching the cars going by on the street in front of Eva's house.

Despite his efforts to stay alert, Finn must have dozed off, because Abernathy's whine woke him up.

"Huh?" He rubbed the grit from his eyes and glanced back at his K-9 partner. "What is it, boy?"

Abernathy had his nose pressed up against the side window of the SUV. A chill snaked down Finn's spine, and he peered through the darkness trying to figure out what had caught Abernathy's attention.

Yellow Labs normally weren't as protective as German shepherds, but remembering how Abernathy had latched onto Roach's leg, preventing him from escaping the window, made Finn take the dog's whining seriously.

He couldn't see anything suspicious. There was no sign of movement from anywhere near the house from what he could tell. Was it possible that Abernathy had seen a chipmunk or squirrel?

Unwilling to ignore his partner's alert, he pushed open the driver's-side door and went around to the back, intending to let Abernathy out.

The dog gave several sharp barks. Finn instinctively turned, lifting his arm to protect his head, but a second too late. Something hard slammed into his temple. Pain reverberated through his neck and skull, and then there was only darkness.

FIFTEEN

A muffled thud woke Eva from a restless slumber. She lay in her bed for several long seconds, straining to listen. Just when she thought the noise had been nothing more than a neighbor coming home late, she heard it again, louder.

She sat upright in bed, her gaze raking through the darkness of her room.

Someone was inside the house!

For a moment she considered the possibility that one of her roommates had decided to come home after a late shift at the hospital, having got fed up with staying at the hotel. Still, she sensed something was wrong. Sliding silently from her bed, she thought about what she might use as a weapon. Grabbing the ceramic lamp off her bedside table, she pulled the cord from the socket, then plastered herself against the wall, holding it ready. If the noise was from her roommates, they wouldn't bother coming to her room.

She held her breath and waited. There was no point in trying to see through the darkness. Her eyes wouldn't help her now. Instead, she focused on the room layout that was etched in her memory.

Should she try to get out through the one window that wasn't boarded up? It was a long drop to the ground, but it might be worth breaking a leg or worse in order to escape from the intruder.

Heart pounding with fear, she decided there wasn't enough time to get out through the window. Inching along the wall toward the doorway of her bedroom, she mentally prepared herself for the worst. Where was Finn? She never should have refused his offer to sleep on the sofa. Her heightened senses made it easy to track the sound of the intruder moving up the stairs to the second floor.

Maybe she should have grabbed her phone instead, but it was too late now.

Dear Lord, help me! Keep me safe in Your care!

The scent of sweat made her wrinkle her nose. She lifted the lamp over her head. When she thought the stinky guy was in the doorway, she brought the lamp down hard against him.

Stinky made a grunting noise, but her aim must have been off, because he didn't go down. The lamp did, though, crashing against the hardwood floor and breaking into pieces. She heard him fumbling in the darkness and made a break for it.

She darted for the opposite side of the room to the window that wasn't boarded up. As she yanked the sash upward, the stinky guy grabbed her roughly from behind, turning and shoving her hard up against the wall.

"No! Let me go!" She screamed and struggled against him, kicking and punching, hoping and praying someone might hear the scuffle. If not her roommates, who were still at the hotel, then maybe a neighbor? Someone out with their dog? Anyone?

Stinky leaned his forearm against her throat, pressing hard. She grabbed at it with both hands, desperate to free herself, realizing in some dim recess of her mind that it was the same arm she'd scratched with her keys the day he stole Cocoa. It was no use. His strength was enough to silence her screams, making her gasp for air.

"Where's the package?" The hint of Southern twang in his tone was more pronounced with his anger.

Eva tried to answer, but nothing emerged from her throat other than a croak. She could feel herself growing dizzy and knew if he didn't move his arm she'd black out.

The stinky guy must have realized she couldn't breathe and eased back some of the pressure. She drew in a deep ragged breath, sucking in desperately needed oxygen into her lungs.

"I don't know where my sister hid the package," she finally managed. "I looked through the entire house twice without finding anything other than five hundred dollars. Is that what you're looking for? Money?"

"Five hundred is nothing," he sneered. "The drug package your sister stole from us is worth over fifty grand."

Fifty thousand dollars? Oh, Malina, what did you do? What were you thinking?

"Why did my sister have the package in the first place?" she asked.

"You didn't know that your sweet sister was one of our best drug couriers?"

Drug courier? Malina? No! When? How? Her silent questions tumbled through her mind like a kaleidoscope, creating a new picture at every turn.

His tone grew sinister. "Until she double-crossed us.

We sent her a message, sideswiping her with the truck. Killing her wasn't part of the plan. We'd wanted to get the package back before eliminating her for good."

Nausea churned in her gut as she realized Malina's death was a direct result of stealing drugs. No doubt, these stupid men had no idea that her sister was going blind and wouldn't have seen the truck swerving toward her until it was too late. Her sister's death wasn't an accident—it was murder.

Swallowing hard, Eva focused on how to keep him talking. Finding a way to get him out of the house was her best opportunity to escape.

"I have a key to the training center," she offered. "I'll help you search for the package. I know every nook and cranny in the place."

He was silent for a moment as if considering her offer. Then he slapped her across the face. The unanticipated blow shocked her. Sharp pain radiated through her jaw, and tears sprang to her eyes.

"Don't lie to me," he spit. "I followed you and that cop boyfriend of yours from the training center. I know you already searched the place."

He followed them? And knew about Finn? Eva's hopes of escaping and being rescued plummeted to the soles of her feet.

Before she could gather herself to ask more questions, he removed his arm and yanked her from the wall. He turned and held her shoulders in a steely grip while pushing her out of her room and into the hallway.

Her attempts to fight against him were like swatting harmlessly at a pesky fly. He fended off her flailing hands easily and wrapped his strong arms around her chest, squeezing hard. Half dragging, half carrying, he took her down to the main level and shoved her onto a kitchen chair. A chair that he must have dragged into the living room, as she could see a hint of light streaming in through the window facing the street.

He'd obviously planned this from the very beginning. Why he'd brought her down here, she couldn't be sure, other than she didn't have any furniture in her room. Less objects for her to bump into, the better.

"What are you doing?" Her voice was hoarse with fear.

His dark shape towered over her. She couldn't help shrinking away from him, anticipating another physical assault.

"Silencing you for good. The police have got too close and our boss is worried Roach is going to turn us in. It's time to get out of Dodge."

Eva tried not to react to his statement but was afraid the truth was reflected on her face. She heard a ripping noise and felt something sticky against her wrist. When she realized he was using duct tape to secure her, she fought him off with every last ounce of strength she possessed.

He used his knee to keep her pinned in the chair, leaning all his weight on her as he finished securing her other wrist. Then he did the same with her feet. "Too bad you never found the package. You could have avoided all of this."

Rendered completely helpless by his binds, she could only watch as he bent over to pull some sort of backpack off the floor. More proof that he'd come prepared. He'd brought his bag of tricks, including the duct tape, to finish her off once and for all.

"This will never work." She tried to infuse confidence into her wobbly voice. "Finn will hunt you down, no matter where you run. And killing me won't prevent Roach from turning evidence against you and your boss."

"Finn? Is that his name?" Stinky surprised her by dropping something furry in her lap. The puppy let out little yips of fear, squirming against her. Cocoa! She hoped the puppy would remember her scent and be reassured by her presence. "Don't worry, I've already taken care of him. And Roach won't live to see another day to implicate us, either. We can get to him even while he's in jail. You should know anything is possible for the right price." After uttering that last statement, he slapped a four-inch length of tape over her mouth, silencing her.

No! Finn! Her heart squeezed as horror washed over her. Was it possible the stinky guy would find a way to kill everyone who knew what they were up to? All because of a package of drugs worth fifty grand?

Cocoa buried his face against her stomach and she wished she could cuddle him close.

Stinky disappeared from view. She thought maybe he'd finally left her alone in the house, and then the acrid scent of gasoline hit hard.

In that moment she knew that he intended to burn down the entire house with her and Cocoa trapped inside.

Smoke wafted toward her. Had he started by putting the living room furniture on fire? Using her shoulder, she rubbed at the edge of the tape covering her mouth. It took several attempts before she could feel it coming loose. She bent her face to her hands and used her fingers to pull it the rest of the way off.

"Help! Please, help!" Fearing no one was close enough to hear her screams, she bent over and used her teeth in an attempt to get the binds loose. Cocoa pushed his nose between her face and her wrist, getting in the way. She didn't want to hurt the puppy—he'd been through enough—so she tried to merely nudge him aside. But he persisted and helped her by using his small sharp teeth to assist in ripping the tape from around her wrist.

Even with Cocoa's help, it was an arduous task, taking far longer than she'd anticipated. Smoke filled the room, burning her eyes and likely Cocoa's, too. They were watering so badly she had to close them while continuing to work at the binding holding her right wrist hostage against the arm of the chair.

After what seemed like forever, the tape gave way. Using her right hand and her teeth, she managed to free her left hand and then her feet. Now the living room was filled with smoke, rendering her completely blind.

A wave of panic hit hard, and she knew that this was exactly what she'd be like in a couple of years. Completely blind. Unable to find her way around without help.

If she lived that long.

Cuddling Cocoa to her chest with one hand, she crawled along the floor toward the door. The increasing sense of heat against her face gave her pause. She needed to get away from the fire, not move closer to it.

Stinky had set the fire near the doorway, effectively blocking her escape route. She turned and crawled toward the wall containing the large picture window. Heat radiated from that way, too.

Which way should she go? Eva cowered on the floor

with Cocoa, fear rising in her throat like a wave of bile. The pup lurched forward, but Eva hung back, fearing it was useless.

They were trapped!

The sound of Abernathy's frenzied barking penetrated the darkness in his mind. It took Finn a moment to realize he was lying on the driveway behind his SUV. With a low groan, he placed a hand on the rear bumper and used that to lever himself upright. His stomach gave a sickening lurch, the pounding in his head matching the beat of his heart. He felt the lump on his temple, his fingers detecting the stickiness of blood. Willing himself to ignore the pain, he opened the back hatch, allowing Abernathy to jump down.

His K-9 partner was beside himself, weaving around his legs, tail wagging as he sniffed at his hands and clothes. As much as he wanted to give his partner some well-deserved reassurance, there wasn't a moment to waste.

"Come, Abernathy." He looked toward the home Eva shared with her roommates, assuming the guy who'd hit him had gone inside to find her. Seeing the flicker of yellow through the window sent his heart up into his throat.

The house was on fire!

Eva!

He lifted his hand to his radio to call it in just as a man darted from the house. Finn barked into the radio as he moved. "This is unit twelve, I need backup and fire trucks to fight a fire!" He rattled off Eva's address. "Get him," he said to Abernathy, using a hand signal to send his K-9 partner after the perp.

Abernathy took off, following the guy down the street.

Finn hated the idea of sending his partner off alone, but he couldn't leave Eva inside the burning house.

He rushed up to the front door and yanked it open, grateful to find that the perp hadn't bothered to lock it on his way out. The kitchen curtains were in flames, and he feared the worst. That he was too late. He took two steps, then tripped over something soft.

"Umph." The muffled sound was followed by several hacking coughs.

"Eva?" Somehow, he'd managed to avoid falling directly on top of her. Relieved she was still alive, yet concerned she wasn't able to talk, Finn scrambled to his feet. He reached down for her, trying to peer through the smoky air. "Are you okay?"

Still coughing from the smoke, she didn't answer, Finn put his arm beneath her shoulders and helped her upright. He was about to swing her into his arms, when he heard a high-pitched bark. Cocoa? It had to be.

The perp had left her and Cocoa in the burning house to die.

"Keep holding on to the pup. I'll get you out of here." He lifted her up, cradling her in his arms as he took her outside into the fresh air. Carrying her to his SUV, he gently set her on her feet, then opened the passenger-side door, so she could sit down. With help from the streetlamp, he could see she still cradled Cocoa close to her chest.

"Are you hurt? Did you get burned by the fire?" He didn't like the sound of her cough and wondered how long she'd been trapped inside while he was lying unconscious on the pavement.

"No." Her voice was little more than a croak followed by several deep, hacking coughs. "Cocoa—helped show me—the way outside. I didn't—want to follow at first, but he showed me the way!"

"I'm so glad you're okay." The wail of sirens grew louder, filling the air as the police and fire trucks arrived, and he knew that help would be there soon. Now that Eva was safe, he needed to find his K-9 partner. "Stay here, Eva. I'll be back as soon as possible."

"Where—" A coughing fit interrupted whatever she was about to say.

"Abernathy is tracking the perp. I'll be back soon." This time he didn't hesitate, taking off in the direction he'd sent his K-9 partner.

Following the sounds of Abernathy's barking was harder than he'd thought. The sound echoed off the buildings, making it difficult to pinpoint his partner's exact location. He hadn't been in the smoky house for long, but he still found it difficult to see through the darkness and realized this was what Eva faced each day.

Still, he pushed on, ignoring the pounding in his head. He went several blocks and came upon a dead-end alley where he found Abernathy barking his head off. The perp was trying to squeeze through a narrow opening between a fence and a brick building.

"Stop! Police!" Finn's voice cut through Abernathy's barking.

The man turned and in that moment Finn realized he had a gun. But instead of pointing the gun at Finn, the perp took aim at his K-9 partner.

"Drop your weapon or I'll kill the dog."

There was a Southern twang in the guy's voice. Realizing he'd found the perp who'd stolen Cocoa, his mind raced. Would he shoot Abernathy? If that was his intent, he could have killed the dog before Finn had even arrived. And he hadn't killed Cocoa, either.

Then again, the stinky guy had left both Eva and Cocoa to die in a fire.

"I said drop your weapon!" Stinky shouted.

Training told him not to give up his weapon, but Finn couldn't risk losing Abernathy.

"Okay, okay." He lifted up both his hands, his gun pointing toward the sky in a gesture of surrender. "There's no reason to shoot the dog. I'm giving up my weapon, see?"

"Drop it. Now!"

Finn hesitated for a moment, then carefully bent over to set the gun on the ground.

"Kick it toward me."

Finn didn't move. The wailing sirens grew louder, and he noticed the perp glance jerkily toward the street as if searching for the red lights.

In that second, Finn jumped into action. "Get help!" He tossed the command toward Abernathy as he launched himself toward the stinky guy, hitting his gun arm hard in an effort to knock the gun loose.

The stinky guy was stronger than Finn had given him credit for. Despite holding the guy's wrist tightly, squeezing as hard as he could to force him to drop the weapon, the perp hung on, using his bulky frame in an attempt to knock Finn off balance. He nearly succeeded.

For several long moments they struggled to gain control of the weapon.

Boom!

The sound of gunfire echoed loudly around them,

giving him one last chance to rip the weapon from the stinky guy's hand.

"Get down! Now!" Finn pressed the gun against the man's temple and he slowly went down to his knees, then stretched out until he was lying facedown on the ground.

Ripping his cuffs off his belt, he grabbed the stinky guy's wrists and locked them together. Once he had the perp secure, he lifted his gaze and swept the area, searching for Abernathy.

He'd hoped his K-9 had gone to get backup, but that wasn't the case. His K-9 partner came toward him, limping as he favored his right back leg.

"What happened, boy?" he asked.

Abernathy was wearing his vest, but as he came closer, Finn could see blood dripping from the animal's flank.

His partner was wounded!

SIXTEEN

The oxygen mask over her face eased her spasmodic coughing but made talking difficult. "Where's Finn?" she asked in a muffled and hoarse voice. She'd asked several times already without a response.

"Just take it easy." One of the paramedics leaned over to check the monitor she was connected to. "You're doing great. The oxygen levels in your blood are close to normal."

Keeping one arm around Cocoa, who was content to cuddle close, she used the other hand to move the mask to the side. "I'll be better when you get one of the officers over here to talk to me. I need to know where Officer Gallagher is and that he's safe."

The paramedic replaced the oxygen mask over her face. "Someone will be here soon," he reassured her.

She didn't want *someone*. She wanted *Finn*. She needed to know he was okay and that someone had gone after him to provide backup.

A loud popping noise had her jerking the mask off her face again. "Was that a gunshot?"

Instant chaos ensued, confirming her suspicion. Dozens of officers and firefighters swarmed the area, apparently searching for the source of the gunshot. Through it all, firefighters continued spraying their hoses at Alecia's house in an effort to douse the flames. Two more hoses were aimed at the houses on each side to protect them from damage. She was horrified about Alecia's house and was thankful her friend's parents had insisted on them paying for good insurance.

The paramedic replaced her oxygen mask, staying close to her side. She appreciated his gesture of support and was secretly glad Pete was home with Mikey instead of being out here, fighting the fire. While she was no expert, the fire appeared to be under control. Maybe because the source of the blaze had been focused in the living room.

Remembering those terrifying moments when she'd feared she was trapped inside the house made her shudder. Cocoa had wiggled out of her arms and had let out several barks while headed toward the doorway leading to the kitchen. She'd followed the puppy, shying away from the heat on her left and keeping far to the right. When the heat was behind them and the floor changed from hardwood to tile, she knew they'd made it. The front door wasn't far. She had scooped Cocoa close and continued crawling toward the door leading outside.

She'd been grateful Finn had literally stumbled upon her in the doorway and that he was all right. His familiar musky scent had calmed her racing heart, but then he'd left her to go after the stinky guy.

Lord, please keep Finn and Abernathy safe in Your care!

Praying was second nature now, and she knew she had Finn to thank for bringing her back to her faith. He was the one who'd shown her the power of prayer.

He was the only man who'd kissed her while knowing her diagnosis.

It was impossible to imagine life without him.

She secretly acknowledged that her feelings for Finn went beyond friendship. But knowing that didn't change her future blindness. With her eyes still burning and tearing up from the smoke, she couldn't see clearly. Being faced with the reality of her future was sobering. Looking back on what had transpired with Malina, she understood that her surgery, along with facing blindness, was the catalyst for her sister's desperate foray into crime.

Nothing else made sense.

"Eva?" It wasn't Finn's voice, yet it was familiar. She squinted through the group of people still milling about to find her boss, Wade Yost, making his way toward her. "You found Cocoa!"

She hadn't exactly found the puppy—the stinky guy had tossed him at her—but nodded anyway. "Yes, thankfully. What are you doing here?"

"I heard about the fire on the news and rushed over." Her boss elbowed the paramedic out of the way, dropping to one knee beside her. The paramedic took a few steps away as if to provide them some privacy. Wade reached out to lightly stroke Cocoa. "I'm so glad you're both okay."

It was odd that he'd come here in the middle of the night. And how had he known this was where she lived in the first place? Her address was on file at the training center, but it was a little creepy that he'd recognized the house from the news. Yet she told herself to get over it. He hadn't revealed the truth about Malina because he hadn't wanted to lose Eva as a trainer. She appreciated his support. "Me, too. Cocoa helped me get out through the fire. He's going to make an awesome guide dog."

"I believe you." Wade smiled, and then she felt something blunt and hard poke into her side. "Now, listen to me. We're going to walk away from here, understand? You make one false move and I'll shoot you right here. With all the chaos, they'll never catch me, and you'll be dead from the blood loss before anyone can help."

A gun? She froze, her mind scrambling to understand what was happening. Wade was her boss. He ran the guide dog training center. Why was he doing this?

"Take that oxygen mask off and stand up. We're going to take a little walk."

After removing the face mask, she rose from her seat at the edge of the ambulance bumper. Casting a furtive glance toward the paramedic, she hoped and prayed he'd notice something was amiss. But he was in deep conversation with another firefighter. She took two steps, then stopped. "I'm still connected to the monitor."

Wade yanked the cords off her in a swift movement. Though the monitor alarm beeped, the sound was lost amid the chaos of people talking and rushing water, and no one seemed to notice. That simply reinforced what Wade had threatened. He could shoot her now and ditch the gun, and no one would be any wiser.

Feeling helpless once again, she walked alongside Wade, still cuddling with Cocoa. They crossed the street, leaving the paramedics and firefighters behind.

"Where are we going?" She did everything she could to drag her feet, unwilling to leave the relative safety of the police and firefighters behind.

"The training center. The big boss wants to meet you."

The big boss? The one in charge of the drug running? Was this how her sister had been led astray? Why would Wade have fired Malina if she was secretly working for him? Did her termination have to do with stealing the package of drugs?

Eva sent one last desperate glance over her shoulder searching for someone, anyone who might help.

Nothing good would come from meeting the big boss. And she knew that this time, there was a good chance she wouldn't survive.

Finn kept his knee wedged in the center of the stinky guy's back as he gently probed Abernathy's wound. It didn't look too deep, thankfully, just a bit of a gash but he still needed to get his partner to the vet ASAP.

"You'll be okay, boy." He gave Abernathy a one-armed hug, then shifted his weight off the prone perp. "Get up." He grabbed the guy beneath his arm, helping him stagger to his feet.

"I'll cut a deal." The guy's twang had turned whiny. "I'll give you the big boss."

"What's your name?" Finn asked, pushing him toward the road. He could see cops milling around, but they hadn't stumbled upon the narrow alley.

Finn wasn't sure he would have found it, either, if not for Abernathy.

"Stu Greer," was the grudging response.

"Well, Stu, you're under arrest for arson and attempted murder of a police officer, among other crimes." He rattled off the Miranda warning, then added, "I'm not sure that a deal is in your future."

"I'll give you the big boss," Greer repeated. "And I

didn't attempt to shoot your dog. The gun went off by accident."

"Yeah, yeah." Finn didn't doubt that Greer's lawyer would play that angle. "Come, Abernathy."

Gamely, his K-9 partner kept pace beside him, and Finn wished he could carry his partner to safety. When he reached the street, he waved a uniformed officer over. "Take this guy for me, would you? My partner is injured."

The officer nodded and took Greer's other arm. Finn bent down and lifted his seventy-five-pound yellow Lab into his arms. Abernathy licked him on the cheek.

He strode quickly toward the spot where he'd left Eva. The cop urged Greer along as well, keeping pace. He noticed the fire crew had doused the flames inside Eva's home, and they continued to pour water on the building to be safe. In the summer heat any spark they missed could easily ignite a second fire.

"Where's Eva Kendall?" He raked his gaze over the area. When he noticed the ambulance in the center of the street, with some sort of wires lying across the bumper, a bad feeling settled in his chest. "Eva? Eva!"

At the sound of his shout, the paramedic glanced over at him, then looked at the empty spot where the monitor was quietly alarming. "Hey, where did she go?"

Finn set Abernathy just inside the ambulance. "I need you to clean him up and put antibiotic ointment on his wound."

"I don't treat dogs," the paramedic protested.

"You do now." Finn wasn't about to take no for an answer. He raked his gaze over the crowd, searching in vain for Eva's blond hair. "How long as she been gone?"

"Just a minute or two." The paramedic was grudgingly using gauze to wipe away the blood from Abernathy's flank injury.

"Abernathy, stay." He gave the command before hurrying toward the street. It wasn't like Eva to wander off, especially since he'd told her he'd return. How well could she see anyway? Her eyes had been watering badly when he'd got her out of the house.

"Eva!" He raised his voice to be heard over the din. Several of the cops and firefighters glanced at him, but there was no sign of Eva.

He returned to the ambulance, where the uniformed officer was still holding Stu Greer. "Tell me about the big boss."

Stu sneered at him. "Not saying anything until I get my lawyer."

The words were similar to what Roach had said, only the guy still hadn't talked. Finn wanted to grab the cuffed man by the shoulders to shake him until his teeth rattled. But of course he couldn't. Instead, he stepped closer until he was invading Greer's personal space.

"If anything happens to Eva, I'll make sure you go down for her murder, understand? Now, tell me who the big boss is!"

Greer stared at him for a long moment before admitting, "We call him Uno. As in he's numero uno in the cartel."

"Number one?" That information wasn't the least bit helpful. He needed a name! "What else does *Uno* stand for? What's his real name?"

"Ulrich." Greer said the name so softly Finn almost didn't hear it. Then it clicked.

"Grant Ulrich? The owner of The Fitness Club and the furniture store?"

Greer nodded. "He owns a lot of places, uses them to launder drug money."

Finn remembered the white powder found in the office at the guide dog training center. "Does Ulrich own the guide dog training center? Is it part of the drug-running organization? Is that where he got the idea to use Cocoa as bait?"

"Yeah." Greer craned his neck to look back at the officer who still had him by the arm. "You're my witness. I gave him information to help his case, so I expect a lighter sentence, understand?"

Finn felt a chill snake down his spine at the implication of the training center. He glanced over at Abernathy lying in the back of the ambulance. The K-9 lifted his head, his dark eyes laser focused on Finn.

As much as he needed to get his partner to the vet, he sensed there wasn't a moment to waste. He crossed over to the ambulance. Cleaning the wound had helped and the gash didn't look deep enough to need stitches, yet he still wanted his partner to be checked out by the vet.

He debated between sending Abernathy to the vet without him or taking him along to find Eva. It wasn't an easy decision, but he needed his partner's keen scent. He lifted the dog and put him back on his feet.

"Come, Abernathy." Finn glanced around, then picked up the oxygen mask, hoping, praying there was enough of Eva's scent left behind for Abernathy to use. He held the face mask to Abernathy's nose. "Find. Find Eva."

Abernathy sniffed at the face mask, then went to work. He made a circle around the area in front of the ambulance, then trotted off in a direction that led across the street.

Finn followed, relieved that his partner was on Eva's trail. As they went down one bloc, then another, he saw the guide dog training center up ahead.

This time he wanted backup, so before they got too close he used his radio. "This is unit twelve, I need backup at the guide dog training center for a possible hostage situation."

There was static on the line, then another officer responded, "This is Zach Jameson. I'm on my way."

"Reed Branson and Jessie, also responding," another voice said.

"Ten-four." He continued toward the training center. Even from this distance, when they were still a few blocks away, he could see a dim light shining from the back of the building.

Interesting that it wasn't from the office area. He quickened his pace, then slowed down when he realized Abernathy was doing his best to keep up with him.

Abernathy alerted just outside the front door of the building. Finn praised him, then glanced over as Zach Jameson and his drug-sniffing beagle joined them. There was no sign of Reed, but Finn hoped he'd show up soon.

"I think Eva's in there with the big boss, a man named Grant Ulrich."

"The owner of The Fitness Club?" Zach's eyes widened.

"Yeah, he owns this place, too." Finn tried the handle and was surprised when it opened. He knew Eva had a key and wondered if she'd left the door open on purpose.

"I'll take the front. You and Eddie cover the back. Tell Branson to meet you there. His K-9, Jessie, will give us added strength." He glanced at his watch. "We'll breach the building in three minutes."

"Three minutes. Got it," Zach agreed. He and Eddie disappeared around the corner.

Finn eased into the building, moving as silently as possible. The sounds of dogs barking helped to cover the noise of Abernathy's pants. He felt terrible about delaying his partner's care, but was determined to get Eva out of here alive.

Above the barking din, he heard a man's deep gravelly voice. "Do you have any idea how much trouble you've caused me?"

"Me?" Eva's incredulous tone would have made him smile under different circumstances. But at the moment, he wanted her to play along rather than antagonize them.

"Where is the package?" The roar was a clear indication that Ulrich was losing his temper.

"I don't know!" Eva's hoarse yell was followed by a hacking cough. "Don't you think I would have given it to you by now if I had it? I couldn't care less about your stupid drugs!"

Finn flattened himself against the wall, edging closer. He held his weapon high near his ear, his attention focused on what he might find up ahead.

"Too bad. Without the package you are of no use to me. And I don't tolerate loose ends, which is why I had Wade fetch you for me. It's time to snip them off, one by one."

Finn's heart stuttered in his chest at the threat. What if he shot Eva before they were ready? The minutes were going by too slowly. Logically he knew he had to wait for Zach and hopefully Reed Branson to get in position, but standing there doing nothing was pure agony. He edged a little closer and risked a quick glance into the room.

Eva was standing between two men, one of them a stranger who was holding a gun on her. His gut twisted as he realized Wade Yost was there, too. Yost also held a gun, which meant he wasn't an innocent bystander. Yost had been involved all along. Finn knew the stranger holding Eva at gunpoint had to be Ulrich.

He rested back against the wall for a moment, committing the location of the principals to memory. With Eva standing between the two men, the likelihood of her being injured was far too high.

A diversion? He thought for a moment about sending a canister of tear gas inside, but he didn't have a mask and neither did Zach. The gas would hurt Eva and their K-9s' eyes, too.

No, they had to use their strength and instincts to take these two perps out, permanently if necessary. He stared at his watch, silently counting the seconds until it was go time.

Three, two, one. Now!

Finn heard the sound of Zach kicking open the back door as he stepped into the doorway. "Drop your weapons!" He waited a second, then yelled, "Eva, get down!" Yost lifted his weapon toward Eva, so he fired his gun at the same time another shot rang out.

Ulrich howled as he fell face forward, hitting the floor with a thud. Finn rushed in, getting to the prone figure of Yost before he could move. Both of their bullets had hit their marks. He stepped on the guy's wrist, pinning the gun to the floor as his gaze sought Eva.

She'd thrown herself down and to the left. Zach rushed over and held Ulrich down, disarming him.

"Eva? Are you okay?" Finn couldn't leave Yost until he had him secured, and since his cuffs were still on Greer, he'd have to use the plastic flex ties.

"Fine," she said in a weary voice followed by a muffled cough. "How did you find me?"

"Greer talked." He used the flex ties to secure Yost's wrists before dragging the man to his feet. "Did you hear that, Yost? Ulrich? Greer told us all about you in exchange for a deal on his sentencing."

Zach cuffed Ulrich's wrists behind him, then drew him up to his feet, too. "Well, look at that. Eddie has caught the scent of drugs. What do you have hiding in your pockets?"

Abernathy had come over to sniff at Eva, licking her face as she rested on the floor as if she didn't possess the strength to get up.

When Zach began digging in Ulrich's pockets for whatever had caught Eddie's scent, the man lashed out with his booted foot toward Eddie and hit Abernathy instead. The toe of his boot connected hard with the injured spot on Abernathy's flank.

His partner yelped in pain as he went flying across the room beneath the force of the kick. His flank wound began to bleed, worse than before, and a red haze of fury filled Finn's vision.

"You just assaulted a police officer," he yelled.

Eva pushed herself upright, scooped Cocoa back into her arms and went to Abernathy. She glanced back at him, concern darkening her eyes. "Finn? We need to get him to the vet right away!"

Inwardly railing at himself for bringing Abernathy

along, Finn nodded and pushed Yost toward Zach. "Call for assistance. We have to go."

Zach nodded. "Backup is on the way. Oh, and here's Reed Branson. We've got it from here—just go."

Once again Finn lifted his K-9 partner into his arms, tears stinging his vision. If anything happened to his K-9 partner, he'd never forgive himself.

SEVENTEEN

The blood coating Abernathy's rear flank was horrifying. Eva held the chocolate Lab puppy against her chest while placing her other hand over Abernathy's wound in a lame attempt to stop the bleeding. As they left the alley, Eva glanced around, then released Abernathy long enough to flag a passing squad car. The patrol car slowed to a stop. She rushed forward and bent down to look at the pair of officers inside. "K-9 officer injured," she managed between hacking coughs. "We need a ride to the vet."

"Sure. Get in." The passenger-side officer gestured with his hand.

Eva didn't hesitate to open the door for Finn. Still cradling Abernathy to his chest, he awkwardly slid inside. She closed the door behind him, then went around to get in on the other side. She was relieved that Cocoa was content to sit in her lap.

The officer driving the squad was on the radio, informing the dispatcher about the need to drive an injured K-9 for care. Afterward, the cop caught her gaze in the rearview mirror. "Where's the vet?"

Eva glanced helplessly at Finn. He lifted his tortured gaze to hers.

"There's an emergency veterinary clinic in Jackson Heights near our K-9 headquarters." Finn's voice was low and husky with emotion.

"Got it." The officer behind the wheel hit the lights and gunned the engine. "What happened?"

Finn didn't answer, his attention laser focused on Abernathy. She could hear him murmuring words of encouragement to his partner. Eva rested her hand on Abernathy's silky fur, hoping and praying he'd be okay, then caught the driver's gaze in the mirror again.

"He was grazed by a bullet, then kicked by a suspect on his wounded flank." She coughed again, wondering if she would sound like a heavy smoker for the rest of her life after being trapped in the fire.

"Man, that's terrible," the officer commiserated. "Hope the jerk rots in prison for a long time. I'll do my best to get you to Jackson Heights soon as possible."

Finn buried his face against his partner's coat, and she knew he was beating himself up over Abernathy's aggravated injury. But the showdown at the training center was her fault more so than Finn's.

Abernathy had been put in harm's way because she'd allowed her boss to dupe her, taking her from safety at gunpoint. Why hadn't she understood that Wade Yost was part of the drug-dealing operation from the very beginning? Looking back, Wade's involvement made sense. Obviously, he was the one who'd exposed Malina to a life of crime. Lured her with easy money and likely convinced her to try their so-called merchandise. Maybe the painkillers she'd taken after her surgery had set her up for switching to cocaine. Eva had heard that it was all too easy to become addicted, that one hit was all it took.

Sadly, she could envision exactly how it must have happened. After things fell apart, Yost had fired her sister. Maybe that was when she'd stolen their package.

If only Malina had come to her for help. Or to Pete. The sister she knew would never have put her son's safety at risk.

Yet that was exactly what Malina had done.

No one spoke for several long minutes. The only noise inside the vehicle was static-filled voices coming through the radio. Eva realized that she could ask the vet to check Cocoa for signs of injury, too. The poor puppy didn't look injured from being stuck with the stinky guy for the past four going on five days, but she wouldn't rest until she knew there were no internal injuries or issues with smoke inhalation, as well.

"Do you have an address for the vet?" the driver asked, breaking the silence. "We're approaching Jackson Heights now."

Finn lifted his head and provided directions to the emergency veterinary clinic a few blocks down from the K-9 headquarters.

When they pulled up in front of the emergency veterinary clinic, Eva had to wait for the officer to let them out of the back seat. She and Finn, along with their respective dogs, went inside.

Finn hit the emergency buzzer with his elbow. "Injured K-9 officer! I need help!"

A veterinary assistant instantly came out through the door separating the front waiting room from the back clinical area. "What's the problem?"

"Abernathy was nicked by a bullet, then brutally kicked."

The tech's eyes widened. "I'll get the vet right away."

Twenty seconds later, a slender woman with curly red hair wearing a long white lab coat emerged through the doorway. "I'm Dr. Ynez Dubois." Her French accent was charming, but Eva could tell Finn didn't notice. "Bring your K-9 officer this way."

Eva wanted to speak up about Cocoa but held back, understanding that Abernathy's wound was more serious.

She settled down to wait, lightly stroking Cocoa's fur while fighting the urge to cough. Her elbow and hip were bruised from hitting the floor on Finn's command. She'd sacrificed her body to make sure Cocoa was safe. She murmured a prayer of thanks that God had watched over them.

The veterinary tech came out a few minutes later. "My name is Anna Lee. Does your puppy also need to be seen?"

While it wasn't exactly an emergency, she was here and liked Dr. Dubois. "Yes. This puppy was taken from the guide dog training center four—well, now five—days ago and I'm concerned they mistreated him during that time. He was also stuck in a fire with me and could have smoke inhalation." She coughed, then continued, "I'd appreciate it if Dr. Dubois would check him out for me when she's finished with Abernathy."

"Of course." Anna crouched beside Eva's chair and held out her hand for Cocoa to sniff. "You're a good boy, aren't you, Cocoa?" She crooned. "And such a lovely name."

"He's learning to be a guide dog," Eva said as Anna

gently took Cocoa from her arms. "He led me out of a burning house. I didn't see any burns on his coat, but if you could ask Dr. Dubois to check out his lungs, I'd appreciate it."

"I will. Although your lungs don't sound great, either." Anna stood, looking down at her.

"I know." She managed to smile while holding off yet another cough. "Thank you."

Anna disappeared through the doorway, and moments later Finn returned to the waiting room. His face was grim and gaunt, the wound on his temple caked with blood. Her heart ached for him.

"Abernathy is going to be fine," she assured him.

He nodded and dropped into the chair beside her. Leaning forward, he propped his elbows on his knees and cradled his head in his hands.

"Finn, don't." She stroked a hand down his back. "It's not your fault. It's mine. I never suspected Wade Yost of being involved. When he stuck that gun in my side and ordered me to leave… I didn't know what else to do."

Finn lifted his head. He shifted in his seat and put his arm around her shoulders, drawing her close. "I'm sorry you had to go through that. I should have figured out the truth sooner. I had no idea Grant Ulrich owned the guide dog training center. And Abernathy's injury isn't our fault—it sits with Ulrich and Greer."

She rested her head on his shoulder, reveling in his comforting scent. Now that the danger was over and the bad guys had been captured, she knew that her time with Finn had come to an end. It was heartbreaking, even though she understood it was for the best.

"Officer Gallagher?"

Finn straightened quickly when Dr. Dubois called his name. "Yes?"

"I need to do a minor surgical procedure on Abernathy. He's bleeding internally, and I need to find the source and cauterize it."

"Surgery?" She felt Finn's muscles tense with anxiety.

Dr. Dubois smiled gently. "It won't take long. Abernathy is in perfect shape. I don't expect to encounter any problems or complications."

"Do it." Finn's voice was low and raspy. "Take care of my partner."

"I will. And when I'm finished with Abernathy I'll check out the chocolate Lab."

"Thank you." Eva wasn't sure the vet heard as she disappeared behind the closed door.

"Surgery," Finn whispered.

"It's okay. As Dr. Dubois said, Abernathy is strong and healthy. He's going to do fine."

Finn surprised her by turning and leaning on her for support. He wrapped his arms around her and buried his face in her hair. "If he doesn't make it…" He couldn't finish.

She clutched him close, in awe that the big strong Finn Gallagher was seeking support from her. "He will. We'll pray for God to watch over him."

"Dear Lord, please keep Abernathy safe in Your care." Finn's anguished whisper resonated deep within.

"And Cocoa, too. Amen," she added, then ruined the moment by coughing. Finn didn't seem to mind. He only clutched her closer.

They stayed like that for a long time, finding comfort and support in each other's arms.

* * *

"Officer Gallagher?"

At the sound of his name, Finn forced himself to let go of Eva long enough to turn toward the vet. "Is he okay?"

The pretty redhead smiled and nodded. "He tolerated the procedure very well. He'll need to stay here overnight, but barring any complications, he'll be discharged into your care tomorrow morning."

A wave of relief washed over him. "Good. Thank you."

"You're welcome." Dr. Dubois glanced at Eva. "I've examined Cocoa, too, and have some lab tests pending. He looks a little malnourished and dehydrated, but I don't see anything more serious. His lungs sound okay, too. I've given him a fluid bolus—you'll see the bulge in the back of his neck—and have given him some moist dog food. He only ate a small amount, so over the next few days I want you to feed him three times a day. I need a little more time for the tests to come back, then he'll be ready for discharge, too."

Malnourished and dehydrated. The words made anger burn in his gut all over again. First Abernathy, now Cocoa. The little pup had proved his worth helping to get Eva out of the burning house. Greer and Ulrich didn't value human or animal life, and frankly, he couldn't wait to testify against those jerks at trial.

"I don't have any wet dog food at home. You'll have to tell me what kind to get."

It was on the tip of his tongue to point out she didn't have a home, but there was time to worry about where she'd spend the night later.

"Not a problem." Dr. Dubois waved a hand. "I'll send

you home with samples. Once those are gone, you can switch back to dry food. I'm sure he'll get his appetite back in no time."

Eva nodded but didn't say anything more. Her coughing seemed to be getting better, but he still wanted her to get medical care.

"I'll get you to the hospital soon," he promised.

"No need. My cough isn't as bad as it was."

Stubborn woman. When the vet left them alone, Finn drew Eva into his arms. She hugged him, resting her cheek on his chest.

She felt perfect in his arms, and in that moment he knew he didn't want to lose her. Ironic how he hadn't thought twice about moving on from one no-strings-attached relationship to the next without realizing what he truly wanted. What he needed.

The thought of losing Eva made his heart squeeze tightly in his chest, making it impossible to breathe. Lifting her chin with his finger, he lowered his mouth to hers, kissing her with all the love he felt inside.

Their kiss lingered for long, breathless moments until she broke away from him. She placed her hand on his chest, gasping for breath in a way that made her cough again. "We shouldn't do this," she managed.

"Because of your cough? I know, I'll take you to the hospital soon."

"Not because of that." She rolled her eyes.

"Then why not?" Finn didn't understand. "The danger is over, Eva. We have everyone in custody. Thanks to you, we've busted up the drug ring once and for all."

"I'm glad about that. Truly." The way she avoided his gaze bothered him. "But we can't be together, Finn. As you said, the danger is over. It's time for you to move on." She lifted her face to his. "Isn't that what you do? Isn't that what has made the Gallagher charm so famous among the other K-9 cops?"

"Not this time." He looked deep into her beautiful blue eyes, trying to think of a way to convince her. "I don't want to move on, Eva. I want you. To be with you. Because I love you. When I realized you were still inside the fire… I nearly lost my mind."

Her smile was sad and she shook her head. "You might think you love me, Finn, but that feeling will fade over time along with my eyesight. You have your whole life ahead of you. You'll find someone else to love. Someone that won't be legally blind in the next few years."

"You're wrong about me, Eva." He couldn't help being upset by her attitude.

"I already had one boyfriend who dropped me because of my diagnosis. I'd rather not go through that again." When he opened his mouth to argue, she lifted a hand to stop him. "Besides, I'm not wrong about your track record with women."

That stopped him because it was true. "Yeah, okay. Until I met you, I wasn't interested in commitment. Cops aren't good husbands or fathers. My mom—" He grimaced, then forced himself to tell her the truth. "Let's just say she couldn't stand being married to a cop. She and my dad fought all the time, until one day she up and left. I was eight years old." The memory of that day had faded over time, but the sense of loss had never left him. "I didn't see her again until I was an adult. No Christmas presents, no birthday cards. Nothing."

Eva gasped and clutched his arms. "Finn. That's horrible!"

He shrugged. "It wasn't easy. But me and my dad became really close. He was a good man and a great cop. I was proud to follow in his footsteps."

"Your mom… Do you think something happened to her?" Eva asked. "I can't believe she'd just disappear from your life like that."

"Not knowing bothered me, so I looked for her. Found her about ten years ago in New Jersey. She's re-married and has two kids. Her husband left the house wearing a business suit, so I figure he's a lawyer or an accountant. Something safe. The complete opposite of a cop."

"Her loss. I think you're amazing, Finn." Eva tight-ened her grip on his arms, then released him. "Your dedication to protecting the people of New York, to upholding the law, is honorable. Don't let anyone ever tell you otherwise. You're a good cop and a good man just like your dad. Your mother was wrong to leave like she did." She tilted her head to the side. "What did she say when she saw you?"

"She didn't." It was his turn to avoid her gaze. "I didn't bother talking to her. She made her choice. I watched her interact with her new family for a while, then turned and walked away."

"Oh, Finn." Eva sighed. "You deserve so much bet-ter."

That made him smile. "You're right about that, Eva." He drew her close again. "I deserve you."

Her internal struggle played across her features. Ironically, it gave him hope knowing that she was pro-testing more because of her impending blindness than a lack of returning his feelings.

Although he desperately wanted to hear her say the words, he silently vowed to be patient.

"I don't know what to do with you," she finally said.

"You could try giving me a chance. To prove I'm better than your loser boyfriend." Now he understood why she didn't trust any man could love her, knowing of her progressive vision loss. But he did. "I love you, Eva Kendall. And I'm happy to spend the rest of my life showing you just how much."

"I love you, too, Finn." Her confession made his heart soar and he swept her up against him, sealing their fate with another kiss.

"Um, excuse me?" The sound of Dr. Dubois's voice broke them apart. "I have Cocoa ready for you to take home."

"Thank you." Eva crossed the room to gather the puppy close. Cocoa licked her face, then greeted Finn exuberantly. The fluids and food had done wonders for the pup.

"Could I see Abernathy before I leave?" Finn asked.

"Of course. But understand he's still a bit sedated."

Finn followed the vet into the back, where he could see Abernathy lying in a crate. There was a small line of stitches along his flank from the procedure. When Abernathy caught his scent, the dog lifted his head but didn't have the energy to hold it there. His tail thumped twice, then went still.

"It's okay, boy." Finn stroked Abernathy's coat. "You're going to be fine. I'll come in the morning to bust you out of here, okay?"

Abernathy's tail thumped again. Finn felt the sting of tears in his eyes and blinked them away. He bent down to press a kiss on top of Abernathy's head, then left, knowing Abernathy was in good hands.

In the waiting room, he took Eva's hand before turning to face the vet. "What time can I pick him up tomorrow?"

"Anytime. We're open all night, remember?" Dr. Dubois smiled.

"Right. Then I'll be here at eight." *Maybe earlier*, he added silently. He escorted Eva and Cocoa outside, then stopped, realizing he didn't have his SUV.

As if on cue, his phone buzzed. Zach Jameson. "How's Abernathy?"

"Healing from surgery. Where are you?"

"At headquarters with Reed Branson. I told Noah about what happened with your partner. He'll be glad to hear Abernathy will be okay. But we have Greer and Ulrich here. I figured you'd want to be here while we question these guys."

He did indeed, and he glanced at Eva. She looked exhausted. "Pick me up at the vet. We'll drop Eva and Cocoa off at my place, then we'll head back to interrogate these guys."

"Be there in five."

"Your place?" Eva pinned him with a narrow glare. "Isn't that a bit presumptuous?"

"I have to work for several hours yet, so I won't be there. Or there's a hotel not far that I could take you to." He hesitated, then added, "Unless you want to go back to Pete's house?"

"No, it's too late. I wouldn't want to risk waking Mikey." She sighed. "I guess that leaves me no alternative other than to take you up on that hotel. Just make sure it's a dog-friendly one as I'm bringing Cocoa."

"I will." He was relieved she'd be close by. Now he just needed to find a way to convince her that a quick engagement and even quicker wedding was the way to go.

But first, he needed to finish the case.

For Abernathy's sake and his own.

EIGHTEEN

Eva awoke the next morning with a sore throat, but the incessant coughing seemed to have disappeared. The room wasn't at all familiar, and then she realized that she was in a hotel near Finn's home.

Cocoa was curled up beside her on the bed. The poor puppy had been so afraid to be separated from her, she'd given in and allowed the puppy to sleep with her.

Cocoa sensed her movements and jumped up excitedly. Eva took the animal outside, then cleaned up after him. Although it was early, she found herself wondering what time Finn might show up.

She hadn't expected to fall asleep after everything that had transpired. But somehow the memory of Finn's kiss and his declaration of love had brought a sense of comfort. Knowing the bad guys had been arrested had helped provide another layer of security.

God had certainly watched over them last night.

Two minutes after she returned to her room, there was a knock at her door. When she opened it, Finn stood there, looking amazingly handsome.

"Hey!" He bent to give her a quick kiss, then flashed

a distracted smile. "Ready to go? I'm making breakfast at my place before we pick up Abernathy."

"Um, sure. I guess." She glanced around the hotel room, found her purse, then saw the cans of wet dog food. She hadn't had a can opener with her so she decided to take it along to Finn's. Last, she picked up Cocoa. "Okay, we're ready."

"Great." Finn ushered her outside and drove them the short distance to his place. When they entered the kitchen, which was surprisingly spotlessly clean, he began pulling out pots and pans.

"Do you need anything? I'm not completely helpless in the kitchen."

"Never said you were," Finn responded. "Have a seat—this won't take long. As soon as we're finished, I'd like to get over to the vet."

She understood his need to see Abernathy. "Okay. What happened last night? Anything you can tell me that won't jeopardize your case?"

He quirked an eyebrow. "How many cops have you dated?"

"Huh?" Had she missed something? "None. Why?"

"It's amazing that you seem to understand what a cop's life entails, that we can't always talk about our cases. I noticed from the moment we first met how you seemed to think like a cop."

She hesitated, then confessed, "I had an uncle who was a cop. My mom's brother. Uncle Jerry. He was my favorite uncle and my mother used to tease me about how much I loved hearing his stories, even the ones I'd listened to over and over. He passed away two years ago, and I still miss him."

"I knew you had to have had some exposure to police," he joked. "Where are your parents?"

"They moved to Arizona. I usually see them a few times a year."

"Hopefully in the winter, right?"

"Right." Her smile faded. "At first I thought of becoming a cop, then decided I was more interested in healing people, so I studied nursing. When Malina was diagnosed with retinitis pigmentosa, the same way our mother had been, I instinctively knew I would have it, too. So I dropped out of nursing school and began training guide dogs. I was diagnosed four months ago."

Finn's expression turned serious. "Eva, I know how difficult it must be for you, but please know that I love you no matter what diagnosis you have. Either one of us could come down with some sort of illness. Cancer, diabetes, heart disease. You name it, it's out there."

She knew he was right, but still believed he was glossing over the reality of her future. "Yes, but being blind is a big deal. It will make having a family impossible."

"Impossible? Not hardly." Finn came over to sit beside her. He took her hands in his. "Challenging? Maybe. But not impossible. The Eva Kendall I know won't let anything stand in the way of what she wants."

That made her chuckle even though she knew he was still taking it all too lightly. "Right now she wants breakfast, so hurry it up, will you? I need to feed Cocoa."

Finn stole another quick kiss and then returned to his frying pan. She opened the can of food the vet had provided and spooned it into a bowl for Cocoa. Reassured by the way the chocolate Lab ate with enthusiasm, she knew the puppy would be fine.

When Finn had their eggs and toast ready, he set the platter on the table, then reached for her hand. "Dear Lord, we thank You for this food we are about to eat. We also thank You for keeping us safe in Your care and healing our wounds. We ask that You continue to guide us on Your chosen path as we get married, have children and live happily ever after. Amen."

"Amen," she answered automatically, then jerked her head up to look at him. "Wait, what? Are you crazy?"

"Crazy in love," he assured her. "And if you're not ready to accept my proposal yet, that's fine. I'll ask every day until you say yes."

"Every day?" She laughed, which then turned into a coughing fit. "Did you get any sleep last night? I think your brain cells have gone on the fritz."

"Four hours, and my brain cells are firing just fine." He squeezed her hand gently, then let go so they could eat. As if he hadn't just proposed, he went on. "After we pick up Abernathy, I'd like to drop by Pete's house to let him know he and Mikey are safe. Oh, and there's an award ceremony next week that I hope you'll attend with me. The brass is giving Abernathy a medal of honor for being wounded in the line of duty."

"So soon?"

"I guess. I thought they'd wait until the K-9 graduation ceremony, but that won't be for six months." He shrugged. "Guess they didn't want to wait that long."

"Okay." Her head was spinning with all the plans Finn was making. Had she imagined his proposal? During a prayer, no less? Goofy man.

They finished their breakfast in under twenty minutes. Finn filled two cups of coffee in to-go mugs and led the way outside to his K-9 SUV. She kept Cocoa with her as she slid in beside Finn.

The trip to the vet didn't take long. When they walked in, she thought for sure she could hear Abernathy barking.

"Calm down," the assistant said, bringing Abernathy out from the back. The poor yellow Lab was wearing the cone of shame and obviously didn't like it. "Here you go."

"Thanks." Finn took Abernathy's leash and dropped to one knee, giving the animal a good rub. "Sorry about the cone, but hopefully those sutures will heal up fast. We'll get rid of that thing as soon as possible, okay?"

Abernathy stared up at him with mournful brown eyes, as if to ask, *Why not now?*

"You're a brave boy." Eva scratched him behind the ears. "I bet Mikey will be happy to see you. And Cocoa, too."

"Next stop, Pete's," Finn agreed.

Eva couldn't deny feeling a bit apprehensive about seeing her brother-in-law again. So much had happened in the short time since she'd left him and Mikey. Logically she knew that Pete didn't hold a grudge against her for Mikey being in danger; at the same time, she knew their relationship might be strained for a while.

Still, she adored Mikey and knew Pete would need help, more so now that Malina was gone.

She prayed that Pete would find solace in God.

Finn parked in Pete's driveway, then went around to the back to let Abernathy out. The K-9 still looked unhappy about the cone, but he didn't try to get it off. Eva carried Cocoa. As they approached the front door, she heard voices from the backyard.

"Pete? Mikey?" she called as she leaned over to the fence. There was a door with a latch on it leading to the backyard. "It's Eva and Finn. We have Abernathy and Cocoa."

"Cocoa?" Mikey's excited voice made her grin. "I wanna see Cocoa!"

"Come on in," Pete called.

Eva lifted the latch and opened the gate. They went into the small backyard to find Pete and Mikey sitting near the turtle-shaped sandbox.

"Cocoa!" Mikey was excited to see the puppy. "You found him!"

"Sure did." She met Pete's gaze and gave a brief nod. "Cocoa is safe now. And so are we."

"We locked all the bad guys in jail," Finn added.

"What happened to Abernathy?" Pete's gaze was troubled.

"Grazed, and then kicked, but he'll be okay." She was glad Finn didn't go into details with Mr. Big Ears listening. "I wanted to let you know personally that you're safe."

"The package?" Pete asked.

Eva glanced at Finn, who shrugged. "We may never know what happened to it. But the guys in jail know that we don't have it, so I don't think there's a reason to worry. The rest of the operation is going down as we speak."

Pete's brow furrowed, but he didn't say anything.

Cocoa jumped into the sandbox with Mikey, making the little boy giggle. "I love Cocoa," he announced.

The puppy began digging in the corner of the sandbox farthest from the house. Curious, Eva went over to see what Cocoa had found. When she saw a hint of plastic, she knew.

The package.

"Finn! Come quick!"

Finn was beside her in an instant. "What in the world?" He knelt down, easing Cocoa aside to finish uncovering the package.

"Is that—" She didn't finish.

"Cocaine," Finn said grimly. He looked at her, then shifted his gaze to Pete. "It was here all along."

Eva let out a low groan. "I never thought to look out here."

"Me, either." Finn hefted the package in his hand. "Looks and weighs about as much as a ten-pound bag of sugar. This is worth a lot of money to those guys."

"Fifty grand," she whispered. "That's what Greer claimed."

"Not worth dying over," Pete said, a faint note of bitterness lacing his tone.

"No, it's not," Finn agreed. "I'm sorry."

Pete blew out a heavy breath. "Not your fault. Just… do me a favor and get it out of here, okay? I can't stand knowing that Malina died because of those drugs."

"Sure." Finn carried the newfound evidence to his SUV, leaving Pete and Eva and Mikey alone in the backyard.

"I'm sorry, too, Pete," she said, breaking the silence. "I hope you'll let me know when you need me to watch Mikey."

He hesitated, shrugged, then nodded. "I appreciate that, Eva. I've been sitting here, berating myself for going to that stupid conference in Atlanta. I hate to admit it, but at the time, I was anxious to get away from it all. But the thought of losing Mikey scared me to death. I need to spend more time with him, and even more so, we need grief counseling. We have to learn how to cope with losing Malina. I've been granted an official leave of absence for two weeks and can use my vacation time to extend it if needed. I'll let you know when I return to work."

"I'm so glad to hear that, Pete. You and Mikey are going to be fine." She bent over and gave Mikey a hug and a kiss. "See you later, alligator," she teased.

"After a while, crocodile!" Mikey shouted back.

Eva carried Cocoa through the gate to where Finn and Abernathy waited near the SUV. She heard him on the phone, no doubt calling in about the drugs. When he saw her, he finished his call and slid the phone in his pocket.

"Everything okay?"

"It will be," she said with confidence. "Pete's strong enough to get through this. He's a good father and will do what's best for Mikey."

"I need to drop this evidence at headquarters. Do you want me to drop you off at the hotel or my place for a bit?"

"Um." His place? Was he serious? First an off-the-cuff proposal and now this?

She was tempted to pinch herself to make sure she wasn't dreaming. The future Finn offered was one she couldn't have.

Or bear to lose.

Finn hid a smile at Eva's poorly masked confusion. He hadn't been joking when he'd asked her to marry him, and he silently promised to prove it by taking her ring shopping as soon as he wrapped this up.

Eva had requested to go to the hotel, but he wasn't thrilled with that idea. Even though she was safe, he didn't like having her out of his sight.

At headquarters, Finn quickly flagged down Zach Jameson. "We found it."

"What?" Zach's puzzled gaze cleared instantly. "The package? Are you kidding? Where?"

"Buried in Mikey's sandbox."

Zach let out a disgusted snort. "I should have had Eddie sniffing around back there. It makes sense now that you think about it. Of course she didn't keep it inside the house. Buried in the sandbox was a perfect hiding place."

"I know. Have they given us anything else?"

Zach nodded. "Names of other players. This is it, Finn. We broke the biggest drug ring in New York City."

"I'm glad."

"I heard Abernathy is getting a medal of honor next week." Zach patted Abernathy's head. "You're going to take the cone off for pictures, right?"

"Right," Finn agreed. "I'll check in with you later, okay?"

"Sure thing."

Finn was making his way through the maze of cubicles when one of his fellow cops, Gavin Sutherland, snagged his arm.

"Finn. Have a minute?"

"Sure. What's up?"

Gavin's expression was grim. "Remember the building that came down due to a boiler explosion a few months ago?"

"Yeah, what about it?"

"I think it's connected to my newest case. The newspaper reported the source of the explosion was the boiler, but I've recently learned the source was really a bomb. The place was blown up on purpose."

Finn's eyes widened. "That's not good."

"No, it isn't." Gavin glanced down at his K-9 partner. "Tommy is the best bomb-sniffing dog on the force, so we're being pulled in to help. I may need backup."

Tommy was a springer spaniel who specialized in finding bombs.

"Let me know and we'll be there to help. You and Tommy need to be careful, Gavin."

"We will."

Finn left headquarters, returning to find Eva and Cocoa waiting outside headquarters in the shade. She was stunningly beautiful, but that wasn't why he loved her.

He loved her spirit, her determination, her independence, her wit, her spunk. He loved everything about her. "Hey, sorry about that. It took longer than I thought."

"Not a problem. Listen, let's just sit at Griffin's for a while. I don't want to be stuck in my hotel room longer than I need to be."

"Okay, I'm up for that," Finn agreed. He gazed into her blue eyes for a long moment, then said, "Eva, I love you so much. I promise to be a good husband and a good father to our children. Will you please marry me?"

She stared at him. "You said you'd propose once a day, not once every couple of hours," she accused.

"I lied." He swept her close and kissed her, longer this time, trying to prove how much he cared. "I'm sorry, but I can't seem to help myself. You better get used to it. These proposals keep popping up before I can stop them. I'll ask until I wear you down."

She laughed and shook her head. "You already have, Finn. Yes."

His eyebrows levered up, hope shining in his eyes. "Yes—what?"

"Yes, I love you. Yes, I'll marry you. Yes, I'll have a family with you."

"She said yes!" Finn scooped her up against him, with Cocoa sandwiched between them, and spun her in a circle. "Thank you for making me the happiest man in the world!"

She didn't answer, but that might have been because he was kissing her again.

Finn had her right where he wanted her. And now that he had her in his arms, he knew he'd never let her go.

* * * * *

With over seventy books published and millions in print, **Lenora Worth** writes award-winning romance and romantic suspense. Three of her books finaled in the ACFW Carol Awards, and her Love Inspired Suspense novel *Body of Evidence* became a *New York Times* bestseller. Her novella in *Mistletoe Kisses* made her a *USA TODAY* bestselling author. Lenora goes on adventures with her retired husband, Don, and enjoys reading, baking and shopping...especially shoe shopping.

Visit the Author Profile page
at Harlequin.com for more titles.

DEEP UNDERCOVER

Lenora Worth

For there is nothing covered, that shall not be revealed; neither hid, that shall not be known.
—*Luke* 12:2

To the men and women of the
New York Police Department. Thank you all
for protecting one of my favorite cities.

ONE

K-9 Officer Gavin Sutherland held tight to his partner Tommy's leash and scanned the crowd, his mind on
high alert, his whole body tense as he tried to protect
the city he loved. People from all over the world stood
shoulder to shoulder along the East River, waiting for
the annual Fourth of July fireworks display. This New
York tradition held a lot of challenges. He searched
again in the park and along the riverfront on the Lower
East Side of Manhattan.

The upbeat crowd grew more rowdy as the late afternoon sunshine began to slowly descend beyond the
Manhattan skyscrapers to the west. Even with the patri-
otic excitement of the crowd, anything could go wrong.
The setting sun hit asphalt and concrete with a laser-
like heat while the merging of people seemed to crush
in on all sides.

The smell of someone's perfume wafted up and out
over the trees to mingle with the scents of cotton candy,
street food and that other unique smell of sweaty humans having too much fun.

His partner, a black-and-white springer spaniel, knew
the drill. Tommy worked bomb detection. People were

always surprised that a springer could be so focused and sharp. Tommy had been trained to find incendiary devices. Period. End of discussion. His quiet, steady work didn't require barking or bringing attention to himself. He knew to sniff the air and the ground. Sniff, sit, repeat. Be rewarded. But Gavin didn't have to get defensive about his partner. Tommy lived for bomb detection, play toys and rewards.

Lately, Gavin had been the one who needed defending. He'd worked hard all of his life and done things by the book and yet a few choice words during a time of chaos and grief had put a target on his back. As a member of the NYC K-9 Command Unit, based in Queens, he took his job seriously and he'd like to keep it.

Pushing aside the bitterness he'd tried to shed over the last few months, Gavin studied the immediate crowd. A woman with a curly-haired baby laughing at the man by her side. A kid in a Yankees baseball cap tossing a soccer ball in the air, his expression bored. A man wearing a plaid cap carrying a dark backpack. Two young girls in jeans and flag-embossed shirts shoving through the crowd to get the perfect selfie with the backdrop of the city.

Tommy held his head up and sniffed. Too many scents. "It's okay, boy. You're doing great."

Glancing up, Gavin spotted his backup, K-9 Officer Brianne Hayes, a rookie who had been paired with him to continue gaining experience. Her K-9 graduation ceremony should have taken place in the spring but had been postponed due to a tragic event that had rocked the entire K-9 Unit.

Back in April, their chief, Jordan Jameson, had been found dead under strange circumstances. He'd been murdered, but the death had been staged to look like a suicide. His administrative assistant, Sophie Walters, had discovered a suicide note, supposedly from Jordan, the morning of the scheduled graduation. Soon after, his body had been found. But they all knew Jordy had not committed suicide. The whole department was on a mission to find out who'd killed him. But a few key officers were *not* on the case. Jordan had three brothers in the K-9 Unit, and though they were naturally more driven than anyone to find the killer, the Jamesons had been assigned to other cases to avoid conflicts of interest.

No one had forgotten how Gavin had complained about being passed over as chief when the position had been given to Jordan. He and Jordan went way back but they hadn't been close in years. Differences in style going back to their days in training at the Police Academy. Ancient history, but Gavin had learned the hard way not to air his grievances—not with so many Jamesons around to remember every angry word he'd uttered about losing out on the promotion.

They'd both graduated and become police officers. Jordan had gotten married to a good woman who was now pregnant and a widow. Gavin had worked with him, practically side by side, and watched him prosper but had always wondered why Jordan managed to stay one step ahead of him. Now Jordan was dead. Gavin's resentment seemed silly and frivolous. The guilt of that ate at him.

When Jordan became chief, Gavin voiced that resentment. Just another thing between them. Then, shortly after his death, Jordan's position had been given to his brother, Noah Jameson. Gavin had complained again, blurting out his feelings without even thinking. So much for not airing his grievances. After that, Jordan's brothers and the department had unofficially deemed him a person-of-interest in Jordy's death. Unbelievable. He'd been easily cleared—he'd been on duty working a big fund-raising event in Manhattan the night before Jordan had disappeared and his roommate had verified he was home the next morning when Jordan went missing on a jog—but things might not ever be the same.

"Hey, Sutherland, want a bottled water?" Brianne asked.

"Sure, Hayes. Bring it."

Gavin tamped down his resentment about not being promoted, then said a prayer for patience and acceptance. He had to take the high road on this and see things through by helping to find the real killer. He might not have been Jordy's buddy like in the old days, but he sure hadn't killed the man. Now he worked twice as hard as anyone in the department to show his worth. So here he stood on a national holiday, hot, tired and wishing he was out on a boat somewhere.

Brianne headed toward him, her auburn hair caught up in a severe bun. He'd noticed her hair when she'd had it down. Straight and sweeping her shoulders in a soft sheen of deep red. That fire-colored hair matched her fierce determination to prove herself since she was one of only a few female K-9 officers in the city that never slept.

Brianne's partner, Stella, was also in training with the K-9 handlers. The gentle yellow Lab had been pregnant a few months ago when she'd arrived in New York, a gift from the Czech Republic. She'd given birth to eight puppies that had all been farmed out to various officers and their families for socialization and possible future training as either K-9s or service dogs.

Brianne had taken on the job of training Stella in the basics, hoping to someday use her in bomb detection. They'd already started practicing—sniffing explosives, getting a treat and then doing it all over again. Once the dog learned she'd be rewarded for finding that particular scent, they'd move on from sit–stay–pay training to seek–find–reward. Stella now trained at the center and soon she'd be training doing the same thing Tommy specialized in—searching out bombs. Brianne had a way with animals from what he'd heard. Her smile had a way of calming him, Gavin had to admit.

"Thanks," he said now as she handed him the ice-cold water, her lips pursed in professional determination.

"I've been along the perimeters of the park," she said, her golden-brown eyes moving over a thousand faces, her heart-shaped face glowing with a sheen of perspiration. "Nothing out of the ordinary. Hot and humid and crowded. Can't wait for the show."

Gavin smiled at the droll sarcasm and gulped down half the water. Then he poured some in his hand for Tommy to drink. The spaniel lapped it up and wagged his tail. Brianne had already done the same with Stella.

Scanning the area again, he said, "I think the crowd grows every year. Standing-room only tonight."

Brianne wiped a hand across her brow. "Stella keeps fidgeting and sniffing. She needs to get used to this."

"Give her time. She's a rookie like you."

Brianne gave him a mock frown. "And you got stuck with me today."

He didn't mind that but he grinned and played along. "I drew the short straw."

Or at least it felt that way at times, but not today. He'd had a thing for Brianne Hayes since he'd noticed her on her first day of K-9 training. But he'd never acted on his feelings because they worked together and because this job demanded his full attention. They mostly picked on each other and flirted in a playful way. Fine by Gavin. He'd dated off and on but most women couldn't handle his long hours or dark moods.

"*I* drew the short straw," she shot back. "I'd rather be sitting on my tiny back porch with the sprinkler wetting my feet. But Stella and me, we can handle you."

As if she'd heard them talking about her, Stella stopped and lifted her nose into the air, a soft growl emitting from her throat.

Brianne held tight to the leash. "Steady, girl. You'll need to contain that when the fireworks start."

But Stella didn't quit. The big dog tugged forward, her nose sniffing both air and ground.

Gavin watched the Labrador, wondering what kind of scent she'd picked up. Then Tommy alerted, going still except for his wagging tail that acted like a warning flag, his body trembling in place, his nose in the air. A whiff he recognized had hit his odor receptors and sent an alert to his somatosensory cortex so he could process the smell. And it had to be a familiar smell.

"Something's up," Gavin whispered to Brianne. "He's picked up a signature somewhere."

Brianne whispered low. "As in a bomb scent?"

"That's his specialty."

Gavin checked her to make sure she wouldn't panic. Instead of panic, he saw something else in her eyes.

Apprehension and anticipation. Brianne's adrenaline faintly shouted at him.

Stella's, too. The rookie knew enough training to expect a reward soon.

"This can't be good," Gavin whispered, watching the crowd. A mass of people side by side. With a bomb nearby, full-out chaos would hit. They'd have to work quietly and quickly to get this situation under control. "We need to verify and contain." He did a sweep of the area. "If we find something, we need to call for backup immediately, okay?"

She nodded and did her own scan of the area.

"We'd better get to work," she said as they both let their partners take the lead, guiding them in a rush through the crowd. "We might not have much time."

It didn't take long to find what the dogs had alerted on. The man Gavin had spotted earlier wearing the plaid cap and carrying a black backpack.

He wasn't carrying the backpack now.

Gavin leaned toward Brianne. "We need to keep an eye on that man up ahead. Don't let him get lost in the crowd. You follow him, and Tommy and I can search for the backpack." Hurrying ahead, he reached for his radio to alert the other NYPD officers in the area.

Brianne nodded, her gaze zooming in on the man pushing through toward the south. "Think he's the one?"

Gavin didn't take his eyes off the man. "Yeah, I do."

The woman he'd noticed earlier sat with her baby girl on a crowded bench, her child in her arms. The kid with the soccer ball kicked it into the air. The ball got lost in the fray, but someone caught it and sent it back to the kid.

"We need to stay calm and see what he does next," he said to Brianne. "See where he goes. The dogs could be wrong, but I doubt that. Stay on the radio."

Tommy alerted again, his eyes on the man ahead but then the dog lifted his nose in the air and changed courses. Gavin pushed his way through shoulder-to-shoulder people, some laughing and ignoring him, some glaring at him full-force. He'd only made it a few feet. Not good.

Gavin stayed focused, trying to keep his eyes on the man who seemed oblivious to all the people shoving at him or to Brianne following him. They got caught up in a large group of teenagers pushing forward around a big oak tree.

Tommy ignored the girls and kept tugging toward the tree. Gavin spotted the backpack, zipped up and sitting on a beach towel by the tree. Tommy headed to it, dug his paws in and lifted his eyes back to Gavin. He didn't need to inspect the bag. If Tommy detected a bomb, Gavin believed him.

"Good work, Tommy."

Gavin called Tommy back away from the area and took in the scene. People all around. He started pushing, trying to guide them away. "Excuse me, folks. Need to clear the area, please."

But he didn't have to say a word. People in New York knew this drill only too well. A man pointed and shouted after he saw Tommy and Gavin—and the backpack. "Suspicious package."

Then someone else started shoving and running away. "Bomb!"

"Go," Gavin called, waving his arms. "Leave the area." Then he stood and spotted Brianne up ahead.

She'd already lifted her phone off her waist clip, her eyes meeting his.

"Get back," Gavin shouted, since people were beginning to whisper and stare. "Clear the area," he ordered, lifting his arms to wave to the people near the bench while he and Tommy kept a safe distance away. "Clear the area. Move away from the riverfront."

Brianne and Stella whizzed back toward him. He heard her radio it in through her mic. "10-33 in progress. East River Park. Intersection of East Houston and FDR."

"Stay back, Bree," he called. "Keep searching for the suspect."

She nodded and, giving Gavin one last glance, turned back to her search.

Gavin kept his hand up to keep anyone from approaching too close and he made sure he and Tommy were a safe distance away. The crowd parted and scattered, parents screaming, searching for children, the group of teenaged girls taking off like a pack to get out of the way, families grabbing each other and pushing through the masses.

In the meantime, he radioed for patrol officers to keep the crowd back and listened in on further instructions until the bomb squad arrived. He could expect to see a whole slew of law enforcement agencies arrive soon, including the FBI, ATF and the New York City Fire Department, just in case. Dispatch had already alerted officers up and down the riverfront on both sides of the firework barges. Unless they found more suspicious packages, the show would go on. But it might be delayed if this turned out to be more than a lone, random act.

Gavin prayed that wouldn't be the case.

* * *

People were running, screaming, shoving. The little boy with the soccer ball fell and cried out in pain. Someone helped him up while his ball went flying and dropped into the frightened crowd. The woman with the baby abandoned her stroller and took off running, holding her wailing child close to her shoulder. Her husband called after her and caught up to hold his family tight.

People shuffled to get away, some tripping and getting up while others stopped to help. An elderly man pushed a woman in a wheelchair. Too close.

Gavin hurried with Tommy toward the couple, hoping to get them away from the backpack, his heart pumping.

But before he could get to them, a boom and flash, smoke all around, people screaming and shouting, calling out to their loved ones. Gavin felt the blowback hit him in the gut, knocking him down. He stumbled while Tommy leaped into the air and fell over Gavin.

His ears ringing, Gavin sat up and rubbed Tommy's fur. "Thank you, boy. Good boy." His partner appeared intact and ready to get back on the job.

Gavin moved toward the smoke, searching for the old man who'd been pushing the woman in the wheelchair. Had they managed to get out of the way?

Tommy sniffed as they neared the area, the acrid smell from the explosion causing people to cough. The backpack had been incinerated. Gone. A black hole covered the spot where the blanket still burned. Searching for the wheelchair, Gavin also looked for Brianne and Stella. The last time he'd seen them they were coming back toward the tree.

The smoke settled enough that he saw the old man

sitting on the ground by the wheelchair, his forehead bleeding. He and the woman held hands. Both safe and sound and looking at each other.

Gavin headed toward them to make sure they were okay. "You folks all right?"

The man nodded, still holding his wife's hand. "Forty-eight years together. We're tougher than we look, son."

Gavin talked to them in a calm voice, making sure they were both okay and telling them help was on the way. Their love for each other was evident—like a punch to the gut but in a good way.

Then he glanced up and saw Brianne and Stella coming from the other direction, Brianne limping. But she gave him a thumps-up.

"Lost the suspect when someone in the crowd accidentally knocked me to the ground. Heading back," she reported over the radio. Brianne turned toward Gavin, Stella dancing at her feet. Shrugging, she held up her hands in defeat.

They'd lost the bomber. But the entire NYPD now had his description from Gavin. The man could easily detonate another bomb at any minute, though. But Gavin had to wonder if he'd planned the attack to hit when the fireworks started going off. Worst-case scenario. Yet the bomb hadn't done a lot of damage. Someone out for kicks? Or sending a warning to the city?

He let out a breath of relief but knew it would be short-lived. He had to go over this bomb scene and do a search for the man they'd spotted. What if he'd planted more bombs?

"Are you okay?" he asked through the radio.

Brianne hurried toward where he stood and nodded

to him, her expression intense as she allowed Stella to do her job.

He hadn't realized until that moment that he really wanted Brianne to be okay.

Glancing back at the old couple, he wondered what it would be like to hold someone's hand at that age and still be in love.

Knowing he needed to search for more bombs, he hurried to meet Brianne, his mind still on that strong, courageous couple.

TWO

Off in the distance and after a long delay, the fireworks finally started. The areas on both sides of the river were now being heavily patrolled by the NYPD and several other law enforcement personnel from various agencies. But thankfully no other devices had been found along the river or in any of the parks, and most of the people on both sides were never aware that they'd searched for bombs. The fireworks barge had been cleared. The show would go on, but the search for the suspect would intensify. Reporters hovered near the cordoned-off areas, wanting the scoop. A few brave people stood behind the police lines, determined to see the fireworks now that the area had technically been cleared. But most of the people who'd been crammed into this area had either gone home or moved to another safer location.

Not a good situation, Brianne thought as they walked the perimeters that had been marked with police tape. The bomb fragments were being gathered, piece by piece, by the bomb squad and so far no other explosive devices had been found. The lab would go over every shred to find clues or markers. No word on the suspect they'd seen earlier. .

Random? Or deliberate? She hoped they'd find the suspect somewhere in the city.

Brianne still shuddered each time she thought about the device that had exploded less than two hours ago in the haze of the coming dusk. If Stella and Tommy hadn't alerted…

But that was the job. Taking care of this city. New trainee Stella had done her part and she'd been rewarded with her treat, which involved a ball and a few minutes of playtime, followed by a doggie treat. They'd have more playtime when they got home. Aggravated that she'd let the suspect get by her, Brianne looked up and found Gavin and Tommy heading toward her. Glad that they were still alive, she tried not to think about how Gavin made her feel.

"What a night," he said, fatigue darkening his eyes.

"And it's not over," she replied. "We don't leave until everyone else does."

"Could be a while."

Brianne had not been happy to be partnered with this man. He had a reputation around headquarters for being an overly ambitious hothead. But she had to admit that today he'd been professional and courageous. And caring. He'd personally made sure the elderly couple that had been nearest to the explosion had both been checked over by the paramedics and cleared. Then he'd seen to it that they had an escort home, not a taxi but a cruiser.

Now Brianne wondered if a big teddy bear hid behind that gruff, fierce exterior. Gavin was good-looking in a don't-mess-with-me way, his hair a rich tousled brown, his eyes almost black, his attitude tough and untouchable. Maybe she'd misjudged her coworker, but then her last boyfriend had explained to her that she needed to work on her trust issues.

Even though she'd caught him cheating with her now-ex-best friend. Yeah, she had a few trust issues. But more than that, her determination and ambition matched that of the man walking with her right now. And that meant no love life. Too messy.

"You might need some downtime later tonight," he said. "It's always rough when things get this heavy."

Whirling to face him, Brianne scoffed. "You don't think I have the mettle to handle this, Gavin?"

"I didn't say that," he replied, clearly confused. "We had an intense situation, but you handled it like a pro."

Anger gaining strength, she glared up at him. "I am a pro. I haven't gotten my official graduation certificate yet, but that doesn't mean I can't do the job."

"I said all of that wrong," he replied, looking adorably sheepish. "You're tough, Bree. We can all see that. You work harder than any of us in training and on the streets."

"You mean, for a woman, right?"

"I hadn't noticed," he retorted, with a trace of a smile.

"Are you laughing at me, Sutherland?"

"No, ma'am."

"Now you're calling me *ma'am*?"

"Look, I'm headed for coffee and something to eat once we're off duty. I'm bushed and I'm starving and my adrenaline has about run its course. You're welcome to come with." Checking his watch, he added, "Our shift should have ended an hour ago."

Feeling contrite and a bit embarrassed, Brianne again

wondered about Gavin Sutherland. She hesitated for her own reasons, but he took it the wrong way.

"Okay, I get it," he said, walking ahead of her. "You obviously don't want to hang around with a piranha like me."

"You don't look that dangerous," she said, catching up with him. "I don't think of you in that way."

No, right now she thought of him in a whole new way. Something that had more teeth than any old scary fish. Mentally doing a shakedown, she pushed all of that away for now. Her adrenaline had drained away, too.

"Then what do you think of me?"

His question caught her off guard. She'd noticed him. It would be hard for any woman to skip right over a man like him. But she knew better than to get involved with a coworker, especially since he was right. She'd worked hard in training and on the job to show everyone she meant business. She'd taken on the task of training Stella to make some points, but now she loved the dog with all of her heart and she planned to make Stella the best bomb-detection dog in this city. Stella had done a good job today, so Brianne knew her gut instincts had been spot on.

"Can't even say it?"

Holding tight to Stella, Brianne shot him another glare and got her mind back on the conversation. "Yes, I can say it. I don't know you that well, but I think you were given a bum rap. You might want to get promoted, but you wouldn't kill anyone to make that happen. You're too loyal to the department for that and besides, you have a solid alibi for when Jordan disappeared."

Giving her an uncertain frown that made his eyebrows shift up, he said, "Thank you, I think."

He took off and followed Tommy, his whole body on alert. Maybe the man just needed a friend.

"Look," she said, tired but still full of enough tension to know that this man made her pulse beat a little faster. "It's been a long hot day and I'm going home when I'm done. Then we get right back to it tomorrow."

He didn't argue with her. "Yep. I need to find some food and then I'm going to go over my report one more time. We have to keep looking for the man in the plaid hat."

"Because he could strike again," she replied, her eyes holding his.

Gavin nodded. "Yes, I have a bad feeling this might only be the beginning."

The next morning, Griffin's Diner was hopping as usual. People still enjoying what was left of the Fourth of July weekend were lined up at the double French doors of the quaint brick building located on a bustling corner near 94th Street in Queens.

Brianne had walked the couple blocks over from the K-9 Command Unit in search of some good coffee and a nice shady spot on the patio.

The old red bricks of the restaurant had mellowed to a deep burgundy over the years. Brianne remembered coming here with her parents as a child and seeing the pictures on the wall of fallen officers, one of them a brother to the owner, Louis Griffin. Most of the K-9s in service now had been named after those who'd died while on duty, including Gavin's partner, Tommy, named after Officer Tommy McNeill.

The diner had been in the Griffin family for generations and easygoing baseball fanatic Louis "Lou" Griffin was a fixture in the place, along with his blunt-talking wife, Barbara, who had a no-nonsense attitude and took care of everything from bookkeeping to settling down unruly customers. Their daughter, Violet, a friend of Brianne's, worked with them when she wasn't at her regular job as a ticket agent at the airport. They'd lost their five-year-old son to meningitis nearly twenty years ago. She often wondered if that's why they all poured so much love into this old building.

Brianne moved around to the right corner where an alfresco area lined with potted dish gardens led to the private space designated for the NYPD and the K-9 team's four-legged partners. She opened one of the matching French doors there, smiling at the etched plaque over the door—*The Dog House, Reserved for New York's Finest.*

She headed inside to see if Violet was working and get that big cup of coffee but stopped when she heard her name.

"Hey, Bree."

Turning, she saw Gavin approaching, Tommy moving ahead.

Holding the door, she tried to hide her surprise. "What are you doing here?"

He pointed to where a big red umbrella cast a shade over one of the square metal tables near a side street. "I never ate last night. I'm going to order a big breakfast." Then he lifted his chin. "Grab your coffee and meet me back out here. It's cloudy and not too hot yet. Lou's got the rotating fan going already."

"Outside it is, then," she replied, again noticing her

good-looking coworker while she wondered why she'd stopped here today, of all mornings. Unless someone else showed up, they had the whole patio to themselves. Not that she minded. More like *too intimate*. Brianne wanted to keep things light and professional. But…a chance meeting over coffee, coworkers did that, right?

When she came back with a to-go cup, Gavin didn't dare hold out her chair, even though he looked as if he might. They both sat down at the same time, facing toward the street, their partners curling up at their feet to wait for water and a special treat from Lou.

"So how ya doing?" he asked, his attitude more relaxed and laid back today.

"Peachy," she replied. "Slept like a rock."

"I never know if you're being sarcastic or serious," he replied, smiling over at her.

"And I'll never tell you which."

She hadn't slept much at all. She kept reliving the moment when that bomb had exploded. But she'd made notes each time she remembered something and she aimed to get back to work. Like right now.

Barbara came out with a coffee pot. "Anyone hungry?" She refilled Gavin's mug, her question causing Brianne's stomach to growl loudly. "What else can I bring you guys?"

"Pancakes," they both said, laughing.

"Pancakes it is," she said, taking her pen out from behind her ear, loose strands of curling brown hair with gray edging escaping her bun. "How 'bout some bacon with that?"

"None for me," Brianne said. "I hadn't planned on staying."

"Double stack," Gavin replied to Barbara.

Brianne shook her head and smiled up at Barb. "Hey, is Violet here this morning?"

"Not yet," Barb said with a smile. "But she's due to stop by any minute now. We're going to talk wedding plans. Have you seen her ring?"

"I have," Brianne replied. "She and Zach seem so happy."

"They are—finally," Barb said. "Took them all of their lives living next to each other and then almost getting killed by some drug dealer to figure it out."

When Barbara walked away, Gavin looked over at Brianne. "Zach needed someone in his life right now. It's been tough on all of the Jameson brothers, losing Jordan."

"I agree," Brianne said, remembering Jordan's funeral and how his brothers had stood so solemn and strong. "Now if we could just find his killer."

"Yeah, I want that, too." Gavin looked down, probably remembering being heavily questioned about Jordan's death since the whole unit knew he'd been bitter about not being promoted to chief. But she didn't broach that subject. He'd been cleared, and that was good enough for her.

He didn't offer up any explanations. Instead, he switched gears. "So you like pancakes, but you don't eat meat?"

"I do but…bacon is addictive. I try to pace myself."

"And why are you in such a hurry to get away from me?"

"I'm not," she said, thinking she needed to do just that. "I came by to get some coffee and chat with my friend. But I remembered some things about last night so I jotted notes to add to my official report. I wasn't planning on hanging around for a big breakfast. I want to do a search and see if I can get a match on that bomber."

He took a sip of his coffee and did the cop scan that came naturally. Trucks whizzed by, vehicles honked, people hurried down the sidewalks. A typical day in the city. "I figured you'd head right to headquarters this morning."

"I went over my report early this morning," she said, nodding. "And I have lots of questions, but I needed some of Barbara's strong coffee first."

"What kind of questions?" he asked. "I have a few of my own but we'll need to see what the lab's found, too."

"That guy in the plaid hat. Gavin, he walked right past us."

"Yeah, I know. Taunting the police? Daring us to see him?"

She took a long drink of coffee. "I did some research online. No other recent reports of bomb threats or bomb scares, but there does seem to be a rash of small explosions all over the city lately."

Gavin tensed up and turned wary. "Such as?"

"In buildings, parking garages, things like that. They've all been explained away as accidents. A boiler explosion here, a garage fire there, several construction fires. But no bomb threats or actual bombs—except possibly at one particular site." She paused. "A site that you and Tommy worked, Gavin. Williamsburg. A boiler exploded in the basement. Why were you called in?"

He didn't flinch, and he didn't look away. "I heard the call on the radio. I happened to be nearby so I went."

"What did you find?"

He looked away this time. She'd read the report. Possible incendiary device. Unsubstantiated. Not enough evidence.

"Gavin, what do you know about that explosion?"

Giving her a confused stare, he asked, "What are you getting at?"

"Nothing. Because I have nothing. But I'm concerned we might start seeing more bombings in the parks or in other big crowded events. Maybe even in buildings. I don't want that to happen but if it does, we'll need to be prepared for a serial bomber."

His expression changed, turning serious and standoffish.

"You think I'm crazy?" she asked, her fingers drumming the table and causing both Stella and Tommy to glance up. That or she'd stepped on his sensitive toes by taking some initiative?

"No. But, Bree, we have bomb threats all the time. It's part of living in New York and most of them are never reported to the public. We handle things to keep everyone safe. This could have been a prank by someone bored and looking for blood or…we could have a terrorist toying with us. We need to be prepared, yes, but we also have to be careful."

"I'm going to be careful," she said. "But I'm also going to find out what I can about this bomber."

When he looked away again, she beamed in on him like a laser pen. "You know something already, don't you, Gavin?"

He shook his head. "I'm not good with words or explaining things. You've seen me blurt out my feelings right in front of everyone."

"Yeah, I have. But now you're clammed-up and this

has to be about last night. You need to fill me in. So start talking."

Gavin took a sip of black coffee, completely unaware of her inner turmoil. But he did seem to have some of his own. "You were a pro yesterday."

Oh, so now he tried to put a spin on this and build up her confidence? "I let the suspect get away."

"No, you didn't. He slipped away with a crowd of people, oldest trick in the book."

"I want to find him."

"I do, too," Gavin said. "And believe it or not, I agree with you. We could wind up having a serial bomber on our hands. And yes, he could be the man who walked right past us yesterday."

"But you weren't going to tell me that because…?"

He looked directly at her now. "I have to sort things out in my mind and make sure I'm right before I jump to conclusions."

"You don't trust me."

"It's not like that."

She shouldn't have been disappointed. This job could be competitive at times and she had to stay one step ahead. She'd given herself a good pep talk on the way over here, so she squelched any mixed messages she might have scrambled in her brain and gave him her I'm-all-in smile. "Then what is it like, Gavin?"

She drank her coffee while she waited, too many questions popping in her head while sweat popped out along her spine.

"I don't know yet. But if you listen to me and let me explain, we might be able to crack this case together," he said, his tone pure business, his gaze steady on her face.

So he did have a plan and he did know more than he'd let on. "How can I help?"

"By pretending to be my wife," he said.

And he was dead serious.

THREE

Brianne swallowed so fast the coffee went down the wrong way and she started coughing.

Gavin watched her, his expression puzzled and confused and kind of comical. She took a sip of water and tried to clear her throat before Lou came rushing out to give her the Heimlich maneuver.

"Would you mind repeating that?" she asked, wiping her eyes.

"Are you okay?"

Nodding, she lifted her right hand to wave him on because she really wanted to hear this. A couple of uniforms came through, nodded and headed inside.

The sky had darkened, and she thought she'd seen a streak of lightning to the west. Traffic noises merged with thunder.

"It's for a case," he said, handing her another paper napkin to wipe her eyes. "I mean, it might be this case."

"Involving the bomber from last night?"

"I don't know yet. We'll have to figure that out together."

"Why me?" she asked, still confused.

"I'm not an undercover cop," he said. "Not even a detective. I can't give up my identity to go undercover but I can snoop around. I just need a cover for a few weeks."

Barbara came out with their meal and refilled their coffee, pretending she hadn't noticed all the coughing drama. But she shot Brianne a knowing smile. "Looks like rain," she said, glancing at the billowing gray clouds. "Better eat up."

Stella and Tommy sniffed the air. *Bacon?*

She felt their pain. Brianne watched Barbara go back inside and then grabbed a slice of crisp bacon. "I think I'm gonna need this."

"I've been following a lead," he explained between bites of fluffy pancakes and the best bacon in New York.

Or at least it tasted that way to Brianne each time she swiped a strip. Stress eating was her thing, after all. She'd have to run the bacon off later. And she'd have to run off the strange currents circulating through her system, too. Why, oh why had she been paired with this man?

Work. Focus on work. "What kind of lead?"

"A few months ago, we established that a person noted as a master bomb-maker might be back in New York and that he could possibly be the one who set off the boiler explosion that caused part of the apartment building you mentioned to wind up in pieces. One person killed and three hospitalized. Tommy and I were the first to arrive on the scene because I had dinner with a friend at a nearby restaurant. Tommy alerted and we found fragments of what looked like the makings of a bomb. Pieced things together but the FBI and Homeland Security took over the case."

"The explosion in Williamsburg?" she asked, gaining

interest. "An older apartment building. They couldn't figure out what had caused the boiler to explode but this report says possible tampering. They never found a suspect."

"*We* never found a suspect. Tommy and I gave it our best shot and we found evidence of an incendiary device but no trace of the person who might have done it." He shrugged and shook his head. "I had to let it go."

"Maybe the department will get a lead soon."

"They won't, and for several reasons," he said. "First, we only have a written report from the other agencies and I had to ask special permission for that. Plus, this possible bomber is like a ghost, but my confidential informant—we call him Beanpole because he's so skinny—told me he's heard things about that explosion being deliberate. Someone wanted that building destroyed. He thinks he's seen the man who did it and he described him to me. If it's who I think it is, he's known as the Tick—a double meaning. His bombs don't always tick but he grips his target and won't let go until the job is done. I'm talking taunting, stalking, harassing and then…boom."

"Like a tick on skin?"

"Yes. Hard to find and even harder to shake."

She almost shuddered but lifted her shoulder instead. "Not a good image."

"No. This man is dangerous. He's not considered a terrorist and he's not connected to any sleeper cells as far as we can tell. But someone could be hiring him to sabotage or damage buildings so they can be condemned. That forces people out so they can buy the property at rock-bottom prices and rebuild on it, making a fortune. That makes him a domestic terrorist in my book, him and whoever is paying him to do this."

He stopped, waiting for her to bolt. But Brianne sat with her eyes on him, giving him her complete attention.

"After that explosion, I did some research and found a pattern that seems to match his MO. I found one report from a building in Chicago—a gas explosion. Blasted but no foul play found. Six months later, the property had switched hands and a fancy new condominium building went up. And another in Atlanta, same pattern. A fire in the basement that got out of hand, ruled as an electrical fire. A few months later, the place had been razed to build a new high-rise condo building."

"So you see a pattern developing?"

"Yes. Those incidents have all the markings of the Tick. He disguises his bombs to make them look like something else—a gas leak, a boiler blowing up, an accidental construction fire. Once that's over and done, the buildings change hands pretty quickly. The previous owners might get an insurance settlement but an offer to buy them out would sure add to that. And I think they're being persuaded in other ways, too."

"Intimidation?" She shook her head. "Violet's mentioned Lou being harassed lately. Something about gentrification."

"Yes, that kind of thing. The threat of another explosion, rumors that scare tenants away."

"So…you've been researching this because…?"

He took a swig of coffee and checked the clouds coming in. "I didn't like leaving the case unsolved, and I need something to prove I'm not just out to get promoted. I really care about this case. I'm ambitious, true.

But…this is dangerous stuff. The Williamsburg explosion turned out to be more powerful—enough to take down a small building and kill a woman. Tommy alerted and our partners are rarely wrong on these things. But… we didn't find enough proof."

"So how is he getting away with this?"

"I think someone higher up is hiring him to scare property owners. He's meticulous in hiding his tracks but now he's getting bolder. Bombers like notoriety, but they don't want to get caught so they prefer to leave little signatures but not much evidence."

"So these real estate agents are trying to scare vulnerable people out of their apartments and homes so they can raze them and build?"

"Yes. They want the property, but not the buildings." He sat silently, as if weighing his next words. "They make people back off on contracts or force owners to sell quietly and quickly. They've got a system of intimidation and bullying tactics and the bomber is just the tip of the iceberg. No one can prove anything so the owners cave and wash their hands of the entire mess."

"So it's not just about the bomber? You want these corrupt real estate agents to end their bullying ways."

"I do, for so many reasons." Looking out over the street, he let out a sigh. "The woman who died in that explosion worked with my grandmother at a nearby hospital. I knew her, Bree. Helen Proctor. She lived in Williamsburg all of her life and most of that time in the apartment she shared with her husband before he died. She was good to me when my grandmother got sick and…after she passed away." Twisting his napkin, he added, "I knew she lived there but…but I couldn't believe it when they brought her out in a body bag."

And right after that, Jordan Jameson had died and Gavin had been put through the wringer as a possible suspect. No wonder he seemed to have a big chip on his shoulder.

More like the weight of the world.

"I'm sorry, Gavin. So sorry." Brianne's heart burned with understanding. She'd heard Gavin's grandmother had raised him after his mother left him as an infant. She didn't bring up any of that, though. "So this is personal for you?"

"Very," he admitted. "At the time, Jordan knew about my connection to Helen, so I asked if I could investigate the alleged bombing on the side, on my own time if needed."

"And he agreed to that?"

"He did after I explained—Helen Proctor didn't deserve to die that way. He knew, Noah knows and now you. I'd like to keep it that way. No one else, okay?"

"Okay." She could see how much this meant to him. But how far would he be willing to go?

"So the chief went along with your plan?"

"He told me to be careful. Jordan and I go way back, but we had a falling out when we were in the academy together and later, as everyone knows, I resented him getting promoted. I think he initially gave the go-ahead to this because we both felt bad about what happened— a stupid fight over a training episode. Just too stubborn to apologize."

Brianne could now see why Gavin seemed so solemn at times. She wanted to hear more about what had happened between them, but she'd save that for another time. "You feel guilty about that?"

"Of course I do." Shrugging, he said, "Then I got put

on the suspect list regarding his murder. That stung, you know. I wish I'd kept my opinions to myself, but I understand how my complaining looked bad."

"We all know you wouldn't kill Jordan, Gavin. And we have proof that you didn't. I read the report. You worked a swanky fund-raiser in Midtown and both the commissioner and the mayor saw you there. Then you arrived home around midnight and your roommate said you guys talked for an hour and both went to bed. Your vehicle never left your yard until after nine that morning, according to the traffic cameras in the area."

"You read the report?"

"Of course I did. Jordan was last seen at six a.m. But I didn't have to read a report to know the truth."

He shot her a look that held appreciation and admiration. And something else she couldn't read. "Thank you, Bree."

She nodded and took a long sip of coffee.

"So now you're on this quest for two reasons—you knew a woman who died at the hands of this possible bomber and…you owe it to Jordan and now the new chief, his brother Noah, to show your true merit?"

He studied her, probably looking for a judgmental frown. When she didn't give him one, he nodded. "Yes, I guess that's it in a nutshell. This is important to me."

Brianne leaned forward. "So you're after the Tick. What's the plan?"

"Well, I'm after him, but I'm also after the people who've hired him. This is a classic case of intimidation. Mafia-style." Glancing around, he made sure they were alone. "After comparing a couple of random explosions around Manhattan, I've been discreetly asking questions, talking to wealthy investors, stuff like that.

We're talking seven figures or more—a lot of money. If someone is sabotaging developers and property owners by bombing buildings so they can step in and take over, it could only get worse from here."

Confused and needing to know the bottom line, she asked, "But Gavin, you're a K-9 cop. You're usually not involved in the investigative part. I can't believe the department agreed to this."

His expression went from hopeful to disappointed in a flash. "I'd been doing this on the side, on my own time, after I got a tip from Beanpole. But I kept Jordy up-to-date." Sighing, he added, "After Jordy went missing and was found dead, I went to Noah to get permission to continue working on this case. You know the rest. This had to be put on hold. We all want to find Jordy's killer. That's top priority for the precinct."

"But you're still working on this, too, clearly."

He nodded and then stared out into the street. "I'm not hiding it from Noah or anyone else. In fact, I think they're all glad I've got something else to occupy me. Even though I've been cleared of any suspicion in Jordy's death, I can't shake the doubters who still aren't sure."

Beginning to understand, she said, "But if you solve this case, you'd look better in everyone's eyes, right?"

"I hope so. Bree, I didn't always get along with Jordy but…I respected him. He was a good cop and a good leader. I need this—not only because of that, but because this man is getting bolder with each bomb. He has to be stopped."

Brianne didn't know what to say. Good officers knew working without backup was never the best plan. Glad he'd been upfront with the chief, she said, "You shouldn't go it alone. Have you talked to the FBI and Homeland Security any more?"

"They've been informed. Those in charge know Tommy and I are good at what we do. As long as I don't interfere in their cases, I'm clear. I have to report back, of course. Besides, I'm not technically undercover. I've just trying to build a solid case—on my own time and in my own way."

"This is an unusual situation," she said. "I know a lot of detectives who are deep undercover. They give up everything to do their jobs."

"Yes, but my job is bomb detection and…I can't let this one go. Tommy found something at that site, and I think he recognized that man yesterday after Stella alerted. I took this on because my gut tells me this man is so close. And based on Beanpole's vague description of him, I think that could have been him. I haven't figured out why he'd bomb the park, but it could have been a distraction. I can't talk to anyone much about it per Noah's orders, but the NYPD is well aware of the situation and they've got people on it, too. I thought I could trust you, though, since you were there."

"And then you got this wild idea that we could both work this case, possibly undercover as husband and wife?"

"Something like that. It's stupid, I know. But…I need evidence, and most of the detectives I know are swamped and all in on their own cases." He took a sip of coffee. "As you know, I rent out a room in the house in Valley Stream I inherited from my Granny Irene. My roommate's so deep undercover, I get rent money from a PO box and I haven't seen him since he vouched for me three months ago—right before he started this new case."

A streak of lightning made a jagged dance over the skyscrapers and then a roar of thunder shook the sky. The flowers in the dish gardens bent in the brisk wind.

"We'd better get inside," he said, his tone gruff now.

Brianne stood. "I want to hear more," she said. "All of it. Then I'll decide."

"Forget I mentioned it."

She slanted her eyebrow up. "Oh, no. This conversation is not over."

The lightning flashed again. Brianne turned away from the street to give Stella a command so they could move inside.

Before she could get to the door, the rain started coming down. Gavin glanced at an approaching SUV and then back at her, his eyes filling with apprehension.

In the next instance, he jumped across the table and covered her, pushing her down, rain pouring around them.

But something else also poured out along with the rain.

Bullets.

FOUR

Gavin didn't have time to think.

He dove over Brianne, his body covering hers as the dark SUV sped by, one tinted side-window in the back open enough to show the tip of a long-barreled revolver. With a silencer.

But even with that silencer, he could still hear the hiss of a projectile coming straight toward them.

While he held her, bullets ricocheted off bricks and iron, one hitting the umbrella where they'd just been sitting, the force ripping the sturdy canvas apart. After what seemed like a lifetime of seconds, the SUV peeled away, wet tires spinning.

For one moment, everything went silent and then everyone moved at once.

The two officers who'd gone inside just minutes earlier came rushing out, weapons drawn.

"Hey, are you guys okay?"

"Shots fired." Gavin looked down at Brianne. He'd knocked her down so quickly, her hair had tumbled out around her face. "You hit?"

"No, no," she said, her breath rising. "How about you?"

"I'm fine."

"The dogs?"

Gavin checked Stella who sat loyally beside where Brianne had landed, her ears up and her eyes on alert. Tommy did the same. These two weren't trained to attack but they wouldn't back off either if push came to shove. "They're good. A tough combo."

Brianne reached out a hand and touched Stella's furry head. "Good girl."

He sat back and then leaped up, offering her a hand. "Are you sure you're all right?"

"I'm fine," she said, grabbing hold, her hand sending little currents of warmth straight to his heart. "My knee is still bruised and cut from falling yesterday in the park and I'll probably have a bruise on my elbow where I hit the concrete when…when you dived over me."

"Sorry," he said, unable to stop staring at her. "I saw the barrel of a gun and went into action."

"We'd better stay in action," she said, her expression hard to read. "We should contain the scene."

Gavin looked around, his mind refocusing. Lou came hurrying out, oblivious to the rain or any shooters, his salt-and-pepper hair standing straight up. "Get inside," he said, worry in his tone.

One of the patrol officers nodded. "Go on. We've called it in. but we didn't see the vehicle or the shooter."

"The vehicle—a black Denali," Gavin replied. "I didn't get the tag numbers. I'll see if I can remember any details when we file a report. Could have been random."

"Right," the younger of the two said. "Two cops sitting on a patio. An easy target."

Lou studied the street, his expression grim. "Who knows these days? We had that shooting when Sophie

Walters was targeted, but that man's dead now. Then Eva Kendall's nephew Mikey got taken from here, remember? Glad they found the boy safe and sound."

He shrugged and then held his hands up in defeat. "Maybe I should just sell the place." He turned to go back inside but whirled around. "This time might have been a warning for me. Someone really wants to buy this property, but I keep refusing to sell. Different real estate agents come by all the time, smart-mouthing."

Gavin shot a glance to Brianne. "Lou, are you being strong-armed?"

Lou shook his head. "I have been but I handled it. Just braggish folks with business cards and big offers. You know, gentrification. As if anyone around here wants to become more refined, know what I mean? I refused all offers, of course. But today, they might have fired their first warning shot directly at me. If this keeps up, we'll lose business and I'll be forced to shut things down."

"Like I said," Gavin replied to the officers. "Random? Or maybe not."

"We've got this," the other one said. "Get inside and dry off."

"Bree, let's go in and talk about what happened."

She fixed her hair, her skin and uniform soaked. "What's to talk about? They shot at *us*, right? Whether they were targeting Lou or us, we're in this. I'm not going inside."

He nodded, worrying, calculating.

Brianne studied the porch and the street. "I don't think this was random, Gavin. So I'd like to help process the scene."

"We can agree on that," he said, his tone grim. "Did you see anything?"

"No. I should have been more alert."

"Except I had you distracted with my lamebrain plan."

"We're not done with that," she reminded him.

The rain softened into a drizzle but since they were both drenched they didn't care. "Let's check for bullet fragments," she said. "The rain might not let up and it's washing away evidence."

"I saw a black SUV, a late model Denali. I didn't get a license plate number. But then we see those all over town all the time. Hired drivers."

"And Lou doesn't have video footage to the street."

"Nope. But the transportation department does. I'll get Danielle's team on that."

They walked the patio, lifting bullet fragments for balistics and taking statements. The rain ended and a hot scalding sun came out to make their wet uniforms even stickier. The patrol officers cordoned off the patio until they'd cleared the scene.

Lou brought out water and offered them coffee. "Find anything?"

"Nope," Gavin said. "But we'll try to figure it out." Then he touched Lou's beefy arm. "I'll need to sit down with you later and hear more about the people trying to buy you out."

Lou shrugged. "People have been trying to buy me out since I opened the diner over thirty years ago. I don't plan on going anywhere. Not without a fight, at least."

Gavin wondered about that. And he wondered if the people who seemed to be targeting Lou might also be after Gavin now, too. Did they know he'd been asking around? Did they assume he was snooping on Lou's behalf?

"Can I get you anything else?" the older man asked, clearly rattled. Barbara came out and tried to tug them all inside, her face etched in worry.

They worked the scene in quiet and then went inside to interview the patrons and Lou and Barb. No one had anything new to add. Most of the diners had been cleared to leave.

"We've had a couple of real estate agents handing out cards and telling us how much we can get for the property," Barb said. "We didn't think anything of it and Lou politely told them we didn't want to sell."

"They weren't polite," Lou told them. "But you know how that goes. Firm and with greed glowing in their eyes. I threw their cards in the trash."

He barely remembered what they looked like, so not much to go on there. "Violet was here the other day when a woman came by and handed me a card. She might be able to describe the woman better. I had people shouting for food so I hurried away."

As if on cue, Violet showed up, pushing her way through the bystanders and the yellow police tape. Hugging her parents close, she turned to Gavin. "What happened?"

Gavin brought her up to speed. "Everyone is okay but I need to ask you some questions."

"Sure," she said, her dark hair caught up in a clip. "What's up?"

"Look, no one was hurt but Lou says they've been approached by some pesky real estate brokers trying to get them to sell out. Lou thinks the bullets might have been a warning for you guys. Do you know anything about that?"

"I talked to a woman once," Violet said, her voice shaky, her arm on her father's shoulder. "She was persistent and maybe a little threatening. Do you think they'd resort to this kind of harassment? Are my parents in danger?"

Barb and Lou patted her on the arm. "Honey, we're fine," Lou said over and over.

Gavin needed to consider that angle, but he didn't have the answer right now. "I think it could have been for Bree and me, but we can't be sure." He thanked her for the information.

Assuring her that her parents were okay, he promised to alert Violet's fiancé, Zach—a fellow K-9 officer—just in case. "We'll keep watch, either way."

"Thanks," Gavin said to Barbara after she'd handed them both a to-go box of fresh food since they hadn't finished their breakfasts. "I'm going back to headquarters."

"Same here," Brianne said. "I drove but I have a clean uniform in my locker."

"I came here first, too, and found a parking place around the corner."

Her brow scrunched. "I'll see you back at the station"

"Okay. Watch your back."

Before they left to go their separate ways, she turned to Gavin. "I don't know why I'm saying this but…I really do want to hear more about your case, Gavin."

"I thought you were against it."

"No, I just like to do things by the book. If you need my help, that's fine. But…we clear it with Noah, understand? Let him know you need me on the case and explain why."

"I don't know—"

"You're already on their radar. If you've been cleared to work on this, that's cool. I need to get clearance, too. We can't be too careful, considering."

"What do you want me to do, Brianne? I took this case and then Jordy died and…I made a mess of things. I need something to focus on."

"We do have something to focus on—finding Chief Jameson's killer and searching for the Fourth of July bomber."

"I want to find the Tick, too. I've just got a hunch that they could be one and the same. And now this. It could all be tied together, especially if they've decided to target Lou, too."

"I want to find that bomber we saw in the park. I don't like this place being shot up, and Lou could be a target now. But we continue to do it by the book or… I'll never work with you again."

She turned and marched off, her shoulders straight, her hair still trying to escape the messy bun she'd managed to fix.

Gavin watched her head to her SUV across the way. He checked the windows of buildings around the area. Had he made a big mistake by telling her what he'd been up to? Now he had to consider someone had just shot at this building. Who? Why?

Lou had been upfront about someone wanting to buy him out, but what if he had been pressured way more than any of them knew?

Hurrying to his vehicle, Gavin got caught up in a traffic jam caused by construction. While he sat there waiting for the workers to finish their task, Gavin thought about his grandmother, Irene. She'd died five years ago, leaving him her home and a modest savings account. His grandmother had raised him after his mother, Phyllis, had given birth out of wedlock. Phyllis, still a teenager, had run away when he'd been only a month old and hadn't come back. Irene, who'd become a widow at an early age, had cared for him and sent him to college, all the while working as a nurse her entire life. She'd only been retired a year or so when her health turned bad.

He'd never had to prove himself to Granny Irene. She loved him with a tough love but he knew he could always count on her. His grandmother lived by faith and she'd planted that seed in his heart. He didn't talk about his faith much, but he tried hard to live up to Irene's strong belief system.

Checking on Tommy in the back, Gavin said, "Hey, boy. We should have walked back to work, huh?"

Tommy woofed his agreement and did a circle inside the kennel. Always ready to roll.

At least he had a solid house with a small yard for Tommy. Small but intact, the two-story wooden row house had a narrow front porch. It belonged to him, no matter how many real estate agents told him he could make a fortune flipping it and selling it.

Maybe that also had something to do with how this particular case bothered him. His grandfather had been a fairly successful businessman and had bought the house, built in the 1940s, for a modest price over fifty years ago.

After his grandfather's death in a traffic accident, his grandmother had raised his wayward mother there.

He'd never sell, even if Valley Stream was now a coveted area. But the place stayed in a continuous state of remodeling and updating. It had a nice backyard for Tommy and room enough for the both of them and his rarely-there roommate. That's all Gavin needed.

Or so he'd thought until Brianne had come into his life. Working with her now and then over the last few weeks, helping her to train Stella and getting to know her better had only made him more aware of her. The woman had a sweet heart behind a solid wall of feminine steel.

Holding her there after the shooting this morning, he'd felt something powerful and true, the kind of emotions a man hides inside his heart. Gavin didn't know how to deal with all the possibilities swirling inside his head. He needed to keep a professional attitude regarding Brianne Hayes.

Now he'd put her in a bad position.

He had to trust her. He needed a partner to help him crack this case. A female who could pose as his rich wife so they could attend open houses and get information on properties without looking suspicious. Brianne had the backbone and the nerves to pull off a high-risk undercover job, but he wondered now if he should put her in the line of fire.

Neither of them had been trained to do this kind of work. Noah had cautioned him against pursuing this, but Gavin wasn't giving up just yet. If those bullets had been meant to scare him, they had not succeeded. A new determination made him want to do his job.

Fifteen minutes later, traffic started moving again and Gavin drove to headquarters, parked, then opened the back to let Tommy out of the vehicle. Together they headed for the indoor practice area like they'd done a thousand times before. As he gave Tommy some play-time, he wondered what Bree was doing. He didn't see her or Stella in the training arena. A few minutes later, his phone buzzed.

Brianne.

She'd said she wanted to know more and that she wanted to help him. Did Brianne Hayes really care at all?

He hit Accept and waited to see, torn between need-ing her help and wanting to protect her.

"Gavin, meet me in the small conference room up-stairs," she said, her words breathless. "We got a call from the FBI. We might have a lead on the Fourth of July bomber."

"I'll be right there."

Gavin put away his phone and forgot about his damp uniform.

He wanted to see if they'd found the man in the park.

Because he felt pretty sure the man who'd placed bombs in the East River Park could also be the same bomber who'd been setting off small explosions for the past few months. First thing, he'd report his suspicions to Noah. This case had taken another turn and since several law enforcement agencies were involved, he wanted full transparency. No mistakes.

They might have found the elusive man everyone on the streets called the Tick. The man knew they'd seen him last night. If the Tick had reported seeing them to whoever was paying him, then Gavin felt sure he'd been made and the Tick's boss had sent someone to rattle him this morning.

Did he dare bring Brianne into that kind of trap?

FIVE

Brianne watched Gavin making his way through the rows of cubicles where most of the K-9 Unit members did their desk work. The chief's office took up most of the back of the big room, its glass windows covered with blinds near a small anteroom where his assistant, Sophic, sat as gatekeeper. The other half of the office space there went to other supervisors and held smaller offices on each side. The conference room filled out the rest of the back part of this top floor. A training arena downstairs gave the K-9s a place to work out and practice mandatory training all year long.

Gavin nodded to several officers but kept walking, Tommy at his side, until he reached the conference room. "What have we got?" he asked without so much as a nod.

She still wore her soggy uniform since she'd hurried up to do a database search of the man they'd seen last night, hoping she might remember something about the shooting this morning in the process.

Gavin looked impatient. "Well?"

The man took his work seriously.

"For now, mug shots," she said, turning to head to the

conference table where a photo she'd printed lay on the table. "One of the images I found looks like the man we saw in the park. A younger version from what I can tell. I sent it to the FBI right away and they called just now. They talked to a witness and that witness remembered seeing the man in the plaid cap. They sent the photo to the witness to verify. She says it could be the same man because of the shaggy hair. But she's not sure."

"Then that won't help us." Gavin stared at the photo of a dark-haired man with brown eyes and heavy brows. "Caucasian and about the same height and weight of our suspect but younger, yes. I don't know. He had on shades part of the time. Hard to say."

He sank down, exhaustion clear in his eyes. "My CI heard two men talking near an older apartment building in Midtown. Beanpole lives on the streets in that area and because he's basically invisible, people stand by where he sits on a corner and talk about all kinds of things. He says the bomber named the Tick is working on something big in Manhattan."

"Well, maybe your CI can ID him, too." She handed him the mug shot.

Gavin stared at the picture. "William Caston? How'd he wind up in the AFIS database?"

"Arrested seven years ago for being with a group of college kids who were setting off pipe bombs in Queens," Brianne said. "But he only got a few years of probation because another kid confessed to setting up the whole operation."

"Maybe the Tick decided to try a better bomb-making career," Gavin said. "I can't be sure if this is him."

She stared at the photo. "That would put his age at around thirty-one. It sounds like the the Tick is around that age, based on what little information I've managed to dig up."

"True, but we can't go on that alone."

"I got up close," Brianne said, hoping he wouldn't make a scene because she'd beat him to the punch. "I saw his face and though he wore sunglasses and that hat, I remember the shape of his face and his hair—scraggly and dark. And those eyebrows."

"Do we have a last known address?"

"No. The FBI says he's always moving."

He stared at the picture. "We keep searching and when we hear from the lab, we can go after him."

"We could leak this picture to the press," she suggested, her voice low.

"Not yet. I'll find Beanpole and see if he can ID this man. If he's sober, that is."

"I've talked to the techs," she said, accepting his decision. "They've got the detonated bomb fragments unpacked and they set up an examination plan. They're taking high-def photos of everything they found and they're going over the fragments from the explosion, piece by piece. But that could take a while. They'll go over every inch of any fragment found on that bomb site and take their time puttingthings together."

"Like weeks." He nodded, fatigue cloaking his face. "Okay. Ilana Hawkins will work with the FBI and CSI to figure it out. She's the best forensic tech we have, and the lab team can discover even the most minute clues. Meantime, I'm going to go back over the Tick's file and see if I can find any markers that might match whatever they find."

Brianne stared up at him. "Do you think they could be the same man?"

"I don't know yet," he replied. "But Tommy picked up on something on that guy in the park and I'm thinking it was more than just the bomb. Like Tommy recognized his signature from another time, which means it could easily boil down to fibers or some sort of scent unique to this person or his clothes."

"Stella alerted, too. Which means her bomb-detection training is paying off."

Gavin didn't argue with that. "Chief Jameson will need a lot of evidence to make a case, but my gut tells me the Fourth of July bomber could also be the Tick."

"Why would the Tick veer off to the park?" Brianne asked, her mind going to places she didn't want to see.

"That's the burning question," Gavin said. "Let's go talk to Noah and explain what we know for now. Then we'll talk to him about this other case."

Brianne nodded and then said, "Hey, go have a shower first. Put on your sweats, and I'll send your uniform out to be cleaned. Then I'll meet you back here."

Gavin actually smiled at that. "You might make a good wife yet," he deadpanned with a grin.

Bristling, she replied, "I don't intend to stay home wearing an apron, Sutherland, so let's get something straight. If I play the part of your wife, I'm going to be a pampered socialite who always gets her way. Don't expect me to cook and clean for you or pick up your dirty clothes."

"But you're willing to help with my dry cleaning?"

"That's easy. I just get on the phone and call someone. Mine needs cleaning, too."

"It's a start," he said. "I think I'll have that shower and then find some of that battery acid we call coffee. Thanks, Bree."

She smiled and watched him head toward the down-stairs locker rooms, her mind whirling between cook-ing and cleaning or running behind a K-9 partner. She preferred the latter.

But she sure wouldn't mind spending some down-time with tall, stubborn and hard-to-read Gavin Suther-land.

Gavin got dressed as quickly as possible, then went back into the training arena to get Tommy. When he saw Tommy curled up in his kennel, he decided to leave his partner there for a few minutes. The springer worked hard and rarely complained.

Gavin called to one of the handlers. "I'm letting Tommy rest a while, okay?"

The handler nodded. "You both need to rest after last night—and this morning."

Gavin agreed with that, but he was too wired to stay still. That park bombing smacked of a setup, as did the shooting, but he needed more to go on before he went to Chief Noah Jameson with his conspiracy theory. They were getting back on an even footing and he did not want to mess that up. Noah liked solid evidence. They all did. He intended to find that evidence.

When he got back upstairs, he went straight to the conference room, surprised to see Brianne had already set up a white board with all the details of last night's bombing. The woman thrived on being knee-deep in any case.

Gavin studied the mug shot of the man Brianne be-lieved to be the suspect. He'd never seen a photo of the Tick since the man always wore black, mostly hoodies, kept his face away from cameras and disguised himself with beards and mustaches, sometimes in different colors. But the eyebrows here were interesting. Real or fake? Hard to say.

Brianne came in with coffee and two big peach Danishes. "Food, Gavin. Eat."

He sat down and rubbed his eyes. "Man, I'm beat."

"I know. Me, too."

She sure didn't look tired with her neat and tidy hair off her face in a tight bun. She wore very little makeup, so he could enjoy the smattering of freckles tossed like sparkled dust across her cheeks and nose. And those eyes—a deep, rich brown that reminded him of the ancient trees up in the Poconos. She had the eyes of an old soul, full of determination and stubbornness, defiance and acceptance. Nothing got past this woman. He'd be wise to remember that and he'd be wise to heed the warning bells in his head. They worked together. Nothing more.

"Hey," Brianne said. "Are you okay?"

Gavin blinked. Had he been staring? "Just putting things together in my head."

Things like walking in an old forest with her, holding her hand, kissing her.

Whoa on that. "It's just nagging me." *True.*

She was nagging him. Being so involved with her and this case—nagging him. Asking her to help him with the other case—nagging him big time. Because he'd given her an in and she wouldn't back down.

"You mean, because now we're dealing with two different bombers or that they could both be the same person?"

"Yeah, that."

"Something else?" She stood, daring him to dispute her.

"You, Bree."

"Me? What have I done? Are you mad that I jumped right into this? Isn't that what we're supposed to do? Are you like all the others, Gavin?"

"If you mean against women officers, no." He shook his head and smiled. "Are you finished?"

"I'm just getting started. I can't believe—"

"Relax, will you?" he said before he bit into the sugarcoated Danish. "You haven't done anything wrong. You've done everything right. I need someone to help me with this—I've been obsessed with the Tick since I realized he had to have been the one who set off a bomb in the Williamsburg building and all the others, too, for that matter."

"So what's your problem?"

"I don't have a problem. Other than Tommy, I'm not used to a partner."

"You asked me to help. Are you saying you don't work well with humans?"

"I'm fine with humans and yes, I did ask you to help, but I don't want to put you in unnecessary danger."

"That's my job. Is this about me being a woman?"

"Do people still discriminate like that?" he asked, meaning it. "That did not enter my mind, other than noticing that you are definitely a woman."

She stopped, staring at him in a new way that almost scared him. "Oh, I get it. You like me? Right? I mean, you did ask me to go for coffee? Just a friendly thing? Are you flirting with me, Gavin? Is that it? I scare you and you don't want to get involved with a coworker, so you're telling me I'm a problem?"

"That's not what I meant." But she was close. He didn't need a work-time romance. Other such notions had taught him to never cross that line, especially now when he'd just been through too much scrutiny already. Romancing a co-worker wasn't wise.

Brianne sat down across from him and attacked her Danish. "First, we *are* working together, so get over the notion that anything else can happen between us." Chewing with determination she stared him down. "And second, this is a juicy case. I know we're on the task force to find Chief Jameson's killer and I'm all over that one, too. But bomb detection is our thing. You and me. Our thing. So I'm in now, Gavin. Unless the chief tells us otherwise. Got it?"

Gavin took it all in. Her magnificent display of letting him have it with both barrels only reinforced that he was in over his head with her. "Yeah, that," he said, wishing he'd kept his mouth shut on asking her to be in on it.

"Oh, I get it. You're regretting asking me, right?"

"Just a tad."

"Gavin, get over yourself. Are we doing this or not?"

"We're doing it," he said, grudgingly. "I need your help and upon further thinking, I'd say you're perfect for the job."

"I do watch a lot of those home-buying shows— you know the ones on the channel that shows people searching for the perfect house. And another show that's all about New York real estate. I can play the part. I just need a designer purse and some kicking shoes and makeup and a fancy car and a big wallet."

"The chief will flip over that budget."

"Go big or go home," she quipped. "I have connections. I think I can pull that part off. Let's go lay out the case for him." Then she gave him that stare of steel. "And, Gavin, I mean the whole case. We have to tell him we think all of this could be the work of one man."

Gavin finished his Danish and coffee, his mind boiling with the hows and whys of these two cases. He needed to talk to Noah. Couldn't leave anything to chance with such a dangerous man setting off bombs all over New York City.

"Let me gather my files and links," he said, admiration for Brianne's spunk giving him hope. He'd either become a better man for having her on his side or she'd do him in, piece by piece.

But for now, he had to trust her.

He needed a fake wife.

The interim chief stared at both of them as if they'd changed into two-headed monsters. "Are you serious?"

"Very," Gavin said, gearing up for a battle. "You know I've been working this case for months and I've contributed to trying to find Jordan's murderer, too. But this is getting out of hand, sir. I need Officer Hayes to assist me with this undercover operation."

"Why Officer Hayes?" Noah asked, his no-nonsense expression intimidating, his green eyes full of doubt.

Gavin refused to be intimidated, however. "She's a good officer, she's trained in bomb detection and she's training Stella—the dog that first picked up the Fourth of July bomber's scent."

"I have the facts, Sutherland," Noah said, his gaze moving between them. "But why do you need a partner now?"

Brianne sat up. "Sir, we think we'd get farther as a

couple. It looks more believable and…two sets of eyes are always better than one."

Noah positioned his stare on Brianne. "And you're willing to do this? Put yourself at risk?"

"I put myself at risk every day, sir," she replied, cool as mint-infused lemonade. "This is no different. I stared into that bomber's face. I agree with Gavin. This could be the same man."

"I'm not buying that," Noah replied, shaking his head. "Coincidence. This is a big city with a hundred threats a day. Threats that we contain while people go about their business, never knowing what we've done."

"We don't think it was coincidence," Gavin replied, aggravated that his superior couldn't trust him. "But until we hear back from the crime lab, we have to go on the assumption that the Tick will strike again. You know how brutal the real estate business is, sir. Especially in Manhattan. We can't risk someone else getting hurt or killed."

Noah leaned back in his chair, his frown weary with fatigue. "And what about finding my brother's killer?"

"We'll continue to do what needs to be done on that," Gavin assured him. "For as long as it takes."

Noah sat silent for a minute. A very long minute.

"All right. This is highly irregular because K-9 officers don't usually go undercover, but using the dogs while you make a few inquiries can't hurt. Just play it safe and don't get too involved in going deep." Waving his hands at them, he added, "Fill out the proper papers on what you need and watch the cost because we don't have much of a budget. Keep me updated and… Gavin, be careful."

Gavin nodded and stood. "Thanks. We'll get this figured out."

"I hope so," Noah replied. Then he looked Gavin in the eye. "I wasn't sure about taking this job and I'm still not sure. I'm trying to do my best. I know we put you through the wringer but...he was my brother. No stone unturned, even when it meant interrogating you."

"I agree," Gavin said, taking the apology as a good sign. "No stone unturned. You have my word on that. If you get any leads, send them to us, sir."

They left Noah's office in silence and didn't speak again until they were outside.

Then Brianne turned to him and gave him an appreciative smile. "You are one tough cop, Gavin."

"Right back at you."

She started for her car, Stella trailing along. "I guess we start fresh tomorrow, right?"

He nodded. "I'll call the next agent on my real estate list and set up a showing with him. He mentioned some apartment buildings in Midtown and the Upper West Side. I'll ask him to show us one of those to begin with and we'll work our way toward a targeted building. Might take a couple of days."

"Meantime, we can do what needs to be done on Jordan's case."

"Good plan."

Then she asked, "How are we going to coordinate this undercover thing?"

He stopped with her near where their cars were parked. "There's a safe house I've been using in Midtown whenever I'm in Manhattan on this case. Approved from the top for certain cases." He gave her the address of a boutique hotel on a quiet side street. "Suite

305. I'll pick you up there each time we're on this case. Be dressed and ready to play your part."

"As your wife," she said, her eyes holding his. "Linus and Alice Reinhart. Catchy names, by the way."

He'd discussed their cover with her earlier.

"Yes, as my wife." Then, because he wanted to get a rise out of her, he added, "But please don't wear any aprons, okay?"

She threw it right back into his face. "No apron, I can assure you. Alice Reinhart doesn't wear aprons, darling."

Gavin couldn't stop his grin. "I can't wait."

He let Tommy into his SUV kennel and then watched as she did the same with Stella, his protective nature taking over.

Tomorrow, they began the real work. The dangerous work.

He prayed he'd be able to keep her safe.

SIX

Two days later, Gavin drove the rental car through the small portico in front of the Gable Hotel. The department used this discreet, out-of-the-way spot as a safe house as needed since it looked more like a Victorian house than a true hotel. The owners were also discreet, and the place had a top-notch security system to boot.

Gavin entered and waved to the desk clerk, then headed up to the assigned room and tapped on the door. "It's Gavin and Tommy."

They'd both agreed to let Stella continue training with another handler for a few days while they used Tommy as Brianne's companion dog. So it would be strange seeing her without Stella at her side. Also it would be a shock to see her out of uniform and actually dressed in civilian clothes.

All of that went out of Gavin's head as he stared at the woman who opened the door and then stood back.

Brianne Hayes sure cleaned up nicely.

She wore her hair swept up in a way that probably required technique but looked like she'd just tossed it together with a big clip. And it looked darker. She wore a red dress. Red with just enough sleeve to be demure and a flowing skirt that showed off her waist before it flowed down to her knees. Pearls coiled around her neck and her shoes were tall with lots of black straps. The purse had some famous designer's initials all over it and shouted money.

"Hi," she said. Then she leaned down and patted Tommy's wiry spotted fur before wrapping a sparkling rhinestone and black leather dog collar around his neck.

"So he looks the part," she said with a shrug and a smile.

Tommy shot Gavin a helpless look but didn't move a muscle. The K-9 was nothing if not professional, but this? *Seriously?*

"Seriously," Gavin replied to Tommy's perplexed stare. Yes, he and Tommy were so used to talking back and forth they could read each other's expressions.

"Doesn't he look like a pampered pooch?" Brianne asked, eying the sparkling leather collar. "I tried to find one that looked mannish."

"Oh, he looks mannish all right," Gavin said, wondering if his suit came off expensive enough to make him look mannish. And he was still stunned by just watching her walk toward him in those shoes and that dress. Giving Tommy a brush of assurance, he whispered, "Don't worry, buddy. A brand new tennis ball is in your future."

She stood and adjusted her purse, a whiff of some sweet, exotic scent flowing around her. "Ready?"

"I don't know. How do *I* look?" he asked, unable to get anything else to come out of his mouth.

"Good," she said in a tone that showed she meant it. "The mustache matches your eyes."

"What did you do to your hair?" he asked, hoping it wasn't permanent.

"Temporary dye. It'll wash out."

Having solved that mystery, he got down to business.

"Did getting here go okay?" he asked as they stepped down the winding staircase to the first floor.

Nodding again to the front desk clerk, Gavin led her out onto the steps of the old brownstone where they both did a scan of the surrounding quiet tree-shaded street.

"I got up early and took the subway in from head-quarters—checked that I wasn't being tailed—and then flashed my badge to the desk clerk, as you instructed. She took me right up to the suite and I spent most of the morning pampering myself and getting ready. This place is nice in an old-fashioned way. I left my stuff here so I need to come back later today, but I do have the room overnight if needed."

Glad to hear no one followed her, Gavin took her arm and escorted her down the steps. At first, she frowned at his gesture. "For show," he quickly explained while he ignored the soft skin that felt warm against his cal-lused fingers.

"Oh, okay then." She took in the car. "Fancy sedan? Did the chief approve this?"

"He did, grudgingly," Gavin admitted, his gaze mov-ing over the sleek gray car before he checked the street. "But it takes money to make money and in this case, it takes a fancy car to flush out corrupt people. Besides, I know a guy who knows a guy at the rental company. I got the friends-and-family rate."

He opened the door for her, causing her to frown. "Part of the cover," he said to hide the fact that he enjoyed doing it. "A gentleman always takes care of his lady."

Brianne gave him a perplexed glance and then let Tommy onto the backseat. Turning, she slid into the car, her actions as prim as any socialite's.

"You sure look nice," he said.

"Just part of the cover," she mimicked, a teasing twinkle in her eyes.

She enjoyed tormenting him!

The woman might be all business on the surface but underneath she was a scamp. Making him squirm while he tried to stay focused.

"You're enjoying this too much," he said. "But I am getting to know the real you."

"You don't know the real me," she said, her tone serious now. "And since I'm wearing borrowed clothes and makeup that costs more than a week's salary, you have to know this kind of getup is so not me."

"Is it okay if I get to know you?" he replied, treading that line between being professional and falling at her feet in surrender.

"I'm good with that," she said. "But right now, we need to go over our cover material. You know the real estate agents will do a thorough background check on us so they can drool over our assets."

"All taken care of," he said to get back on track. "Since I set up my own background months ago, and some of them know I've been single, I went back and added you as my new bride. We met in the Hamptons and fell in love, had a whirlwind marriage and honeymooned in Europe. Now we need a place to live in Manhattan."

"Do I work?"

"Not anymore, darling."

"What if I have a career and I'm a highly independent woman?"

"We can go with that, too."

"And what do you do, Linus, my new husband?"

Loving the way that sounded on her lips, he said, "I'm an entrepreneur who dabbles in real estate investments on a big scale. So we'll look at the penthouse, but we'd like to buy an older building and tear it down. Progress, of course. We need to drop that into the conversation, by the way."

"Perfect. So we're covered there."

"Solid. Danielle and our other techs enjoyed setting this one up for us."

Brianne scanned the road ahead. "Dani is like a fairy godmother and with her curly blond hair and all the bling she wears, she would know. She gave me some great fashion tips and she knows this guy who sells purses. Don't ask."

Gavin silently thanked their eclectic tech analyst, yet again. Then he got down to business. "The park bombing concerns me in more ways than one. What if I've been made already? What if we're walking into a trap?"

"We have to make *them* believe *us*, Gavin," she said. "And if it is a trap, then we find a way to get out and bring them down."

"You shouldn't sound so bold and brave."

"We both look completely different today than we did at the park the other night. Even if the bomber noticed us, we were in uniform with patrol hats covering most of our hair. And today, we won't come face-to-face with the alleged bomber, right?"

"I sure hope not. Not yet, anyway. I want to get to the person hiring the man."

Brianne watched the road and kept looking around at the interior of the car. "We have to be bold and brave. It's our job. So don't make it sound like you're not the same way. I've seen you in action. I can take care of myself, but I'm also going to watch out for you. You'd do the same for me."

He couldn't argue with her spot-on logic. "Okay, but if things get out of hand, promise you'll be careful."

"I'm always careful," she replied.

He worried she liked this stuff too much. She was good at her job, yes, but the adrenaline rush could take over sometimes. She could become reckless. He prayed against that. He wasn't reckless. Maybe that's why he got passed up for promotions. He wasn't scared of taking matters into his own hands, but Granny Irene had taught him to be thorough and always do what was right. While Brianne seemed to have those same values, he knew this job could go to a person's head, too. Or mess with a person's head. One slip and it would all be over.

"Bree, I mean it. This is dangerous work."

"I know that," she said. "I'm not so careless that I'd put myself or you and Tommy in danger. I've done my homework. I memorized your files on this case and I've done some research on my own. These people target buildings in transition, the kind that need a quick sell. Explosions can bring that about easily enough." Then she shrugged. "This is New York. For someone with a lot of money, anything is possible. Buyouts are common here but then so is corruption."

"Okay then." Impressed, he shifted the car and

headed through the Manhattan traffic, his heart tripping over itself while he hoped he wouldn't regret this.
They had a part to play, but he preferred real life.

And maybe way down the road, a date so he could
relax with the real Brianne Hayes.

As they got closer to the property, he said, "This is
the Sherriman Building, owned by Sherriman Properties. Our real estate agent is Justin Sanelli from the
Rexx Agency, a hotshot playboy who brags about getting the best deals in town. If a seller won't come down
on the price, Justin makes it happen. He is the big dog
at Rexx and has about twenty agents under him."

"So he's not first on our list. I read in your report
you'd already ruled out three others since they didn't
fit the mode."

"No, he's number four. He might not be the last, but
he got on my radar after I met him at an open house. I
did some research on him but couldn't pin anything to
him. After attending business school and getting his real
estate license, he hired on with a small agency in Chelsea and worked his way up. Now he travels in high-up
circles and works the room with his charm."

"I'm guessing his persuasive tactics are enlighten-
ing," she said, "in a booming way."

"That's what I think. Just as you said, his firm
swoops in when a building is in trouble, buys out the
frustrated person or company holding the deed to the
entire property or pushes the owners out. Then Sanelli
gets a good deal and a prime piece of real estate, touting that he *rescues* distressed properties and flips them
to make them million-dollar investments."

"I can't believe someone hasn't noticed this pattern before."

"Think about it," Gavin said as he maneuvered the smooth-riding car through the stop-and-go traffic. "All the buildings for sale in New York and accidents happening every day—easy to let something like this slip right on by. We got a break with that explosion in Williamsburg when Tommy picked up on what remained of the bomb. Before that, we were just working with what looked like a boiler explosion in the maintenance room. Now that scent is embedded in his system. The Tick isn't careless, but something went wrong there and he left us just a trace of his bomb-making DNA. And now I'm onto him."

"And if he's also the Fourth of July bomber, Tommy and Stella both have his number, too."

When they arrived at the building, Brianne stared up the redbrick structure trimmed in white stone and intricate molding. "It's not as tall as most."

"No, just fifteen floors, but exclusive. Prewar at its best with those tall ceilings, big rooms and solid walls. We're looking at the penthouse—three bedrooms and three baths—and many millions of dollars. It used to be four apartments, but someone had a big family and combined all of them."

"Who has that kind of money?"

"It's passed hands several times and been renovated. The original owners made a pretty penny when they sold it about five years ago. But the rest of the building needs a lot of work."

"So Justin sees an opportunity here."

"Yes. The company that owns the building is holding out for a high price, but Justin assures me he can get them down. So first we focus on the penthouse and then we tell him we'd like to buy the entire building."

"Yeah, right," she said. "Why do people have to be so greedy? He'll get the current owner to come down but then he'll still make a profit because he'll turn around and broker the whole building."

"Especially if he blows up part of the building and sends down the property value because of structural problems. The current residents will be so ready to sell, one by one. The Tick thrives on being a domestic terrorist."

Gavin shot Brianne one last look as he pulled the car up to the curb in front of the complex with its adjacent garage and gave his name to the valet attendant. "Linus and Alice Reinhart, here to see Justin Sanelli."

The dour guard at the door gave them and their vehicle a once-over and nodded to the young valet. They were in.

There would be no turning back after this.

Once they were out of the car, the burly guard studied them and then sent a text upward. "Go ahead," he finally said after getting a reply, seemingly bored with all of it.

After the valet took the car, they made their way to the spacious lobby where a fountain gurgled and soft music played. The place looked rundown but held a patina of elegance. Another guard behind the rounded desk nodded and walked with them to the elevator. He, too, eyed them in a money-hungry but bored way. "Mr. Sanelli is on his way down."

"Fancy," Brianne whispered, hoping her eyes didn't pop out of her head. She tried to look as bored as the guards they'd just encountered, but her heart raced and she couldn't stop the awe in seeing such a historic and expensive building. "Very art deco."

Tommy did his part. He sniffed as any dog would but stayed near her since she held his leash. She had to control herself or the K-9 would pick up on her nervous energy. But Tommy knew all the tricks of the trade and he could handle a fake out same as they could.

Gavin kept his voice low. "Sanelli's meeting us here because, as I mentioned, a while back I encountered him at an open house in another building similar to this one. After we'd talked a while, I explained what I was looking for."

Gavin had told her earlier that Justin had hinted about his unique ways of getting stubborn sellers to cave and agree to any offers. *He has ways*, Gavin now reaffirmed. Business was booming.

Gavin had honed in on Sanelli, his gut telling him this might be their man. "I've been watching him for weeks but nothing out of the ordinary. He's a hustler but I can't pin anything definite on him."

"Ah, the setup," she replied, her smile serene as they waited for Justin to come down and escort them to the top of the building. "I'll pretend I'm interested in the whole building. I mean, only the best for my sweet boy."

Gavin rolled his eyes. "You'd buy a building just to please your dog?"

The elevator dinged, and she went into full-on fake mode.

"Linus, you know T-Boy is more than a dog," she said, her voice rising as she stared over at him. "T-Boy is my companion, a sure comfort when you leave me alone and go off on yet another scouting-for-real-estate trip."

Gavin obviously figured their man would be interested and went with it. "Alice, I have to travel for work, darling. But if you think buying a building will make you and T-Boy happy, then that's what we'll do. And I'll try to find more business ventures in the city so I can stay home with you more."

Alice sent him an air-kiss and then giggled, pushing past him to the average-looking man standing behind Gavin. "You must be Justin. Did you hear us bickering?"

Justin Sanelli laughed and gently shook her hand, his frosty blue eyes wide with obvious glee. "I call that negotiating," he chirped. "And if you're serious about wanting the entire building, I can work with you on that."

"Let's talk upstairs," Gavin said, shooting his wife an indulgent smile.

They got in the elevator with the blond-haired man who wore what looked like a tailor-made suit. Brianne watched the elevator stop on the P level. Penthouse.

Brianne winked at Gavin, her arm on his, her heart doing funny little skittish leaps. "This is an impressive building. I love the crown molding and the big windows."

Justin did an elaborate bow. "Then you're really going to love the penthouse." With a flourish, he opened the doors and stood back. "Best view in the city."

Brianne looked through the massive rooms and out into the city beyond, her gaze moving past the buildings and toward the Hudson River.

Then she clapped her hands and giggled. "I can't wait to see the rest of this place."

Gavin gave her a brilliant fake smile.

But Brianne wished he'd really smile at her. He looked handsome in his nice suit, his dark hair shining and combed.

She might be living in a fantasy world right this minute, but her mind wandered beyond large apartments with beautiful views. She thought of a small fenced yard and dogs running along with children, dinner on the table and her man by her side. Why did she have to envision Gavin in that role?

Impossible.

"Let's go inside," Justin said, bursting her bubble.

Giggling again, she purred down to Tommy. "What do you think, T-Boy? Could this be our new home?"

The dog woofed, but she couldn't be sure if he agreed with her or if he was just disgusted. She was sure of one thing. Tommy had not alerted on the real estate broker, which meant he didn't have any trace of explosives on him today.

Gavin grinned and took her hand. When he squeezed it reassuringly, Brianne felt an explosion inside her heart.

An explosion every bit as scary and dangerous as the real thing. For the first time since she'd signed up for this mission, Brianne had to wonder if she'd made a huge mistake.

SEVEN

Justin Sanelli primed himself like a dancer trying to win a competition, full of superlatives and over-the-top bragging rights. "We grossed close to half-a-billion dollars last year and we should surpass that this year. I have an outstanding team, fabulous and ruthless. We get properties moving."

"Thank you for personally meeting us here," Gavin said, his expression showing pretend-fatigue. "We are certainly impressed."

Brianne went to the windows again to stare out at the view. Exposure to the north, south and east. Central Park wasn't that far from here and Fifth Avenue flowed just around the corner. There was a concierge, a doorman and those guards they'd endured…a fitness center and rooftop pool… Luxury. The way the sunshine shot through these big windows showed a different side of life. This sun highlighted beautiful furniture and expensive artwork, not the grit and grime she saw down there on the street. The deck—covered with wrought iron, cushioned furniture, thriving dish gardens and parlor palms that would have to be moved inside come winter—was bigger than the basement apartment she lived in.

Gavin came up behind her and put his arms around her. Brianne almost decked him and then remembered he was her pretend-husband. So, for just a moment, she leaned into the strength of his arms and enjoyed the view, her heart hurting for all of the people who didn't have this panoramic indulgence.

"What are you thinking, sweetheart?" he asked, his fingers covering her hands.

Brianne put away her thoughts, his endearments and went back to work. "I'm thinking I love this penthouse and I want this whole building." Then she turned and put on a good show for Justin Sanelli. "I mean, this is prime property. Think of what we could do if we tore this building down and started from scratch." Looking up into Gavin's questioning eyes, she touched her hand to his jaw and felt his pulse quicken. "Let's keep this one in mind but maybe we should tour a few more. I know we can afford this but... I also know how to negotiate."

"You are very good at negotiating and saving money is important," Gavin responded, his tone husky. "And yet I want to give you the world. Everything you've ever dreamed of."

Something in his words caught Brianne and held her, but the look in his dark eyes made her dream of that house in the suburbs again. The best view was the one you could treasure each and every day, a blessing, a home, a safe haven. She couldn't see that view here in this over-the-top fancy environment.

But she sure could see that view in Gavin's eyes.

Justin coughed, not wanting to miss this opportunity. "I can work on the owner. He's sentimental since his mother lived in this building until the day she died. And since you mentioned the whole building, I can make sellers see the light. Just name your price and we'll get everyone who's still left here to agree to your offer."

Gavin shot Brianne a warning glance. "We'll consider this one, Justin. But we'd like to look around over the next couple of weeks. I have a good feeling we'll be back, but we never buy the first thing we look at."

Justin hid his disappointment well. "I'll see what else I can find. So you're interested in the best for less, correct?"

"Correct, and we are very interested in buildings such as this one—the whole building," Gavin said, his eyes on Brianne. "Keep doing what you're doing and I'm sure we'll find a property that meets our needs very soon."

They left on good terms. Justin would shake down the whole of Manhattan to find them a bargain—one that would ultimately bring them all what they wanted.

And maybe bring jail time for the broker.

Brianne waited until they were back in the sleek sedan before she let out a breath. "If he is our man, he's going to have a very hard time adjusting to a jail cell."

"Yep." Gavin watched the traffic and kept checking the mirrors for any tails. "Tommy didn't alert on him, so I know he's not our possible bomber, but I had hoped for something to come out of this. I could be wrong all around."

"Well, he could be working for someone. Same as the Tick. We need to get to the big guy."

Gavin nodded and watched the road, concern clouding his handsome face.

Wondering why he remained so quiet, she tried again. "I'm starving. Let's find some food."

"We need to change first. Unless you want me to take you to a restaurant I really can't afford."

"We can change at the safe house," she suggested. "Then I want to go home. I'll take the subway back to get my vehicle from headquarters."

"I'll take you after we change and eat."

"No, I don't expect that," she replied, thinking she could just eat at home by herself. Then she went on without thinking. "I live with my parents, but they're visiting my aunt and uncle out on Long Island for a few weeks. We can order a pizza and unwind at my house."

Gavin gave her a panicked glance. "Uh, I don't know…"

From the look on his face, he obviously didn't like that idea. "I mean, I guess we could do that but—"

"Okay then, forget it. I'm beat and I can't wait to get out of these clothes."

"I could go for pizza," he finally said. "I'm trying to figure out the logistics. I have to hide our fancy car in a secure parking garage that has excellent surveillance. My vehicle is parked around from where I need to leave our rented car."

Relaxing, she understood his hesitation. "You don't want to blow your cover."

"Right."

"Sure, you can give me a ride to headquarters. Makes sense. I'm dying to ditch this dress—it's a loaner so I can't keep it. At least I can bring Stella home with me if we swing by headquarters."

"Too bad you can't keep the dress," he said and then looked sheepish. "I mean, it's nice."

"Nice? Danielle borrowed it from a sample sale at Saks. She knows people there. This is more than nice. It's an original—a designer dress."

"I should have said that it's a knockout dress and I can tell by the cut and the thread that it's worth *every* dollar—several hundred—someone might spend to buy it."

"That's better."

Sending her an appreciative glance, he asked, "Are you sure you don't want to walk through the training yard to get Stella wearing that outfit?"

That made her laugh. "I'm not going anywhere near the training arena until I've changed. Do you want to eat pizza at my house or not, 'cause I'm ordering one with or without you, Sutherland."

He studied her and then nodded. "I'm in."

"Change first. Garage second. Headquarters third. Pizza at my house—finally."

"That's a good plan, Bree," he said. "We have to be careful with this whole operation."

"Then let's take the long way back to the garage," she suggested. "Just in case."

Gavin nodded and meandered through the city to switch cars. Careful, they made their way out of the garage on foot and headed toward his official SUV. The sun began to descend behind the buildings to the west and the streets filled with commuters on their way home from work.

Why did the night seem so sinister? The heat sizzled over the asphalt and concrete in hot waves.

"So far, so good." His relief was obvious after they were in his vehicle and going through the Queens–Midtown Tunnel. "I don't think anyone followed us," he said an hour later. They turned toward the K-9 Unit building. "We can meet back at our vehicles after you get Stella. I'll follow you to your house."

"Okay, it's not too far from headquarters," she replied. "I live in Corona."

"Will you be safe?"

Wondering why he worried so much, Brianne stiffened her spine. "Gavin, seriously? I'll see you back here and I'll have Stella with me. We'll meet at my house for pizza."

Once they entered the lobby, Brianne kept her head up and took the stairs down to the training arena, the sound of her sturdy heels clicking an echo that sounded too loud in her ears. Taking a quick shower in the women's locker room where she'd stashed her clothes earlier, she rinsed the dark color out of her hair.

Being a rich wife had zapped her.

The locker room looked empty so she hurried to her locker and made sure she had everything in order before she left for the day. Then she ran a hand through her hair and twisted it up into a damp bun.

"Free," she said, hurrying to find Stella. When she ran into Noah Jameson near the stairs, she nodded. "Sir."

His gaze swept over her. "How did it go, Officer Hayes? Give me a report."

She didn't want to steal Gavin's thunder, but her superior had asked her a direct question. "We made contact with a man who could be one of our suspects." She went on to explain Justin Sanelli. "But this is just the beginning. It's possible he's hiring the Tick to make things happen."

"I sure hope we find that bomber," Noah said.

"You're both going out on a limb here and this is highly unusual. But I'm learning sometimes we have to bend the rules to find justice."

Brianne worried about their interim chief. Noah wanted justice for his brother, Jordan. Would his grief cause him to do whatever it took, no matter the cost? She'd said a lot of prayers for the three remaining Jameson brothers. They were tough but sooner or later the grief could cave in. "Yes, sir, but we'll stay within the rules so we don't mess up."

Noah nodded, and then he gave her a twisted smile. "You sure seem to be in a hurry to get home. Long day?"

Embarrassed, she lowered her head. "Uh…you saw me coming in?"

"I see everyone who comes and goes," Noah replied. "Just be careful. We've all been dealing with a lot lately."

"Yes, sir, I plan to stay alert. And Gavin's got my back."

"I hope so," the chief replied. "I'm counting on it."

Now she could see why this case meant so much to Gavin. He still had a lot to prove to the Jameson brothers.

Her heart hurt, knowing he had no one to turn to.

That's wrong, she thought. *He has me now. And I've got his back, too.* She didn't know when she'd come to that conclusion but…she wouldn't let Gavin down. She'd start a new prayer thread for Gavin—asking the Lord to protect her temporary partner.

After checking her phone for any messages—one from her mom telling her they were having fun and reminding her to stay safe, but nothing else much—Brianne followed the chief to the K-9 training area. She saw Gavin standing with Tommy, talking to Carter Jameson. Of all the brothers, Carter reached out to Gavin the most. They seemed close again, at least.

She nodded at them and after chatting with the chief a while, went to find Stella. Rookie K-9 Officer Lani Branson greeted her. "Hey, we need to have another girls night soon. I sure could use one."

"I need that, too," Brianne answered as she walked toward her friend and saw Stella running toward them from the kennel area. "It's been crazy lately, but I'll try to squeeze one in soon."

Lani, blonde, buff and so New York, looked more like a model than an officer of the law. She handed off Stella to Brianne, her graceful and easy moves reminding Brianne she'd once been an actor and a dancer. But she'd given that up, taught self-defense classes and then decided to become a K-9 officer. Talk about a career turnaround.

"Heard you're on a job with Gavin Sutherland," Lani said with a knowing grin. "How's that going?"

Not wanting to give too much away since the unit members assumed they were working on Jordan's case and the bombing in the park, Brianne said, "It's interesting. A little nerve-wracking."

Lani gave her an unabashed stare. "I'm thinking you'll be good for Gavin. He's intense."

"He can be," Brianne admitted. "But then so can I. We're working through it."

She'd heard rumors that the chief and Gavin had once been friends and Gavin had confirmed that. But something had happened years ago to drive them apart. An argument about how to conduct a training session had come between them, but Brianne didn't plan on trying to get the details out of Gavin until he wanted to talk.

Maybe Brianne could get Gavin to open up about that. Maybe over pizza or, if not, then later when he trusted her more. She'd suggested a meal and some down time so she could get a better read on the man. She liked knowing she could trust a person and so far she trusted Gavin. But she wanted him to trust her and not worry about her. She could handle this.

Well, she could handle the case and the danger.

Her erratic feelings regarding her temporary partner? Another matter altogether. She'd have to keep a close watch over her heart with this one.

"Hey, you okay?" Lani asked. "Is Gavin already giving you grief?"

"You could say that, but this is only a temporary partnership, so I'll be okay."

Lani discreetly dropped the subject of Gavin and gave Stella a parting pat. "We had a good workout today. She found bomb materials we'd planted in the locker room and out in the training yard. This girl definitely has a nose for explosives."

"Good to know," Brianne said, pleased. "Ready to go home, Miss Stella?"

Stella danced around to give Lani a goodbye smile. Then she looked up at Brianne for further instructions.

Laughing, Brianne said, "Let's go then."

Brianne took her leash, noting she wore a black training vest to get her acclimated to wearing a bulletproof vest later. "Dinner soon, Lani. And we'll invite Faith, too." The single mom, also a K-9 officer, had a cute four-year-old named Jane. She could always use a break.

"That's a plan," Lani said, her gaze moving from Brianne to where Gavin and Carter stood. "I think Gavin's been waiting for you."

Brianne didn't tell her friend she was having pizza with Gavin Sutherland. Lani would jump to the wrong conclusion. So she just waved and headed toward Gavin and Carter. And noticed the chief hurrying back upstairs, walking right past the too-curious Lani without a word.

Gavin walked with her out to her vehicle and did a thorough scan of the surrounding area.

Brianne did the same. Someone could be watching them right now. Ignoring that feeling, she said, "I'll pick up the pizza. You have my address, right?"

"Got it," he said, his gaze moving back and forth. "You should take Tommy with you, too."

"I have Stella. She can bark, you know."

"I know that but… Tommy is a seasoned K-9."

"Gavin, stop it. If you keep this up, you'll have me changing my mind. You have to trust me to do my job."

"I can't help it. This is dangerous, and I shouldn't have dragged you into it."

"Well, too late to worry about that." Cutting him some slack, she added, "My dad bought an alarm a couple of years ago. And Stella and I like quiet time when we first get home. Girl talk and all."

"So you can talk about me?" he quipped.

Tommy's ears lifted. "See, Tommy wants to hear, too."

"Of course. He's probably wondering why you and I were so lovey-dovey earlier."

The shrewd dog looked from him to Brianne, his

tongue hanging out in what could only be described as a smile.

Gavin watched as she let Stella into the kennel and then turned to open the SUV door. "I'll lay off but... be careful."

"Always. I'll see you soon, with pizza—one pepperoni and one veggie."

He walked backward to his vehicle. "Don't eat all of the pepperoni before I get there."

A bit later, Brianne had the pizza and drove home, keeping an eye on any vehicles behind her. But no one turned off to follow her up her street. Careful when she got out, she once again did a scan of the quiet area and saw nothing out of the ordinary. So she opened the door and turned on the lights.

"Search," she told Stella, to test the newbie and to reassure herself. Stella took off, glad to have a command but came back to stare up at her. "What's wrong?" Brianne asked, her heart rate accelerating. Placing the pizza on the counter, she tugged at her gun holster. "Search," she said again, moving behind Stella through the empty house.

Stella took her downstairs, to the door that opened from her basement apartment to the backyard. Not waiting, Brianne opened the back door, noticed the motion detector light was on and sent Stella out. "Find."

Stella took off.

Brianne thought she heard a noise out by the back fence but before she could check it out, the doorbell rang upstairs.

She jumped.

Stella barked.

Another noise, shuffling and then footsteps running away.

Brianne started out the back door but the bell rang again. Should she go after the intruder or shout out to Gavin? Hurrying since she didn't even have her phone, she held her gun in front of her and used the security light to check the backyard. Nothing.

But Stella sat by the far fence, a soft growl emitting from the dog's throat. Someone had been here and left, probably hopping over the fence. But the outside door to her apartment was intact. No damage.

Maybe Gavin was wise to be so cautious, she decided.

But she couldn't let him see her doubts or fears.

She had to stay strong and alert because Gavin wasn't the only one who had something to prove. Her focus had to remain on two things—finding that bomber and finding Jordan Jameson's killer.

There could be no room for a third in there. Even a good-looking third named Gavin.

EIGHT

"The backyard is clear," Gavin said after Brianne told him Stella had alerted and she'd heard something earlier. "You should have let me bring you home."

She sent him a controlled glare and went about finding plates and drinks. "Stella and I handled it, Gavin. I think someone had been in the yard and then hopped the fence when I sent Stella out. But they're gone now."

Gavin ignored the feminine glare and took in her home.

Small but tidy, showing signs of wear and tear, the living room consisted of a dark couch and a dainty side chair across from a broken-in, manly recliner with a table that held several television remotes. Family photos lined the walls—Brianne and her parents traveling together, her playing softball, taking karate lessons and winning awards in track and basketball. He noticed a tiny dog bed near the window. Surely not Stella's. Tommy noticed, too, and immediately starting sniffing.

"I could have gone over the fence to search."

"I told you I checked the yard and I did," she reminded him while she slapped pizza slices onto floral plates. "I also checked my apartment. The door was locked, and nothing has been tampered with." Seeing the direction of his gaze and Tommy's nose, she added, "My mom has a lap dog. Serpico is also an excellent guard dog, all ten pounds of him. But he's with her at the shore."

Obviously, he'd gone and made her mad with his heroic efforts. Her comments were terse and her movements precise. She might throw a whole pizza at him.

But what should he do now?

She'd told him she thought someone had been in her yard the minute she'd opened the front door. He'd ignored her request to wait, and headed out back with Tommy to the small fenced yard, seeing it through the muted yellow of the security lights. A big oak and some shrubs, potted plants along the covered patio, and a door and a small patio to what must be her downstairs apartment. A door that made him nervous. The door where Stella had alerted. Tommy had gone over the entire small backyard and found no one and nothing. Just as she said—the door was secure.

"And I told you I'd do the same, so I did," he reminded her, still concerned about that vulnerable entryway. "It doesn't matter which one of us cleared the yard. We're here together."

"There's a thought," she retorted. "Us *working* together. I wanted to talk to you about that."

"Oh, so you bribed me with pizza to get me alone so you can remind me how you're just as capable as I am?"

She handed him his portion and then looked sheepish. "Something like that."

Tommy and Stella both lifted their heads. *Pizza?*

Gavin grabbed a big slice oozing with cheese and pepperoni. "I can't help being protective, Brianne. My grandmother was strong, but I always worried about her. It's my nature."

"Do I look like your grandmother?"

"Uh, no. She was pretty but you two are nothing alike."

"Maybe you can tell me all about her when we aren't both so tired and hyped-up?"

"Maybe I can and maybe I will," he replied, his eyes holding hers. "And maybe you can explain why a woman who grew up in a good home with solid parents decided to become a K-9 officer."

"Does that bother you—women in law enforcement? Is that why you can't let go and trust me?"

"No, no," he said, wishing Granny Irene had taught him how to talk to women without making them angry. "I'm all for women who want careers in law enforcement. It's not that at all. I admire you. I've told you that."

"Then what is it, Gavin?" she asked, her pizza chilling on the plate. "I can't shake the feeling that you're uncomfortable around me."

"I told you, I've never worked this closely with a female. Do you get that? I'm fighting that age-old problem—I'm attracted to you. I can't let that come between us but that does change things," he admitted. "You're pretty and scary-smart and determined. But we have to toe that line."

"You're right." Then she lifted her hand toward the back of the house. "I'm sorry. We rarely get intruders around here."

"Exactly," he said. "You handled it and the intruder is long gone. Your security and Stella worked, and you did your job."

"Except I overreacted about you," she said, lowering her eyes.

Surprised, Gavin shook his head. "So…you feel it, too?"

She looked flustered for about two seconds and then the wall came back down. "I've never worked with a man like you, Gavin. You stand out from the rest and you've stood up to the rest. But you give off a lot of mixed signals and I can't read any of them."

"I could say the same about you."

"My only signal is to do my job. That's it for now. I'm still a rookie. I can't afford any mess-ups. Especially the tangled-up-in-emotions kind. Get it?"

Yeah, he got it all right. That and the fact that someone had been snooping around her house. "We're a pair—full of our own angst and insecurities."

"Hey, speak for yourself," she teased. Then she nodded. "I think everyone has those issues but we all manage to hide our turmoil behind a wall of pride and determination."

"So can we work together and be professional, in spite of…whatever this is between us?"

"Can't be anything between us. Let's keep reminding ourselves of that."

"I guess I can do that." But inside, Gavin knew he'd be fighting a lot of battles while they were on this case. Something about holding her this afternoon in that mock embrace they'd shared just for show had made him think about her way too much. Her perfume, sultry and exotic.Her skin, warm and smooth. Her dress, so pretty and so perfect. Or the way she sighed, maybe without knowing she'd done it.

Gavin did a mental shake. He glanced up at her, trying to put a blank expression over some of that turmoil she'd mentioned.

Brianne handed him a soda and then sat down on the couch centered across from where he sat in the old recliner that had to be her father's favorite spot. The dogs settled at their feet, hoping for crumbs.

At least they weren't alerting. The intruder had obviously run away. But would he be back?

"We're in this together, Gavin. If you want me to have your back, you have to trust me to do my job."

"You still think I don't trust you? I just told you the truth."

She chewed her veggies-and-cheese and nodded. "Yes, and all of these feelings between us might get in the way and cause resentment and distrust. If you get aggravated and wish I wasn't around, you'll mess up by trying to do both our jobs. You'll consider me a distraction, a deterrent. That isn't going to cut it. So don't use that excuse again, okay?"

He sat there weighing his options. "You can walk away. No hard feelings."

"Are you having second thoughts?"

"First and second thoughts. This is an odd operation and I'm surprised Noah agreed to it. But he wants our department to shine, and so do I. If we nab the Tick, we all win."

"Not to mention we'd have something good to celebrate—getting an evil bomber and a corrupt real estate millionaire behind bars."

"That is cause for celebration. But we still have to help search for Chief Jordan's killer, too."

"We can do both, together. I'm good to go, Gavin.

But if you're having doubts, all the more reason to tell me now. I can't fight that kind of waffling."

"The only waffling I do is at Griffin's on weekends when the price is reduced on a stack of 'em, Bree."

"Okay then. We can add an intruder in my backyard to our growing list of strange incidents. I could dust for prints or have the neighborhood searched, but we both know how this works. He's gone. I don't have a description and I can't even prove anyone was here."

"I'll search near the fence and see if he left anything. Footprints or something dropped."

"I'd feel better if we both did that." She waited a beat, but he didn't try to dissuade her.

Progress.

"About Griffin's," she said, not missing a beat. "Do you think what happened there has anything to do with the Tick and this case?"

"I think it might," he said, glad to be off the personal stuff. "Lou said he'd been approached about selling. I've got Danielle and her crew looking at Lou's video footage and the traffic cams since a couple of the real estate agents came into the café and handed Lou cards. Maybe we can ID one of them."

"Good idea." Brianne took another bite of pizza. "Maybe Lou will remember more. Violet might not know about the details of the threats they could have received. They'd want to protect her, though."

"Lou didn't want to tell us from what I could see."

"I'm glad he did, even if the brokers weren't that threatening. More reason for us to be aware."

"But that means if they're after Lou, he and the whole staff as well as customers could be in danger. We were there, and the shooter saw, but I don't know if they specifically targeted us. Either way, that ups the danger on our play at being undercover." Giving her a frustrated stare, he added, "Now we have someone possibly snooping where you live, Bree. I don't like this. Maybe I should stay here with you."

"That would be a no," she quickly replied. "I can protect myself, Gavin."

"What if someone recognizes you while we're checking out apartments?"

"We're just looking at apartments. It's a free country. We can attend open houses like anyone else."

"Not so free if we snoop in the wrong places—together."

"Not so scary if we truly trust each other to the bitter end and stay alert and cautious until we have them behind bars."

Gavin picked up his third slice of pizza while he marveled at her reckless bravery. "I want to trust you, Brianne. But I brought you in on this. That means I feel obligated to watch out for you…"

"We can't let that get in our way, remember?" she said, dropping her pizza back on the plate in her hand. "You can't see me as anyone other than your current partner."

"I've never had a partner before. It's all new to me. But I believe you're the best person for the job."

"You mean, you believe I can stay professional? I can do that. Can you?"

He wondered at the blankness of her face and the darkness of her eyes. Could she really do that? Or would she put up that shield to protect her own confused feelings? "I'm working on being professional, yes. But it's different. We're playing a very real game."

She hid her surprise behind a stunned glare. "A little late to admit that, don't you think?"

"I'm not admitting anything." He sure wouldn't admit that he enjoyed being with her. "Are you still in?"

"I'm in," she replied. "In way too deep, but I'm in."

They finished their pizza, played with the dogs a bit, talked about their next plan of action and discussed the stall out on finding Jordan's killer.

But an awkward lull hung in the air, a sure sign that sooner or later, one of them would slip up and cross that line.

Gavin didn't want to be the first one to cave. When his cell buzzed, he gladly answered it.

"It's Danielle," he told Brianne.

She nodded and took the leftover pizza over to the kitchen and started cleaning up.

"What's up, Danielle?" he asked, hoping for a break.

"Nothing good," the fast-talking techie replied. "We can't get a read on the license plate of the Denali, Gavin. The surveillance camera in that area around Griffin's seems to be on the blink."

"You're kidding me, right?"

"I wish. A malfunction."

"That just figures," he said, frustration making him gruff. "Thanks, Danielle. I know you tried."

"It happens," she replied. "Those things are not one hundred percent accurate all the time."

"I know." He thanked her and closed his phone. Then he told Brianne. "We got nothing to go on yet on the shooting. Probably a rental vehicle. I'm sure whoever did this knows to cover their tracks but I worry that they sent someone here tonight."

Brianne came around the kitchen counter. "Danielle's right. Half the time, the cameras don't work or read false. And we don't know for sure a person was in my yard." Then she shook her head. "Who am I kidding? I heard footsteps—someone was running away."

"Just stay alert and keep the security lights on full blast. Set your alarm. We'll have to focus on the other evidence and hope we hear better news."

"And we have a plan," she reminded him. "That should keep us busy."

"A good plan," he said as she walked with him to the front door. "Lock up."

"And set the alarm," she repeated, but he saw the concern in her face. "Want me to follow you home and order you around? They might have paid your place a visit, too."

"No. I'm good."

He wasn't good, though. More like worried, confused and wide-awake. So he checked every corner of the rectangular Hayes house and did another sweep of her apartment door. Gavin didn't want to leave her there alone, but she wouldn't like him staying. At least Stella would alert on any noises, and she did have a motion-detector light on the back porch and a good security alarm.

But he circled the block two times before he headed home. The surrounding streets were deserted and quiet. Brianne was smart, and she knew what to do if anyone returned to her house. So why was he so concerned?

Later this week, they'd tour a few more residential buildings and hope to get a lead on the Tick. Was he crazy for pursuing this?

Or was he crazy for letting Brianne Hayes get under his skin so quickly?

* * *

"We got a call about a possible sighting of Snapper near a construction site," Noah told Gavin the next morning. "I want you and Brianne to go and check things out. See if the dog is really Snapper."

"Okay," Gavin said just as Brianne came into the chief's office. Snapper was Jordan Jameson's missing partner. The dog had gone missing when Jordan had and though sightings had been reported, no one was sure if the German shepherd was really Snapper. He was still out there. They all desperately wanted to find the K-9—in honor of Jordan and because the dog was part of their family, part of their team. There was always a chance that finding Snapper would lead to a clue about Jordan's killer's identity. But at this point, they didn't know if the killer had taken the dog and let him go or if Snapper had been on the streets the entire time.

"You wanted to see me, sir?" She glanced from Noah to Gavin, her eyes wide with questions.

"Someone spotted a stray German shepherd," Gavin said. "Might be Snapper."

"Since you two are working together, I want you to partner up on this, too," Noah said, nodding. "Take both dogs with you, just in case. You can let them sniff around. ."

"Where?" Gavin asked, hoping the site wasn't one he'd been investigating.

The chief named a place near Flushing. "Let's go," he said to Brianne. "No time to waste."

Brianne nodded and made sure Stella had on her protective vest. Gavin could see the adrenaline in her bright eyes and stern expression. The woman was seriously into her work.

But then so was he. This tip could lead to nothing, but it might be another chance to help in solving Jordan's murder. If this dog turned out to be Snapper, it might lead them to evidence, somehow, some way. A long shot, but clues or not, the whole unit wanted Snapper back, safe and sound. Tommy and Stella were trained in bomb detection, but they could help out here, too. Tommy would recognize Snapper's scent and Stella would alert to another dog.

Work would keep his mind off Brianne and how she made him feel. Even if she stayed right by his side, Gavin knew one thing—they were both pros. He'd just have to tamp down these crazy currents of awareness he felt each time he got near the woman.

"Let's go together," she suggested. "I'll drive."

He didn't argue with her. She took off out the back door and headed to her vehicle.

"I'll check the area," he said, pulling out his phone. "I'm pretty sure I haven't done any searching or surveillance in this particular location but I do know some buildings in that part of the city are being gutted and renovated. Gentrification again."

"Let's hope not by our man," she replied as she gunned it through traffic like an expert race car driver.

Soon they were at the location. Nothing special but definitely not livable yet.

"An older building that's being renovated," Brianne said, her eyes wide. "Interesting."

"This one is not on my list," Gavin replied. "But that doesn't mean an accident didn't happen months or years ago. I think this broker acts quickly and gets new construction going fast, probably cutting corners and breaking all kinds of union rules regarding safety. But I can't prove that on this one."

Brianne whirled into an open parking spot, the official vehicle giving them leverage if anyone complained. But the street around this area looked deserted, the building covered in scaffolding and construction dust.

This one stood at least twenty stories high. It had creamy old stone and black wrought-iron trim on the small balconies, rows of ornate windows and a quaintness that couldn't be denied.

"Let's check around the building first," Gavin suggested. "Looks like it covers half the block, at least."

They managed to find their way into an alley behind the main building. Tommy and Stella sniffed and glanced around but both appeared bored with the whole thing.

"I wonder if they *can* pick up Snapper's scent, like the chief said," Brianne whispered low.

"Maybe. But this could be a wild goose chase."

"Let's see."

They found an empty lot full of construction materials. Heavy plastic flapped in the moaning wind that flowed throughout the open, deserted building. But nobody seemed to be working here today.

"Odd, don't you think?" Gavin said, his words echoing out over the gutted building.

"Maybe they took a break or had a shutdown."

They kept moving. Brianne called out, "Snapper. Come."

Nothing happened except the haphazard rustling of plastic hitting against bricks, the sound of a few birds chirping in nearby trees and the constant noise of traffic out on the main thoroughfare.

They'd gone inside to check the gutted lobby area when they heard a yelp and then a bark. A scrawny, skinny dog came toward them at a slow bounce. When Tommy and Stella saw the other dog, they alerted and growled low.

Gavin gave Tommy the quiet sign. Stella calmed down after Brianne did the same.

Handing her leash off to Gavin, Brianne pulled out a treat and slowly made her way to the dog. "Here you go, boy. That's right. I won't hurt you."

She inspected the dog, careful to let him smell her knuckles and get to know her scent. Gavin watched, thinking the dog sure looked like Snapper but even from the distance of a few yards, he knew the truth. This dog wasn't a purebred German shepherd. Just a mutt out on the loose. They'd have to take him with them or call the pound to pick him up.

Brianne must have realized the same thing. She turned back to Gavin and shook her head. "It's not Snapper."

Disappointed, they told their K-9 partners to stay while they corralled the frightened, hungry animal, bribing him with treats until they had him inside the kennel in the SUV.

Leaving a vehicle window down, they turned to call their partners. "We'll put them in the backseat," Gavin said. He'd ask one of the trainers to evaluate the stray. The skinny mutt seemed calm and friendly, and maybe he could be trained as a service dog.

Gavin hated to tell the chief they hadn't found Snapper. Frustration heated him right along with the hot July sunshine.

They were headed back to the vehicle when Gavin

heard a scraping noise, followed by several thuds and thumps above them. The dog waiting in the SUV went wild, barking and snarling, his head held up toward the roof.

Gavin glanced up and saw a steel beam barreling over the edge of an open high-up balcony—a beam coming down right toward them.

NINE

Gavin grabbed Brianne and shouted, "Go!" to the dogs.

Brianne looked up, her eyes going wide as the huge beam came tumbling toward them like a torpedo.

The dogs ran toward the SUV and turned to wait.

The stray barked from inside the open vehicle. His growl echoed out after the beam landed on the hard concrete with a deafening hit, cracking the pavement into chunks.

"Bree, are you okay?"

Brianne blinked and looked up at the man holding her, inhaling air full of dust and debris. Nodding, she said, "And you've saved me yet again."

Gavin moved away and then sat up at the same time she did. They'd landed in the grass near the alleyway. She already had enough bruises from being around this man.

"I see your wit and sarcasm are still intact," he said, getting up, craning his neck to squint up at the roof. "But your new pal there in the vehicle saved us. Apparently, that dog knows whoever was on that roof."

"Did you see someone?" She hopped up before he

could offer her his hand. "We need to search this whole place."

"I didn't see anything but the beam coming down." Gavin stared up toward the balcony. "But by the way the stray barked, I'm thinking that beam didn't just fall off the roof by itself. Someone had to have pushed it."

"Only one way to find out," Brianne said, courage she didn't feel coloring her words. "We call for backup and go up there in the meantime."

They took Stella and Tommy and hurried into the building to the service elevator. "It's working," Gavin said as he punched buttons.

The rickety contraption made a groaning climb and caused Brianne to consider the stairs. But they didn't have time for that. Soon they were crawling at a snail's pace toward the roof.

Brianne followed him out onto the scorching hot rooftop, the view grabbing her. She could just make out the East River off to the west. She scanned the area, noticing building materials and a stack of beams like the one that had fallen.

"Gavin," she said, indicating something she'd spotted in a corner.

He followed her gaze. "Let's go."

They hurried the dogs over to the corner. Tommy immediately alerted, his doleful gaze on Gavin.

"He's picked up something," Gavin whispered.

"I know what it is," Brianne said, already snapping photos with her cell. "A plaid baseball cap."

Stella caught the wind and gave Brianne her own signal that she recognized this item, too.

Gavin did a sweep of the entire roof. "No one. No

place to hide and we came up the only working elevator."

He leaned over and checked below. "Whoever did this sure got away fast."

"And left his hat behind," Brianne said, grabbing a pen out of her pocket and lifting the hat with it. "We can bag this when we get back to our vehicle."

"This was no accident, Bree," he said, a frown coloring his sweat-drenched skin. "And it wasn't a coincidence that we were sent here."

"Nope. The Fourth of July bomber could have been here."

"Or someone wearing a plaid hat and trying to mess with us was here. Someone who doesn't want us to find Jordan's killer." Gavin turned and went to another door leading into the building. "This is locked tight, but they could have had a key and they might have taken the stairs."

"We'll have to take the elevator again and check the stairs from the ground up."

They made it down without any more mishaps. After bagging the hat and placing it on the floor behind the passenger seat, Brianne checked on the dog in the SUV, gave him some nibbles and made sure he had water and that the windows were open halfway.

Then they headed to the first set of stairs, only to find the door locked.

Hitting her hand on the steel door, she said, "He planned this so he could take the stairs and get away while we rode that old elevator."

Gavin looked around. "We can take the elevator again and search floor by floor until backup arrives."

"Good idea, but what about the dog in the SUV? Scrawny."

"Bring him just in case they're still lurking," Gavin said, noting the nickname. "Scrawny is now an honorary member of the K-9 Unit, plus he might find the intruder. We'll deputize him."

Brianne ran to the SUV and got the dog out. When she heard sirens echoing out over the street, she breathed a sigh of relief. With a little effort, she had Scrawny leashed and ready to go, giving him treats to entice him.

They started the long, rigorous climb on the rickety iron-gated elevator. On each floor, they moved through the open units, letting the dogs lead the way.

Gavin talked into the radio to the patrol officers who'd arrived, telling them to search down below.

An hour later, nothing. The dogs had sniffed the air and the ground. Scrawny seemed to get the importance, the poor boy lifting his head like a pro. They did find a water dish and bowl on the fourth floor.

At least the dog had been taken care of while the suspect waited for them to show up. Nothing else there, though.

Bree took an evidence bag from one of the other officers and wrapped the dog bowls inside it. "Maybe we'll get a hit on a print."

Gavin rubbed a hand down his face. "I doubt it."

Brianne felt his frustration. "We were set up."

"Yep," Gavin said. "Now it's personal. He knows about Jordy's death—or someone involved in this knows and called in a fake sighting of Snapper. Noah picked us randomly to check it out, but whoever was waiting probably recognized us."

"Do you think the two are connected? The bomber

and Jordan's death? Did someone set this up because we're looking into real estate? Or does someone want to distract our unit from finding out the truth about Jordan's murder?"

"Good question. I don't know. But I do believe our suspect is keeping up with the news updates and he—or whoever they sent to do this today—knew that Snapper is still missing. So they used Scrawny to lure someone from our department here."

"So what now?" Brianne asked. Scrawny seemed to fit right in. The two K-9s sniffed him with a keen interest and he returned the gesture. He might make a good service dog yet. Or maybe a K-9.

"We didn't find any scent of a bomb, so that's that. He's long gone and the only evidence we have is that cap."

Walking in a pacing circle, she turned back to Gavin. "Well, the dogs were smart enough to pick up on that hat. Maybe, just maybe, the lab can, too." Then she pointed to Scrawny. "Stella and Tommy picked up his scent. He might have some evidence in his fur."

Gavin moved toward the SUV. "We need to get Scrawny to the vet. I'll dust the door to the stairs for prints, but I'm guessing I won't find much. Then we'll turn over the evidence to the lab."

Brianne wiped at her wet brow. "Always exciting, working with you, Sutherland."

"Same here, Hayes."

"I need a hamburger," she decided. "Too many near-death experiences have made me see the light."

"And what do you see in that light?" he asked after they had the animals watered and settled in the back of the SUV.

"Besides my maker?" She gave him a soft smile. "That life is too short not to really live. And living means eating a burger when under stress."

"Amen to that. Hamburgers it is. But after we get all of this squared away."

Brianne wondered if they'd ever get any of this squared away. She glanced at Scrawny. "Gavin, I can't stop thinking about the setup."

"What about it?"

"Someone wanted us to think we'd find Snapper at this location, right?"

"I believe we've established that, yes. Noah told me about the dog first thing this morning."

"But *who* called Noah? No one could guess he'd send us. But whoever it was wanted us dead. Because we're investigating Jordan's murder? Because we're investigating the Fourth of July bomb? Was it the same guy who shot at us at Griffin's? What is going on?"

Gavin met her gaze head-on. "All very good questions we don't have the answers to. But we'll have to find them—soon."

"An anonymous tip," Noah said an hour later after the whole team had gathered for their daily reports on Jordan's murder. He'd brought his assistant, Sophie Walters, in to verify that. "I find it hard to believe your bomber or anyone connected to my brother's death left that dog there."

"Do you think that beam falling was coincidence then, sir?" Brianne asked.

Carter Jameson tapped his fingers on the table. "Noah, you have to see this isn't a coincidence. What would cause a beam to fall like that? It's not that windy out today. And no one was around working. Sounds like a setup to me."

Gavin shot Carter a thankful glance. Brianne's gazed moved from Carter to his brother Noah. The chief remained quiet.

Gavin spoke up. "I don't think this incident has anything to do with Jordan's death but I do believe it has everything to do with the Fourth of July bomber. He knows Brianne and I saw him at the park that day. Brianne and Stella gave chase but lost him in the crowd. He's probably been keeping up with our entire department and Jordan's case. The only way he'd know we'd be the two to show up is if he's been following us. Today he had an opportunity to do something. It started with the shooting at Griffin's—whether the bullets were aimed at us or to harass Lou, we don't know—and Brianne had a breach in her backyard last night."

"Honestly, you believe that?" Luke Hathaway asked.

Luke, of all people, should know anything was possible. He'd saved Jordan's administrative assistant, Sophie Walters, from the man who tried to kill her after she witnessed him leave a phony suicide note from Jordan in with some of Jordan's paperwork. Claude Jenks wouldn't reveal who'd hired him, and had been struck by a car and killed while running from police.

Luke and Sophie were engaged now. When she'd reported on the anonymous call about Snapper earlier, she'd smiled at Luke in passing. Their love shone so brightly that Gavin had wanted to look away. Instead, he'd looked at Brianne.

"I do believe that, Luke," he said. "We got shot at the other day at Griffin's. And the morning after the park bombing at that."

"Yeah, but we all agree Lou might have been the target. We're keeping a close eye on his place," Noah said, his arms crossed in a firm stance.

"We think someone is after us," Gavin replied without going into detail about his undercover plan.

Noah sent him a hard stare. "We can't trace the call. They didn't stay on the line long enough."

"I figured as much," Gavin said. "I think it was a setup. We checked the roof and there is no way a beam could have just toppled over. Someone had to have placed it near the edge and then tossed it down."

Brianne stood up. "We found a cap that looks like the same one the bomber wore—red, white and blue plaid. The lab is testing it along with some fibers found on the dog. Gavin dusted for prints around the door to the first-floor stairs and we have two dog dishes that could hold some DNA or prints. We think the Fourth of July bomber was at that building today because he's been tracking us since we spotted him in the park."

Gavin stood with her. "I agree, and I stand by everything Brianne and I have reported."

Noah dismissed the others and then stood with them. "Do I need to take you off this real estate bombing case?"

"No, sir," they both said at once.

"We're making progress," Gavin said. "A week or so more."

"Okay," Noah said. "I have to admit today's incident does sound fishy but we need solid proof that any of this is connected. We'll see what the lab says, all right?"

They left defeated. Gavin wanted to hit a wall. "What do I have to do to prove to him that I'm not crazy?

"We'll make him a believer," Brianne replied, steel

behind that declaration. "The bomber doesn't know we went undercover. He might only know us as two K-9 officers who got a good look at him."

Gavin wished he hadn't gotten her involved. Now Noah had her on his radar, too.

Brianne kept walking, but he stopped her when they neared the back entrance to the building. "Hey, you don't have to keep at this."

Brianne turned to give him a frown. "I'm not quitting, Gavin. I know someone is after us so we have to stay one step ahead of them. Do you honestly think I'd just walk away after you've come to my rescue twice now?"

Gavin's heart did a funny little leap. Joy, maybe?

"No one's ever said anything like that to me before."

Brianne's frown softened. "Your granny had *your* back."

"She did, but she never needed rescuing."

And the frown came back. "But I do, right? I need rescuing, Gavin?"

"No, Bree, I do," he said. Then he turned and headed out the door before he did something stupid like tug her close and hold her tight.

TEN

Brianne couldn't get Gavin's words out of her head.

Did he need rescuing?

The man seemed so confident and sure at times, then demonstrated the same insecurities and frustrations that hit her almost every day.

After letting Stella sniff the backyard and clear the upstairs, she went down to her apartment and made sure everything was as she'd left it. Stella sniffed here and there but didn't indicate anything out of the ordinary.

"I don't know, Miss Stella," she said, glad she had someone to vent to. "How's it coming with Tommy? I mean, I know he's not as tall as you but that dog has a heart of gold and he has that striking brown mask-like pattern on his face with matching brown spots. And those floppy ears—so adorable. He's a true hero. You guys make a cute couple."

Stella stared up at her with somber golden-brown eyes, then plopped on her big dog bed and put her nose down on her paws.

"Now you look as confused as me," Brianne noted. "Males can do that. Both the human and the dog kind. I'm going to take a shower and then we'll decide about dinner. Because Gavin never did take me to get a hamburger."

A few minutes later, Brianne stared at the empty refrigerator in her apartment and thought about going upstairs to raid her mom's freezer. But while her parents often invited her up for meals, Brianne insisted on paying for her own groceries and her part of the utilities. Her father had recently retired after working for the city for twenty-five years.

She hadn't mentioned this to Gavin, but hearing her dad's stories when he'd worked in the transportation department had shaped her career choice. His proud talk about the brave men and women of the New York Police Department had been the main reason she'd decided to become a cop. That and her love for animals had sealed her decision to become a K-9 officer.

Now she had finally begun living her dream job, frustrations aside. She'd made it to the top of her class and the only mar had been the chief's horrible death. She didn't mind holding off on the official graduation ceremony but…she wished their class hadn't been hit with such a tragedy right out of the gate.

And somehow she'd also stumbled into an unusual assignment with an interesting, slightly uptight partner.

Stumbled, or had a push from the Big Man upstairs?

Lord, if You want me here, could You steer me through? she prayed.

"I didn't ask for a partner."

Stella lifted her head.

"I'm not talking about you, Miss Stella," Brianne corrected. "You are the best partner in the history of partners."

Stella did a little woof and then got up to stare at

her food bowl. Brianne took the hint and fed her loyal friend.

When her phone rang, Brianne hurried to grab it. Probably her parents calling in with a report on how much fun they were having. They often stayed for weeks during the summer in her aunt and uncle's beach house. Brianne usually visited them a couple of times on weekends, but another visit would have to wait for now.

Not bothering to check the caller ID, she said, "Hayes."

"Uh…it's Gavin. I have a bag of burgers and… I'm parked in front of your house. Are you hungry?"

"Starving," she said. "Come in the door to my apartment. Just go around to the gate and come through the yard."

"I'm on my way."

"Gutsy of him," she said to Stella. "Driving across town and showing up unannounced."

When she heard a knock at the door opening to the tiny porch that served as her private sunning area, she looked through the blinds to make sure it was Gavin.

He shook the white bag at her.

Brianne opened the door and smiled. "You went to the Shake Shack?"

"Yes. Is that okay?"

She yanked him inside and shut the door, Tommy on his heels. "Only if you got me the cheeseburger with all the trimmings."

"I did."

Stella perked up and stood to greet her friend Tommy. The smaller dog yelped at her, his curly brown-and-cream spotted fur almost bristling with delight. Stella played it cool but gave him a doggie smile.

Brianne wished humans could figure each other out so quickly.

Gavin glanced around and she cringed at her messy home. "I'm not good at domestic stuff."

He took in the small kitchen where a few dishes sat on the draining board, and the living area cluttered with books, magazines and training manuals, before giving Brianne a thumps-up. He smiled at Stella who stood with Tommy, both curious about what came next, then pointed to the superhero-embossed throw on the bright blue loveseat. "That's interesting."

"It makes me feel safe," she said with a shrug, glad she'd at least lit a spicy-smelling candle. "Since I seem to need saving a lot."

"You don't need a superhero, Bree," he said, his gaze moving over her.

"But I do need a burger."

Soon, they were sitting at the tiny kitchen table inhaling burgers and fries, the dogs hovering nearby after they'd both been fed their rations for the day.

"You didn't have to do this, Gavin," she said. "Driving all the way over here and stopping to get food, too."

"I wanted to apologize for how we left things this afternoon."

She chewed on a fry. "You mean, the fact that we didn't get lunch and now I'm woofing down this food too fast because I'm starving?"

"Yeah, that and how I implied certain things."

"Oh, the part about me rescuing you?"

"That, yes. Just one of my moods."

"*I* never get moody."

He took her seriously. "You don't seem to. In fact, you seem to have life figured out."

"Ha. I don't have anything figured out." She wiped her fingers on a napkin. "But Gavin, you *do* need rescuing—from yourself."

"Excuse me?"

"You want what you want and there is nothing wrong with that. But you can't seem to see that you're good and you're kind and you work hard. Surely your grandmother taught you all those things, so you must see them in yourself."

He frowned and put down his burger. "My grandmother was a good, hardworking woman who sacrificed a lot for me."

She could tell he wanted to say more but wasn't ready to spill his guts to Brianne.

"She raised you, right?"

He nodded, his eyes dark with emotion. "Yes, but…"

"But what, Gavin? I need to understand why you seem to have a big chip on your shoulder."

He dropped his napkin and stared over at her. "Why do you need to pry? You had a family, Bree. Two parents, married and solid. A good house to live in. Stability. You didn't have to second-guess everything you did or said."

"And because of that, I'm somehow okay?" She laughed. "I've had to fight and scrape for all of it, Gavin. I had to beg my parents to let me try out for the Police Academy. My dad had seen the worst of this city and he hated the idea of me being out there on the streets. But I wanted it—because he'd also worked those streets in the transportation department. He knew them in and out, and I loved hearing his stories. But he didn't want me to know or see that kind of life."

"Bree—"

"No, let me finish. My mom worked as a school secretary and dealt with the worst of teenagers and my dad saw a lot of horrible things. They tried to protect me, but I felt stifled at times. So I haven't had it all that great but I had a pretty good life with parents who loved me and now, even with their concerns, they support me."

Gavin got up and turned to stare down at her. "Granny Irene loved me, too. But…she never got over how my mother just up and left me at her doorstep, an obligation to her."

Brianne's stomach clenched. "I didn't know that."

"I don't talk about it much."

"Well, your grandmother had to have loved you and apparently she took good care of you. Did she live long enough to see you join the force?"

He nodded. Then he shrugged. "But I never felt as if I measured up to her dreams—the dreams she had for my mother."

"Maybe you're wrong," Brianne said. "Maybe she loved by actions, not words. And that counts for something."

He stared down at her and shook his head. "You amaze me. You're full of bluster and sarcasm but underneath, you have a big heart."

"I could say the same for you. Now sit back down and finish your burger. We're still a team, okay?"

"Okay."

He'd just reached for his burger when his burner phone rang.

"It's Justin Sanelli," he told Brianne after glancing at the caller ID. "I think things are about to get rolling."

Brianne stood beside him and nudged him to answer. "I'm ready. I've got your back, Gavin."

* * *

Gavin gave her an appreciative glance and took the call. He turned to Brianne after he'd disconnected. "He wants to show us another property. This one in a building in Tribeca."

Brianne cleared away the remains of their meal. "That's gonna be pricey."

"Yes, this is an open house, so others will be around."

"Do you think the Tick will show up?"

"If he does, he'll be in disguise just like us."

"What if he remembers Tommy?"

"There are a lot of springer spaniels in New York."

She smiled at Tommy. "I'll find him another interesting dog collar."

Tommy's eyes widened in protest. Gavin thought the dog always stayed one step ahead of them.

Brianne motioned to the love seat and she took the cushioned rocking chair across from it. "Why a new building?"

"I'm wondering about that," he admitted after he settled onto the comfortable little sofa. "I can't see anyone bombing such expensive property."

"Maybe Justin wants to impress us with his clients. We might see some celebrities or high-ranking New Yorkers."

"We need to be careful, though."

"Okay, so we go to the open house, act impressed and make our way around while stressing we want in on any property that needs to be torn down. And we watch for the Tick."

"I think that's a good plan. The Tick could be scouting us out, too."

She pushed at her hair, which was down tonight. A

treat for Gavin—he wanted to run his hands through all those reddish-brown waves. Her hair had to be so soft.

"And still no word on whether the Tick is William Caston—the man I thought looked like him in his mug shot?"

"Nope. We can't find him to bring him in, which makes me think he has to be the Tick. That man knows how to go to ground."

"Well, if he's working for Sanelli, he might be attending the open house and could soon be high in the sky with us," she quipped."

When she got up to put her glass in the sink, Gavin gently held her wrist. "Bree, we have to be careful."

She studied his hand on her and nodded. "I will be careful, Gavin. You have to trust me."

He stood and held her gaze. "I keep telling you, I do trust you and appreciate you. But that doesn't mean I don't worry."

"We aren't in the business of worrying," she retorted. "We never have time for that. And I'd rather not think about it and just do the job."

"And I'd rather be prepared and think things through." He shrugged. "My grandmother always had her ducks in a row. When my mother left and never looked back, it shattered Granny Irene's methodical, controlled little world. She lost her husband early on, so she had reason to worry and fret but she held it together. Too much at times, I think. I guess I inherited some of that resolve and pride."

"And…you never got closure with your mother, right?"

"That is another whole conversation," he said, wishing he could let go of the shadow that seemed to follow him around. "Let's save that for another time."

Her expression softened and she pulled away. "Okay, back to the case then. I'm the rookie, so you do the heavy strategizing and I'll do what I need to do when it's time to make a move, all right?"

"As long as we're on the same page."

"I'm there, Gavin. I just want you to see that I'm there. I'm not going to abandon you or let you down."

He motioned to Tommy and headed for the door, uncomfortable with her pointed promise. "I see more than you think," he said. "I'm gonna go home and do some research on this apartment building so I'm prepared."

"And I'll do the same," she said, her tone firm. "Plus, I have to figure out what to wear."

"It's Tribeca," he reminded her. "Understated and hip."

She made a face at his effort to talk uppity. "I think I can handle that."

"You'd look good in a flour sack."

"Nope. Not gonna happen."

He nodded at her and Tommy barked at Stella. "I'll see you tomorrow."

"Thanks for the burgers." Brianne shut the door with a thud.

"Search," Gavin whispered to Tommy. She might think she had it all together but…he had the right to watch her back.

"What she doesn't know won't hurt her, right?"

Tommy seemed to bob his head, but Gavin knew the dog was doing a ground-to-air search.

They covered the whole backyard but Tommy didn't alert. The only sound came from a rickety swing under a mushrooming oak tree. The dog turned to stare up at Gavin. *What next?*

"Good job, Tommy," Gavin said, keeping his words low.

For now, Brianne was safe.

ELEVEN

At the briefing on Jordan's murder case the next morning, Noah told the team they still had nothing much to go on. "We've had sightings on dogs we thought might be Snapper, but we haven't found him yet. We thought we had a solid lead yesterday but while Gavin and Brianne found a dog similar to Snapper, he turned out to be a mix—part German shepherd and part hound, we think."

K-9 Officer Lani Branson spoke up. "His nickname is Scrawny, but we'll get him healthy and change that," she said with a smile. "I'm working with him to see if he has K-9 or service dog capabilities. I'm thinking the latter since he's calm and has a big heart. He's been checked out and given his shots and he's had a couple of decent meals. Ynez says he's malnourished but she's taking care of that."

Everyone smiled. Ynez Dubois, one of the best veterinarians in the city, took care of all of the K-9s and any strays they brought in, too.

"Well, at least we have a new prospect," Noah said, his tone full of disappointment about the dog not turning out to be Snapper. "We'll make sure the stray finds a good home, whether inside the department or in the service dog capacity."

"We have to find Snapper. For Jordan. And we have to find Jordy's killer," Zach reminded them, his blue eyes flashing with anger over his brother's death. "Snapper is out there somewhere. We can't stop looking."

Gavin gave him a sympathetic glance. Jordan's brothers were still grieving. It would take a long time to deal with his death, but they needed solid answers and some closure. At least Zach had Violet to help him through. Those two had been neighbors growing up, but a threat on Violet's life that involved a drug dealer and a reluctant coworker smuggling shipments into the airport had brought them together as a couple.

Once they were dismissed and heading out for the day, Gavin called out. "Brianne?"

Brianne turned at the door to the parking lot. "Hey."

Waiting until they were alone, he nodded to her. "So let's meet at the Gable again. The building we're going to is on the corner of Hudson and Reade in Tribeca. I'll pick you up at the safe house so we can pull up in the car together. There's valet parking."

"Okay. What time?"

"It starts at six. So around that time. We don't want to look too anxious and be the first to arrive."

"Oh, no, of course not."

"Just so you know, I can't locate my CI, Beanpole. He must be on the move. He has different corners where he hangs out but no one's seen him for a while."

"So no verification on Plaid Cap being the man he heard discussing this with another man."

"No, not yet. But I'm thinking the other man had to be Justin Sanelli."

"And we still don't have the DNA results, if any, from the fibers and other evidence we sent to the lab."

They parted, and Gavin saw Brianne stop to talk to Lani and their friend Faith, a seasoned K-9 officer who'd helped train Brianne. The women's expressions changed from happy to curious to surprised to intrigued. He had to wonder what *that* conversation was all about.

"What gives, Bree?" Faith asked, her dark eyebrows slashed up, her short hair curling around her jawline.

"What are you talking about?" Brianne asked, glancing from Lani to Faith. She'd neglected her friends lately and now they wanted answers.

"You don't have time for a night out and I heard Gavin making a date with you."

"It's not like that," she tried to explain as they left the building and headed to their vehicles.

"Then what is it like?" Lani asked, tossing her blond ponytail. "You two seem awfully chummy lately."

Brianne glanced around. How to handle this?

"She's hedging," Faith said. "What are you not telling us?"

"We're still working this case," she said on a low whisper. "The Fourth of July bombing case I mentioned before. For our protection, we're trying to keep details under wraps."

"Oh, for your protection," Lani teased. Then she turned serious. "We get it. You don't need to explain since we're all concerned about this so-called bomber."

"Can we talk later?" Brianne said. "I have to do some training with Stella this morning."

"I'm headed that way myself," Lani said. "I want to take a look at Scrawny."

"I have to hit the street," Faith replied. "Lunch soon?"

"The Pizza Palace? Friday?" Lani said, giving Brianne a questioning stare.

"I can do that," Brianne replied, hoping she'd be able to keep that promise.

She hurried toward the training center with Lani, glad her friend didn't push for more information. She wanted to work off some steam with Stella this morning since the Labrador wouldn't be with them tonight. She also wanted to check on Scrawny.

"Maybe we should have nicknamed our new dog Brawny since he'd obviously been dumped on the streets and left for dead," she said to Lani. "He's a scrapper, no doubt. A survivor."

"He'll be fine once we get him fattened up with good food and get him into training." Her friend gave her a worried glance. "Hey, are you okay, Bree?"

"Just thinking about that poor dog. He went with us up to the roof, you know. He bonded with us right away. If he hadn't made such a fuss, we might not have seen that beam. He probably saved our lives."

Lani gave her an empathetic smile. "You survived and so did the dog—an animal probably abused at the hands of this person. Your kindness to Scrawny made him immediately bond with you and the K-9s. A lesson for all of us."

"Jordan was brawny and tough," Brianne said, the image of the chief being forced to write that horrible suicide note moving through her head. "Why didn't he survive? Why would someone kill him and make it look like a suicide?"

Lani shook her head. "I don't have the answer to that, but each time we get a lead, it's another opportunity to find out the truth. We might find something on the dog you brought in or on the hat and those food dishes. It's not over yet."

"You're right. We're still waiting on the lab for DNA from the bomb fragments we found after the Fourth of July... We've got a name, but we can't find the man. Maybe something will develop with that, too."

"Is that why you're not quite yourself?" her friend asked while they headed down the hall to the outside training facility. "Are you still shaken from the bomb scare?"

"Maybe," Brianne admitted. "Made me stop and think."

"About mortality and men?"

"About mortality and one man," she admitted.

"I knew it," Lani said. "You and Gavin have a certain chemistry."

"I *don't* know it yet," she retorted. "Or rather, I'm trying to ignore that chemistry. That's not easy and I'm not ready to talk about it."

Lani nodded. "Tell me when you're ready, because it's becoming more and more obvious to all of us."

Brianne wanted to say more, but then she wasn't ready to tell her friends much about her feelings for Gavin. She wanted to see where they went with this case and then...later they'd decide about that chemistry Lani seemed to think they had.

Brianne's gut burned for answers on the bomber and on finding the person responsible for the chief's murder. It didn't matter how many times they went over what little evidence they had, getting a fresh lead would really help all of them right now. Yesterday, finding that dog had given her hope. But then almost getting crushed by a beam had dashed those hopes.

"Maybe today will be the day, Lani," she said. "Maybe we'll get news that can help all of us to understand why Jordan had to die."

Lani nodded. "I'll pray for that end, Bree."

Brianne followed her friend out onto the training arena. This spot always brought her calm and peace. She loved working with the handlers and watching the dogs grow and become confident in what they were trained to do. After one of the trainers brought out Scrawny, Brianne gave him a rub and grinned at the eager dog.

"Go on, boy. You're already a hero in my eyes."

Brianne took over with Stella while Lani patiently learned what kind of stuff Scrawny was made of.

Brianne and Stella worked the obstacle courses and went through their paces on hide-and-seek so Stella would continue to improve on sniffing out incendiary devices. One of the lead trainers who'd worked with Stella came over to talk about how far she had come.

"You *are* a smart girl," Brianne told her furry partner a couple of hours later. "You found the goods so now we have playtime."

Stella's ears perked up. She'd worked hard after being a good, attentive mother to her puppies. Now they were all being fostered by various members of the K-9 team to learn socialization before they started intense training. When Brianne played a game of tug-of-war with her, Stella growled and snarled in a playful way, determined to hang onto the prize. Then they played fetch for a while. Stella loved running after a soft plastic ball but Brianne didn't allow her to keep it or chew on it. If

Stella swallowed a chunk of the ball's shell, she could die from a stomach obstruction.

"Let's go get cleaned up," Brianne said. "And we'll get a treat."

Stella knew what that word meant.

At the end of the shift, Brianne left Stella clean and fed inside the kennel room. "I'll be back to get you later tonight, I promise."

Brianne had to go and get gussied up for the big open house in Tribeca.

Would she come face-to-face with a bomber?

Gavin stood in the hotel suite doorway, admiring Brianne's outfit. She grinned at him, looking like she was waiting for a friend. She'd dressed in a beige lightweight T-shirt with a black scarf looped over a flowing paisley skirt with black strappy sandals. Her hair was dark again but down, cascading around her face in a casual toss, her bangs hooding her eyes. Dangling gold earrings swung against her neck. And she carried another expensive-looking purse with some designer's initials on it.

"Hello, beautiful."

Shaking her head, she asked, "Is that part of the act?"

"No, you *are* beautiful. But, yes, I know the rules."

"Tonight, we pretend there are no rules."

"You look different," he said to push past that statement. "I mean, you really are in disguise."

"That's what layers of mascara and eyeliner can do for a person," she quipped.

"Maybe I should ditch the mustache and try that," he retorted.

That made her laugh. "I kinda think the mustache is a better look on you."

She had her look down—expensive but bohemian, understated but fashionably cool. While he liked her red hair better, he had to admit the dark brown looked real good.

Sure beat their official uniforms. He followed her to their waiting car. Tommy did a tailspin and stared out the window, his happy face greeting her.

"I feel the same way," Gavin whispered before she slid into the car.

"You clean up nicely, too," Brianne said once they were buckled in.

"I dress this way when I'm off duty."

She laughed again, the sound dancing around him like tiny bells. "Sure you do."

He'd worn jeans and a sport coat that would have cost a week's salary, except he'd found it at a thrift store with the tags still on it. His dark shades helped to hide his eyes. "It's showtime."

He weaved in and out of side streets jutting off from Broadway to avoid traffic.

"The Bec-Off-Broadway," Brianne said as they came to a stop about thirty minutes later in front of the chrome-and-glass lobby. "A brand new building. So this is what happens when people get bombed out of their homes."

"Collateral damage to the person responsible. They don't care about people being forced out of their homes, or buildings having to come down because of corruption."

"Well, we do," she reminded him. "I hope we find something to help us."

"Yeah, I hope so, too."

He got out and came around to open her door, surprised that she let him. But when she stepped out, he understood she was playing her part. She held the seat up so Tommy could jump out of the car. Then she placed a black leather dog collar around the K-9's neck and winked at Gavin.

"I like having matching accessories," she said with a feminine grin, her finger pointing to the wide leather band on her left arm.

Gavin laughed and nodded. "That's so you, darling."

To prying eyes, they looked like a happy, flirting couple.

But Gavin could see the shimmer of intensity in her dark eyes, could feel the heat of excitement running through her veins. Brianne lived for this stuff while he only wanted to do the job and get back to being a K-9 cop.

Tommy felt it, too. He might be playing a pampered pooch but the K-9 also knew he had work to do. He danced and watched Gavin's face for his orders.

The valet took the key to the car. "Nice ride, dude."

"Thanks," Gavin said, giving him the alias of Linus Reinhart. Then he handed the kid a big tip. "Take care of it for me, will you?"

The young man bobbed his head. "Don't you know it!"

Gavin held Brianne's arm as they made their way into the glimmering lobby of the building. An agency rep showed them the private elevator to the top floor of the ten-story building.

"Based on the history of this location before this place came up, I'd say the older building was cozy and could have been salvaged," Brianne whispered. "It's a shame that it had to be torn down."

Gavin nodded. "Yep. A fire destroyed the bottom three floors. They had to condemn the building."

"But no one found the truth."

He shook his head since the elevator had stopped. "Not yet." Then he leaned close, as if he were whispering sweet nothings into her ear. "But we're here to take care of that."

When the door opened, Brianne was staring into his eyes, her smile frozen on her face. Gavin held her gaze. "Be careful," he reminded her. "Please."

TWELVE

Brianne followed Gavin's lead. She kept her gaze on him for a brief moment and then turned to find several sets of curious but cool eyes on both of them.

Inhaling, she let go of Gavin's arm and held Tommy by his leash, steadying him as they entered the ritzy crowd. People dressed in glittering clothes, torn jeans with diamonds, bright blond long hair with short red dresses, short dark bobs and all black clothing, men in button-up shirts and polished loafers, some in suits with glee in their eyes. Some ignoring everything and everyone while they stared at the incredible view of historic townhouses and the Hudson River off in the distance.

She noticed a woman doing just that, a champagne glass in her hand, a diamond tennis bracelet sparkling against her porcelain skin. Her inky black hair fell in expensive layers down over her shoulders. Her cream-colored suit shouted Armani.

And when she turned, her eyes caught Brianne's. A cold smile and then the woman moved on.

Something about the other woman left Brianne cold, too. Too rich to be friendly.

Before she could say anything to Gavin, Justin

Sanelli hurried toward them. "The Reinharts. So glad you came. Grab some champagne and I'll personally give you the tour. I think you'll like this place."

Brianne made a face. "But, Justin, this is all new and shiny. We wanted to find a fixer-upper. You know, a building we can put our own stamp on."

"Of course," the agent said. He twisted the gold ring he wore on his left finger. "Just see what you think and then I'll explain how to make that dream come true." Then he laughed. "The previous building on the property was in a mess when we bought it. Crumbling and out of date and most of it destroyed by a tragic fire. We've built one of the most sought-after properties in Tribeca."

"I'm impressed," Brianne said with a smile, while she sent Gavin a knowing nod. Justin obviously loved making things happen in the real estate world.

He moved them through the crowd with ease, smiling and patting people on the back as he went. Brianne had worried about people wanting to pet Tommy but others had brought lap dogs in huge purses, while some held tiny dogs in their arms, so what was one more animal in the crowd?

Tommy marched along with her. Gavin warned her Tommy might not pick up a scent with so many perfumes and other scents merging in the spacious living and kitchen areas of the apartment. The dog, used to crowds, had been trained on how to react and not react, but this crowd was different.

Tommy, however, did his job in a subtle way, sniffing here and there, his head going up and then down. So far, he hadn't alerted on anyone in particular.

"Let's start with the master bedroom," Justin said

as he moved up a short staircase. "It covers the entire top floor, closet space is huge and the bathroom is like a spa."

They passed the dark-haired woman on the stairs. Justin stopped, twisting his ring. "Liza, I'd like you to meet the Reinharts. They're interested in renovating property in Manhattan."

"You've come to the wrong place," the woman he'd called Liza said, her voice cultured and crisp. "We just finished this building. We had to start from scratch but…don't you think the results were worth the effort?"

Brianna shot Gavin a quick glance and then held out her hand to the woman. "It's a beautiful place."

Justin moved to say something but was interrupted.

"Liza Collins," the woman said, her hand cold against Brianne's skin. "Justin mentioned you two just the other day."

"Did he now?" Gavin asked, looking bored. "We thought we'd stop by, but we're looking for something a bit different—Alice has a thing for authentic art deco and prewar designs."

"Maybe we can persuade you on this one," Liza said, her cold eyes assessing them.

"Liza owns the Rexx Agency," Justin explained.

Gavin nodded. "Ah. So you're the famous Mrs. Watson Collins."

"I am," she replied. "But I'm a widow now as most of New York knows."

Gavin lowered his head. "I'm sorry for your loss."

"So am I," the cold woman replied. "But yes, the Rexx Agency is still going strong in spite of everything. And Justin is my top broker," she said, almost cooing.

"You're in good hands. Come and have more refreshments after your tour."

Brianne wanted to shudder but she held herself erect. So Liza was *that* Collins. The name had sounded familiar. A big scandal a few years back regarding corruption and embezzlement in the real estate world.

Tommy danced and sniffed, shooting a glance up but someone came by laughing and then Justin took them toward the open doors of the huge master suite.

Gavin nudged her, his eyes moving down.

Brianne turned on the small landing to stare down into the crowd. A man dressed in black with dark hair and heavy brows stood near the entry hall, his back to them.

Tommy did his little dance again. And alerted.

But on who?

Brianne glanced around to Justin. He smiled and waited. "Ready to be wowed?"

"More than ready," she said.

Gavin took Tommy. "I think spoiled sport here is trying to tell me he needs to take a walk. I'll be right back."

With that, he gave Brianne a quick kiss. "I'll hurry."

"Oh, you're so sweet to take care of my T-Boy," she said for Justin's benefit. "Is that our man?" she whispered against Gavin's ear.

"I think." He lifted away and spoke loudly. "I think I'll need another drink after we get back. You two behave."

Justin grinned like a Cheshire cat and twirled his expensive ring. "I'll take good care of her."

Brianne gave Justin a brilliant smile but wished she could follow Gavin and Tommy downstairs. Would Gavin be able to get close to that man?

Had they finally found the Tick at last?

* * *

"Find."

Tommy heard Gavin's one-word command when he whispered it. The dog knew hand signals enough to know they were officially on the case.

Tommy moved through the noisy crowd, pushing past people only to stop and turn back. The women thought he was adorable but they didn't bother to touch him. Just smiled and gave Gavin thorough come-hither gazes.

The men in the room focused on the chase—who would get this penthouse first. He heard snatches of Wall Street discussions, some rants on politics, the reviews of the latest musical on Broadway, the tall tales of a weekend in the Hamptons.

And while he listened and smiled and worked his way toward the elevator, he searched for the man in black with the heavy eyebrows. Where had he gone?

Gavin turned toward the kitchen where a white marble island covered with an array of food faced another city vista and the cabinets and appliances still smelled fresh and new. Tommy did a ground sniff and then lifted his head to a set of solid glass doors centered in a glass wall.

The terrace.

"Let's get some fresh air," Gavin said loud enough for anyone nearby to hear.

Taking Tommy out through the glass doors and into the heated dusk, he glanced around, admiring the view. But his eyes did a search of the entire terrace and the surrounding buildings. Up above, the master bedroom's ceiling-to-floor windows were covered in sheer curtains. Then he turned to the left, facing north toward

Broadway. A door stood open at the other end of the penthouse.

"Let's try there," he said to Tommy.

The dog moved ahead with purpose. But when they reached the room, they found an empty office. *No one in here.*

The place shined with the same gray and white tones of the other rooms, with just a touch of red popping out. Tommy did a search, his nose hitting the lush white rug underneath the oval glass-topped desk. He lifted his snout to the gleaming white wood cabinets lined with artifacts and trinkets.

Tommy looked up before turning back to give Gavin a cue that meant he'd found something.

On the top of the massive built-in cabinets lay a plaid baseball cap. Red, white and blue with a sparkling row of white gemstones across the rim.

"What?" Gavin asked the K-9. "Are you saying—"

"There you are."

Gavin turned to find Liza Collins smiling at him, her arms elegantly crossed over her white suit jacket. "Did you like the master?"

"Impressive," Gavin admitted, still wondering about that hat and this room. "T-Boy here needed some air. I was headed out the elevator but saw the terrace. The last rays of the sun slipping over it kind of drew me out there."

The woman's cool gaze moved from the sun-dappled terrace back to Gavin. "And yet, you're in here now."

"Yes, the door to the terrace was open."

She moved to close it. "Someone must have been in a hurry." Shutting the door, she turned back to Gavin. "It's still a bit warm out there."

Gavin noticed how the woman stood away from him and his partner. Maybe she didn't like big dogs.

Tommy did a little dance and lifted his snout. Had their man gotten away through the terrace doors? Gavin hadn't seen anyone on the terrace but Tommy had alerted on this room.

"Yes. I'm taking this one for his walk and then I'm going to find my wife and make sure she hasn't bought this place already."

"I'll see you back in the kitchen then," Liza said. But she turned and gave him one final glance. "I hope we can find what you're looking for, Mr. Reinhart. I hate to disappoint clients."

"From what Justin tells me, he knows how to make things happen," Gavin replied, wondering if she knew what her top salesman was really up to. Or if she cared.

"He's good at what he does," she said with an eloquent shrug. "I don't ask questions."

Did she have a clue or was she playing her own part in all of this? Gavin couldn't be sure.

He left her standing in the middle of the office and took Tommy down the elevator, hoping they'd pick up a scent.

But he had to wonder if Brianne was holding her own with Justin.

Gavin had a feeling she could do that with ease.

And he prayed she'd heed his warning and be careful.

Because right now, he had no idea what their next move would be.

Brianne didn't move. Justin had her cornered but she refused to be intimidated. The man had flirted, offered her wine and food, suggested they get together for lunch sometime and then practically begged her to buy this penthouse.

"Don't you think you'd rather live here?" he asked, his arms opening wide toward the view. "It's Tribeca after all. Some of the most sought-after property in all of Manhattan."

"I love this area," she admitted while she took in every detail of the room and this man. She couldn't see him as a bomber, however. He'd do the hiring but not the dirty work. "But as we've told you, we have a hands-on approach to buying properties. We've talked about Williamsburg—it's going through such a change these days. And, of course, we adore the Upper West Side and Central Park. But it seems everything old is going and all these new high-rises are appearing. I like to take old and make it new again, but the location is the thing. We need a good piece of property. Do you understand what I'm saying?"

"I make that kind of stuff happen," he said, moving closer. "I can find exactly what you want." His eyes danced over her with too much intimacy to suit Brianne. She held her spine tight so she wouldn't shudder.

"We're back."

They both whirled around to find Gavin standing there with Tommy. "And, Alice, darling, we're late for dinner." His gaze indicated they needed to hurry.

"Oh, well." She smiled at Justin. "Just when things were getting interesting. You will call us, right?"

"Of course," the real estate agent said, disappointment chilling his promise. "Don't worry. Soon we'll all have what we want." Then he shook Gavin's hand. "Good to see you again, Linus."

Gavin guided her down the stairs. "I got in a conversation with Morticia."

"Who?"

"Liza in the white suit. She reminds me of the matriarch of *The Addams Family.* Surely you watched that sitcom."

"Oh, her. Yes, I watched that show. This one is kind of creepy in a sophisticated way. That nickname fits her but I'll have to pull up all the news reports on her real life."

"Once I excused myself from her, I saw the man in black heading toward the elevator. If we hurry, we might catch him."

Keeping her voice low as they crossed the crowded room, she whispered, "Did Tommy alert?"

Gavin nodded. "I'll explain once we're out of here."

Brianne glanced back and saw Liza Collins watching them. "Morticia at your six."

"Keep walking," Gavin said. "I don't think she's our problem right now."

They didn't find their man in the elevator but Tommy seemed agitated, his snout in the air.

When they came out into the lobby, Gavin spotted their man moving toward the front doors. Tommy went still and stared after him.

"Gotcha," Brianne said, hurrying with Gavin toward the front doors. But a crowd of laughing people pushed through, forcing them to wait.

When they got outside, Gavin saw the man disappearing around the corner. "Let's go," he said.

Brianne followed him into the dusk.

"What are we going to say when we get to him?" she asked.

Gavin gave her a quick glance. "I haven't gotten that far yet."

"If it's not him, Gavin, we'll blow our cover."

"Then we'll follow him and find out where he's headed."

Brianne nodded. "I believe Tommy and he seems to want to stay on this course."

"I agree," Gavin said, his stomach roiling. "I think we might have found our man but I need to see his face."

"You don't think he left anything back there, do you?" she asked.

"No bomb, but Tommy alerted on a plaid cap on a shelf in the bedroom, similar to the one the park bomber was wearing."

"I hope we can finally pin him down."

"I hope so, too," Gavin replied. "I want this to be the beginning of ending this thing."

Or…they'd been set up to chase someone who only wanted to lure them away and possibly kill them.

THIRTEEN

They tailed the man up Hudson for three blocks.

Gavin made sure they were well behind so he wouldn't notice. The man walked briskly, weaving in and out of people moving along the sidewalks, his stride purposeful. He never went inside any of the shops and he barely glanced around.

When he abruptly turned a corner to the right onto Leonard, Gavin grabbed Brianne to hide inside a doorway, his arms shielding her in case the man saw them when he whirled to the right.

Holding her there, Gavin stared down into her eyes, thinking he'd like to kiss her. Which was crazy and impossible right now. "That was close."

She nodded, her breath shallow, her gaze moving over his face. "You scared me."

"I thought he was turning back."

Tommy sat hidden with them and never uttered a sound.

Gavin checked the street on both sides. Nothing out of the ordinary along Hudson. "Let's go."

They turned the corner onto Leonard and Gavin spotted their suspect up ahead. Then Gavin slowed, careful to make it look like they were taking an evening stroll.

Then the man headed toward the subway station.

"Hurry," Gavin said, tugging Tommy along and holding Brianne's hand. "He's taking the Uptown 1 Line."

The man disappeared down the subway stairs.

Brianne rushed to keep up, but Gavin held her hand and kept Tommy tight on his leash while they hurried down the stairs to the train platform. "There," she whispered.

They saw the man moving through the crowd waiting for the next train, his head down and turned away.

Gavin found a spot next to a support column, mindful of keeping out of sight.

When the incoming train arrived, a mob of passengers started disembarking. The man shoved through people still trying to exit, knocking them out of his way as he squeezed through the train doors. By the time they'd reached the doors of the train, the man had barreled through the crowds inside, his face disappearing in a crush of commuters and tourists. They made the door just as it shut, leaving them standing on the platform.

"I don't see him anymore," Brianne said.

Gavin tried to find the man. "We can't get to him. Even if we'd made the train, he'd have spotted us."

"So that's it?" Brianne asked, her tone full of aggravation.

"For now," Gavin said, feeling the same. "We can't halt the train without a warrant or order from someone higher up. We've got nothing to go on but a scent and a description."

"He might have made us. The way he hurried onto that train shows he's up to something."

Gavin let out a sigh. "I don't think he saw us but yes, he could be in a hurry for a reason."

"I hope that reason has nothing to do with us." She didn't look so sure.

"No, I watched. He never turned his head," Gavin replied as they pivoted to walk back to the Bec-Off-Broadway. "I don't think he spotted us."

"Or he could have been pretending," Brianne pointed out. "If he's the Tick, he'd know how to blend into a crowd and he'd know the busiest subway lines this time of day."

"Good point," Gavin said, aggravation coloring his words.

"It's a start," Brianne said as they walked back the way they'd come. "Our hands are tied, Gavin. We can't do much more without bringing in actual detectives."

"I think it's time we did that," he said, hating to admit it. "We're out of our league and…we still need to chase leads on Jordan's murderer. Not to mention, we have patrol duties in various other places."

They were almost back to the valet station when Brianne stopped and stared at a flyer on the window of an art gallery.

"Look, Gavin. 'Dog Days of Tribeca.' At the Washington Market Park this weekend."

"What does that have to do with us?" he asked, tired and irritated.

"Sponsored by the Realtors of Rexx."

That got Gavin's attention. "Interesting. Trying to impress the neighbors?"

"Neighbors with dogs," Brianne replied. "We have dogs. We saw a lot of people there tonight with dogs.

Maybe we can snoop around a little bit and spot some of the other brokers we saw there tonight."

"Another walk in the park," Gavin said. "It sure can't hurt."

"Linus and Alice strike again," she said, smiling now.

"Okay, I'll pick you up—"

"Not at the safe house. It'll take far less time for me to get ready at home and take the subway directly to Tribeca."

"How about we meet near the park? There's another garage between Greenwich and Reade," Gavin said.

She nodded. "I'll text you, so we can walk out of the garage together."

"Okay, but be careful."

"Always," she said.

The valet went to the parking garage around the corner to find their car. Gavin glanced around out of habit. No one watching or lurking about. But Tommy's head went up as they waited at the entryway of the apartment building.

"Bree, we've got something."

Tommy sniffed the air, but the dog faced away from the building and looked to the left.

To the parking garage.

"I hear you," Brianne said. "Let's see where Tommy takes us."

"Go. Find." Gavin's word weren't out before Tommy took off into the garage. "He's following the same route as the valet."

"The valet? I can't believe he'd be involved in this."

"I can," Gavin replied. "Anyone here today could

be involved. Money makes people do strange things. Maybe we've been following the wrong man."

They reached the exit from the garage when Gavin saw the parking attendant bringing back their luxury sedan.

Waving the man down, Gavin stopped him at the entryway.

"Maybe he picked up something on the street or in the garage," Brianne said, determination clear in her words. They hurried to meet the man.

Tommy barked and tried to move forward toward the car. "Let's see." Gavin held Tommy back. "He'll let us know if something's not right with this attendant"

The young attendant got out, standing with the car door open, confusion clouding his face, but Tommy ignored him.

Gavin came up with an excuse. "We thought we'd save you some trouble, so we strolled up the block. Our dog is restless."

The man nodded and shrugged, but he started toward Gavin. "Whatever, man."

Tommy zoomed in on the car and kept tugging.

"He's alerting on the car, not the man," Gavin whispered, giving Brianne a surprised frown.

The attendant was about ten feet from where he'd left the car running and pulled up just inside the exit. Tommy pivoted to Gavin and whirled back to stare at the car.

Gavin shouted, "Run. Get away from that car!"

The kid looked up, surprised. He stopped and looked back.

"Hurry!"

Gavin jumped into action and hurled himself toward

Brianne and pulled her back, Tommy going with them as they ducked behind a wide concrete and steel pillar.

Before the valet could move, a loud boom hit the night air, echoing against the buildings all around.

Shrapnel flew out through the air, dinging and sputtering against parked cars on the street and hitting the windows of nearby buildings. Gavin felt a sharp, searing pain near his right temple. Brianne gasped and ducked her head, her arms going over Tommy to shield the dog.

Then the place went silent.

Gavin jumped up and dropped Tommy's leash, then took off running to where the unconscious valet attendant lay near the burning wreckage of the car, dark smoke surrounding them.

With a grunt and a tug, he pulled the bleeding man away from the destroyed car. Through the buzz in his ears, Gavin heard Brianne calling in their location and giving directions to the 911 dispatcher.

"Hurry," she shouted into her cell phone. "The vehicle could start leaking fumes."

Then she ordered Tommy to stay and ran toward Gavin and the injured attendant. Grabbing the man's legs, she helped Gavin move him off to the side, out of danger from the still-burning car and out of the path of any vehicles that might emerge around the corner. Alarms were going off everywhere. People came running. Cars skidded to a stop.

Gavin worked on keeping the man alive, checking his pulse and giving him chest compressions.

Brianne looked up and into Gavin's eyes. "I guess we won't be using the fancy car again."

"Nope." He turned his head to scan the area. "And we need to get out of here before everyone comes down to see what happened. We don't want Sanelli or Liza Collins to see us here."

Brianne stared up at the building down the street. "They won't like this kind of publicity."

Then she saw the blood running down his face near his left eye. "Gavin, you're hurt."

"Tell me about it. Burning like a bed of ants attacking me."

"You need help," she said, trying to reach out.

"No, *he* needs help. We'll worry about me later." Then he checked her over. "Are you all right?"

"I'm good," she said. "And so is our partner."

Gavin nodded and went back to counting compressions.

"I've got a pulse," he said.

By then, the first responders had arrived and someone moved them out of the way so they could get to work on saving the young attendant while the fire department put out the vehicle fire. After showing the first responders their IDs, Gavin and Brianne watched from a distance, careful to stay hidden inside one of the squad cars that had responded. Soon the firemen had the burning vehicle hosed down. Since the car had been in front of the building and away from most of the other parked cars, they were able to contain the explosion.

Gavin grabbed one of the firemen. "What's the status?"

"We haven't located the source yet, but I'd say a small incendiary device, probably triggered remotely. Could have been a lot worse. If it had exploded inside the garage and caused the gas tank to leak, the gas fumes probably would have ignited this whole place."

Brianne took Gavin farther away, around the corner and out of sight. "We need to get that gash on your temple checked."

"I'm fine," he growled, not used to being pampered. Then he looked into her eyes. "This is my fault, Brianne. If that boy dies, it's on me."

"No, it's not," she argued. "You know who did this. The Tick. He must have doubled back to leave an explosive on our car."

"I brought the car here."

"But you didn't place that bomb on it. You do realize he wants us dead?"

"I do, yes. That's why I'm so mad right now."

Brianne took his hand. "Don't be mad. We have to get even. Now we have proof someone is trying to kill us, Gavin. This is the third time, at that."

"And it won't be the last," he finally said. "Are you willing to stay with me until the end, Brianne?"

"I want you both off this case," Noah said when the whole team had gathered in the conference room the next morning. Noah explained the situation, bringing some surprised grunts and glares from several people.

"But, sir, we're so close," Gavin said, shooting a glance at Brianne. "We have to finish this thing."

"We can't stop searching now, sir," she echoed, frustration scraping across her frazzled system.

"He blew up your car," Noah reminded them. "No, wait, he blew up a car Gavin rented from a friend."

"A friend who has good insurance since he deals in luxury rentals."

"I'm not worried about insurance on the car," Noah replied, his tone hitting Brianne like nails on tin. "You two have been threatened enough and we're thankful that the attendant survived and is okay. I'm bringing in detectives for backup and I'm ordering you both to take it easy for the rest of the week." Glaring at them, he tossed them a stack of files. "See what you can find on the details of my brother's death."

"Desk duty?" Gavin said, anger coloring his words.

Brianne shot him a warning glance. "Good idea, sir. Things are too hot right now."

"Agreed," Noah replied, glancing around at the other officers. "Now…let's get to work. And you two, in my office so we can talk about how to proceed when you turn this case over to the detectives."

Gavin and Brianne exchanged looks. He wouldn't want to let go of the Tick. She'd promised to stand by him. Somebody needed to have his back.

Once they were inside Noah's office with the door shut, Brianne and Gavin sat down and waited for Noah to let them have it. Instead, he stared out the window.

"Sir?"

"I know, I know," Noah said. "You want to stay on this. You're close to finding a possible bomber. But… we don't know if this is the work of the Fourth of July bomber or the Tick, do we? Or if they are both the same man."

"I'll get on the lab to get DNA results," Gavin said.

"And I'll see if they found any trace evidence on Scrawny," Brianne added.

Noah's eyebrows shot up. "Scrawny?"

"The mutt we found at the building site the other day," Brianne said. "We think the person who shoved the beam had been with the dog before. The way the dog acted and sniffed the air made me think he caught the man's scent." Her hands on the arms of her chair, she added, "We might find some trace evidence on the dog—human hair, epidermis, fibers, anything."

"And that person could be one of our alleged bombers?"

"Yes, sir." Brianne nodded. "Or…it's not connected and just someone who doesn't want us to find your brother's killer."

"None of this makes sense," Noah admitted. "I had my doubts about letting you two do this on your own since you're not trained in undercover work and now I'll hear it from everyone up the chain of command. As if I don't have enough to deal with."

"We don't mind bringing in a couple of detectives, sir," Gavin replied. "I wanted to talk to you about that very thing."

"Well, that's something to be glad about," Noah said before sitting back in his chair.

Gavin went over their plan again. "We need to meet with Justin Sanelli one more time and seal the deal. That means we'd have to make a huge down payment on the property we pick—if we get that far."

"If these people are on to you, how do you plan to do that?"

Brianne sat up straight. "If we get in, we can possibly catch the bomber in the act. Set up a sting."

"You'll need help with that."

"We agree," she said, daring Gavin to argue with her.

Noah tapped his fingers on his calendar pad. "The commissioner's not happy about the car exploding but I assured him you are both all right and the City of New York will not be held accountable. The fire department managed to contain the fire to that vehicle. Not much damage but we'll have to pay for a few repairs on the parking garage."

"We need one more try, sir," Gavin said.

"So you think this bomber is working on his own, or with one of the brokers?"

"We don't know. We're trying to follow the information and piece things together, but we think Justin Sanelli could be involved. He could have distracted us at the open house while the bomber found our car. Tommy alerted at the open house and we tracked the man we believe to be the bomber until he got onto the subway.

Noah rubbed his chin. "So you think the man you saw at the open house watched you two arrive and slipped into the garage to plant the bomb?

They both nodded. "Or he took us on a merry chase so someone else could plant the explosives," Gavin said.

"Did anyone see you after the car exploded?"

"Not that we know of," Brianne replied. "We waited for backup and showed our IDs, then went around the corner. We didn't mingle with the crowd."

Noah studied his notes. "And we still can't find this William Caston who Brianne ID'd as the possible Fourth of July bomber. Did you get a look at the face of the man you followed today? Could he be the Tick?"

"We don't know, sir," Brianne said, shaking her head. "We never saw his face. We need solid evidence."

Noah sat silent for a minute. "Desk duty until the weekend, then come back with a plan, including discussing this with the detectives on Monday, okay? You're not going out on this again without sufficient backup, understood?"

"Understood," they both said in unison.

Once they were out and about and going to their

FOURTEEN

"So we're doing this?"

Gavin glanced over at Brianne after they met up in the designated spot, glad to see she was okay after two days of being tied to her desk and the training yard.

Brushing her fingers through Stella's shining golden coat, she said, "Sure, Sutherland, let's go have some fun."

Gavin pivoted to get a good look at her. They'd both changed up their looks yet again. "Aren't you glad to be out in the fresh air on a Saturday morning?"

"You know I'm grumpy in the mornings," she quipped. "Especially when I'm chasing after an elusive bomber in the middle of New York."

They stopped on the street, their eyes meeting.

For a brief moment, the noise of traffic and sirens and planes overhead, the sound of honking horns, children laughing and dogs barking—all of the things that made up New York City—went out of his head.

And he saw her. Only her.

He'd like to see her every morning, just like this. Grumpy or not.

He'd never been able to keep the world away, to be so

desks to dig into files, Brianne turned to Gavin. "What about the park on Saturday?"

He gave her a solemn glance. "Nothing says we can't go to the park, Bree, and take our dog for a walk."

"As Linus and Alice?"

"No, but disguised. Hats, sunshades and whatever else will make us look like normal people. We'll stay on the fringes of the crowd."

"Okay, I'll bring Stella since they might recognize Tommy. No one knows her and it'll be a good teachable moment for her. But, Gavin, normal is not in my vocabulary."

"I'm beginning to see that," he replied before he turned to his cubicle. The red welt on his temple reminded her of how close they'd come to being blown to smithereens.

But did he see everything? she wondered. Did he see the truth of her feelings each time he looked into her eyes?

calm and sure that he could focus on one thing and one thing only. Even when he worked, Gavin's mind worked along with him, like a roller coaster that couldn't stop running. Granny Irene used to tell him to focus and he'd learned how to do that on most days. But he always had a hard time trying to find complete calm and peace.

But with Brianne he felt calm and secure, although he worried about protecting her, even when the world seemed to be closing in on him.

"Gavin?"

"What?"

"Why are you staring at me like that?"

"I don't know. How is *like that*?"

Her eyes went dark with awareness. "As if we're still Linus and Alice and you'd like to kiss me."

"I'm not Linus right now, Bree. But yes, I am thinking about kissing you."

She backed away, causing Stella to give them a surprised stare. "That would be stupid."

She always made him laugh.

"You're something, you know that?"

"I'm your partner and we're walking a thin line with the entire police department. Yesterday, I had a quick lunch with Lani and Faith. They grilled me about us. People are talking."

"People are always talking."

"Stop flirting with me."

"You think I'm flirting? Really?"

"You said you wanted to kiss me."

"I'm being honest. I'd have to be dead not to notice you."

Today, she wore torn jeans and a high-necked sleeveless white blouse covered with rows of colorful necklaces and chains, a pair of strappy tan sandals and a big floral tote bag with a pair of black sunshades peeking out of a side pocket. A pretty blue scarf covered her messy now-red-again bun.

"Well, stick with me and we could both be dead," she replied with her sarcasm intact. "Each time I'm around you, someone tries to kill me."

"Bree, I'm being serious."

"I can see that. But aren't we here for pretend fun?"

He didn't understand why she tried to push him away. She'd said she didn't want any tangled relationships and he'd felt the same at first. Maybe he needed to grasp that and get back to work. Or it could be that she sensed that unease that covered him like an aura. He'd never fit in with her world because he didn't know how to do family stuff or people stuff. Always a loner. Always waiting and wondering and asking himself why he'd been abandoned by his own mother.

Would he ever be able to let go and just live, really live?

He needed to talk to the Big Man upstairs about that. Ask for some guidance on getting his life right before he turned into a perpetual bachelor.

He'd always felt the same way about work as she did—all business and no time for a love life—until he'd asked her to be his pretend wife. Dangerous territory.

Focus.

"Fun it is," he retorted, tamping down his anger and his awareness. "Fun while we try to find a bomber and his boss."

"Now that's my kind of Saturday at the park," she said, grabbing him by the arm. "Let's go explore the farmer's market and then we'll let Stella run with the big dogs."

Gavin shook his head and followed her. Her brave, carefree nature always amazed him. And scared him. He could take care of himself. He'd been doing that for years. He could be ruthless and daring. He'd learned that in high school and had come close to a crash-and-burn. But Granny Irene had nipped that in the bud by getting him a part-time job as an orderly at the hospital.

Seeing the ER on Saturdays had made him choose the law enforcement path where he'd learned to be cautious and conscientious. But the driving need to help people had carried him through.

Brianne seemed to thrive on being relentless, a good trait, but sometimes being concise and sure could win the day.

Which left him trying to figure out how to protect a woman who had too much gumption for her own good.

Well that was the thing—she'd warned him over and that she truly didn't want a man trying to protect her.

Or maybe at least not this man.

She'd wanted that kiss.

Brianne realized, while she hid behind her sunglasses and browsed through a booth full of colorful Bohemian clothes, she might be pretending a lot lately, but she'd been serious when she'd stared into Gavin's eyes an hour ago. It would have been so easy to give in, but she'd been burned by being too impulsive with her last boyfriend and too trusting with her best friend. They'd gone off together and done a number on her.

Burned and hurt and disillusioned. She charged ahead in life, but not in her love life. Not anymore.

Being a part of this case could make or break her career in law enforcement and she wasn't letting up now. She was too deep into pretending on so many levels.

It was one thing to pretend because of an undercover operation but quite another to pretend she didn't have feelings for Gavin Sutherland. She refused to let those feeling get in the way of keeping him safe and bringing in a domestic terrorist.

She had to stay the course and maybe, later, they could revisit a possible kiss. In the meantime, she would hold tight to the memory of his eyes filled with hope and passion and awareness. She'd hold on to that moment they'd shared, with the world so alive and colorful and brimming with possibilities all around them, while they were just two people fighting the good fight and fighting their own battle to keep away from each other.

"Hey, you okay?"

Brianne looked up and saw Gavin through her sunglasses. "Yes, just trying to decide if I need this tunic." Holding up the colorful, sleeveless cotton garment, she asked, "What do you think?"

He smiled and did another scan of their surroundings. "I think it's time to make our rounds."

Brianne paid the older woman manning the booth the twenty dollars for the tunic. A keepsake, colorful and bursting with life, to remind her of being in the park with Gavin.

After tucking the paper bag holding the tunic into her tote, she checked the gun nestled in the side pocket hidden inside.

Gavin wore a NY Yankees cap and dark shades, an old faded T-shirt and worn jeans, a five-o'clock shadow giving him a rugged look. He looked good and blended in with the crowd. She tried to do the same. She could pretend they were a couple strolling through the park while Stella sniffed and worked her scent grid.

When they reached a spot near the big overhead banner close to the gazebo that read Welcome to the Dog Days of Washington Market Park, sponsored by the Realtors of Rexx, she glanced around and immediately spotted Liza Collins standing near a table holding a tiny Yorkie in her arms. Liza wore crisp white jeans and a black-and-white striped cotton T-shirt, her sandals tall-heeled and expensive-looking, her Wayfarers black and dark. The tiny dog yelped and put on a fierce front despite the pink bow around her little neck.

"Gavin."

"I see. We can't get too close."

"Okay, so we stroll around the perimeters and keep our eyes open."

"Yes, and our ears. We might hear tidbits here and there."

"I don't think she'll notice us. It's getting pretty crowded."

People with their dogs were everywhere. Several booths touting dog food and chew toys were set up along the tree line, offering everything from treats to comfortable doggie beds to demonstrations on how to exercise and train animals or keep them calm during storms and other traumatic events.

"Quite an array of interesting products," she whispered close, hoping no one noticed them.

"Yeah." Gavin laughed as if he didn't have a care in the world. "You'd think people would figure out dogs only need love and a chew toy."

"That's a good start."

"Maybe that's all people need, too. To be loved and to have something or someone to comfort them and make them feel useful."

Her heart did that strange bump. The one that made her want to pull him close and hold him tight to show him he had someone on his side. "Listen to you, oh, wise one."

"I'm learning," he said, his smile soft and real. "I'm a loner but I could get used to this."

Stella halted and sniffed the air, then looked toward the big information booth.

Brianne glanced over to where Liza stood talking to a group of people. "Gavin, check it out."

Gavin looked over. One guy shifted his position, and Gavin froze. "Well, would you look at that?"

The Bushy-Brows Man. The one they'd followed into the subway and lost.

The Tick—maybe.

"The guy from last night! And he's talking to Morticia."

Gavin nodded. "And Stella recognizes him."

"She smells his scent, even if he's not carrying a bomb. Or is he?"

"I don't think the man would bomb this park. He looks too chummy with Liza."

Brianne took out her cell and snapped away, being careful to get pictures of the scenery while taking in the crowd. But she got two close-up shots of Liza with Bushy-Brows Man.

"William Caston?" she asked, her voice low and steady. "Sure looks like the mugshot."

"My gut says yes—and that he's the Tick," he replied. "We should have lab reports next week. We need a connection to that man and the Fourth of July bomber. Something to indicate they're one and the same guy."

"And now, we need to find out more on Liza Collins, too," Brianne said. "She made a big deal out of her husband's death. Blamed other brokers for the stress that caused his heart attack."

They strolled as close as they could get without being obvious. Brianne watched the people gathered around the information table. Justin Sanelli was nowhere to be found but Liza definitely worked the crowd. And the Bushy-Brows Man seemed to follow her around, listening and watching.

"Maybe he's her bodyguard," she said to Gavin.

"Then why did he abandon her at the open house and take us on a merry chase the other night?"

"To protect her," Brianne said. "Maybe just like with our suspicions about the Fourth of July bombing, that man could be a decoy and a distraction. But we still don't know if he deliberately tried to lead us away after he placed a bomb on the car or if he was just leaving the open house while someone else placed that device in our car."

Gavin gave her a nod. "I'm beginning to see the logic in him being a decoy." Glaring at Liza through his dark shades, he added, "And I'm wondering if she's the one calling the shots."

"Now we just have to follow the evidence and prove that theory," she replied.

Gavin and Brianne did hear tidbits of conversations while they strolled around the event.

"Yes, we just moved to Chelsea. Love the quaintness of the neighborhood."

"No, we decided against the efficiency in Midtown. The association wanted too much personal information."

"Yes, I talked to Justin just the other day. It's a go on the Central Park West property. Justin says things will get moving there very soon. I can't wait to see what he does with the place."

Brianne and Gavin smiled and spoke to people, talking about dogs in general, but stayed toward the back of the crowd. Bushy-Brows Man shadowed Morticia and her overly excited dog. They never once looked toward Brianne and Gavin.

"I think we should go," Gavin whispered, his head almost touching hers. "We need to find out more about Liza."

"I agree," she said after they'd ordered some iced tea from a coffee shop near the park. "At least we've established that Bushy-Brows is a dead-ringer for the Fourth of July bomber."

"And that he is highly involved with the Rexx Agency. Which supports our theory that both bombers are one and the same."

"Okay," she said as they scrolled back to the parking garage. "Let's take him in for questioning."

"Not yet," he replied. "We need to form a plan to finish this. We need to do as Noah told us and set up a sting. Besides, we're not here officially."

"Why don't we catalog this and talk about Jordan's death? What are we all missing there?"

"I don't know," he said. "We've been helping the team follow leads for months now and the only thing we've come close to was possibly finding Snapper, as if that could give us any answers. That turned out to be another setup or maybe something else to taunt us."

"We know a thug named Claude Jenks planted the suicide note and now he's dead," Brianne said as they entered the parking garage. "He can't tell us who hired him."

"We've gone over the woods where Jordan was found and didn't find much there to go on, either."

"I hope the lab techs can find something on Scrawny, so we can figure out if Jordan's killer planted the dog there to mess with part of the team or if our bomber is responsible."

Gavin guided her toward where he'd parked on the second level, using his personal vehicle today.

When he went to unlock it, Brianne stopped him. "Wait, Gavin. Let Stella get in some practice."

She guided the dog to the car and commanded Stella to search. The big girl worked her way around the car, sniffing and lowering her snout to the garage floor and then lifting her head to sniff the air and the vehicle's exterior. When she didn't find anything, Brianne breathed a sigh of relief.

"We're clear."

Then they heard footsteps hitting hard against concrete.

Someone came running toward them.

FIFTEEN

Gavin grabbed Brianne and tugged her away from the plain tan SUV. Commanding "Quiet" to Stella through a hand signal, he quickly moved them three cars away and pushed Brianne down behind a huge pickup truck.

The footsteps slowed, moving with a light tap that hit the concrete with an eerie cadence, grating against Gavin's nerves. He held his breath while he kept Brianne and the K-9 out of sight. Was someone lost? Or searching for them?

Brianne lifted her weapon out of her tote bag, checked the magazine and nodded to him. Stella sat attentive but didn't make a sound.

Gavin silently thanked God that Brianne and Lani were such dedicated K-9 officers. Stella proved to be as good as Tommy at following orders and sniffing out bombs.

He held a finger to his lips as he stayed low and took a quick glance around the truck's heavy grill. Then he held up one finger to Brianne to indicate he only saw one person.

A man moving from car to car. When the stranger

came up on Gavin's SUV, he stopped and stared at the vehicle.

Gavin held his breath. He waited, held back and watched, fully expecting the man to plant a bomb or place a tracker on the SUV.

The man leaned over and stared inside the locked car. Gavin noticed he held something in one hand but he couldn't surmise whether it was a weapon or a phone. The man glanced around, but he wore dark shades and stayed in the shadows. After a moment, he turned back and studied the vehicle again. Then he squatted near the front driver's side tire.

When a nearby vehicle cranked and started backing out, the man whirled and disappeared back toward the garage stairs and took off down toward the first floor.

The other car drove around, exiting the garage, the driver unaware that he'd probably just stopped a crime.

"Stay here," Gavin told Brianne on a curt whisper.

Her eyebrows slanted up, the questioning expression telling him she didn't like that command.

But Gavin didn't stop to argue with her. He stood but stayed low, the weapon he'd hidden at his waist now in his hand, and trotted toward where the man had gone down the stairs. Gavin leaned over the railing by the street and glanced below to the stairs and the sidewalk. But he didn't see anyone lurking about and no one left or right on the street who matched the person he'd seen earlier.

Families with laughing children, a couple walking hand in hand, an older woman pushing a stroller.

Gavin studied all of them, looking for the man who'd been too interested in his vehicle. The old woman with the stroller looked a little off. Gavin watched, waiting.

But the old woman turned and greeted a younger woman. They hugged and the older woman lifted a beautiful baby out of the stroller and handed the little girl, all dressed in pink, to the woman who was obviously her mother.

Pushing away the pangs of anger and hurt that image brought out, Gavin hit the railing and turned to hurry back to Brianne and their partner.

Once again, the bomber had come and gone. If that had been the bomber. Hard to tell in the dark muted lights of the parking garage if he'd actually left something on the SUV.

Frustrated, Gavin headed back to the spot where he'd left Brianne and Stella.

But she wasn't waiting there.

Brianne did yet another sweep of the garage, her eyes adjusting to the dark hot place while she watched Stella going over Gavin's vehicle for the third time.

If that man had planted anything, Stella would sniff it out. But she sniffed the ground around the SUV and kept moving, trying to follow the stranger's scent out onto the street below. Brianne had checked the tires and hadn't found any kind of damage there. What had that guy been doing? Would she suspect everyone for the rest of her life and chalk it up to being a police officer?

When she heard footsteps and realized someone was approaching, she signaled Stella back and raised her weapon.

Only to find Gavin rushing toward her.

"What are you doing?" he asked, clearly out of breath.

"I'm checking your vehicle for bombs or trackers," she explained. "Did you find anyone?"

"No. Gone. Again."

So he wasn't in a good mood and why should she blame him? "Well, your SUV is clear. I've searched it thoroughly."

"I told you to stay behind the truck."

The man was seriously stubborn in the protection detail department. She didn't need a detail or his protection and while it touched her each time he tried to take care of her, it also irritated her to no end. But she'd let that slide for now.

"I'm a cop, Gavin. I'm just as capable as you in checking out this scene."

He let out a sigh and shook his head. "Yes, you are. I overreacted."

"But you're still not happy with me."

"You're still a rookie."

Brianne couldn't believe he'd just said that. "Gavin? Honestly?"

"I'm sorry, Bree. But you need to learn to follow procedure."

"Follow procedure? I did follow procedure. I took our bomb-sniffing K-9 to a site that I thought might have been compromised. Your personal vehicle. What if the bomb had gone off?"

He stared into her eyes and then looked out toward the street. "Okay, all right. I'm frustrated because I don't know what's going on. Is the bomber following us? Or does this have something to do with Jordan's death? I want things resolved."

"We all do," she said, changing her tone from defensive to accepting. "But we have to work the cases as they come. You know that. We get called out every day on nothing cases and now we've got two major ones going on. It's hard and it's stressful and none of us have had time to grieve for Jordan."

He placed his hands on his hips and gave her a softer stare. "I'm sorry. That rookie comment was uncalled-for. You've gone above and beyond."

"Yes, it sure was and yes, I've tried. You're welcome, by the way."

"For?"

"For me making sure you didn't get blown to pieces just now."

He actually cracked a smile. "Thank you, Bree, for doing your job."

"And thank you, Gavin, for trying to protect your team. But we are a team, right? We work in tandem to get things taken care of and sometimes that means we have to break a few rules."

"As long as breaking the rules keeps you safe and sound and is within the guidelines."

"I'll do my best on that."

He glanced around again and then leaned close. "Bree, I'm a pain. I know that. But…you're one of the few people in our unit who seems to trust me enough to work with me. I won't forget that. I won't forget you."

"I don't want you to forget me," she said, wishing she could let go and tell him how she really felt. But he couldn't know that her feelings for him were changing and growing deeper every day. "I won't let you forget me, Gavin."

He nodded, but neither of them spoke, that silent but swift undercurrent charging through them and bonding them in a way no words of explanation ever could.

Finally, he said, "Okay, we made progress today, at least. We've got some homework to do."

Yes, they'd made progress on the case. But with each other? Still at a standoff point.

"I'm going do some digging on Liza Collins and I want to talk to Violet again tonight," she replied. "See if they've had any more brokers trying to get her and her parents to sell Griffin's."

"Good. I've tried to pin her down but she's either on her way to work at the airport or on her way to help out at the diner. She told me again she'd seen a couple of real estate brokers talking to her dad but said it all seemed civil and there was no pressure."

"Maybe the brokers seemed that way but we know different," Brianne replied. "She might be more willing to talk to me."

"Why? Because you're not as uptight and gruff as me?"

"Something like that, yeah."

His grin caught Brianne and took the breath right out of her lungs. The man really should smile more often.

Hitting the key fob to let Stella in the back, he looked over at her again. "I'll pester the lab until we get something on the Fourth of July bomber—anything that can tie him to the Tick. I can't find Beanpole. I'm beginning to worry that he's skipped town."

"You can drop Stella and me at the nearest subway station," Brianne said once they were in the SUV.

"No way. It's our day off, Brianne. I'm taking you home."

"You're not gonna do a sweep of my house again, are you?"

"Maybe. Just to be sure."

"Gavin…"

"Bree, humor me, okay."

"Would you do that if I were Carter or Finn?"

"No, but they're not nearly as pretty as you."

"I think you like being at my house. Pizza, hamburgers and now giving me a ride home."

"Maybe it's not the house I like, but the woman who lives there."

That remark flowed over her, warming her in a way that she hadn't experienced before. He did make her feel safe and secure. But this kind of security had nothing to do with bad guys or tracking explosive devices. This security had to do with her heart and how she needed to keep it safe.

Gavin might just be the one man who could give her that kind of security. Giving in to that feeling, she said, "Okay, big guy. You can come in and explore to your heart's desire."

He nodded, clearly pleased with himself. "Good. That's good, Bree. I feel better already."

Brianne decided Gavin needed to feel secure. And he needed to make others feel secure.

Her parents had given her security and a good home. She always felt safe with her parents around.

He'd never had that kind of security growing up—not the kind she'd had with two loving parents. His mother had abandoned him and his grandmother, while providing him with the necessary things he needed, had obviously tried to show her love for him in the most practical of ways.

But had she forgotten to show a scared, confused little boy the kind of emotional love that all humans craved?

Brianne said a little prayer for her big hunky partner

while they traveled across the city. She didn't mind the bumper-to-bumper traffic or the long commute. From now on, she'd try to appreciate him more. That's what the man needed—respect and appreciation.

She could show him that, at least. High time someone did.

They talked. Really talked. About New York, about why they both became police officers.

"So you have different reasons than me," she said.

Gavin checked the GPS for the quickest route and took a bridge across the river.

"Yes." The heavy traffic moved at a brisk pace. "My grandfather died in a horrible wreck. He worked in Manhattan and made a good living. My grandmother often talked about how busy the city could be. She admired the police department. She encouraged me to be of service, so she got me a job working with her in the ER. I mean, she was a hardworking nurse who saw the underbelly of all of New York. I got a good look at that, too, working in a hospital during my last year of high school."

"But you didn't become a nurse or a doctor."

"No, I wanted to be a cop. I watched police roaming the halls, filing reports, holding down meth addicts, some bringing tough-as-nails K-9s with them. I was hooked."

"My daddy would talk about the people we never notice when he'd describe his day to me," Brianne admitted. "He always had praise for law enforcement. I think they both influenced us in their own way."

"Sounds so," he replied. "I loved animals, but Granny didn't want a dog in the house. Too much trouble. I finally convinced her to let me get one when I mentioned

I wanted to become a K-9 officer. She seemed impressed when I trained a mutt from the city pound by myself."

"I always had a pet," Brianne said, holding a hand on the dash when they came off the bridge to follow 287 into Queens. "I tormented them into being trained, too." Then she laughed. "My mom has a tiny Chihuahua. Serpico is fierce. He sleeps with Stella and me and travels with them."

"We are a pair."

When they finally pulled up at Brianne's house, she noticed the door to the one-car garage stood open.

"That's odd. I know that door was down when I left. We never open it since we don't park in there."

"All the more reason for me to go inside the house with you," Gavin said, putting the SUV into Park and hurrying around to let Stella out. Giving the Quiet signal, he met Brianne as she slid out of her seat.

Slowly, they made their way to the open garage and moved around boxes of Christmas decorations and pieces of old furniture until they'd made it to the door leading to the kitchen.

Gavin went first, and Brianne didn't argue with him. Someone was clearly inside since they heard pots and pans banging.

"On three," Gavin said, waiting for Brianne to open the door so he could charge in.

He counted and she followed his lead, grabbing the doorknob to slam back the door.

Gavin rushed toward the door Stella on his heels.

Brianne followed. Then he heard a loud scream followed by an agonizing male groan and several sharp yelps and Stella's excited barks. Brianne went into action, her weapon drawn.

But the scene she saw in the kitchen stopped her cold.

SIXTEEN

Her mother stood holding a frying pan up in a defensive mode.

Serpico yelped and bared his teeth while he danced in a ranting circle, his short light-brown fur on edge.

Gavin stood by a happy-barking Stella, both of them wide-eyed, holding his weapon down.

Stella stopped short and then yelped at seeing her little friend. Serpico yelped back, but trembled in place.

Gavin rubbed his right shoulder. "Your mom knows how to use that frying pan."

Brianne took one look at the scene and burst out laughing.

"What is so funny?" her frightened mother asked, still holding the frying pan.

"I'm wondering that myself," Gavin added. Then he glanced at her mom. "May I put my weapon away?"

Her mother nodded, slowly. "Yes, and I shall do the same."

They both stared at each other while Gavin put his gun back underneath his T-shirt and her mother lowered the ridiculously huge frying pan onto the counter.

Stella sniffed. Gavin blushed. Serpico snarled. Her mother didn't move.

Brianne pushed past Gavin. "Serpico, hush up. Mom, are you all right?"

"Other than having my nineteenth heart attack, I am perfectly fine," her mother said, her salt-and-pepper short hair seeming to stand straight up on her head. "Who is this man?"

"I'm Gavin Sutherland," Gavin said, offering his hand in peace. "I work with Brianne."

"Officer," her mother replied, taking his hand with all the grace of a queen. "Nice to meet you."

"Same here, ma'am," Gavin said.

"Gavin, this is my mother, Janet Hayes," Brianne said, still smiling.

Gavin nodded and dropped her mother's hand. "I'm sorry for startling you."

"I'm fine," Mom said. "My heart rate is going down, at least." Then she glanced at his shoulder. "I've assaulted a police officer. I'm sorry."

Motioning to Serpico, Janet watched him trot over and then lifted the little imp up and soothed him with soft words. Serpico shot Gavin a petulant pout, followed by another snarl, his little body shaking despite his bravado.

Brianne knew she'd have some explaining to do. But first she had some questions. "Mom, I didn't know you and Dad were coming home today. Where's your car?"

"Your father went to get milk and eggs," Mom said, waving her hand in the air. "I told him that could wait. And I did try to call you. Many times."

Brianne winced. "I had my phone muted for part of the day."

"Oh, well, that explains it," her mother said with that infamous tone Brianne knew so well. Then she put Serpico down and told him to find his bed. The little fellow tapped across the room and hopped up onto his tiny doggie bed, his big brown eyes daring anyone to mess with him.

"We were on a case, Mrs. Hayes," Gavin said, clearly respectful of that frying pan. "It's my fault. I told her to silence her phone."

"And she listened?"

Now Gavin burst out laughing. "For once, yes," he said.

"You'll stay for dinner, then." her mother replied, not really forming it as a question.

Gavin glanced at Brianne, his body language shouting panic.

"Mom, Gavin was just dropping me off."

"Nonsense," her petite mother retorted, pulling things out of the refrigerator. "I'll make meatballs. Are you hungry, Gavin?"

"I could eat but—"

"It'll be about an hour. Just have to warm up these homemade meatballs. You know, I use Italian sausage and special herbs."

Brianne could almost hear the poor man's stomach growling.

"Mom, we have some reports to file and work to do."

Janet gave her an as-if glance. "You can do that while I cook."

Brianne knew when she'd been beaten. "Okay then."

Her mother stopped everything and came over to give her a hug and kiss. "How are you, baby?"

"I'm good," Brianne said, shooting Gavin an apologetic look over her mother's shoulder. "We've just been so busy with this investigation."

Janet held up a hand. "I know you can't discuss it. And I get that. I'd hoped you'd come out to the beach and visit with us."

"I wanted to, but work."

"Yes, work. So go down and work and I'll call you when it's ready." Then she leaned down. "Hello, Miss Stella. How are you today?"

Stella barked and pranced, knowing a treat might be in her future. Serpico lifted his little head and snarled again.

"You are a good girl," Janet purred to Stella. Then she got busy again, pulling out frozen things and humming to herself. "It's so good to be home. I love my sister, but you know how that goes."

"I'm glad you're home, too, Mom," Brianne said. Then she motioned to Gavin. "We can go down to my apartment. Mom, can I help with dinner?"

"No. Go do your work so we can visit later."

Brianne obeyed her too-interested mother and indicated to Gavin to get moving. They hurried down the stairs, the K-9 following them. Serpico got up and inserted himself into the fun, too, Stella playing with him in a friendly fashion.

When they were downstairs, Brianne turned to Gavin. "I'm so sorry."

He grinned and leaned down to show Serpico he was not the enemy, letting the scared little dog sniff his knuckles. "Why apologize? I'm the one who frightened your poor mother."

Brianne giggled. "As you can see, my *poor* mother can hold her own."

"Good point," he replied. "So...I'm staying for dinner?"

"Yes, you are."

She moved around the kitchen and found them two sodas. "Meantime, make yourself at home and prepare to be interrogated."

"This should be interesting," Gavin replied, his eyes soft on her.

Brianne decided he made this apartment seem so small. He filled it and her life with a definite presence that enveloped her in a tingly, charged awareness.

"Are you okay with this?" he asked, misreading her silence.

"I don't think I had a choice," she replied, meaning more than just another meal with him. "But you sure seem to be hanging out at my house a lot."

"I know," he said, serious now. "I could get used to this."

"One day, I'd like to see your home, Gavin."

"That can be arranged. But I don't cook much."

"I don't, either, but once you've had my mother's famous spaghetti and meatballs, you won't go hungry again. She'll want to feed you forever."

"That sounds like a fair trade."

She nodded. "Okay, let's get down to work."

He stretched and took his weapon out of his waistband and laid it on a high shelf. "Where do we start?"

His question should have been regarding work, but Brianne sensed he was asking her a personal question.

Where would they start, once they were finished?

They found a lot of interesting information but nothing criminal regarding Liza Collins.

Gavin read off the findings. "Divorced twice. Daughter to a real estate mogul and third marriage to yet another real estate success—Watson Collins. With her older husband, she became a New York socialite and a powerhouse in the real estate world, but her husband suffered a fatal heart attack after his firm was investigated for embezzlement and fraud."

Brianne nodded along with each word. "Not so much as a traffic ticket on her, but I remember the investigation and how Watson Collins almost lost everything. Liza went to the Wharton School of Business, not to mention making millions in record-breaking housing market sales at a very young age. I'm impressed."

"She's still creepy," Gavin said, his gut burning. "Something about her doesn't sit well with me. And then I told you about that plaid hat I saw on the office shelf in that fancy apartment."

"Yes. Why was it there?"

"Why was a similar baseball cap lying on the roof of that building?"

"And the bomber in the park definitely was wearing the same kind of hat." Brianne looked up at Gavin. "Why would the bomber leave a dog at a construction site?"

"He wanted to lure us there to get rid of us, because you saw him up close and we're both searching for him. But we don't know yet if this was our bomber, although the hat indicates that."

Brianne stared at her notes. "Yes, and he later rigged our vehicle to explode at the garage entrance near the fancy open house." She paused, her brow furrowing, her pen tapping. "But, Gavin, he had a good opportunity to harm us when we followed him to the subway. He could have called for help or turned to attack us."

"He's too smart for a full-on confrontation, Bree. I think he was testing us to see if we'd blow our cover."

"Do you think he planted Scrawny at that building site?"

"You know, the tip about the dog could just be coincidence, like someone suggested."

"True but when we got to that building, someone did try to kill us. What if a random person called in the tip—not knowing anyone else was around. Then Plaid Cap followed us and hid until the other person left and then he tried to kill us with the only weapon he could find—that beam."

Serpico came and nudged Gavin's boot. Gavin lifted the little dog and held him in his lap. The munchkin sure liked to be in on the action.

"He could have tossed one of us off that building or trapped us in the elevator while he put an explosive device on our vehicle again. Or better yet, he could have blown up the building with us in it. But he didn't do any of that."

Brianne's eyes widened, the frown and furrow back. "Maybe he got interrupted by whoever else was there? The person who called in the dog tip?"

"If the bomber tracked us there and tried to get to us, but realized someone else was already there, he would have tried to hide or get away."

"And in his hurry to do that, he lost his hat?"

Brianne twisted a strand of hair falling out of her bun. "Or left it to tease us a little more."

Gavin dropped Serpico down and grabbed his cell

phone. "I'm going to find out about surveillance on that building and see if the lab has anything for us yet."

Brianne took Serpico and held him tight, whispering sweet things to the scrappy little Chihuahua. She had a way with animals. And she had a way of making Gavin more centered and focused, too.

He called the lab, knowing someone would still be there. That place never shut down. When Ilana answered, Gavin explained what he needed.

"I was about to call you," the tech said. "We ran the prints you gathered, but we couldn't find a clear set on the doors. Too many to distinguish since it's a construction site."

"And the baseball cap we found? Any DNA on that?"

"Nothing significant on DNA, no. Sorry. However, we did find some synthetic fibers."

"From what?"

"Possibly from a wig. We thought we had a couple of good hair fibers but they turned out to be synthetic."

Gavin let that settle over him. "So our man could be wearing a wig under the hat?"

"Yes. Which means not much to find on the hat." Gavin heard her rustling through some papers. "I'll let you know about anything we find on the dog bowls."

"And the evidence from the park bombing?"

"That's gonna take a few days longer, Gavin."

"Thank you," Gavin said. "I'll check with Danielle about the possible surveillance video on the building site where we located the dog."

Ending the call, he glanced over at Brianne. "They found wig hair on the hat."

"Wig hair?" Brianne gave him a surprised stare. "So our bomber is definitely wearing a wig?"

"Yep—someone was wearing the plaid cap over a wig. Makes sense it could be our bomber since he doesn't want to be recognized and he avoids facing cameras straight on. Probably fake eyebrows, too."

"But we can't prove any of this."

"No, and Noah is going to make us turn this over to the detectives next week. We have to find something soon that can match the Fourth of July bomber with the Tick and the Rexx Agency."

Brianne tapped her pen on her notes. "Liza Collins and Justin Sanelli appear to be clean—and I use that word *appear* loosely, since I think Sanelli is sneaky and too suave and she's creepy and as cold as a frozen salmon. But we've seen someone who looks like our bomber with Morticia. And we think he was at the open house." Shrugging, she said, "Maybe she sends several of them out like minions. Who knows?"

"All we need is one—a strong connection if we can prove it."

"Then we need to keep at it," Brianne said. She picked up her cell phone and called her friend Violet, and told her she was sending pictures of a couple real estate brokers to see if they'd visited Griffin's.

"I'll look them over," Violet said. "Other than what we've told you guys, nothing regarding real estate has escalated. We've had a couple of scary moments with other issues lately but this is a new one. I hope you find these people."

Brianne ended the call and waited for Violet to respond to the photos of Justin Sanelli and Liza Collins.

I don't recognize either of them, Violet texted.

Brianne texted back a thank-you.

Gavin watched Brianne work, knowing she wanted

to solve this case, same as him. He wanted to warn her again to be careful but he wanted this bomber, too. Someone was playing a game of cat and mouse with them.

"I'm going to contact Justin again and tell him we're getting impatient. Maybe he can make something happen."

"And we'll be there to make something happen, too," she said, her tone low. "Like several arrests."

Gavin nodded. "Bree, I appreciate all your hard work."

"It's my job."

"Yeah, but—"

"Your dad's home, Bree. Dinner!"

They both sat up in their chairs like guilty teenagers. "My mom has a good set of lungs," she said with a laugh, her tone shaky.

Gavin had been about to go personal, so he was glad her mother had stopped him from doing something stupid like sharing his feelings. *Keep it professional.*

So he said, "And I have a good appetite. That smells so wonderful."

"Okay, let's go eat and then we'll get back at it."

Gavin couldn't argue with that. "Let's do some more searching on Morticia. My gut tells me she's up to her false eyelashes in this mess."

"We'll start there," Brianne said as they moved up the stairs, two four-legged buddies following them. "Meantime, prepare to meet my dad."

Gavin took a deep breath. "Can't wait."

Already in too deep with Brianne, now he was meeting her folks. *Just dinner with a coworker,* he told himself.

But he sure wouldn't mind it becoming more than

that. If he survived this dinner and they solved this case, he might have a glimmer of hope about things moving to a new level with Brianne and him. At least that little gatekeeper Serpico liked him.

SEVENTEEN

Monday morning, Brianne headed to the break room and saw Faith pouring herself a cup of coffee to go with the bagel she had already started nibbling.

"Hey there," Faith said, smiling over her shoulder, the coffeepot in her hand. "Want me to pour you a cup of rocket fuel?"

"Please," Brianne said, Stella at her feet. She rubbed her eyes and stifled a yawn.

"Rough weekend?" Faith asked, her dark curls tucked and pinned behind her ears.

"Up late working through some things."

"Alone or with Gavin?"

Brianne did a mock frown. "Who wants to know?"

"Just about everyone who works here," Faith admitted, "but especially Lani and me."

Brianne took the steaming cup of dark coffee and held it with both hands. "We hung out for a while Saturday. Then I went over everything about this case again last night. So many details to piece together even if I'm officially on desk duty."

"That's every case," Faith said. "Are you still working on Jordan's murder case, too?"

"Yes, but…it's hard to figure that one out since we don't have any solid leads. We didn't have much evidence to work with at that building site where we found Scrawny and we're not even sure if the call was related to Jordan's murder or our bomber."

She wouldn't discuss the details past that information.

"Drink up," Faith said, knowing not to push. "Scrawny is going to have to get a new name soon. He is fast becoming a handsome boy. I think he'll do great as a service dog."

"That's good to hear," Brianne said, her mind on the construction site.

"Want half my bagel?" Faith offered.

Brianne shook her head. "No, I ate at home. Just needed some more caffeine."

Faith left, and Brianne sank down on a chair and thought about having Gavin eat dinner with her parents the other night. Her dad hit it off with him immediately. Soon they were into a long discussion on sports. Baseball was her dad's favorite and Gavin spouted off stats and predictions for the World Series that had Ronald Hayes nodding his head and laughing.

Her dad had winked at her, meaning he approved.

Mom had stood behind the kitchen counter like a judge overseeing a courtroom, her smile serene, her gaze moving with laser-like precision from Gavin to Brianne and back.

Brianne knew that mind. Her mother was probably picturing grandchildren. Several of them. Drat. Now she was picturing a cute baby with Gavin's big brown eyes.

"Stop it," Brianne said. As if she could.

"Excuse me?"

Brianne glanced up to find Sophie Walters staring at her.

"Oh, hi, Sophie. Didn't hear you come in." Or she wouldn't have been talking to herself.

"I guess not," Sophie said, her smile as pretty as ever. Her blue eyes missed nothing, though. Brianne liked Sophie and she was happy for Sophie and Luke and all of her other friends who'd found love despite their tough jobs.

That might not work for her, however.

"Sorry, I was talking to myself." She glanced at the box of doughnuts someone had kindly left on the counter. "I want a doughnut, but I have to refrain."

Brianne had been eating way too much lately. Her mom's meatballs were her favorite and she'd had another plateful last night. But she'd especially enjoyed watching Gavin's face on Saturday during his first bite of a meatball with her mom's homemade spaghetti sauce.

He'd looked like a little boy on Christmas.

"Seriously good," he'd said, still chewing.

Her mother had fallen in love with him at that moment.

And maybe, Brianne had, too.

Stop it, she said to herself this time.

But no one heard her thoughts. Except maybe Stella. The astute dog lifted her head and stared at Brianne, hoping for a doughnut but offering feminine appreciation.

"Don't tell," Brianne whispered. "We need to get to work."

Okay, now Sophie was looking at Brianne like she'd lost her mind.

Her radio crackled to life. A robbery in progress

at a nearby shopping center. Perpetrator getting away on foot.

A 10-31. Robbery. Commercial.

Dumping the rest of her coffee in the trash, she let Sophie know she was responding, grabbed Stella and took off. Even though Stella was being trained for explosive devices, the patrol officers who arrived on the scene would need backup. They could help search to give Stella more out-in-the-field experience.

Brianne got in her SUV, with Stella in the back, and drove the three blocks over.

When she got to the small shopping strip and skidded to a stop, she saw several of New York's finest already on the scene.

Then she spotted Gavin with Tommy walking the perimeters of the small parking lot. They hadn't talked since Saturday night, not even about work since she hadn't found much else on Liza Collins. If the woman was involved, she'd covered her tracks completely.

"Hey," she said, suddenly shy after the way he'd stood at her door Saturday night and smiled at her like a goofy teenager. She'd smiled right back at him, too. Putting that memory away when he only nodded at her in a curt way, she got down to business. "What's the situation?"

"Two males. One, blond and tall, and the other dark-haired and wearing a yellow shirt." He studied the street and watched Tommy for signs of any alerts. "Took off on foot to the east."

"Why aren't we searching?"

He shrugged and readjusted his cap. "We're on standby. Zach and K-9 Eddie took the lead."

"Drug detection?"

He nodded, staying alert, not looking at her. "The store clerk said they both were high on something. They stole cash, bashed her over the head and ran out when she managed to sound an alarm."

Brianne glanced around. The store's front had been cordoned off with crime scene tape and was closed to the public. Patrol officers, K-9 officers and crime scene techs walked in and out, evidence bags in hand. A woman sat in an open ambulance, a wide piece of white gauze covering her head.

Feeling awkward, Brianne smiled at Gavin. "My parents enjoyed meeting you."

"Yeah, they seem like great folks."

So he didn't want to be goofy this morning. Well, she'd told herself to be professional. But that didn't mean they couldn't be polite. *Forget polite.*

She was about to find out what his problem was when they heard a ruckus around the corner. A dog snarled and barked and a human screamed in fear.

"Looks like Eddie found one of our suspects," Gavin said, taking off so fast to check things out that he left her and Stella both prancing in a circle.

Brianne followed, thinking it was going to be a long day. And why was he acting so strangely?

Gavin tried to keep his mind on providing backup while Zach came out of an abandoned building, a cuffed man stumbling and mumbling in front of him. The tall one. Eddie trotted along, clearly proud of apprehending a dangerous drug addict.

But Zach had things under control and the other assailant had been found cowering behind some shipping crates in a corner of that same building, a wad of cash-register money sticking out of his pocket. Nothing much for Gavin to do here.

And nothing to take his mind off Brianne and how she'd somehow made him feel right at home with her folks. Too at home. He'd never felt this way before, as if he belonged. So he'd decided to step back.

Way back. But he needed a lot of distractions.

This kind of work happened on a daily basis. Sad but true.

The busy morning had cleared his head and now he wanted to move on to the next crazy thing that came across the radio.

But he couldn't stop thinking about this weekend and that night around the dinner table with Brianne, her parents, Stella and that little bundle of hair named Serpico.

They'd laughed and joked with each other, the loud love surrounding them a sharp contrast to the quiet his grandmother often demanded in her gentle but firm way. He didn't resent his upbringing and he loved his grandmother, but he'd missed out on that loud love, that flexible, always-going-with-the-flow kind of family dynamic that he'd felt at Bree's house.

He'd felt that love the minute he'd walked in with her that first time. He wished he'd stayed away. It would be hard to walk away now and go back to the silence of his life.

That ache in his heart had subsided last night and now this morning it had come rushing back with all the swift sharpness of a knife cutting through his soul.

"Are you okay?"

Brianne. She'd want answers and he didn't know how to explain things to her without hurting her.

"I'm fine. Just tired."

"Me, too." She started walking with him toward their SUVs. "Can't find anything on Liza Collins, other than she's ruthless and aggressive on winning real estate deals. A good businesswoman but not a people person."

"I set up another meeting with Justin Sanelli," he said before they could move back into a personal conversation. "Thursday at 3:00 p.m. He said he's found some properties that fit what we're looking for. Are you up for it?"

"I'm ready to finish this," Brianne replied, her tone all business, her gaze holding his in a definite challenge. "Are you ready?"

"Yes," he admitted. "I want to get this solved and over with."

"Want to get rid of me, Sutherland?"

He could be honest in his answer. "Not you, Bree. Just this having to look over our shoulders, trying to chase down a man who has no scruples and the amoral people who pay his salary."

"Then I'd say we're both ready," she replied, her tone softer now.

"By the way, Noah cleared us per our last discussion with him. Let's meet at the safe house again." He turned to leave, thinking this was for the best—this pulling back, going neutral, trying to pretend he didn't want more.

"I'll be there."

He could feel her eyes glaring at him. Telling himself he was a coward in the relationship department, Gavin wanted to turn back but he kept walking.

Yep—a long week.

The week turned out to be a busy one for Brianne. Once they were back from the robbery call, she and

Gavin updated two detectives sent from high up on what they'd been doing and what they'd found so far.

The detectives agreed to let them take the lead and they'd be their eyes and ears on the street, as well as backup.

"I don't want you two out there on your own again," Noah had explained in a tone that indicated they'd better not argue with him. They didn't.

Freddie Alverez, a well-liked detective who'd transferred to Queens two years ago, asked Gavin what he could do to help.

"Find Beanpole," Gavin said. "I'm worried about him. He's not showing up in the usual places and he's not answering the burner phone I gave him a month ago."

"You know how street people are," Freddie replied, his dark eyes piercing and steady, his inky hair spiked and shaggy. "They like to hide sometimes."

"I'm still worried," Gavin replied. "Beanpole is usually predictable."

"I'll do what I can," Freddie promised after taking what information Gavin could give him on the wayward homeless man. "And I'll be your driver come Thursday."

Noah had insisted Gavin and Brianne have a driver each time they went to meet Sanelli. No argument. No more fancy *borrowed* cars.

Several more routine calls, inlcuding one involving a bomb scare in Times Square that turned out to only be a backpack a teenager had left on the bleachers there. Then a possible bomb threat in a building in Chelsea that had her heart pumping and Gavin and Tommy out the door with Stella and Brianne.

Nothing. They'd found nothing in the five-story

apartment building near 24th Street and Waterside Park, two blocks from the High Line. But both Gavin and Brianne agreed the call had been odd since the building was full of renters and not scheduled for a sale or demolition.

A prankster or someone toying with them again?

"They could have set that up to flush us out," Gavin said to Brianne and Noah later. "Maybe to do some surveillance and identify us as Linus and Alice?"

"We were in full uniform with our hats on," Brianne told Noah. "And no one was around. The entire block was cleared."

"But a nervous bomber has ways around that," Gavin said. "This is another one of those non-coincidence things like the shooting at Griffin's and the report of the dog at that building site. Just too close for comfort."

"Finish this," Noah replied. "These people could be on to you or maybe this was random, not connected to your investigation."

Someone had called in a bomb threat, either way, and it had been their job, along with others in the area who'd answered the call, to check things out. Brianne had to hope that with so many uniforms taking over the area, she and Gavin hadn't been singled out. They'd worked hard to disguise themselves each time they met with Justin Sanelli.

Now, in plain clothes but a disguise nonetheless, Brianne rode the subway from Queens to Manhattan, headed for the safe house just off Broadway. She'd already put the rinse on her hair again and done her face and eyes in heavy makeup. She had an overnight bag with her regular clothes so she could change and go home on the subway and take a cab from the train hub to her house.

As usual, the afternoon commute was crowded. Brianne had her hair covered with a large floppy hat and she wore big dark sunglasses.

Don't act like a cop, Brianne thought. Stella would be waiting for her with a handler at the safe house—to help protect Brianne while she was there alone. Since regular pets had to be in a carrier to ride the subway, this was the best plan. Usually when they were both suited up in their uniforms, people on the subway made a wide berth. No one wanted to be taken down by a K-9 officer and her four-legged partner. Dog bites hurt. But Stella would guard first, and only bite if ordered.

She missed her K-9 partner. Having Stella with her as much as possible gave the dog training hours and gave Brianne some protection. A precaution Gavin and she had agreed on, at least. But Brianne had her weapon nearby, and she covertly studied the passengers getting on the train.

Nervous about being on assignment with Gavin again today, she watched the crowded car and wondered why he'd pulled away after what she considered a successful meeting with her overly protective parents. Maybe too successful. Or he didn't like having family so involved in his work. Or just her family? Did he want to be a loner the rest of his life? Or did he not want to be with her?

Brianne couldn't figure it out, but she used the hour or so on the train to consider Gavin from every angle. She came to one conclusion.

He was afraid of loving anyone. He'd lost so many

people in his life, why would he want to risk everything for her?

I should be worth it.

She wanted to be worthy of someone's love but this life, this job made that hard. Maybe they were too much alike, too determined and ambitious and stubborn to take things beyond work.

Glancing around, Brianne tugged her hat close and watched people at each stop.

Then she noticed a man with dark shaggy hair and heavy eyebrows getting on at the station. He looked a lot like The Plaid Cap man!

Brianne snuggled down in her seat and kept her hat low. If she could get a good look, she could ID him and report this. Or follow him.

Gathering her wits, she watched as he sat down a good distance away, many people between them. As far as she could tell, he hadn't noticed her. But would he spot her when she had to exit? Or should she follow him?

Brianne took a breath and formed a plan. She'd stay on until the man got off the train and then she'd alert Gavin to send one of the detectives to tail Plaid Cap. She couldn't take on this man on her own, as much as she wanted to. She texted Gavin and told him which train she was on and who had joined her.

On it, he texted back. Be careful.

When Plaid Cap stood to exit, Brianne knew she had to do as Gavin asked. This was her exit, too.

EIGHTEEN

Gavin got out of the car he'd brought to take them to meet Justin Sanelli and hurried up to the Gable Hotel's double front doors. Detective Freddie Alvarez sat in the driver's seat, wearing a chauffeur cap and dark clothes. There as backup, he'd make sure no devices were put on the car.

Glad for the help, Gavin hurried to get Brianne, who should be in their room. Noah had put patrols all the subways around Manhattan based on what she'd texted so that Plaid Cap could be tailed, but so far nothing. And he'd heard nothing from Brianne, either.

He went through the front door of the old hotel and nodded to the front desk clerk, also an undercover detective taking over for today only. They'd covered all the bases.

When he knocked on the door of the suite, Gavin steeled himself. Tommy looked up at him with loyal eyes, always ready to do his job.

The door opened, and he took in the sight of Brianne in a flowing floral summer dress and strappy sandals, a small shoulder bag hanging over her arm, the gold designer initial on it winking at him. Just big enough to get a weapon in, he imagined. She wore her hair up in a messy bun and long swaying earrings hung like miniature wind chimes from her ears.

Breathless, she said, "Let's go."

"Are you all right?" he asked, thinking he sounded neutral while his heart was anything but neutral. And she smelled like summer, fresh and clean.

"Fine." Turning to Stella, she ordered the curious Lab to stay and pointed to the doggie bed the hotel had provided for their suite. Their friend downstairs would check on Stella and take her for a walk. "I got here late. I followed Plaid Cap into the crowd but...he slipped out a side door."

"Brianne..."

"Don't fuss, Gavin," she whispered as they headed out. "I had to keep an eye on him until I saw one of our detectives nearby."

"He could have turned and recognized you."

"I was heavily disguised in a huge floppy hat and my sunglasses."

They got into the backseat of the sedan, the detective turned chauffeur at the wheel.

"The building is in Chelsea," Gavin said, deciding he wouldn't chastise her, but later he'd have to discuss this with her. "Three blocks from where the bomb threat happened earlier this week."

"Hmm, that's interesting," Brianne added, keeping her voice low. "I think the Tick sent us a calling card." Then she sat up. "What if he's going to the same place?"

"We'll know soon," Gavin replied, his expression going dark. "If they're playing us, I'd rather meet them head-on than let them walk."

"I don't want these people doing their dirty work anymore."

"We can agree on that," he replied, his gut churning.

"So what's the building?"

"The CHL—Chelsea-Highline, but Justin called it the CHL Condos. He says the building is *vulnerable* and needs a lot of work. But the seller's asking price is high."

"So a perfect building for him to mess with," Brianne said, her gaze moving over the traffic.

His phone buzzed. Gavin answered and then thanked the detective on the line. Turning to Brianne, he said, "Plaid Cap got away again. Turned into an alley and managed to disappear."

"I hate not knowing where he is and what he's doing."

"Ditto. But we have strong backup and we have to play our parts."

Freddie pulled the sleek black car up to the redbrick building that shot toward the sky.

"This one really does look like a bargain," Gavin said before they got out. "Maybe fifteen floors."

Brianne stared up at it, her eyes dark. She'd gone off on her own today—following Plaid Cap until she'd spotted a cop on his trail. What if she hadn't seen their backup? How could he get past that?

Work. Focus on work.

"I'll be around the corner," Freddie said with a final nod.

They both had tiny wireless mic pieces hidden in their clothing. Bree's was in the neckline of her dress, and Gavin's was taped onto the handkerchief in his lapel in case they needed to warn the two detectives assigned to watch out for them.

Gavin guided Brianne and Tommy into the small lobby, noticing the exits down hallways each way and the two elevator bays behind the unmanned reception desk. No doorman and not much security. Justin waited next to the mailboxes near the elevators.

"Hello, you two," Justin said, all sweetness and light, his dark shades hooked on the pocket of his white button-up shirt. He air-kissed Brianne and gave Gavin a quick, firm handshake. "I think I've found the perfect place for you."

"It's drab," Brianne said, doing a sweep over her pulled-down sunshades. "But I can see the potential."

Justin nodded, his icy blue eyes twinkling. "I believe you know how to overcome drab, Mrs. Reinhart."

"Linus, what do you think?" he asked, shifting his weight from one Italian loafer to the other before tentatively reaching out to pet Tommy. The spaniel allowed it, his head up while Justin scratched between his ears.

So Tommy didn't think Justin was a bad guy—or at least had no scent related to making bombs. The man did like his aftershave, however.

Gavin watched as Brianne steered Tommy back by her side and then gave the place his full attention. "I think I should be able to get the best possible price— a low bid. This place needs some serious tender loving care."

"Good, good," Justin said, beaming. "Let's take the full tour."

He took them past the shabby unmanned desk, explaining that most of the former tenants had moved out and the building was slowly becoming empty. The owner wanted to sell, but he was being stubborn about the price and refused to negotiate.

"But I have one ace left in the hole," the bubbly broker said as he hit the tarnished elevator buttons.

Gavin's gaze met Brianne's. They both knew what that ace might be. This investigation was about to move forward.

Finally.

Once he had the Tick behind bars, Gavin had big plans of his own. He planned to find a way to overcome the solid wall of fear he had each time he thought about being with Brianne.

There had to be a way to crack that wall, same as cracking a major case. He hoped. He prayed.

Brianne held Tommy's leash tightly when they exited on the fifteenth floor. The penthouse.

"This whole floor could be your apartment," Justin explained. "It's four different apartments with hallways running between them in a four-square design. Tear out three of the kitchens and knock out a couple of walls and you'd have close to six-thousand square feet, several large bed and baths and a view of different areas of the city from every room."

Brianne could hear the gleeful greed in his words. "Yes, this could work," she said, smiling to hide the anger whirling through her. "Or we could just tear down the building and start over." Spotting the Hudson River, she added, "I'd kill for this view."

Justin gasped and put a hand to his mouth. "We won't have to go quite that far for you to get it."

Brianne smiled knowingly at Gavin, not even having to pretend. "I would hope not."

Justin moved them through the main apartment, pointing out the pros and cons. "There's the High Line.

It's just around the block. You can stroll to your heart's desire. Tommy here would love that, right?"

Tommy woofed right on cue.

They all laughed. "I think he agrees," Gavin said.

"And you have dining on one of the piers by the river at sunset—just two blocks to the west. And, of course, Chelsea Market on Ninth Avenue, again with the High Line passing through on Tenth Avenue."

"You're reeling me in, Justin," Brianne said, her hand on Justin's buff arm. "Keep talking."

He showed them another apartment on the other side, smaller, but with more panoramic views. "There's the Empire State Building."

"Amazing," Gavin said, his tone just below giddy.

"Not to mention the Flower Market and Chelsea Park," Justin added. "This place is going to shine. It has everything nearby you'd ever need." Then he did a mock-pout. "But *it* needs someone to give it the attention required to turn it into a gleaming modern apartment building. Who says gentrification isn't a good thing?"

"Not me," Brianne replied, wanting to strangle him. "But brand-new is always good, too."

They finished viewing the entire top floor and came back to the biggest of the four apartments.

"Impressive," Gavin said. "What do you think, Alice in Wonderland?"

Brianne chuckled. "Darling, I think I'm *in* Wonderland."

"Justin, I think we have a winner," Gavin said to the eager man standing there with them.

"I do, too," Brianne said, her arms opening wide. "I can see it now. A huge gourmet kitchen here, open to the fabulous den and living area. We'll add more windows and glass doors so I won't miss out on any part of this incredible view. And the bedrooms… What, maybe four or five, at least? And the baths. We'll redo all of them and add bigger closets, of course."

"I hear the swish of my money leaving my hands," Gavin said with a laugh.

"So do I," Justin chimed in. "I hope a large chunk of it lands in my hands."

Gavin pulled Brianne close. "Is this the one?"

"Let's look at the entire building," she replied. "We'll have to bring in people, inspectors, surveyors, the works, but this building has good bones. I think we should make an offer."

"Strong bones," Justin quipped, sensing a deal. "I'm guessing it can withstand anything."

Gavin kissed Brianne. "I'm thinking that same thing." Then he told Justin their low-end price, a sum that boggled Brianne's mind but made the greedy broker wince.

But the kiss had boggled her mind *and* her heart. It was quick, efficient and…wonderful. What would a real kiss from Gavin do to her?

How would they ever pull this off? And how would she ever get over her feelings for him?

Later at Griffin's, Gavin sat down with Brianne inside the Dog House, the room reserved for NYPD's best. They were both exhausted, starving and glad they'd made the next move with Sanelli. No sign of Plaid Cap, however. Why did the man keep slipping away?

"So everything is in place since I filled out paperwork on this months ago and got clearance to make an offer within a certain amount. We can deliver the down payment by Tuesday," Gavin said once they'd ordered their meals. "They will never cash the check, however."

They'd left Justin Sanelli a very happy man. Now they both decided on Barb's baked chicken and rice with string beans on the side. A good hearty meal.

"That's a lot of zeroes," Brianne said after sipping her iced tea. "But Sanelli won't get his hands on any of the department's cash."

"Not with us to stop it."

They sat talking for a few minutes, Tommy and Stella lying at their feet. The place wasn't too busy tonight. Only a cluster of other officers in plain clothes in a corner and several tables of loud patrons in the main area.

"You charmed Sanelli," Gavin said, thinking she'd already charmed him. She had a good laugh and a great smile. He'd given her a spontaneous kiss while pretending.

He wondered what it would be like to kiss her in the quiet when they were alone and off duty.

But would they ever reach that point?

He was working two undercover operations here— the bomber case and the case of slowly falling for a woman he couldn't have. How long could he keep pretending?

The kitchen door next to their table swung open. The waiter bringing their food stopped, his body holding the door while one of the chefs asked him about an order. The scents and sounds from the kitchen wafted through the room.

Tommy and Stella both stood, lifted their heads and stared at the kitchen door.

Gavin sent Brianne a glance. "Time to move."

"Get out of the doorway," Gavin said to the surprised waiter.

The young man stepped out into the restaurant and then set their food, tray and all, on the table. "What's wrong?"

The chef stood inside the door, holding it. "Hey, officers, what's up?"

The other officers immediately stood, too.

Brianne motioned them to the door. "We got an alert from our partners." Turning to the chef, she said, "Get Lou and everyone out of the kitchen. We need to search it now."

The off duty officers knew what to do.

"I'll call it in," one of them said.

"I'll clear the main room," another one called, heading toward the closed glass door between this room and the other dining area. His voice boomed, "NYPD. People, clear the room. Get out now!"

Gavin and Brianne hurried through the swinging door. "We need to search the kitchen," Gavin called, seeing Louis coming toward him. "Lou, stop everything and get everyone out of here."

Lou didn't asked questions. "Turn off the stoves and burners and get out," he ordered.

Two other officers arrived and shouted, "Let's go. Now!"

His staff did as he told them, knowing when two K-9 officers came into their workspace that something was up.

"Search. Find."

Tommy and Stella trotted around the long square kitchen, their snouts moving from ground to air. When

Tommy alerted on one of the storage rooms, Gavin knew they were in for trouble. Stella immediately did the same, sniffing, sitting and then looking back at them.

"Come," Gavin and Brianne ordered, getting the dogs away as quickly as possible.

They rushed out the side doors and hurried onto the street, sirens wailing in the distance and patrol cars skidding to a stop down the street.

"Everyone out?" Gavin called.

"Yeah," Lou called back, holding Barb by his side. Their daughter, Violet, stood with them, her eyes wide and her hand to her mouth.

Gavin hurried Brianne and the dogs out to the cordoned-off street. Before he could turn to look back, Griffin's Diner exploded.

NINETEEN

Brianne's ears rang with all the force of a thousand crickets chirping against her skull. She lay flat, waiting, the acrid smell of something burning bringing her out of her fog.

"Bree?"

She lifted and felt two strong hands pulling her around.

Gavin. He had another gash, this one on the left side of his jaw. The man would be scarred for life if they didn't end this. Soot rained down on them, but he sat back on the concrete and held her close with a hand on each arm. His eyes and his expression full of shock and worry.

"Are you all right?" he asked, his words echoing as if from far away.

She nodded and pointed to her ears.

"Me, too," he said, shaking his head.

Paramedics came running and pointing the ambulance. "Here, let's get you to a bus."

"I'm fine." She managed to stand on wobbly legs, then held out her hand to help Gavin up. Tommy and Stella stood a few feet away, watching and waiting.

Once they were standing, the action around them came to her full-blown and chaotic. "Gavin," she whispered. "I'm so sorry this happened." Touching at her head, she whispered, "I shouldn't have let him out of my sight earlier today."

"This is not your fault," he replied, his hand pushing at her messy hair. "Are you sure you're okay?"

"Just another bruise to add to my collection." She touched a hand to his cut. "You're bleeding."

"I'll be fine. Let's get to it."

They turned to see the damage. A hole gaped in the roof, fire shooting up out of it. The fire department hosed it down in minutes, but the building had suffered damage.

"The kitchen is toast," Lou said when they went to find him. "Pun intended." He held his hands up in the air and then dropped them down. "I don't know if we can come back from this."

Barbara wiped at her eyes. "We always come back, Louis Griffin. Don't let them run us out."

"No one is going to run you out," Brianne said, her ears still full of what felt like cotton, her head throbbing.

"We'll find whoever did this. In the meantime, you two get checked and make sure your employees and customers are safe."

Barbara shot her a thankful smile. "She's right, Lou. Let's see how your blood pressure is holding up."

No loss of lives, but the place would be closed until they could rebuild.

Violet stood by, tears in her eyes. "Zach is on his way," she said, reaching for her mother and falling into Barbara's arms.

"Everyone got out alive," Barbara said. "If Bree and

Gavin hadn't been here with their partners, we might not have survived."

Gavin breathed in a long breath. "I'm going to talk to the fire chief."

Brianne sense he wanted to do that alone, so she called for Stella. "I'll do a search for shrapnel and maybe find something to help us."

"No, you need to be checked over first," Violet insisted. "Some people are being sent to the hospital. Let one of the paramedics make sure you're okay."

"Later," Brianne said. "Right now, it's important to find evidence before this place gets contaminated even more."

"Bree," Violet said, stopping her with a hand on her arm. "Do you think this was aimed at my parents?"

Brianne couldn't lie. "We don't know yet, but yes, we think so." She couldn't tell her friend this might be because of Gavin and her. They didn't know yet and she needed to keep the details hushed to protect all of them.

But she knew in her heart, this had been deliberate.

Brianne took Stella to walk the perimeters of the block, ignoring reporters and people gawking. She was searching for something and someone. But she didn't see anyone who matched their bomber in the crowd. He'd probably detonated the explosive from a cell phone. She'd let him slip away.

Turning back, she told herself she wouldn't stop until she found the person who'd done this.

Once she'd finished, Brianne found Gavin and they let the dogs do another sweep inside the building, keeping busy while the bomb squad finished investigating.

Tommy stopped again near where the storage room had once been. Now only a few beams of the wall around that area remained. The wood, drywall and the supplies stored there had all been blown into jagged pieces and tiny particles.

"What is it?" Gavin asked. "Find."

Tommy sniffed and lowered his snout, staying close in a corner. "He's got something."

Brianne turned to a patrolman standing nearby. "Hey, send someone from the bomb squad over here."

Gavin took a still-smoking fragment of lumber and carefully shifted through the pile of rubble at the dog's feet. When he saw a rectangle black box with wires twisting away from it, he patted Tommy on his head. "Good dog. Good find, Tommy."

"What is it?" Brianne asked from behind.

"I think Tommy found the detonator," he replied.

A member of the bomb squad came over and looked at the device. "I'd say this did the deed, Gavin. Let's get it to the lab pronto."

Gavin nodded. "It could match the one we found on the Fourth of July bombing site in East River Park."

After the bomb tech left, he turned to Brianne. "This might be our break." Staring at the corner where they'd found the device, he added, "I think the Tick just made a big mistake."

This latest explosion had shifted things into full speed ahead. From the commissioner on down, Gavin and Brianne's undercover work now had the approval of the whole department, the FBI and any other agency that had an interest in this investigation.

"You'll finish it with our full backing," Noah told them two days later. "The money is in place for the down payment. Don't hand over that check until the

last minute. We need concrete proof of what these corrupt individuals have been doing for years now." Then he added, "I had to call in some favors with a couple of friends in the FBI to keep them from taking over this case. They'll be watching, and they expect a full report on your activities. Do your best and come out of this alive, okay?"

"Yes, sir," they both said.

Gavin and Brianne left Noah's office and quickly walked toward the training arena.

Gavin took her by the arm and tugged her into an empty office. "Bree, before we finish this, I need to talk to you."

"What's the matter?" she asked, those incredible eyes drenching him with a heart-wrenching longing.

He wanted to tell her what he'd realized yesterday— that life was too short to fight against what your heart was shouting to you. But it sounded cliché in his mind. And he wasn't good with words.

Maybe if he just showed her.

"I just wanted to—" His phone buzzed. Groaning, he said, "Don't go anywhere."

"Okay." She stood still and waited, her pretty face frowning.

"Hey, Ilana," he said. Then he listened. "We'll be right there."

He hung up and took Brianne by the hand. "They've found something on the Fourth of July bomber. Ilana says they've got something that indicates matches to the Williamsburg bomb and the one at Lou's two days ago."

She followed him but pulled back. "Gavin, what did you want to tell me?"

Gavin stopped and took a breath, his gut moving

ahead of his logic. Tugging her close, he kissed her on the lips, not caring right now who might see them.

When he pulled away, he was rewarded with a stunned gaze and what looked like the same longing that churned inside of him. "Just that," he said. "Just in case."

"In case of what?" she asked, breathless.

"In case this thing goes bad," he replied.

Then he hurried her back out to their vehicles. "Maybe the lab found something we can use to end this."

Brianne gave him another stunned glance. "Then we should pray that this case won't go bad."

That comment gave Gavin hope that she'd liked kissing him.

But before he could explore that theory closer, they had a lot of work to do.

"So you see these little wires right here?" Ilana asked, her magnifying glass in her hand.

Gavin squinted and pointed. "Yes. Did those wires cause the explosion?"

"Partly," Ilana explained, her brow furrowed. "You know that bombers have a signature. Sometimes it's easy to find, sometimes impossible. This one is really good at hiding his work, but ego gets them every time. He left us a distinguished design and it's all there in these little wires."

Brianne took the magnifying glass. "What are we looking at?"

Ilana beamed and held her hands together. "So bombmakers have a tendency to do special curls and twists in the wiring when they're creating an explosive device."

She moved to her microscope. "The device you're seeing has an interesting wire twist."

She pointed to the microscope standing on a nearby table. "Gavin, look at this."

Gavin leaned down and looked through the microscope. "Is this the same device?"

"Nope," Ilana said on a proud note. "It's the one the techs found at the Fourth of July bombing."

Gavin stood and let Brianne look into the microscope while he studied the other device through the magnifying glass. "And this one came from Griffin's, right?"

"You are correct," Ilana said, pushing at her dark glasses. "They match almost completely. So I was curious and I went back to the device you and Tommy found at the Williamsburg explosion."

"But that scene didn't show anything definitive," he reminded her. "The fire department decided what we'd found was part of the boiler panel."

"Or so we thought," Ilana replied, moving to a table where she had pictures of both the scene and the fragments laid out.

Pointing to a particular photo, she said, "We found some wiring, but the tech thought it came from the boiler's system—the breaker box."

"And you're saying it didn't?" Gavin asked.

"Yes, I'm saying that," Ilana replied. "I think your bomber is left-handed, Gavin. Whoever it is, they like swirls in their wires. Very intricate, dainty swirls."

Brianne's gaze hit Gavin. "So we've got a match on the same bomber for all three locations?"

"Yes, we do," Ilana replied. "And…I saved the best for last. We also found some epidermis on this last device. Just enough to compare to the touch DNA we found from the Fourth of July bombing."

"Did you get a match?"

"William Caston, aka the Tick, is your bomber, Gavin. At all three sites."

Gavin couldn't speak. He nodded and stared down at the evidence. "Now we have to find him."

"Well, when you do, you'll have some interesting comparisons to show him," the proud tech said with a grin.

"Thank you," Brianne said, giving Ilana a little hug.

They left the lab, quiet until they were outside alone. "This is huge," Gavin finally said. "We need to report this to Chief Jameson."

"I agree," Brianne said. "We need to set up our final meeting with Justin Sanelli. We have proof that the bomber was at all three sites. Now we need to find the person who hired him to do this."

"And set up a sting to finally bring the Tick to justice," Gavin added.

Gavin's phone rang before they made it back to the department's main floor.

"Sutherland," he said.

"Gavin, this is Freddie Alverez. Listen, I have news on your CI."

Gavin motioned to Brianne to wait. "You found Beanpole?"

"Yeah, but Gavin, it's not good. We found his body in some bushes near Battery Park. I'm sorry, but looks like he's been dead for a week or so, according to the ME."

Gavin hung his head. "He had a favorite spot near Battery Park. Do you know what happened?"

"Blunt force trauma. He has a deep wound in the

back of his head. The ME said he probably went with the first blow."

Gavin closed his eyes. "Thank you, Freddie. I'll want to see the report and the body."

"Understood," Freddie replied. "Got to go."

Gavin hung up and stared over at Brianne. "Beanpole is dead. Blunt force trauma. I have to go and see him and get the details."

She grabbed his arm. "Oh, Gavin, I'm so sorry. Someone killed him?"

"It looks that way," he said, his heart sick. "And I think we both know who that someone was."

TWENTY

A day later, Gavin stood with Brianne in the Gable Hotel suite. "Ready?"

She smiled up at him, her hair caught up in a twirl on her head, the dark strands almost as much a part of her as her brilliant red tresses. But he liked the red best.

"As ready as ever," she said, the smile going to steel. "I want to end this."

He looked her over, enjoying this pretending but anxious to get on with the real deal—her. She wore a sleeveless olive green high-necked sweater and a full black long skirt over shimmering gold-burnished heeled sandals.

"You know," he began, "I've never noticed fashion much before, but you sure know how to pull off these designer looks."

She laughed and patted her hair, her gold hoop earrings winking at him. "I'll miss these fancy clothes but I like my jeans and T-shirts just as much as this overpriced getup."

"You look good in any outfit, Bree," he said, taking her hands in his. "And before we get wired for our own protection, I just wanted to continue our discussion from the other day."

"Which discussion?"

He grabbed her close and leaned down to kiss her. "This one."

Gavin placed his hands in her hair and pulled her close, loving the way she sighed and fell into the kiss. Did she feel the same way? Did she want this to keep going?

They parted, and he looked down at her, the feel of her soft curls warm against his hands. "Bree, I don't want anything to happen to you."

"Nothing is going to happen to me," she said. "Except my hair is now messed up."

He held his hands in place. "You look liked you've just been kissed."

"Oh, part of the cover?"

"No. A real kiss." Then he dropped his hands and stepped back. "I guess it's silly, but I never knew what happened to my mother. If she's dead or alive or if she ever thought about what she'd done. That unresolved uncertainty makes me cautious and too protective."

Brianne's gaze filled with understanding. "Did you do this with Granny Irene? Did you watch out for her?"

"I tried but she had a large dose of pride. She thought she needed to be the one taking care of me."

"Well, Sutherland, she did a fine job on that and I'm thinking you did, too."

"So you get it?"

"I get it. I'm touched and amazed and… I like this discussion. But we've got business to take care of."

She seemed to be shutting him down. But she turned back before he could say anything else. Grabbing him by his white button-up shirt, she leaned up. "You take care, too. You're not the only one who's protective around here."

Gavin nodded, unable to say anything more.

Then he said a silent prayer for their protection and thanked God for partnering him with a woman who could not only match him but outshine him, too.

"Okay, Brianne, let's get this done. This should be our last meeting with Justin Sanelli."

"I sure hope so," Brianne replied.

Freddie knocked and came in to wire them. "So we can keep track of you two and communicate," he explained. "But anything you do or say will be heard, so keep that in mind."

No more personal talk, Gavin thought, smiling at Brianne.

Soon they were on their way out the door. On the ride over, Brianne tried to absorb that kiss. This one had been deep and meaningful and full of a sweet warmth that left her longing for more. But would they get a chance to explore these feelings without the guise of pretending?

Freddie watched them settling into the dark sedan and turned to man the wheel. "We'll be in Chelsea in about twenty minutes since we're early for rush hour. Rest up and get your heads in the game."

Gavin sat quiet with Tommy tucked against his jeans wearing a leather collar with some hardware on it to give it a moto edge.

The dog had been a trouper, doing what he needed to do and staying out of the way unless told otherwise.

Stella would be with them when they took in the Tick. If that happened according to plan.

As they entered the Rexx Agency offices, she smiled, but inside her nerves dinged and banged against her system, giving her a buzz that was part adrenaline and part anticipation. She would be careful.

Because she had a good reason to fight to the finish on this one. It had taken a lot for Gavin to confess his worst fears to her earlier. He had a scar on his heart that needed to be healed. She wanted to be the one to help with that.

Freddie pulled the car up to the lobby of the modern steel-and-chrome building. "This is it, my friends. Remember the code word for help: 'no deal.'"

"I'm planning on getting the deal," Gavin replied.

The dark shining in his eyes reminded Brianne of the building they were about to enter.

Unyielding.

"So this is it." Justin Sanelli looked like he might pass out from pure greed. "Soon, your name will be on the CHL building."

"It's happening," Brianne said with the same greedy glee. "I can't wait to put our stamp on it."

Justin's glee went south. "The seller tentatively agreed to your price, but the paperwork hasn't arrived yet."

Gavin gave the man an intimidating glare. "Make it happen, Justin."

Looking nervous, Justin made a call. "Speed things up. My clients are tired of playing games."

He listened for a moment and then ended the call and turned back. "I hate to tell you this but...one of the tenants is waffling. He's threatening the building owner with a boycott or something. The seller is getting cold feet since this tenant is standing in the way of the deal.

"What?" Gavin asked, real frustration clear in his words. "We agreed on this, Justin. We're about to hand you a very big down payment and sign the rest of the papers."

Sanelli shrugged. "The hold-out is a tough old bird."

"Obviously." Brianne went into full Alice-mode. "This won't do. I thought we had a deal."

"And we still have a deal," Sanelli said. "I told you I will make it happen. Give me twenty-four hours to talk both the seller and the tenant into this."

"I don't know." Gavin stood, pacing and shot Justin a rage-fueled stare. "You'd better come up with something, Sanelli."

Justin stood, too. "I'll be right back."

He left the room with an abrupt swish.

Gavin kept up the facade. "Don't worry, honey. We can offer more money. You know I'll do whatever it takes."

The door opened, and Justin came in with Liza Collins.

"I'm so sorry," she said, her dark hair held to one side with a wide clip that allowed it to cascade over her shoulder, the scent of something spicy lingering around her. Wearing a crisp white blouse and cream linen pants, she held up a white sheet of paper with something typed on it. Sitting down, she signed the paper with an elegant burgundy pen, her jewels flashing. "The building is nearly empty, but there's always someone who wants to make a last stand. This is my signature. My word that we will make this right—a good faith document that I rarely give out. If we don't please you, we'll find something else for you within the week."

Gavin took the paper and stared down at the swirls in her signature. "I'll hold you to that." Handing the paper to Brianne, he asked, "What do you want to do, darling?"

Brianne stared at the paper, her eyes going wide. "I think we should give the Rexx Agency one final opportunity to give us what we're asking for." Then she glanced across the table at Liza. "Twenty-four hours or we walk."

The other woman's expression filled with rigid surprise, but something dark and daring passed through her eyes.

They left, not having to pretend disappointment and anger.

"We'll surveil the building in question," Gavin told Freddie when they were back in the car. "If the bomber compromises the building, the seller and the unhappy tenant should both be ready to make a deal."

"Already called it in," Freddie replied. "This is where we take over. We'll convince the tenant to get out—a gas leak or pest control excuse—and make sure the building is empty."

"When the Tick is inside doing the deed, Bree and I want to take him," Gavin said.

Freddie nodded. Gavin told Brianne he'd be watching the monitors for the next twenty-four hours. "The bomber is going to make a move. I'm pretty sure the person Sanelli contacted is giving the orders. They're not only sabotaging buildings but also gouging clients."

"I'll watch with you," she replied. "I won't be able to sleep, anyway."

Gavin nodded, his face washed in shadows, his eyes rimmed with fatigue. He tugged her close but stayed silent.

They went back to the safe house and then waited until dark to leave separately in unmarked cars driven by fellow officers.

Once they were at headquarters, they headed into the tech department and took seats behind the IT experts who'd sent out two other detectives to monitor the building.

Brianne came in with coffee and sat with Gavin. "Hey, I noticed something interesting about Liza Collins today."

"Okay, what?"

"She's left-handed," Brianne said, her gaze meeting his.

Gavin let that sink in, remembering the swirls in her penmanship. "Swirls," he said. "Swirls and twists."

Brianne nodded. "Just like the wires used to set off these bombs."

"Left-handed and has a thing for making swirls."

"That can't be coincidence," Brianne whispered. "Do you think we've been after the wrong person all along?"

Gavin let out a breath. "It all makes sense now, doesn't it?"

"The bomber didn't show."

Gavin hated saying the words, but he and Brianne had spent a long night piecing this investigation together.

"Is he onto you?" Noah asked, while the other team members sat listening.

"We don't know," Gavin admitted. "But we're not

giving up yet." Looking over his notes, he added, "We've learned a few things."

"Such as?"

"We think there were two people on that roof when the beam came down the other day."

Brianne added her thoughts. "We think someone deliberately brought the dog there and reported it, but meantime the Tick could have been at the building already and had to hide from the other person."

Noah mulled that over. "So this other person knows something about Jordan's murder and was messing with the department by bringing a German shepherd-mix there?"

"Yes, and they didn't care which of us showed up. The bomber might have been watching Gavin and me, followed us and had to hide once he realized someone else was already there."

"So we still don't know who pushed that beam off the building?" Noah asked. "It could have been either person."

Gavin glanced around the room. "Not sure, and we didn't get any good prints off of the dog bowls or the stair doors."

Brianne leaned in. "We do believe someone wanted us dead. Maybe to distract the unit from Jordan's death, or maybe the bomber wanted to take out Gavin since Gavin and Tommy found what they believed to be the remains of one of his bombs after that explosion in Williamsburg."

"Oh, and one other thing," Gavin added. "We don't have proof yet, but the Tick could be a woman."

Noah let out a grunt. "What?"

Gavin's phone buzzed. "It's Freddie, sir. He's still watching the CHL building."

"What's happening?"

"We've got action. One person entering the building through a back door. Dressed in black, shaggy hair, plaid hat. Building cleared and empty."

"We're on our way," Gavin said. Turning to Noah, he explained, "They only have a couple of hours left before we check in. So they'll blow part of the building today and halt the deal to get a better price."

"Then you need to stop them," Noah said. "Go."

Gavin and Brianne grabbed their gear and hurried to the kennels to suit up Tommy and Stella. "This is the real deal, boys and girls," Gavin said to the dogs after their official protective vests were on.

The two animals stood at attention, ready to do what they'd been trained to do. When the vests went on, the real work began.

"This is it," Brianne said as they rushed out and got into Gavin's vehicle. "This has to be the end of it, Gavin."

"One way or another, it will be," he promised. "Man or woman, we're taking down this person today."

TWENTY-ONE

"All systems go."

The command came over the radio loud and clear, but the plan had changed. Justin had called an hour ago, asking to meet them at the building to give them the good news. The stubborn tenant had caved, and the seller would accept their offer.

"It has to be a setup," Gavin said to Brianne. "Either the seller strong-armed the tenant or they have other plans."

"But we need to go, this time with backup."

She wasn't about to let these people slip away again.

So they got dressed in street clothes and decided they'd take both Tommy and Stella with them, minus their official vests. Carter and Luke and their dogs, Frosty and Bruno, two of the best in their unit, would serve as backup along with the other detectives monitoring the whole thing in an unmarked construction van.

Add to that several uniformed police officers parked nearby and a bomb squad on alert and they were ready to get going. If this was a setup, they'd act as bait and the team would move in and take over.

"If something goes wrong," Gavin said as they

strolled toward the CHL building, "promise me you'll take Stella and run."

Brianne did an eye roll. "I promise you I'll draw my weapon and do as I've been trained as a cop and a K-9 officer."

"I don't like that promise."

"What would you do?" she countered, knowing he'd take these people head-on.

"Good point," he replied.

"So we're ready?"

He nodded. "Stella is our new dog. You needed more than one to comfort you and keep you company."

"What if they know we were at the park that day?"

"Yellow Labs are very popular. Stella won't stand out. But it doesn't matter now."

Nothing mattered now, except that she'd fallen in love with him and she wanted to keep him safe. But he might not ever know that.

They entered the building and looked around, "Since we're the 'buyers,' we have good chance of surviving this," Gavin quipped. He stared at his watch and checked the elevators and the desk. "I don't see Sanelli."

Then they heard footsteps. Clicking footsteps.

Liza Collins came toward them, dressed in a bright red tunic over white pants. She wore red leather flat sandals.

A chill went down Brianne's spine, but she shook it off. Both dogs stood at attention, a sure sign that they recognized something in her nearness.

"You have two animals now, I see," Liza said with a sly smile. "You must be dog lovers."

Tommy turned his head, sniffed, glanced back at them.

"Stay, boy," Gavin commanded. "He gets nervous around people sometimes."

"We love animals," Brianne replied, her voice calm, her gaze holding the other woman's. "Dogs make me feel safe. They both need more training so ignore their jitters. It's so nice of you to come here and take care of this, Liza."

Liza motioned for them to follow her. "Oh, I sometimes have to clean up messes and this has turned into a big one."

Gavin chuckled. "Nothing we can't fix, correct?"

"Absolutely," the woman said, her laughter like sharp needles hitting against Brianne's skin. "Let's go into my temporary office, shall we?"

"Where's Justin?" Brianne asked, mainly to alert the team that Liza was alone.

"He's indisposed," Liza replied with a shrug, her creepy laughter echoing around them in a pleased cackle.

She took them to a small room in the lobby that wasn't much bigger than a closet. "Have a seat."

They sat in two folding chairs in front of an old desk. A storage armoire stood in the corner. Tommy again gave Gavin a look. Gavin held the dog's leash tight.

"Did the seller change his mind?" Gavin asked.

"He will before the day is over," Liza said. She didn't sit. Instead, she paced around.

Gavin shook his head. "We came here for a deal. If you don't have one, we're leaving."

Her back to them, Liza stared out the one dingy window that offered a crack of light in this sad little room.

"You won't be leaving at all, Mr. *Reinhart*," she said, whirling to face them.

Then the door slammed behind them.

They turned to see a dark-haired man with bushy eyebrows grinning at them. The Plaid Cap man—minus the hat—held a nasty looking handgun at their backs.

"What's going on?" Brianne said, while the two dogs grew restless. "You're upsetting my babies."

"Cut the act," Liza said. "I've been on to you two for weeks now."

"What do you mean?" Gavin asked, indignation in his words. Then he glanced back. "Who is he and why is he holding a gun on us? What's the matter with you?"

Liza leaned over the desk. "What's the matter with *me*? I'll tell you. You've been lurking about, pretending to be who you aren't, asking a lot of pointed questions. And I want to know why."

Brianne shot Gavin a quick glance. "You already know who we are. You're stalling."

"You won't scam me," Liza said, her voice shaking with anger. "Justin wouldn't confess but I think he's been working with you two to undermine my whole company."

"Excuse me?" Brianne asked. "So you brought us here because you think we're scam artists?"

"No. But your whole marriage and real estate thing is a scam. I saw the way you acted at the open house so I looked you up. Quite impressive. You claim you've come to New York to take over my business. But then, I also spotted you at the park with this Lab. So I did even more research."

Brianne realized the woman either believed they were trying to scam her or had figured out they were cops. So she played along. "What did Justin tell you?"

"He wouldn't talk. But he's been acting strange

lately. I have ways of taking care of people who betray me."

"Why would we betray you?" Gavin asked. "We only met you a week or so ago. We just want to find a building to renovate." Laughing, he said, "This is New York. Plenty to go around."

"Not in this market," Liza said with a frown. "Not for you. You followed Bill after the open house. He told me."

"Bill?" Gavin asked, pretending confusion. Then he looked at the silent man behind him.

"My brother," Liza replied. "My twin brother who suffered a head trauma years ago. He does odd jobs for me, hangs around to protect me and occasionally takes care of things."

"Things such as?" Gavin asked.

"See, you're trying to get information out of me. Bill helped me figure this out."

Gavin shrugged. "How do you know you can trust *Bill*?"

Liza hit a hand on the desk. "He's my brother. He wouldn't betray me. I take care of him since his injury left him lacking. Justin was a scaredy-cat, always nervous and wanting to do things by the book. But Bill does anything I ask him to do. It's been that way all of our lives, even after I went through two divorces and an ugly scandal since my last husband died. Justin won't be a problem anymore. You're dealing with me now."

Brianne felt sick to her stomach. Justin Sanelli was probably dead. And this woman was quite mad.

Gavin studied Liza with a cold glare. "It's obvious you have a problem with us, Liza. Justin promised us we'd get this property so we'd like to talk to him."

"I knew it," Liza said, hitting the metal desk so hard she snapped a lacquered fingernail and caused both dogs to twist and bark. "I knew he was double-crossing me."

"How so?" Brianne asked, calming Stella with a soft command.

"Never mind," Liza replied. "Now that I know the truth, I have to go. You've both been interesting, but let's cut to the chase. You're not into real estate. You're cops and not very good ones since I discovered that early on. Still, Justin went behind my back to show you this dump. A fatal mistake."

She opened a drawer and took out a cell phone, staring at the too-bright screen. "I'm going to make the rounds and then I'm leaving."

Gavin gave Brianne a warning glance. "You're right, Liza, we are cops and we've got this building surrounded. You walk out of here, and you'll be shot on the spot."

Liza went pale but motioned to her brother. Bill held the gun closer. Close enough for Brianne to know this man was the Tick. "Bill?"

She stood, too, but Liza pushed her back down.

"If you move, I'll start the fireworks right now."

"Fireworks?" Brianne looked around. "What are you talking about?"

"In fifteen minutes, something tragic will happen here," Liza replied, calm again. "An unfortunate accident. Another gas leak or maybe a faulty wire in the mechanical room. Holding up her phone, she said. "I just call it in. Boom. Boom."

Rushing around them, she opened the door and screamed, "Run, Bill! Get out!"

Bill, who had never uttered a word, did as his bossy sister asked. He handed her the gun and took off running.

Liza held the gun as she backed out the door. "So nice *not* doing business with you, Officers."

Then she slammed the door shut and Brianne heard the clicking of a lock.

"Gavin?"

"I know." He did a mic check. "Freddie, did you get all of that? She's onto us."

"Got it. We're moving in."

Gavin unleashed the dogs and told them to Find. "By the way, we're locked in and there's a bomb about to go off in this building." He gave their location.

Gavin and Brianne went into action. The dogs alerted on the armoire in the corner of the hot, tiny office. Tommy touched his paw to the door and whined. Stella sniffed the door handle and turned to stare at Brianne.

Gavin shot Brianne a look that told her everything she needed to know. He loved her. She saw it there in his dark eyes.

This man loved her. Too much.

He'd die for her.

"Gavin?"

"Bree, I'm going to open the door. We have to know what we're dealing with here."

She nodded, held back tears.

"Get behind the desk," he said. "Keep the dogs with you."

"Gavin, wait."

Then they heard something. A soft moan coming from the cabinet where the dogs had alerted.

"Get back, Bree."

Gavin pulled out his hidden weapon and gently opened the door to the closet-like cabinet.

Then he stood back.

Brianne looked up over the desk and gasped.

Justin Sanelli was tied up in the cabinet.

And he had a bomb strapped to his stomach.

Gavin turned to Brianne, a million scenarios going through his head. "We have to get this thing off of him."

Justin moaned, his eyes wide with fear. Gavin didn't try yet to remove the tape covering his mouth.

"Listen, Justin. Listen to me, okay?" Gavin leaned close, studying the three bars of C4 strapped and wired across Justin's midsection. "We're with the NYPD, understand? We're going to get you out of here, do you hear me?"

Justin moaned again and gave a slight nod, but the fear in his eyes didn't go away. He tried to say something.

Sirens sounded all around. Loud shouts echoed through the building.

"Our backup is here." Gavin turned to Brianne. "I'm going to get this tape off."

She nodded, her weapon drawn, the dogs behind her. "I'll work on the door."

Gavin turned back to Justin. "Don't move," he said. "And don't scream."

Justin moaned again. Gavin counted to three and yanked off the tape, praying all the way.

Justin didn't scream, but he started talking. "She's a madwoman. She thinks I'm in cahoots with you. She's a bomb-maker. How can I work for a woman and not know that she's the one who's been sabotaging half the buildings we buy? And how could I not see that you two are cops?"

"Calm down," Gavin said. "It's okay. We're gonna get you out of here but I need your help. We've only got about ten minutes."

"Do something!" Justin said, sweat covering his ruddy face. "She plans to blow us up with her phone."

"Is her brother involved?"

"He delivers the bombs, sets them up. But he's tired of her ordering him around. He messed up on the Fourth of July. Went to the wrong building and panicked."

"So he deliberately moved through the crowd at the fireworks," Gavin said to keep Justin talking. He could see the twisted wires on the bomb, the same loops and swirls as the others. They'd been after the wrong man.

The Tick was a woman.

"I don't know, but I heard them talking. He rarely talks to anyone but her. She's always bossed him around. But I know he did something she wasn't happy about."

"Just hang on, Justin. We'll be out of here soon."

Brianne touched Gavin's arm. "The door is solid and locked tight. Maybe the window."

Justin stared up at Gavin, sweat shimmering on his skin. "She'll go out the basement door to the street. You won't leave me?"

"I won't," Gavin said. Then he stood up and went to the window. After trying to pry it loose, he used the butt of his gun to knock out the old panes. Fresh air filled the room.

"Bree, send the dogs out and go with them."

"No. I won't do it."

Gavin saw the tears in her eyes and he also saw the

bravery. "You need to get out of here. We don't have much time."

"No." She backed away, shaking her head. "Gavin, no."

He hurried to her, guiding her. "Get out, Brianne. I mean it."

She gave him a hurt look and then glanced at Justin. "I'm going to find Liza. I'll make sure she's put away for a long time, Justin."

Then before Gavin could warn her to be careful, she grabbed a chair and climbed up into the open window. She looked back once, her eyes holding his while she commanded the dogs to Go.

Gavin watched as she dropped down onto the ground into an alleyway, his heart breaking when she glanced back up at him. He might not see her again.

Turning back to Justin, he stared at the frightened man.

"Are you two the real deal?" Justin asked in a quiet voice.

Gavin nodded, cleared his throat. "Yeah, we are. We're the real deal."

TWENTY-TWO

Brianne wanted to take off her mic and throw it on the ground. She couldn't bear to hear the bomb exploding in her ear. But she had to report in and she needed backup, so she listened and prayed they'd get to Gavin in time.

She did, however, want to find Liza Collins. That need burned through Brianne and cut through the pain she'd seen in Gavin's eyes when he'd demanded she leave.

The woman's perfume had lingered in the air of that stifling little room, so she ordered the dogs to Search. Liza's scent—the scent they'd zoomed in on—was that of a bomber.

Tommy had tried to warn them at the open house. They'd misread his signals. And Stella had picked up the bomb's scent on William Caston—Bill—when he'd walked into the crowd to dispose of a bomb he'd taken to the wrong place—a bomb both his sister and he had handled.

She'd seen the whirls and twists of this bomb's wiring. Liza was an evil woman who had two major talents—selling real estate and making bombs. But her ego had given her away in the form of dainty bomb wiring.

Why hadn't they picked up on her sooner?

Because she'd used her own brother as a decoy and as her runner. She'd sent him through the open house to lure them away, already paranoid that they planned to take over her territory. What a horrible life Bill must have had, always lurking about doing her dirty deeds. Creepy and evil.

Brianne followed the dogs until she reached the back of the old building. Another alleyway, but near the High Line. She could hear people laughing not far away. But she also heard sirens and, from the chatter coming through her earbud, knew the bomb squad was in place. She heard Gavin reassuring Justin. Checking her watch, she prayed they'd make it in time. She couldn't think about what would happen if they didn't.

She radioed her location and followed the two K-9s, surprised when they reached Gansevoort and Tommy wanted to go onto the High Line. Had Liza taken the popular green space that used to be a train track?

A lot of places to hide there.

The dogs were rarely wrong, so Brianne ordered them to keep going. They made it up the entryway and moved through the crowds, the afternoon heat beaming down on them.

Tears moved in a quiet stream down her face, but Brianne kept reporting her moves. They passed The Standard, High Line Hotel. She searched in all directions. How would she ever find Liza in this crowd? Brianne looked to the right, her heart doing that little flip when she thought she saw Liza up ahead. They kept moving. The High Line was a little over a mile long but she felt winded and feverish in the heat, pushing past strolling people. She prayed the dogs would hold out.

When they came near Chelsea Market, Tommy lifted his snout and picked up the pace. The High Line cut underneath buildings here. Tommy alerted, and Stella soon followed.

But where had Liza gone?

They moved to the Observation Deck after crossing Tenth Avenue and Brianne stared down into the street below. And she saw Liza strolling along, her phone in her hand.

Five minutes. Liza had told them she'd hit the button in fifteen minutes and ten of those were gone. Liza would denotate the bomb if she couldn't get to her.

Five minutes to save Gavin and Justin.

"Gavin?" she said into her mic. "Officer Sutherland?"

"Bree?"

"I see her. Tenth Avenue Square. I'm going after her."

"Bree? Wait! Wait! I'm coming, I'm coming!"

"Are you out?"

"I'm still with Justin. The bomb squad is here. We've got eyes on you and the bomb squad is working to defuse the bomb. I promised Justin—"

"That you won't leave him."

"I promised, Bree. But I should be with you."

"I know, I can do this."

She hurried to the exit at 12th and 34th and then backtracked. She came up on Liza sitting on a bench, watching her phone.

"It's over, Liza," Brianne said, easing closer with her weapon drawn.

The woman looked up without surprise. "No, you're wrong about that, *Reinhart.* I can't let you live. You're cops—Bill followed you two to a vacant building site, but he ran away when he heard a dog barking. Undercover cops—that's an uneven playing field, don't you think?" Holding the phone up, she said, "It won't be over until I finish it."

Liza gave Brianne a smug smile and put her finger to the phone.

Brianne moved in. "Drop the phone, Liza. Drop it or I'll shoot you."

Liza shook her head. "I don't really care about that right now. I just want to watch your face when the bomb explodes."

"Don't," Brianne said, holding her breath, expecting an explosion somewhere behind them. She prepared to make the shot.

Liza went to hit the button at about the same time Brianne shot her in the upper arm She wouldn't give the woman the satisfaction of a forced death-by-cop.

Liza screamed, blood seeping down her arm and onto her white pants.

Brianne waited, her heart pounding, tears blurring her eyes. The bomb didn't go off.

For a brief instant after the shot, birds scattered and people screamed and hurried away. but soon the city kept moving. Horns honked, dogs barked, sirens screamed and the sky was a brilliant blue.

Liza let go of the phone and grabbed at her bleeding arm, her gaze hitting on Brianne. "What have you done?"

"She's done her job" came a winded, masculine voice behind them. "She's bringing in the Tick. Finally."

Brianne didn't dare turn, but she gulped in a breath that she'd been holding for the last fifteen minutes.

Gavin rushed forward and commanded Tommy to Guard.

His partner obeyed, growling at the stunned woman sitting on the bench.

"Where is my stupid brother?" Liza asked.

"Sitting in a NYPD squad car singing like a bird," Gavin explained as he hauled her up and cuffed her. "Take a good long look at this view, Liza. It'll be the last time you see it."

After that, everything went by like a movie in Brianne's mind. Gavin guided her to an ambulance to get her checked out. Stella stayed by her side, guarding her. Freddie rushed by, taking over for Gavin. Luke and Carter showed up, helping to get a screaming Liza to a waiting ambulance with a guard to escort her to the hospital. FBI agents swarmed the scene.

Brianne sat and heard people rushing by, talking. "Just heard about a bomb scare right here in Chelsea."

"They stopped it with seconds to spare."

"God bless those K-9 officers and the bomb squad."

"God bless New York City."

Brianne closed her eyes and held tight to Stella. *Thank You, Lord.*

She felt a warm hand on her cheek. "Gavin?"

"It's over, Bree," he said, taking her into his arms and holding her close. "It's over."

Two days later, Gavin sat in the training yard with Carter Jameson watching Carter's little six-year-old girl, Ellie, play with a hyper puppy.

"Daddy, we need to take this one home, too," the cute dark-haired child said.

"Sweetie, we already have two puppies, remember? We're running out of room."

Gavin felt for Carter. His wife had died during childbirth and the man still had the shadow of grief about him. And now his brother, too. All the more reason for Gavin to grab on to love and hold tight. Which he planned to do soon.

"What a week," Carter said, passing Gavin the doughnuts someone had brought out to the picnic table earlier. "I wish I could keep Ellie this innocent and free forever."

"Yep," Gavin said, anxious to go and see Brianne. The chief had made them both take a day but Gavin had come by headquarters to sign reports and tie up loose ends before he headed to her place.

"Hey, Gavin," Carter said, "we're all sorry about even thinking you could be involved in Jordy's death. Chalk it up to grief and shock, man." He extended his hand, hope in his eyes.

Gavin shook his friend's hand. "I get it and I'm sorry for not handling my ambition a little better. Jordan and I had our differences, but he was a good man. I won't stop searching for his killer."

Carter nodded. "Thanks for that. And now that we know there were two people on that roof the day you found Scrawny and you and Brianne almost got hit by that beam, we know someone out there wants to get the jump on us finding his killer."

"Also look into the shooting at Griffin's," Gavin said. "Liza Collins claims after Justin told her about us, she had her brother start following us. But she realized we were police officers the day her brother tracked us to that building. He told us another man was there with the dog. So we think the person who killed Jordan was behind the shooting at Griffin's. He started going after whomever he could find to keep us all guessing. However, the bombing there was set up deliberately—to threaten Brianne and me. Liza pulled out all the stops."

Carter nodded. "You and Brianne did a good job."

"Yeah, we make a good team," Gavin replied.

"In work or in life?" Carter questioned with a soft smile.

"We have a thing," Gavin admitted. Then he took a breath. "And if I have it my way, we'll be together for the rest of our lives."

"That's great," Carter said. "How are you gonna handle working together?"

"I've mulled that over," Gavin said. "I thought about asking for a transfer, so I talked to Noah and spilled my guts."

"And what did my brother say?"

"He told me I wasn't going anywhere and that both Bree and I and our partners would be honored soon for stopping that bomber. We just can't work the same cases anymore."

"So a kiss every morning and off you go in different directions."

Seeing the pain in his friend's eyes, Gavin nodded. "I guess you were used to doing that, huh? Kissing your wife every morning."

"Yeah," Carter said. Then he looked at his little girl. "Now Ellie and I share that kiss." Turning back to Gavin, he added, "Grab tight, Gavin. Don't let go, okay?"

"I won't," Gavin said. "But first, I have to see how Brianne feels about this idea."

Carter laughed and stood up. "Well, what are you waiting for? Get going."

* * *

"Bree, you have a visitor."

Hearing her mother's words, Brianne turned from watching Stella chase yet another ball out in the back-yard and saw Gavin walking toward her.

Her heart ran toward him before her feet could move. "Hi," she said, watching as Stella took off toward her friend Tommy and danced around him with delight.

"Hi," he responded when he met up with her near the swing underneath the old oak. "Got a minute?"

"I might," she said, motioning to the swing. "Come into my office and we'll check my schedule."

He sat down with her and smiled at their partners. "Those two knew right away, didn't they?"

"About the bomber? Yes."

"And about us, silly."

Her heart beat too fast. "Is there an 'us'?"

"I sure hope so," Gavin replied. "Justin Sanelli wants an invitation to our wedding and he's offered to give us a discount on a house, if we decide to buy a new one."

Letting that soak in, she asked, "Is he okay?"

"He will be. He'll testify against Liza Collins and her brother, William Caston—and he's been cleared of any wrongdoing. He thought his boss just had a talent for bringing in deals. He was clueless as to how she did it."

"Really?"

"Really, he's clean. He just bragged a bit too much and one of the people he bragged to was me, thank-fully."

"Okay then." She looked Gavin in the eyes. "Now back to that other part…"

"You mean—how long will the wig-wearing bomb-toting twins stay behind bars?"

"No, I mean that part about a wedding and a house and…whatever comes after that."

Gavin turned and pulled her close, the old swing creaking.

"Do you want all of that, Bree? With me?"

"Is that your way of asking me to marry you?"

"We were good together as Linus and Alice, but don't expect designer purses or a penthouse in Manhattan, okay? But I do have a solid house and I will get you a ring, I promise."

"I'll take the ring and I can't wait to see the house. But the only thing I expect, Sutherland, is to spend the rest of my life coming home to you and those two amazing K-9s. Can you make that happen?"

"I've already worked out the plan," he said, telling her about his talk with Noah. "We're all clear."

"So…we're getting married?"

"We're getting married," he said, bringing her close. "I love you. I almost lost you."

"You almost lost yourself," she replied. "But I love you because you chose to stay with a frightened man strapped to a bomb when you knew you could die. That is a true hero, Gavin."

"And I love you because you did what I asked you to do—leave—and then went after an evil woman, knowing that you and I might not ever be together. That is a true heroine, Brianne."

She stared crying. "No aprons, okay?"

"No aprons. I'll cook for you, how about that?"

"I love you so much."

He kissed her and held her close. When they heard a loud squeal from inside the house, they pulled apart and started laughing.

"My mother," Bree said with a grin. "I sure am glad she didn't smack you too hard with that frying pan."

"So am I," he said. Then he stood and lifted her up and kissed her again. "Let's go inside. Your mom's making meatballs."

Together, they walked toward the house, their K-9 partners trotting behind them. Brianne glanced back and saw Stella giving Tommy a big doggie smile.

"I feel the same way, Stella Girl," she said, smiling over at Gavin. Looking up at the blue sky, she'd never felt more happy. Gavin had found peace at last and…a family who loved him.

* * * * *

WE HOPE YOU ENJOYED
THIS BOOK FROM

LOVE INSPIRED SUSPENSE
INSPIRATIONAL ROMANCE

Courage. Danger. Faith.

Find strength and determination in stories
of faith and love in the face of danger.

6 NEW BOOKS AVAILABLE EVERY MONTH!

LISHALO2020

SPECIAL EXCERPT FROM

LOVE INSPIRED SUSPENSE
INSPIRATIONAL ROMANCE

*With his K-9's help, search and rescue K-9 handler
Patrick Sanders must find his kidnapped secret child.*

Read on for a sneak preview of
Desert Rescue *by Lisa Phillips,*
available January 2021 from Love Inspired Suspense.

"Mom!"

That had been a child's cry. State police officer Patrick Sanders glanced across the open desert at the base of a mountain.

Had he found what he was looking for?

Tucker sniffed, nose turned to the breeze.

Patrick's K-9 partner, an Airedale terrier he'd gotten from a shelter as a puppy and trained, scented the wind. His body stiffened and he leaned forward. As an air-scent dog, Tucker didn't need a trail to follow. He could catch the scent he was looking for on the wind or, in this case, the winter breeze rolling over the mountain.

Patrick's mountains, the place he'd grown up. Until right before his high school graduation when his mom had packed them up and fled town. They'd lost their home and everything they'd had there.

Including the girl Patrick had loved.

He heard another cry. Stifled by something—it was hard to hear as it drifted across so much open terrain.

He and his K-9 had been dispatched to find Jennie and her son, Nathan. A friend had reported them missing yesterday, and the sheriff wasted no time at all calling for a search and rescue team from state police.

The dog had caught a scent and was closing in.

As a terrier, it was about the challenge. Tucker had proved to be both prey-driven, like fetching a ball, and food-driven, like a nice piece of chicken, when he felt like it.

Right now the dog had to find Jennie and the boy so Patrick could transport them to safety. Then he intended to get out of town again. Back to his life in Albuquerque and studying for the sergeant's exam.

Tucker tugged harder on the leash; a signal the scent was stronger. He was closing in. Patrick's night of searching for the missing woman and her child would soon be over.

Tucker rounded a sagebrush and sat.

"Good boy. Yes, you are." Patrick let the leash slacken a little. He circled his dog and found Jennie lying on the ground.

"Jennie."

She stirred. Her eyes flashed open and she cried out. *"We need to find Nate."*

Don't miss
Desert Rescue *by Lisa Phillips,*
available wherever Love Inspired Suspense books
and ebooks are sold.

LoveInspired.com

Copyright © 2021 by Lisa Phillips

LOVE INSPIRED
INSPIRATIONAL ROMANCE

UPLIFTING STORIES OF FAITH, FORGIVENESS AND HOPE.

Join our social communities to connect with other readers who share your love!

Sign up for the Love Inspired newsletter at **LoveInspired.com** to be the first to find out about upcoming titles, special promotions and exclusive content.

CONNECT WITH US AT:

Facebook.com/LoveInspiredBooks

Twitter.com/LoveInspiredBks

Facebook.com/groups/HarlequinConnection

LISOCIAL2020

HARLEQUIN

Heartfelt or suspenseful, inspiring or passionate, Harlequin has your happily-ever-after.

With new books published every month, you are sure to find the satisfying escape you know you deserve.

SIGN UP FOR THE HARLEQUIN NEWSLETTER

Be the first to hear about great new reads and exciting offers!

Harlequin.com/newsletters

HNEWS2020

Get 4 FREE REWARDS!

We'll send you 2 FREE Books plus 2 FREE Mystery Gifts.

Love Inspired Suspense books showcase how courage and optimism unite in stories of faith and love in the face of danger.

FREE Value Over $20

YES! Please send me 2 FREE Love Inspired Suspense novels and my 2 FREE mystery gifts (gifts are worth about $10 retail). After receiving them, if I don't wish to receive any more books, I can return the shipping statement marked "cancel." If I don't cancel, I will receive 6 brand-new novels every month and be billed just $5.24 each for the regular-print edition or $5.99 each for the larger-print edition in the U.S., or $5.74 each for the regular-print edition or $6.24 each for the larger-print edition in Canada. That's a savings of at least 13% off the cover price. It's quite a bargain! Shipping and handling is just 50¢ per book in the U.S. and $1.25 per book in Canada.* I understand that accepting the 2 free books and gifts places me under no obligation to buy anything. I can always return a shipment and cancel at any time. The free books and gifts are mine to keep no matter what I decide.

Choose one: ☐ **Love Inspired Suspense**
Regular-Print
(153/353 IDN GNWN)

☐ **Love Inspired Suspense**
Larger-Print
(107/307 IDN GNWN)

Name (please print)

Address   Apt. #

City   State/Province   Zip/Postal Code

Email: Please check this box ☐ if you would like to receive newsletters and promotional emails from Harlequin Enterprises ULC and its affiliates. You can unsubscribe anytime.

Mail to the **Reader Service:**
IN U.S.A.: P.O. Box 1341, Buffalo, NY 14240-8531
IN CANADA: P.O. Box 603, Fort Erie, Ontario L2A 5X3

Want to try 2 free books from another series! Call 1-800-873-8635 or visit www.ReaderService.com.

---

*Terms and prices subject to change without notice. Prices do not include sales taxes, which will be charged (if applicable) based on your state or country of residence. Canadian residents will be charged applicable taxes. Offer not valid in Quebec. This offer is limited to one order per household. Books received may not be as shown. Not valid for current subscribers to Love Inspired Suspense books. All orders subject to approval. Credit or debit balances in a customer's account(s) may be offset by any other outstanding balance owed by or to the customer. Please allow 4 to 6 weeks for delivery. Offer available while quantities last.

Your Privacy—Your information is being collected by Harlequin Enterprises ULC, operating as Reader Service. For a complete summary of the information we collect, how we use this information and to whom it is disclosed, please visit our privacy notice located at corporate.harlequin.com/privacy-notice. From time to time we may also exchange your personal information with reputable third parties. If you wish to opt out of this sharing of your personal information, please visit readerservice.com/consumerschoice or call 1-800-873-8635. **Notice to California Residents**—Under California law, you have specific rights to control and access your data. For more information on these rights and how to exercise them, visit corporate.harlequin.com/california-privacy.

LIS20R2